In Darkness, There is Still Light

Sara Butler Zalesky

Cover design by R.L. Rebach

Dedication

For my Muse,
And Jude Law

Disclaimer

Please be advised this novel contains adult language, intense situations, sexually explicit scenes, and violence which are not intended for sensitive readers.

The views, thoughts, and opinions expressed herein belong solely to the author, and not necessarily those of the author's publisher or employer, any particular organization, committee or other group or individual depicted.

This is a work of *fiction*. For the good and the bad, the names, businesses, places, events and incidents are either products of the author's imagination or are used in a fictitious manner. Any resemblance to actual persons, living or dead is purely coincidental.

That said, portions of this novel are derived from actual names, characters, businesses, places, events and incidents, and as such, are meant as *fictionalized* depictions and/or *dramatizations* of those names, characters, businesses, places, events and incidents. The use of such names, characters, businesses, places, events and incidents are not intended to disparage or harm any such person, place, business or event, unless said person, business or organizer replied to the author's contact and consented to the use.

Speaking of persons, the individual characters in this work are fictional and/or inspired by several individuals and/or are from the author's wildly creative imagination. That is, unless said person replied to the author's contact and agreed to have a cameo.

Otherwise, the use of such personal characteristics is not intended to injure or vilify that individual personage. You have the author's sincerest apologies if you feel injured or vilified. Hit me up on Twitter and we'll hug it out.

3 October

New York

It's not over. It's not.

Loren Mackenzie let out a sigh, her eyes following the blinking lights of a jetliner as it disappeared into the distance over Kennedy International Airport. *He's just going back to work in California, and I'm going home, to England.* She let out an even longer sigh. *Two more races and I get to take a real break. How perfect would it be to go lie on a beach somewhere with him.*

Her gaze refocused on the reflection of a man approaching her in the window. His long, confident stride and athletic form quickened her pulse. She turned to face him, but her smile dissolved into a hard frown when he was stopped by a bunch of fawning teenagers, begging for autographs and selfies with him.

Yep, I had to fall in love with an A-list actor. As Graham Atherton separated himself from the group to continue toward her, Loren forced a smile, but it didn't stick as he stopped again to become engrossed in his mobile. He looked up from the screen to continue on his way.

"Sorry about that, love," he said to her. "Just a text from Ron. He said he'll ring you when he gets into London to discuss setting up a meeting. Is that alright with you?"

She squinted an eye. "So, I have *people* now?"

"I do come as somewhat of a package deal. All that, you know." He thumbed at the disbursing crowd behind him. "And Ron's a bit more than just my agent. He's my best mate, and I trust him." She nodded, turning back to the window as Graham came up behind and wrapped his arms around her.

"Talk to me, love."

"This is the longest we've been physically together, and I don't want it to end." Her shoulders drooped. "I'm sorry I'm whining. I'm just tired."

"No, darling, you're not just tired," he murmured. "You've been completely shat on." He kissed her neck then tightened his arms around her. "You won the time trial Championship in Richmond, but you had to put up with all the nonsense from the press. And then losing the road race, which even that BBC reporter, Theo Arnold agrees was not your fault." Graham released her to face her with pinched brows.

"But if that weren't enough, you had to deal with me throwing your past in your face." He cupped her cheek. "I still feel awful for that, and I want to help you, but I have no idea how." Loren kissed him, then put her arms around his waist to hold him close.

"I want this, and more of it when I see you again." He gave her a squeeze then drew away to glance around them, frowning. "Graham?"

"Grab your bag and come with me." As he bent to pick up his carry-on, she drew her messenger bag over her head, then he led her to a private seating area, far away from prying ears and eyes. He motioned for her to sit on the small sofa, putting down his suitcase and sat next to her. Her stomach jumped to her throat when he took her hand with both of his.

"Darling, I know how hard it was for you to talk about your mother and sister with your aunt, and I'm awfully proud of you for doing that," Graham said and glanced down at their clasped hands. "And I know Maggie gave you all the photos and documents she found in the attic, and I gave you the file my father's man put together." He breathed in. "I would ask that you don't look through all that again by yourself."

She blinked. "Is that all? Here I thought you wanted to have a quickie or something." His stare was somewhere between being shocked and wanting to laugh; his laugh won.

"I love you." But his mirth died out as his bright blue eyes studied her. "I have a present for you, and I was going to save it for your birthday, but it's burning a hole in my pocket." He leaned to remove a small red velvet box from his jacket.

Her jaw dropped. "What are you doing?" He didn't move from his seat, only handed her the box, smirking.

"I'm not asking; I'm giving. That's all." Her hands shook as she took the box and opened it. Nestled inside was a platinum ring of two clasped hands holding a red stone shaped like a heart, capped with a crown.

"It's a Claddagh. It's beautiful," she said, smiling at him. "What's the stone?"

"It's a garnet," he replied. Taking the ring out of the box, he slipped it on her left ring finger, with the hands facing outward. Graham held her gaze as tightly as her hand. "With this crown, I pledge to you my loyalty. With these hands, I offer you my service, and with this heart, I give you mine." Loren stared at him as her brain reset.

"I don't know what to say."

"You don't have to say anything, love," he chuckled. "The stunned look on your face says it all." A laugh mixed with a sob bubbled up her throat.

"I didn't want to cry in public, dammit," she hiccuped, covering her mouth with her hand. He pulled her into his lap and cuddled her close, but she suddenly pushed him away. "Wait a minute. You had this with you the whole time we were together, and you're just giving it to me now?"

"Well, yes and no," he replied, avoiding looking at her. "It belonged to my great-grandmother, so I've had it for a while, but it needed to be resized. It's a complicated process, you know." Loren huffed a chuckle and kissed him, then moved off his lap to the sofa next to him.

"It's beautiful. Thank you." She settled her head on his shoulder, his cologne sending ripples through her. "I don't want you to go," she whispered, brushing her lips against the scruff under his jaw.

"I don't want to either, but we both have jobs to do." Graham held her tighter. "I'll be home before you can miss me."

I miss you already. She squeezed her eyes closed against the sting.

"Loren," he cleared his throat, "about the file–."

"Who am I going to talk to, other than you or Maggie?"

"You can't talk to Cece about it?"

"How can I talk to her about something I've never told her?"

"Then, perhaps you should," he said, and Loren let out a breath.

"I need to talk about all of this with my brother, my real brother," she replied. "I need to find him." Graham moved back to see her, the corners of his mouth curling down.

"Will you wait until I come home to do that?"

"Yah, I can wait. Hell, I don't even know where to start looking," she grumbled, and he kissed her forehead.

"I do love nothing in the world so well as you," he murmured.

"*Je connais.*" Loren slid her arms around his neck and kissed him.

***

When Graham's flight was announced, neither he nor Loren spoke as they gathered their bags and returned to the gate area. They held each other tightly until final boarding was called when he drew away to caress her cheek.

"Love looks not with the eyes, but with the mind," he whispered, his blue eyes welling up. "I'll see you in my dreams."

"In Cleveland," she replied, but he didn't move away. She kissed him, her arms circling his neck to deepen their connection, then broke away to gently press her forehead to his. "Go, before I don't let you." Loren gave him a little push even as her throat tightened.

Graham walked away from her but turned back at the gate. He gave her a tight smile, a little wave, and then he was gone. She closed her eyes and envisioned the pink jewelry box she had as a child in her mind.

I will not cry in public. Breathe. Let it in, then put it away. The ache was still there when she opened her eyes, letting out a soft groan as she picked up her messenger bag. Two young women standing near the seating area caught her attention. One was holding up her phone, and both were crying.

Ah, fuck. Loren slung the strap of her bag over her chest, eyeing the girls with a deep frown as they approached.

"That was Graham Atherton, wasn't it?" the blonde asked.

"That was the most romantic moment I've ever seen," the brunette sighed. Loren kept a tight rein on her emotions, but as she took a breath to speak, the blonde stepped closer to her.

"I recorded you, and I'm really sorry I did." She turned her mobile around to show the thumbnail view of the video directory. "I haven't shared it, and I'm not going to. Nobody needs to see it." The girl selected the video and pressed delete, then went into her 'recently deleted' folder and deleted it permanently.

"Thank you," Loren told them and turned to escape through the exit. The long walk to International Departures gave her the time to pull herself together and once at her gate, she kept to the furthest corner of the seating area, away from the other passengers. She sat down, facing the windows and put on her headphones, but when she opened the music app on her mobile, she gawked at the name of the playlist that was queued. *Graham's Mixtape for his Lady Love?* She blinked. *He made me a mixtape.* She covered her face with her hands and let out a quiet sob.

When her flight was called for boarding, Loren mechanically followed the other passengers into the queue. A flight attendant met her at the end of the gangway and accepted her ticket.

"You're this way, Miss Mackenzie," she said and escorted Loren through the forward section, stopping before a first-class capsule. "Here you are."

Loren frowned, glancing around. "I'm sorry, but isn't this first class?"

"Yes," the attendant replied, smiling. "This is your seat assignment."

"There must be some mis–." Her mouth popped open, recalling Graham's smirk when he relayed a message from Ron. "No, he couldn't… Oh, I can't believe him," she muttered, then smiled at the woman. "I'm sorry. My mistake. What were you saying about the seat?"

As Loren got settled into her capsule with a glass of champagne, her mobile pinged a voicemail message from Graham.

"He is the half part of a blessed man, left to be finished by such as she; and she, a fair divided excellence, whose fullness of perfection lies in him. I wish I were going with you instead, but if wishes were horses, beggars would ride. Three weeks, my love. Three more weeks and I will be in your arms again. I love you and have a safe flight."

"Damn you," she mumbled, quickly dialing his number, but it went straight to voicemail.

***

Midway through his flight to LAX, Graham received an email from her.

> My Apollo:
> I held it together after you left, even when two girls came up to me to say they were sorry for recording us at the gate. But then I

4

found a playlist on my phone that I didn't make and started blubbering. Nobody's ever made me a mixtape before. I've loved every song so far, which is surprising, considering what's usually on my playlists.

And I've never flown Upper Class before, mostly because it's a $9k upgrade. I can't believe you did that and didn't tell me. The champagne is good, and they'll give you as much as you want. I'm sure going to take advantage of that.

The little capsule thingies are neat too, but if you're with somebody, you have to hang over the partition to talk. Kind of like the way some young actress in the next capsule has been talking to me non-stop since the plane took off. I even put the partition up, but she's still chatting away. I have no idea who she is, and while she made sure to tell me all the TV shows she's been on, they're American shows, and I haven't heard of them either.

But if I were flying with you, I'd rather be in Economy so I could snuggle up with you.

However, if it wasn't you that upgraded my ticket, then I'm going to have to track down Jude Law and thank him for being such a wonderful boyfriend.

Three weeks is too long.

He took off his glasses and rubbed his eyes against the sting. *This hurts so much worse.*

***

4 October

London, England

Loren shuffled out of baggage claim at just after ten in the morning with her head down, dragging her silver bike carrier behind her. Before reaching the main concourse, she ducked into the ladies' room and recoiled when she caught a glimpse of reflection in the mirror.

"Yikes." Dark circles shaded her eyes. She splashed cold water on her face, then pinched her cheeks to get some color back in them. She traded her team warm-up jacket for her favorite of Graham's pullovers, a dark gray Burberry with patched elbows, then headed out to the concourse. She passed through security unnoticed, but neared the airport exit, she picked her head up to look for Graham's driver. A small group of photographers were near the doors. Loren ducked her chin and followed a larger group of travelers heading in the same direction.

Don't see me. Don't see me. When the clamor from the paparazzi began, the passengers scattered in all directions like pigeons. *Walk fast. Don't look up, just keep walking.* Cameras were shoved in her face, while photographers shouted questions and comments at her.

"Congratulations on winning the time trial, Loren. Too bad about the road race."

"Was your team leader, Amber Moll upset that you took fourth, ahead of her?"

"Did you and Graham Atherton break up over his affair with Cortney Goodwin?"

That comment brought her head up, and Loren was blinded by a camera flash. She jumped when an arm went around her shoulders and turned to the tense face of her friend, Anthony Ainsworth.

"Just keep walking," he grumbled, shielding her with his arm as they forged through the gauntlet. Once they reached the doors, airport security restored order and Anthony took over pulling the cumbersome bike carrier.

"What the hell was all that about?" She shot a glance over her shoulder.

"Don't worry about it," he told her. "I can take your duffle."

"No, it's okay. Thanks." She slung the strap over her head, hugging it to her chest. He directed her to cross the pick-up/drop-off lanes to where his Range Rover was parked in the taxi area. The front passenger door burst open, and a young woman with short dark hair jumped out and darted between a few cars. Loren's teammate and best friend, Cece Taylor grabbed her in a rib-crushing hug.

"Charlotte, you're hurting me," she groaned, and Cece let her go.

"I'm sorry, but, it's just... look!" She pointed to a headline on page two of the crumpled newspaper in her hand.

Atherton Leaves Her! Is the Actor's whirlwind romance with the Pro Cyclist over?

The article featured a photo of Loren, sitting alone in the International terminal waiting area with her hands over her face.

Just wonderful. She rolled her eyes. *I hope Maggie doesn't see that.* She didn't bother reading the copy and handed it back to her friend. "Yes, Charlotte, he left me. In the airport, to fly back to California." Cece grimaced as Anthony put his arm around her shoulders.

"I told you," he said. "She would have called one of us." Loren peeked over her shoulder to the exit.

"But that explains the ruckus back there." Several people with cameras were on the sidewalk, watching them. "But, why are you guys here and not Graham's driver, Jim?"

"Ah, well..." Cece made a face. "Graham sent me a text this morning asking if we could retrieve you."

"And yet you still thought he broke up with me?"

"I don't know!" she whined, shrugging her shoulders.

"I don't get you," Loren muttered and headed to the Rover.

***

She jerked awake when the SUV came to a stop and blinked at her house on Essex out the window.

"How embarrassing," Loren muttered hoarsely, rubbing her forehead. Her car door opened, and Anthony caught her elbow as she stumbled out with the weight of her duffle and messenger bag.

"Mind the gap," he snickered. "I'll get your carrier."

"Yah, thanks." She stiffly walked toward the house when his voice stopped her.

"Ah, Loren, we need to talk." She dropped the heavier duffle to the ground and pinched the bridge of her nose.

"You haven't changed the house again, have you?"

"No, but–."

"Great." She dragged her duffle behind her to the front door and stopped. Cece and Anthony were holding hands as they came around the house. "I'm happy you guys got together, honest." Her shoulders rounded as she sighed. "Could you just open the door, please?"

"We're headed to Colin and Emma's in a bit," he said as he entered the security code into the keypad and the door unlocked. "Would you be coming?" Loren heaved a bigger sigh.

"Can I clean myself up first?"

"Yah, sure."

"Great." She trudged through the front room and up the stairs, her duffle and messenger bag banging off the steps to stand at the threshold of her bedroom. The king-sized bed dominated the room, draped with a turquoise paisley duvet cover accented by pale blue and beige curtains. A single photo of them together was in a frame on her nightstand surrounded by pictures of her family.

"I'm home." Loren heaved a sigh and entered the room to flop face first on the bed. "Wonderful softness," she moaned and turned over to her back. Her thumb brushed against the cool metal of the ring on her left hand and she held it up to stare at it.

He gave me a ring, but he didn't ask anything. He pledged. He promised. Then, she heard Felix's voice echo in her ears. *He plays at love, Loren. He's an actor!* She pushed aside the ache then narrowed her eyes at the slightly askew dome light on the ceiling.

"Huh. I keep forgetting to fix that. But not right now." She groaned rolling off the bed to her feet, towing her duffle into the bathroom. Loren stood under the gloriously hot shower until the water grew tepid, then bundled in a towel and sat down on the bed with her toiletries bag. She rummaged through it, searching for her comb when she found a small bottle of Graham's cologne. Tears sprang to her eyes.

"I'm fine. I'm just tired," she croaked, spraying her chest with the scent. "I can miss him without falling apart. I can do it." She took a deep breath and stood up to don her underclothes when her tablet pinged a video call. Checking the ID, she connected as she slowly pulled Graham's Hyrule T-shirt over her head.

"I was just thinking about you, but shouldn't you be sleeping?" She chuckled at his wide-eyed expression as she sat down.

"It's a good thing I'm alone with a view like that."

"I could show you a little more," she purred, taking hold of the hem of her shirt to pull it up a bit.

He groaned. "As much as I would thoroughly enjoy that, it's not the same as me removing it myself. With my teeth." She laughed as a smirk formed on his lips. "And that's my T-shirt."

"I nicked it." She bit her lip, hugging the cotton fabric to herself. "I found the little bottle of your cologne in my bag. Thank you."

"Don't use it all. That's expensive stuff," he grumbled, making her smile return. "Did you spend all night looking at pictures of Jude Law?"

She huffed and shook her head. "No, but that girl was off the wall. She talked to anyone who would listen for the entire flight."

"I'm sorry, love," Graham said, grimacing. Loren gave a little shrug, but they didn't look away from each other for a long moment. His frown returned as his gaze slid away. "I knew I would miss you, but I didn't realize how much until I was lying here in bed and I was cold," he said quietly and touched his chest above his heart. "There's a deep ache, right here, where your head should be."

"*Mon Coeur*," she murmured. "I feel it too, but you know it will all seem different in the morning." She squinted an eye. "Or later."

He laughed softly. "I know, it's just–." Loren turned around at a knock on her bedroom door.

"Sorry, didn't mean to interrupt," Cece said and started to turn around.

"No, no, it's alright," Graham called out. "It's late, and I need to get some sleep."

Cece came closer to the screen. "I'd say so. You both look like death." She turned to Loren. "You don't have to come, you know."

"I know," she replied, then turned back to the screen. "It's Sunday luncheon."

"It's alright, love. Go," Graham told her. "I'll see you in my dreams."

Loren winked. "In Cleveland."

***

5 October

Loren woke in her bed, in her house, alone and without the birdsong that had accompanied the dawn for the past five months. She looked up at the window above her head.

I miss those stupid birds, then promptly smacked herself in the forehead. *What the hell am I thinking!* She rolled over to pick up her mobile and saw there was an email from Graham.

> My sweet:
> I did dream of you, but we weren't in Cleveland, and I did *not* want to wake up from that. I was late for a meeting, but that isn't a new thing.
> My assistant, Karen told me she and her boyfriend signed up for a triathlon relay next summer, which got me to thinking. I run fast. We both swim quite well. You are the time trial World Champion. What damage could we do to the age-groupers if we did a relay together? I know it might be difficult with your racing schedule, but if we found one somewhere close when you had a break, would you do it?
> Have a wonderful day, and I love you.

She touched her fingers to her lips, holding in her mind how it felt to kiss him. Remembering how he looked rising out of the pool in a Speedo sent hot chills running through her.

"He sure looked good in those tiny briefs, even though I wasn't in any shape to appreciate it." Loren sighed and typed out a reply.

> My graham cracker:
> We're back to the lovey-dovey greetings, huh?
> A lot of egos would be bruised if we did a relay tri. I'll have a look at the calendar to see where there might be a break.
> Holly's done triathlons before, so I could pick her brain a bit to see which ones are good for beginners. I've done a few 5ks so I can run, I just don't like it. I might like it better with you, if you promise not to leave me in the dust.
> You, in a Speedo. Speechless. Okay, not true. I would have lots of things to say about you in that teeny swim brief again. Most notably, removing them, very slowly.
> Ahem. That's enough of that.
> I'm looking forward to today's ride with the team. It's funny, but other than the two times I went out with Kevin and his friends in Rochester, I haven't been on my bike since the road race. I'm ready to get back to work.
> I love you too.
> p.s. I can't stop thinking about you in that Speedo. I might not need that electric blanket tonight.

Loren was giggling as she pressed send, then glanced at the list of text reminders. There was one from Graham's friend and agent, Ron Hudson, asking her to ring him.

He sent this at three in the morning? He answered just before her call went to voicemail.

"Eh, whadda want?"

"You told me to call you," she said, holding back her chuckle. "I'm sorry, were you sleeping?"

"Loren?" He coughed. "Yes, sorry." He coughed again. "Good trip?"

"Yah, until I got to Heathrow. I was accosted by paparazzi."

"Yes. I'll assume you saw page two of The Sun?"

She curled her lip. "It was shown to me."

"Well, my advice is to be certain those close to you know the truth and don't bother with the rest. We can discuss all this later this afternoon if it suits you."

She sat up in bed. "Okay. Where?"

"I'm in Glasgow at the moment, but I can meet you at Graham's in Northaw this evening."

"Alright then," she yawned, which made him yawn.

"Gawd, would you stop that!"

"Sorry," she laughed. "I'll send a text when I'm on my way." She disconnected and rolled out of bed to gather her gear. When Loren made her way downstairs, Holly was fiddling with one of her bikes in the front room.

"Hey! You're back."

She smiled at her younger teammate. "You've settled in quite nicely, I see." Loren pushed her chin to the three additional road bikes that hung on the wall.

"Yeah, I can't get rid of them," Holly replied and stood up to admire her bikes.

"I know what you mean," Loren said. "Graham made fun of me because I still have my Cervelo from college. I set two records on it. I can't get rid of it."

"Regular people don't get it." Holly tilted her head. "We're riding over to the center, right?"

"I don't have a car yet," Loren answered over her shoulder, heading into the kitchen. A small stash of mail was in a cubby on the wall, and she took the bulk out to sort through it. "Bill, bill, junk," she muttered, then picked up a white envelope addressed to her, but without postage or return address. She glanced over at Holly, holding up the envelope. "When did this come?"

"I don't remember that," she replied, opening the refrigerator.

Loren tore open the envelope and pulled out a single piece of white paper with three words on it.

I see you.

"*What the fuck?*"

"What is it?" Holly asked.

"Nothing." She crumpled the paper and shoved it in the rear pocket of her jersey. They both turned at stomping feet coming down the stairs.

"I don't know what I'm going to do with you two early risers," Cece grumbled entering the kitchen. "I could hit the snooze a few times with Ingrid." Loren narrowed her eyes at the unusually dark circles under her friend's eyes and stopped her before she followed a laughing Holly out the back door.

"You okay, after what happened yesterday?" Cece nodded but found her shoes more interesting.

"Yah, I just didn't expect Colin to get so upset."

"Well, it is a little weird, you dating our landlord," Loren replied, squinting. Cece opened her mouth to retort but just blew out a breath.

"Yah, I reckon. Anthony's not gonna give us a break on the rent, though."

"Like you pay rent to begin with," she laughed.

"That'll change when you move out," Cece answered and Loren's humor evaporated.

"Who says I'm moving out?" Cece pointed at the ring on Loren's finger.

"But, that–."

"It doesn't mean anything," she snapped, turning on her heel and walked out.

"If you say so," Cece muttered and followed her out the door.

***

The trio stood in line at the local coffee shop to place their orders, and Loren glanced at an empty table under the bay window. She smiled, recalling the first time she saw Graham there.

I think I was even standing right here when he looked at me, and I completely froze. She huffed. *He wasn't smiling at me, though. His sister, Moira had walked in behind me.*

"Stop your wool gathering and order," Cece quipped, bringing Loren back to the present.

With their insulated mugs safely tucked into spare water bottle cages, the trio made their way to the main road through Enfield, heading toward the training center. They rolled to a stop at an intersection, and Loren turned to look behind them and scowled. Two motorcycles were a few cars back, and one of the passengers quickly pointed a long lens camera at her.

You've got to be joking. The light turned green and she took off, pushing hard to leave the motos stuck in traffic.

As the three women rolled through the open bay door, their *Directeur Sportif,* James Parker was standing with the rest of their teammates. He turned and waved to them.

"Good morning, ladies! Welcome back Loren." She smiled at Ashley, Elsa, and Chantal as they all came together, but it dissolved, counting only six. James addressed the group then.

"Our route today has a hill with a ten percent kick at the top, just like the San Luca in our next race," he said. "I reckon that could be where Elsa can make a break for it, so we're going to take a few runs at it, to work out the timing."

"I like it," Loren said, nodding, but Elsa frowned at both of them.

"Me? But Loren is lead rider."

"The other teams might be watching for something from her," James explained. "But you could be our ace in the hole."

"It's your time to shine," Loren added, nudging Elsa with her shoulder. "Besides, I'm not Italian."

The younger cyclist grinned. "Thank you. I won't let you down."

As the team prepared to leave, Loren caught up with their Director at the car.

"James, before you left Richmond, we were discussing expanding the roster," she said. "What's changed?"

His smile tightened. "We'll be meeting about that tomorrow," he replied and opened the car door. She put a hand on his arm.

"Please tell me what's going on."

"As much as I would like to, that's for Ulrik and Darren to explain," James said, a hint of anger in his voice. "Let's get going."

Loren moved away as he slid into the driver's seat and closed the door, ending their conversation.

Darren's got some explaining to do.

***

The six cyclists kept a tight double pace line behind the team car as they left the center. They headed north on the busy local roads, in the opposite direction of the morning traffic; to keep the riders safe, and to appease local drivers. Once further out into the countryside, their formation loosened, and Loren glanced back at the two motorcycles following them. She squeezed the mic hidden in her jersey to talk with the team car.

"The motos that followed us to the center have made an appearance."

"I see that. We'll drop back," James replied. The Volvo pulled over to the roadside, and Loren caught the concerned look of their mechanic Sven, from the passenger seat as they glided past. The car then came out behind them, cutting off the photographers.

Loren rotated through to the front of the group with Holly, and together, they picked up the pace in the crisp morning air. Her teammates' laughter and lively chatter kept her mood from turning dark and eventually, Loren slid back for Ashley and Cece to take over and formed up with Elsa.

"Congratulations on your win in the time trial," the Italian said as she flicked her dark braid over her shoulder. "We watched your run on TV at Ulrik's house."

Loren's mouth dropped open. "You guys went… I've never been to his house!" Elsa gave a soft chuckle but came in closer.

"What happened to Amber in the road race?"

She shook her head. "It was like Philadelphia all over again," Loren replied. "Three riders were drafting me on Governor Street, and one of them was Amber. I went all out at the top, but she couldn't stay with me, and I didn't have anything left." She pulled a grimace. "I hate to admit it, but that's our strategy for this race, too. It's either me or Holly for your lead out on the San Luca."

"Don't worry about me," Elsa told her, putting a hand on her shoulder. "I'll be with you all the way."

"Then let's get going!"

Loren led the younger climber in two attacks on the hill, with everyone but Holly countering along the loop back. She traded places with Holly to work on the charge, while Ashley, Cece, and Chantal went on the attack again. Loren was bringing up the rear of the group when one of the motos slipped past the team car and came alongside her. She glared at the two men and zipped up her wind vest.

"Really, guys, nobody wants to see my sweaty face," she called out, but they didn't back off, and her frown deepened. She momentarily considered taking the offensive and passing the rest of the team just ahead of them but nixed the idea.

They'll just catch me anyway. She stopped pedaling and glanced back at James in the team car. Luckily, he got the point and inched closer to the motorcycle, forcing it further over the yellow line until it retreated. Loren slid to the left-hand passenger side and held onto the frame of Sven's open window. They both eyed the motorcycle behind them.

"Maybe I should take a dive, so they have something to photograph," she said dryly, making Sven and James chuckle.

"We'll try and keep them at bay," James told her.

14

After the team's fifth time around the loop, their DS called the group back together at the crest of the hill.

"Nice work team," James said and nodded to Holly and Loren as they pulled up. "Since your times are similar, I reckon it will be who has the best position once you get to the climb for the lead out." He squinted at the motos parked a short distance from them. "That's enough for today."

"I'll stick to the back," Loren told him. "It's me they want anyway."

The riders held to single file coming into the more populated neighborhoods near Enfield, with Loren as the last rider before the car. The photographers had already buzzed past twice, then doubled back to come at her from the opposite direction when they came upon signs for a sharp bend ahead.

The cyclists slowed down with traffic, but the whine of a motorcycle came from behind as it swerved past the team car and into the oncoming lane. The screech of tires on asphalt followed, along with the startled shouts of six women, and several car horns.

"I've had enough of this." Loren stopped pedaling to let the Volvo pass her then tucked in behind it for a moment or two before squeezing the brakes and coming to a stop. She yanked off her sunglasses to scowl at the photographers.

"You fuckers are going to get us killed out here! Back off, or I'll have you arrested for harassment."

**

Later that afternoon, Loren sent a text to Ron that she was on her way as she headed out to the shed in the rear garden. She stopped short to stare at the keypad.

"Dammit." Fumbling with her helmet and her mobile to look up the code, she pressed the number into the keypad then pushed the door open but dropped the helmet. As she bent to pick it up, the dying sunlight glinted off something hanging from the handle of her BMW. She squinted, taking a step closer to reach for it, only to snatch her hand back. A tiny turquoise bison dangled from a silver chain.

"Oh, my god. My necklace." Loren grabbed her throat and backed out of the shed. *It was locked. Nobody else has the code. What do I do?* She spun around, gasping for breath.

"Stop it. Breathe. Call Anthony." She let out a groan. "Fuck! He's in London!" She banged her fists against the sides of her head. "No. I can do this. I'm the fucking storm. I can do this." Inch by inch, she forced her legs to move closer to the motorcycle. She grasped the chain and put it into her pocket, then shoved the bike out of the shed.

Halfway to Northaw, she couldn't ignore the tingling sensation on the back of her neck anymore and took a left without signaling. She caught sight of a dark sedan and her heart skipped when it veered off to make the same turn.

Loren shook her head. *No. That can't be the same car. I'm just freaking out.* She couldn't shake her unease though, and a few minutes later, she dove to the right, across the lanes of traffic and onto a country road. Rolling the throttle hard, her nimble BMW shot away. Two miles down the lane, she pulled off into a residential development to turn around. She activated the camera mounted on her helmet and waited, her stomach churning. A dark blue sedan slowed down as it passed her position, then took off.

Her lip curled. *Oh, no, you fucker. You're not getting away from me.* Loren rolled the throttle, her tire spraying dirt and stones as she headed in pursuit, getting close enough to see the tag number clearly, then veered down another side street. Loren came to a stop and pulled out her mobile, then pressed a contact. Ron answered on the second ring.

"Hey, where are you?"

"There's a pub on the corner of Vineyards and Northaw, called The Two Brothers," she said. "Meet me there."

"I'm always up for a pint," he said and disconnected.

***

Ron Hudson squinted entering the dimly lit, wood-paneled taproom of the Two Brothers Pub and it took a moment for his eyes to adjust. She was sitting at the corner of the bar, encased in a black leather motorcycle suit with bright blue striping outlining her curves. He smothered a grin at an older male patron giving him the stink eye as he made his way to her.

Her reddish-brown hair was tucked back in a loose braid that curled over her shoulder. Fading pink pressure marks were on her cheeks and forehead, with bluish half-moons shadowing her eyes. Her fingers loosely curled around a tumbler of amber whisky over ice and she didn't look up when he sat down. The barkeep moved over to him.

"What can I get ya, sir?"

"I see you have Wells Bombardier on tap."

"Aye, that," the man said. "Fetch'a pint?"

"That'd be perfect." When the keeper returned with the beer, Ron took a sip and sighed in happiness, then nudged Loren's arm. "That must be the moto suit Graham can't stop talking about you wearing." She raised her storm gray eyes to him, and the seriousness of her expression gave him a cold knot in his chest. "What's happened?"

"I found this hanging on my motorcycle," she replied, her hand shaking a little as she passed him a necklace. "And then I was followed here." She slid her mobile toward him with a clear photo of the sedan's tag number was onscreen.

"How'd you manage to get this," he tapped the photo, "and what do you mean, you found this?"

"I know how to ride," she said, her pitch going higher. "Graham gave me that necklace, and I never took it off until it was ripped from my throat. No one could find it, but now it just magically appears in a locked shed?"

"Alright, alright, steady on." Ron patted her hand even as his heart rate went up. "Perhaps your new roommate found it."

"Maybe." She squinted an eye at him. "How did you know I got a new roommate?"

"Graham tells me everything," he replied, smirking.

"Hmm." She pursed her lips as she studied him. With a hint of a smile, she reached out and brushed his jaw with the back of her fingers. "You didn't have this when we met in Richmond. I like it." He rubbed the five-day growth on his cheeks.

"Ah, well, I have a bit of a baby-face. I wasn't sure how I'd look," he said, but his humor dissipated. "Keepin' your chin up, after all that nonsense, then?"

"I'm fine," she said and refocused on her glass. Ron went back to his beer and was almost finished with it before she spoke again. "I appreciate that you're here to help me, but I think I'll be okay by myself."

"You think you can handle the media crush alone, huh?" He raised his brows, and she shrugged a shoulder.

"If I don't like a question, I won't answer it."

"And if you're pressed?"

Loren gave him a little smirk. "I'll tell 'em to fuck off."

"Not using those words, I should say," he chuckled. "You have an image to protect."

She frowned. "I don't have an image."

"Yes, you do. You're not known for being emotional. That's why they call you the Snow Queen."

She rolled her eyes. "The Ice Queen."

"Whatever," he drawled, then downed the last sip of his beer. "The point is, you can't be emotional."

"But that's not who I am." He looked down his nose at her.

"Be that as it may, you put on that uniform, that's who you become."

"You think Graham would get involved with such a cold bitch?"

"We try not to have an opinion of each other's relationships," he replied, glancing around at the other patrons.

"And I thought you tell each other everything," she shot back. He ducked his chin to cover his smirk.

"Fine. I've met all but two of the women he's been involved with, and they each fit a certain profile, a Damsel in Distress. He's attracted to people who need to be saved." Ron held up his hand as Loren took a breath to interrupt. "I'll admit, being with you has changed him, and it wasn't just me who noticed; Benny saw it, as well. He seems more grounded, and I hoped this time might be different because *you* seemed different." His gaze dropped to her hands, closed tightly around her empty whisky glass.

Well, well. He gave her the ring after all. He took a breath, aiming to push her buttons. "But then I read what was in the file Graham's father gave him." Her cold glare hit him like a slap and while her voice was calm, he could swear her eyes grew darker.

"You think you know me because you read some fucking file. I have spent the better part of my life overcoming what's in there, all by myself. I don't need a man to save me."

Ron licked his lips. "I believe you, Loren, but you didn't mind the gap before you hopped on the conclusion train," he quipped. "That's something we need to work on."

She reared back from him. "You're testing me?"

"Yes, and you were doing quite well until that last bit there when I dangled the carrot." He nudged her with his shoulder, then sat back in his chair. "If you're asked a question that sets off a reaction, it would be preferable that you don't answer. Even though you didn't raise your voice, you were rattled, and became defensive and slightly threatening," he said, his voice rising an octave. "It's a knee-jerk reaction; I understand." He patted her hand and moved away again.

"I think it was after La Course; you stared at the reporter who asked about Graham, then you went back to the bloke who asked you a question before that and reiterated your answer. I liked that." He signaled to the bartender and ordered her a refill. When the barkeep returned, Ron felt his brows hit his hairline when she tipped back her drink in one gulp. The bartender touched her hand.

"Thanks, Calvin," she said before he moved away, and Ron did a double take.

"You know the bartender?"

"He's my neighbor." She looked to him, her eyes glistening. "He's the one who called the police when he heard…" His mouth popped open, flicking his gaze to the ruddy-faced man.

"I had no idea."

"Yah, I don't know how to thank him," she whispered. "I've always been friendly with him and his partner, Dean, but not close, you know. I feel a little safer now knowing they're watching out for me." She swished the ice in her glass when her mobile pinged a text. A flash of heartache crossed her face as she glanced at it, but it disappeared just as quick.

"All's well?" he asked.

She rubbed the bridge of her nose. "Yah, I'm getting a headache."

"Well, as much as I'd like to sit around here for the rest of the evening, I have some things for you to go through back at the house."

"That's why I'm here." She pushed a fifty across the bar, and Calvin handed over her helmet.

Loren followed Ron out of the pub and glanced around the parking area, then down the street.

Good, I don't see that … Oh. A deep pain hit her in the chest at the sight of the gray Jaguar parked next to her motorcycle. *Knock it off. It's just a car. But, it's his car. Dammit.* She pulled on her helmet before Ron could see her tears.

She kept an eye on her rearview following the Jaguar down Vineyards Road when Ron pulled up to the gate too far to the right. She clutched at the brakes and stalled out, narrowly missing the back of the car.

He lowered the window. "Sorry. I reckoned you would want to go in first." Loren flipped up her visor to give him a black look, then got off her bike. After entering the code to open both the gate and the garage, she proceeded down the cobblestone driveway and rolled inside the open garage door. She cut the engine and set the stand, then dismounted the BMW, placing her helmet on the seat to see him get out of the car.

"This is the first time I've been here without him since he left," she told him. A dull ache spreading through her and she dragged her feet following Ron into the house.

"Say, you reckon' you know how to…" She stopped at the edge of the great room and his voice faded away. Loren turned toward the door leading to the study, her breath catching in her throat. The door opened, revealing Graham standing there, his bright blue eyes creasing with laughter as he held his arms out to her. She flinched when Ron touched her shoulder.

"You're looking a tad lurgy," he said. "You want to lay down?" She turned back to the door and it was closed.

Wishful thinking. "I'm fine," she replied, wiping her cheeks with her hands and sat down at the island. She fiddled with the ring on her finger as she focused on her breathing.

"Hey." She slowly raised her chin to meet Ron's emerald green eyes. "Mother in heaven, don't look at me like that. I might have to hug you or somethin'," he grumbled, and she burst out a sob mixed with a laugh.

"Yah, like that'd happen," she muttered, sliding her gaze away.

"Right," he scoffed and opened the slim case laptop in front of him. She shuddered when her mobile sounded with Graham's ringtone next to her on the counter. Loren stuck on a smile before connecting the video call.

"Hey, you."

"Hello, love," Graham said, smiling brightly. "You're in my kitchen."

"Yes, I hope you don't mind. I'm having a chat with Ron." She turned the camera on him, and he flipped Graham the bird.

"Why would he mind? I have my own suite here," Ron groused.

"Getting along then?" Graham laughed.

Ron snorted. "I'll have you know, the locals much prefer *you* with her than me."

"Ah, you went to The Two Brothers, did you?"

"Yes," she replied, turning the camera back to see him. "I had a bit of a tail, and I didn't want to bring it back here."

"Oh, that's not good." His concern was clear, but she shrugged a shoulder.

"I'm sure it was some photographer or whatever," she told him. "They were giving us a problem on this morning's ride, as well."

His frown deepened. "I'm sorry you have to deal with all of this by yourself."

"She's not by herself!" Ron countered.

"Isn't there anything you can do about that?" Graham asked but Loren answered for him.

"Hey, this all comes as a package deal, remember? So long as they keep their distance, the only shots they're getting are of my Lycra-covered ass." Graham shook his head at her smirk.

"I'll let you get back to your conversation," he said. "You'll ring me later?"

She nodded. "Will do."

"Love you."

"Love you too, darling!" Ron yelled over her reply. Graham's laugh echoed through the house after he disconnected, leaving her with a hard knot in her chest.

"Alright, down to business." Ron cleared his throat as he shuffled papers around. "I've received several requests for interviews, but there's one I want you to consider. ESPN Magazine."

Loren squinted at him. "Why?"

He held up his hand. "Hear me out, yah? I've worked with Cara Smith before, and I like her. Her interview would be about you, not *him* and you, like the others, and we can review her questions beforehand. That way, we're in control."

"How are we in control?" she bit back. "It's called editing. They can just splice shit together, and there's nothing I can do about it."

"She's not like that Montgomery woman," he replied and leaned toward her. "Do you trust me?" Loren raised her chin and studied him for a long moment.

"He trusts you. That's good enough for now."

***

London, England

"Mr. Lalonde?"

He blinked at the therapist, his mind sluggishly rolling over and the rest of the room began to come into focus. Beige walls, dark wood office furniture; a man with glasses perched on his nose staring at him.

"Mr. Lalonde?"

He heaved a sigh. "What were you saying?"

"We were discussing why you have requested a transfer to inpatient treatment," the man replied, flipping through a file on the desk in front of him. "You state you've had difficulty staying sober as an outpatient."

"What else have I to do?" he sneered, anger rousing him. "I have no income; I have no life. Everything has been taken from me."

"You don't deserve punishment?"

"It was a misunderstanding," Felix snapped back.

"And what was it that you misunderstood?"

He sat up straight. "I misunderstood? I merely wished to speak to her; to reason with her." The man's eyes held no emotion behind his glasses.

"What did you want her to know?"

"She should be with me, not that actor!" Felix leaned toward the man. "He pretends to love her, but he could never know her the way I do. She and I are the same. We have lived through the same hell." The therapist folded his hands before him.

"And what kind of hell was that?"

"It matters not." Felix turned away, folding his arms over his chest. Trying to manipulate the man wasn't going to work. "It changes nothing."

"Why did you go to her house?"

Leave me alone, you imbecile. "It was as I said before. My contract was terminated. I was distraught. I needed to talk to her."

"Your blood alcohol was 0.25. That's almost lethal."

"I drank anything I could get my hands on," he replied, his voice soft. "I just wanted to forget. I wanted to drown. I needed her." He saw her then, as he paced before the door of her house; the fear in her eyes. "It hurt to see her, and when she told me to leave, I went mad. I grabbed her arm, and she hit me." He lifted his head to the therapist. "The next thing I recall is being in hospital, in handcuffs."

"You don't remember striking her? Choking her?"

"I don't know," he murmured. "I see flashes of her face in my dreams and a terrible darkness pressing on my skull." Felix closed his eyes, wiping a shaking hand over his mouth.

"Yet you have accepted a plea agreement."

"I want this to be over, for me, for her," he muttered, pinching the bridge of his nose. "I can't face her."

The therapist cleared his throat. "You've been sober for twenty-four hours. The difficult time has only just begun," he said. "You're in the right place if your goal is recovery, but you must work the program, or you will end up in prison. Do you understand? This is your last chance."

"Yes," Felix choked. "I swear, I never meant to hurt her. I love her." His eyes slid away. *I cannot go back to that hell.*

6 October

"I can't believe I'm fucking fifteen minutes late," Loren muttered as she sat down next to Cece at the conference room table.

"That's what you get for giggling on the phone all night."

"I didn't know Graham was going to call me, and I miss him." Her voice cracked over the last words, and Cece gave her a shoulder bump.

"I know. I get it." They both snapped to attention when James and the team's silver-haired manager, Ulrik Vislosky entered. He was followed by their impeccably dressed team owner, Darren Wickersham. "What's he doin' here?" Cece mumbled.

"Ladies, good morning," Ulrik spoke as the three men sat down. He looked around the table. "Welcome back and congratulations again, Loren, on your Championship win in Richmond." Darren cleared his throat, bringing all eyes to him.

"Now that everyone is all together, I can officially announce that we will be moving you all to IDC's facility in Harrow by the middle of next month," he said. "We have a much larger support staff, and the design and production crews are eager to have you all assist in the redesign of their women's specific models. You will also be training with the men's team and utilizing our staff through December, then joining us for camp in Majorca, Spain in January." Cece nudged Loren with her elbow.

"I've seen the plans for the new bikes," she whispered. "They're feckin' brilliant."

James sat forward in his seat. "As some of you know, Ulrik, Darren and I have discussed sending a mixed team of six to Australia for three races next month. Holly and Ashley have volunteered to go, thank you, ladies. I know Josh is looking forward to working with both of you. He's a capable DS and I reckon you'll learn a lot from each other." He winked at Holly.

"Alright team, it's performance testing day," Ulrik said, clapping his hands. "Tomorrow will be long and easy." The teammates were grumbling as they followed him out of the conference room, but Loren, Darren, and Ulrik stayed in their seats. None spoke until the room cleared and her manager coughed softly.

"Loren, did you enjoy your vacation with your family?"

"Yes, thank you," she replied, her eyes sliding to Darren. "We were talking about going to nine riders before I left. Is that not happening now?"

He let out a long breath. "We've had some complications with the budget and–."

"You cut our budget?" She leaned into her hands on the table. "We're third in the team standings this season, and the new World Tour has more

Elite level races. How are we supposed to compete–." He held up his hand.

"I know that; however, the team lost several minor sponsors." She stared at him, her eyes flicking to Ulrik and back.

"Because of me." She sat back in her chair, turning away from the two men.

"We can't say that for certain, but it was recent," Ulrik replied. "I'm sorry, Loren."

This is my fault. An idea sparked, and she pressed her lips into a hard line. "What if I could make up the difference?"

"You intend to bring in more sponsors?" Darren asked.

"Perhaps," she said, licking her lips as the possibilities rolled around in her mind. "But what if I could fund the difference, personally."

"Loren, we know your boyfriend is wealthy but–."

"Graham has nothing to do with this," she snapped back, then took a deep breath. "I have a trust fund that I can use to make up the difference."

"Why would you do that?"

"Because." She met Darren's gaze briefly. "They're my teammates; my family, and maybe by investing in them now, I'm investing in my future."

"I see." He ran his hand through his short hair. "I would have to review the rules about having a team owner as a rider."

She sat up quickly. "Hang on! I didn't say anything about being a team owner."

"What else would you be?"

"I don't know, but not that," she replied, clenching her hands. "It's your company. I don't want to be involved like that." They were quiet for a moment, then Ulrik cleared his throat.

"The trust is from your parents' deaths, isn't it?" She focused on her hands. "It's tainted." Her jaw clenched as she forced the words out. "When my father murdered my mother, their farm went into a trust for me," she said. "I've never had to tell anyone, but because of Sylvia Montgomery and her microscope on my life, it might come out in the tabloids now."

"My god, Loren. We had no idea." She winced at the pity in Darren's voice. "It is inexcusable for them to reveal something so personal. I'm so sorry," he told her.

"Thank you." She stood, tightening her fists at her sides. "I have to go." Darren stood up, reaching out to stop her.

"Jon told me you tend to carry too much on your shoulders," he said. "My door is always open to you, Loren." Her ears flamed and she stepped away.

"Thanks, Darren," she mumbled and bolted from the conference room.

He then turned to Ulrik. "Did you know about any of that?"

"I knew something happened to her, as a child," he replied, rising from his seat. "Gabi told me she had terrible nightmares, and I had meant to talk to her about it, but I never did." Darren nodded and put his hand on his shoulder.

"It wasn't you," he said, his voice heavy. "I took Felix at his word. This is on me."

***

Loren rolled to a stop between Cece and Holly at a traffic light on Southbury Road, her anxiety burning a hole in her stomach. She glanced over her shoulder again, her eyes widening, and quickly turned back.

It can't be the same car from yesterday. It can't be.

"Cripes, I feel like I got hammered by a lorry," Cece muttered, then nudged Loren. "Are we still working at the Church tonight? Because I'm thinkin' I might have a kip. Hey." She pushed Loren's shoulder. "You're not even listening to me. What's up?"

"Nothing," she muttered, clipping back into her pedal, then pushed off the curb, but Cece cut her off at the next intersection. She got her cleat out of the pedal just in time to stop herself from falling over. "What the fuck, Charlotte!"

"You're hiding something," she hissed, poking her arm with a finger. "Now spill." Loren glanced at Holly, then out at the main road. The rock in her stomach jumped to her chest when the dark blue sedan slowly passed the corner they just left.

"What is it?" Cece turned in the same direction and grabbed her arm. "Is that the car you said followed you yesterday?"

"I don't know," Loren croaked, and Cece moved closer.

"Listen, if we take the next right, we can cut through the neighborhood to the Police Service building on Baker."

Loren shot her a look. "And what am I supposed to tell them?"

"That you're scared," she countered. "That'd be enough."

"I just want to go home," Loren bit back, then clipped into her pedal and took off.

***

The Church Pub was packed for a Tuesday night as Loren, Cece, and Holly entered. Loren led the way to the kitchen, where Anthony was a maestro in the chaos and waved them toward his office.

"Where do you need us?" she asked him as he sat down behind his desk.

"I need Cece in the kitchen, she has the most experience," he said and smirked when Loren stuck out her tongue at him. "You and Holly can help

Nigel behind the bar. It's going to be a brisk night. The Refinements are playing."

"Oh, boy," Loren muttered, and Holly turned to her.

"Who are they?"

"A local ska band," she said, as they left the office. "They're great, but it's going to get a little loud."

"Oh, boy is right!" Holly laughed and pushed open the swinging door to head out in search of Nigel.

As the night went on, Loren found herself smiling more and more. The music and atmosphere lifted her spirits, and she didn't mind the few times she was recognized. Her honor guard of regulars kept to their seats around the bar, discouraging any further conversation past a drink order. When the bar closed just after midnight and cleanup began, she was surprised to feel a little disappointed. After gathering up the trash, she grabbed two bags and turned to the barkeep.

"Nige, I'm going to take these to the dumpster."

"Alright, but mind steps. The light over the door is out," he replied. "I saw it earlier and told Anthony. I'll replace it in the morning."

"Got it," she said and backed through the kitchen door. Anthony was writing out the next day's menu on the blackboard.

"Hey, be careful going out there. The light over the stairs is out," he told her as she passed.

"Yes, yes, Nige just told me," she muttered and pushed open the door to the alley behind the pub. It was darker than she expected as she stepped down and the door closed behind her. The dumpster was lit by a street light shining from the parking lot on the other side of a ten-foot wall. It was bright enough to get there, but dark shadows clung to the walls for the length of the narrow alley. Loren pitched the bags into the bin and started to the door when a voice came out of the dark.

"Aren't you that bird fucking some actor?"

She froze. Her mind raced through hundreds of scenarios, but each one ended with her getting hurt. Bad.

"I saw you wiggling that sweet ass of yours on the TV," the man sneered. A crunch of stone came from her left and Loren took a slow step to the right. "My car's just over the wall there. You gonna get me off in the back seat, too?" He laughed. "Fuck, I'm gettin' a stiffy just thinking about it." A hulking figure was silhouetted from the street light several yards behind him. The door to the Church was fifteen feet beyond him.

I can get past. Big sprint. She balled her fists, tensing. *Three, two, one!* She took off, intent on bolting past, but his reach was longer than she anticipated. He seized her left arm painfully tight and yanked her to his chest.

If you can't get away, remember the details, Anthony's instruction echoed in her mind. She eyed the man through half-closed lids.

Plaid shirt. Big muscles. Slicked back hair. Big nose. Not English. His breath was thick with onions and lager as he pressed his mouth against her cheek. She turned away, wanting to wretch.

"Where do you think you're going, pretty girl? Daddy wants some sugar." His taunt lit the fuse of her rage.

"You do not get to touch me!" She clutched at his shoulder, digging her thumb into the hollow of his clavicle. His bellow echoed off the bricks but was cut short by her knee applied to his groin. Loren readied to jab at his throat with her pointed knuckles when the back door opened, and the alley was flooded with light.

The man shoved her away, and her trainers slipped on the damp cobbles. Pain shot up from her elbow as she fell to the stones. Shouts and running feet, then a hand touched her shoulder. She yelped and turned with fists swinging. Anthony backed away with his hands raised.

"Whoa! It's me!"

"I'm sorry, I'm sorry," she gasped, and he knelt next to her.

"Did he hurt you?"

"No. I don't know." She clutched at his jacket. "He knew who I was," she whimpered. "He knew who I was." Sirens echoed off the brick walls.

"It's alright, he's gone now," he said, brushing her hair out of her face. "Hey, I'd like to be all chivalrous, but I need your help to get up." She nodded, moving to her knees and together, they half-dragged each other up the steps. Once inside the tavern, Anthony sat her down on one of the stools at the bar. Nigel came over with a shot glass filled with amber whisky.

"Here, drink up. Stay calm."

"Right," she muttered and gulped down the shot, coughing as it burned down her throat. Anthony and Cece's hushed conversation was becoming heated, then he turned to glare at her.

Great. Fucking snitch. He moved to stand in front of her, his arms crossed over his chest.

"Were you going to tell anyone else about the car following you?" She turned to scowl at Cece when two uniformed officers came into the pub, followed by a tall woman in a dark overcoat.

"Everyone alright?" the woman asked as she strode over to the bar. "Loren? Are you injured?" She looked up into the dark eyes of Detective Sergeant Theresa O'Dowd.

"I'm okay," she muttered, turning her hand over to inspect her scraped palm. The DS patted her shoulder.

"Let's get your scrapes cleaned up regardless." O'Dowd nodded to a tall, dark-haired uniformed officer and a shorter blond, then addressed the other employees gathered. "Ladies and gentlemen, Officers Gilligan and Neuland are here to coordinate taking your statements. Please, do not leave until you have spoken with one of them." She glanced at Anthony, then gave Loren a slight push.

"Let's go into the office." The DS led the way through the kitchen to Anthony's office where she closed the door. She then grabbed the first aid kit from the wall behind the desk. "Do you want me to tend to your scrapes?"

"I can do it, thanks." O'Dowd handed her the kit, then perched on the corner of the desk. Loren sniffled her way through cleaning the scrapes on her right hand, then the shallow gash on her knee. "These were my favorite jeans," she muttered.

"Having holes in the knees is all the rage, I understand," O'Dowd replied. "Some cost hundreds of pounds. I don't understand that."

"Yah, I don't either," Loren replied, picking at the fraying cotton, unable to quell the fear choking her. "He knew who I was, Theresa."

"Take a deep breath, then tell me what happened." Loren clenched her hands in her lap.

"I was taking the trash out to the dumpster. Nige and Anthony both warned me the light over the door was out," she said, her breath coming faster. "I couldn't see when I was coming back, and some guy came out of the dark and grabbed me." She looked up. "I kicked him in the nuts."

"Good show," O'Dowd said, smirking, then softened her tone. "I know you don't want to, but I need you to tell me as much detail about him as you can." Loren nodded and closed her eyes.

"He wasn't English, that I'm sure of," she replied. "He was big, but not tall. Muscular. His trapezius was well developed. I had to work to get my thumb in there." She touched the muscles near her neck. "Plaid shirt. I didn't see his face clearly, it was too dark, but his hair was slicked back." She shifted in her seat and felt the crinkle of paper in her back pocket. There had been another note in her mailbox that afternoon. *Tell her. Do it. You're not safe.* She let out a shaky breath.

"Um, I've been finding strange notes in my mail." Loren took out the envelope and handed it to her. "This one was in the box when I got home today. No postage, no return address. I haven't opened it." She started wringing her hands as O'Dowd carefully tore open the envelope and read it.

"I hear you."

Loren swallowed hard. "The first one said I see you." She then brought out the necklace from her front pocket and handed it over. "Yesterday, when I went to get my motorcycle out of the shed, this was hanging from it. Graham gave it to me, and I never took it off until Felix…" She held her breath for a few seconds. "I've cleaned the front room and the kitchen several times without finding it, but then to have it hanging on my bike, in a locked shed, months later?" The tight knot in her throat began to grow, stealing her voice.

"When I was headed out to Northaw to meet with Graham's agent, a dark sedan was following me. I got a photo of the tag." She handed over her mobile with the picture of the car. "Today, we were heading home from the training center, and I saw that car again." O'Dowd's expression tightened as she stood and opened the office door. Officer Gilligan was in the kitchen, chatting with Holly.

"I'm sorry to interrupt your lovely date, Hamish, but please jot down this tag number and ring the station for a search."

"Will do," he replied, his grin widening at Holly. The DS shut the door and sat down on the corner the desk, studying Loren for several moments before speaking.

"I'm going to take you home, but I think you should gather up a few things and stay with Anthony," she said. "Or, if you'd rather, I can take you to Colin's or perhaps another friend?" Loren turned away, her panic rising, but O'Dowd moving to sit next to her snapped her out of it.

"I was going to ring you tomorrow about some developments in your case, but I don't want to add to your stress."

"Just tell me," Loren whispered. O'Dowd dropped her chin and let out a breath.

"The Court has offered Lalonde a plea bargain, and if he accepts, he'll plead guilty to a lesser offense. There won't be a trial, and you won't have to testify." Loren's hand jumped to her throat.

"He attacked me in my home, Theresa. He needs to be held accountable for that."

"I agree," she said grimacing, "but, if there were a trial, his defense would dig into every past relationship to paint you as something you're not."

"He called me a whore," she whispered, turning her head away.

"If he takes the plea, your character can't be scrutinized," Theresa said. "Loren, he made a statement that you struck him first, and he was merely defending himself."

Her mouth dropped open. "What?"

"Lalonde's had witnesses come forward to offer testimony in support of leniency," she said, her frown deepening. "It's despicable, I know, but he has no criminal record, in any country. No complaints have been lodged that we could discover. Not even a parking ticket. Do you know of anything–."

"No," Loren choked. "I don't know anything." She started to rise, but O'Dowd put a hand on her knee.

"Are you certain?"

"I don't know anything," she repeated, louder, but the DS didn't let her go.

"Graham's agent must have used a security firm before. I think it might be–." Loren pushed her hand off and stood up.

"I'm not going to have some bodyguard following me around again," she hissed. "They did that to me in Richmond after that Montgomery woman stirred up shit. All it did was set me further apart." She made for the door, but O'Dowd blocked her.

"You're frightened, and perhaps not thinking clearly."

"I will not be intimidated," she snarled and walked out. All heads turned as Loren burst through the door to the kitchen, followed by O'Dowd.

"I got word from Clark," Officer Gilligan said, stepping forward. "The plates on that blue saloon came back stolen."

"Thank you, Hamish." O'Dowd turned to Loren. "Please, rethink your stance." She crossed her arms over her chest, leveling a scowl at the DS.

"I'm going home," she countered. "I will not be chased out of my house again." Hamish adjusted his utility belt, puffing out his chest.

"Well, I'm about to clock out," he said, glancing at Holly. "I can, um, hang around, in case somebody decides to bother you."

Holly grinned back at him. "Heck, I'd feel a whole lot safer having a police officer around."

***

7 October

It was late morning when her bedroom door open, and a dog's snuffling came from the other side of the room. The bed shook, and a cold nose was shoved in her face.

"Leave me alone, dog," Loren muttered and turned over. Alfie sniffled at the back of her neck, and she shrugged him off. "Seriously! Get off." He whined and pawed at the blanket, then gingerly stepped in a circle before settling down with his head draped over her side.

"Anthony let you in to get me out of bed," she grumbled. A few minutes later, her mobile pinged another text message from Graham. She picked it up and gave a soft laugh at a short video of him goofing around on a child's tricycle, his knees in his chest as he tried to pedal. Loren sent a reply of 'LOL' and turned over to hug her pillow again.

Soon, the scent of frying bacon wafted through her room, and her stomach began to make a case for eating. She groaned, threw off the covers and got out of bed. Anthony was at the stove when she entered the kitchen with Alfie at her heels and she sat down at the table.

"Why are you here?" she grumbled. The dog bumped his head against his master's elbow.

"About time you came down," Anthony said, glancing over his shoulder at her. "I wasn't sure you were alive."

"Very funny."

"Cece rang me. She's worried about you." He set a plate with bacon, toast and three eggs, sunny-side-up, on the table and sat down across from her. She narrowed her eyes as he buttered the toast, then dipped a corner in the eggs and glanced up at her. "Sorry, did you want some?" He chuckled when her mouth popped open, and he slid the plate to her. "I'm joking, but I'm keeping the toast."

She pushed it back. "I can make my own."

"No, you can't."

"Yes, I can." They glared at each other until Alfie tried to grab the bacon off the plate. "Alfie, no!" She pushed him off, but broke off a piece for him, then pushed the eggs around with a corner of toast.

"Are you alright?" Anthony asked.

"No, I'm not. Every time I close my eyes…" She took a breath. "How did you know I was in trouble?"

"You can be pretty loud when you want to be," he replied. "What do you recall about him?" She put the toast down, unable to eat it.

"He was big, like Colin, but not as tall. Six foot, maybe," she replied. "I think he ate at the pub. Your shepherd's pie has a lot of onions in it, and that's what his breath smelled like."

He narrowed his eyes. "My shepherd's pie is perfectly balanced."

"Yah, right," she scoffed, rubbing her arm. "My arm still hurts. And my knee."

"You got him in the plums?" She nodded, biting her lip. "Good show," he chuckled, but it died quickly at her strained voice.

"He knew who I was. He said he saw me with Graham in Ingrid's car and asked if I was going to get him off, too." She squeezed her eyes closed as the man's words echoed back. *Where do you think you're going, pretty girl? Daddy wants some sugar.* Her hands clenched as bile rose in her throat. "He was… he was going to…"

"Easy." Anthony stood and drew her to her feet to take her in his arms. "You're safe. We're not going to leave you alone."

Loren held back her tears. "I'm not safe. Not anymore."

***

8 October

Loren was packing to leave for Bologna when her mobile pinged a video call. She heaved a sigh, plastered a false smile on her face and answered.

"Hello, love," she said, but Graham was not smiling, and his voice had a hard edge to it.

"One-word replies to my texts are not enough, Loren. Why haven't you gotten back to me?" She sat down at her desk but couldn't meet his gaze.

"I was busy," she replied. When she finally looked at him, his scowl was scorching.

"You were busy," he repeated, a little muscle in his jaw jumping. "Because you didn't ring me back, I had to find out from Charlotte what's been going on with you. Someone tried to attack you the other night?" His blue eyes bored into her at her silence. "I've had Ron arrange for a security agent for you, and you will comply. Do you understand me?"

Anger flashed through her. "You have no right to tell me what to do," she bit back. Graham winced away, pressing the back of his hand against his mouth.

"Please," he croaked. "Please, Loren." She bit her lip as a tear slid down his cheek.

"You will not speak to me like that again."

"I'm sorry," he said, his chin trembling, "but it's killing me that I can't be there to protect you."

"That is not your job!" She squeezed her eyes shut. "This is exactly why I didn't want to tell you."

"Please don't do that. Please don't hide things from me." The pain in his voice was almost too much for her to bear.

"Don't you get it? When you freak out, I freak out more and then…" Loren pinched the bridge of her nose. "I understand you want to be the knight in shining armor for me, and if you were here, I would probably let you, but I don't need you to save me, Graham. I just need you to love me." He met her gaze, his eyes glistening.

"I do, I swear, but please, please do this for me. I'm afr–." He shook his head. "Please, just cooperate."

"Fine," she muttered and let out a shaky breath.

"Thank you," Graham said quietly, then glanced over his shoulder. "Dammit. I have to go. Ring me in the morning, please, before you leave. I don't care what time it is."

"I will," Loren replied, then disconnected to stare at the Claddagh on her finger. *I don't want this.* She took a breath. *Just breathe. Let it come. Breathe in and let it go.*

***

It was after ten that night when voices echoed from the kitchen, and Loren came down to find Ron Hudson with his head stuck in the refrigerator. She crossed her arms over her chest and leaned into the door frame, pointedly ignoring the other man seated at the table near the back door.

"I don't think there's much in there," she said, and Ron jumped back and shut the door.

"Oy, hey." He rubbed his beard, which was growing in much redder than the brown hair on his head. She glanced down at his electric green suede shoes.

"Nice shoes." She kicked out a foot to show off her neon green trainers.

"I knew there was a reason why I liked you." His slight smile disappeared. "Keeping your chin up?"

"Yah, I'm fine." Movement brought her eyes to the man seated at the table, and as he stood, his head rose several inches above her and Ron. His lean, muscular physique was well-defined by his slim cut charcoal suit. Thick brows framed almond-shaped eyes as dark as his artfully tousled hair. But it was the tiny smirk on his face that set her off.

"Loren, this is Derek Graves of Lester Security," Ron said.

"I don't want you here," she said, her voice low.

"I understand your anger, Loren, but I'm here to provide for your safety," he replied in an annoyingly proper British accent. He crossed his arms over his chest. "I've had many clients in your situation–."

"You're only here because Graham has some fucking hang up about protecting me," she growled, stalking toward him with clenched fists. "I don't need your protection. I can take care of myself." He stooped slightly to meet her hard gaze.

"You reckon so? You've been lucky so far, but the next time someone comes after you, and there will be a next time, you won't stand a chance by yourself." She moved fast; punching him hard in the jaw, and Derek stumbled backward, into the kitchen table.

"Whoa! Steady on, now!" Ron jumped in front of her, his hands on her shoulders. She pushed against him, swearing in three different languages as Holly and Hamish walked in through the back door.

"Oy! That's enough!" Hamish barked, stepping in front of the much taller stranger and flashed his badge. "What in blazes is going on? Who are you?"

"Derek Graves, Officer. I'm with Lester Security," he said, rubbing jaw as he righted himself. "I was hired by Graham Atherton."

"Well and good then. He's taking the threat seriously," Hamish replied. "I'm certain you have a permit for that Taser on your belt."

Loren lurched away from Ron, the voices around her drowned out by the harshness of her breath. Her lips were tingling, and her muscles primed to flee.

Run! We'll be safe if we run! Her brother screamed. She put her hands over her ears and turned, her gaze locking on Derek.

"I'm not safe," she gasped. "I'm not safe." Her knees buckled, and all went black. When she came to, she was lying on the sofa in the living room, with Derek sitting on the coffee table next to her. Ron, Holly and Hamish were gone. She pushed up on her elbow.

"I passed out, didn't I?"

"Take it slow," he replied, helping her to sit up, then handed over a tissue. "How long have you had panic attacks?"

Loren sniffled. "I've had them my whole life to varying degrees. This was only the second time I've passed out. I-I need to get some air," she croaked, her eyes darting around the room.

"Excellent idea." He got up from the table and gave her a hand up, then led her through the kitchen. She grabbed her parka from the closet near the door, and they settled across from each other at the bistro table outside. She fiddled with the zipper pull on her jacket, glancing up at him.

"He trusts you, why?" she asked. Derek sighed, leaning his forearms on the table to link his fingers.

"I was part of Graham's security team in Africa two years ago. We found ourselves in a few tight spots and got to know each other fairly quickly," he told her, giving a tight smile. "He's typically level-headed, even when under duress, but when I spoke with him today, to say he is concerned about you is putting it lightly." He leaned forward a bit more. "From what he told me, you've been through hell." She crossed her arms tightly over her chest, averting her eyes.

"He told you, about me?" she whispered.

"Don't be angry with him. I needed to know," he told her. "Ron's group is very good at what they do, but their focus is Graham. You are ours." They were quiet for a few moments as Loren fiddled the Claddagh around on her finger.

"I'm sorry I hit you," she said, grimacing.

"Don't be," Derek told her, rubbing his jaw. "Your reflexes are quick, and you've got a good right cross. We can build on that."

***

10 October

Bologna, Italy

Loren woke to the sound of her mobile buzzing on the nightstand and rolled over to grab it before it vibrated off. She smiled at the caller ID and connected.

"Hey, you." She cringed at the harshness of her whisper and coughed.

"Hello, darling," Graham replied. "Did I wake you?"

"That's okay. My alarm was going to go off soon anyway," she said.

"Gawd, shut feck up," a voice grumbled from the other side of the room.

"Sorry, Cece," Loren muttered and got out of bed to head to the bathroom. "I'm sorry we didn't connect yesterday."

"It's alright. I got your message. Ron and Derek showed up, then?"

"Yes," she replied, rubbing her nose. "And then I had a panic attack."

"I'm sorry, love."

"It's not your fault," she said, then narrowed her eyes. "Oh wait, yes, it is." He gave a soft laugh but then was silent for a moment.

"I don't know what to do, which leads me to overreact." She ran her hand over her face.

"I don't think you're overreacting. I think it's me, underreacting. I'm being an ostrich with my head in the sand."

"Ostriches don't put their heads in the sand," he said flatly, and she shook her head.

"Alright, Mr. Smarty-Pants, I'm in denial," she retorted.

"You're in Egypt? But I thought you were going to Bologna." She held in a laugh, then tucked her lip in her teeth.

"You're trying to be shiny and distract me, but it's not going to work. Something's bothering you, I can sense it. What is it?"

He gave a long exhale. "I don't normally pay much attention, but it appears TMZOnline is reporting you've replaced me rather quickly."

She lowered her mobile to eye level and entered the website. The first images were of her, huddled under Derek's arm, or holding his hand as they walked through the airport the previous day. The headline read: *Has the love affair run its course?* She put her hand over her mouth.

"Oh my god."

"Don't worry, darling," he told her. "I know it's not the truth."

"It's so not the truth," she whined.

"Loren, it's alright," he said, his voice gentle.

"How can they make shit up and get away with it?" She pressed her hand to her chest and turned around. "It's not fair!"

"I know it's not fair, but it will pass, it always does," Graham told her. "Maybe Jude Law will start dating someone else, and they'll focus on that." Her mobile buzzed against her cheek.

"Dammit. I'm sorry, I have to go."

"I understand. I love you. Good luck."

"I love you, too." Loren disconnected, then placed her hands on the counter to meet her pinched expression in the mirror. She focused on her breathing, and as her muscles relaxed, all trace of fear disappeared.

"I am the storm. I will not be afraid."

***

Giro dell'Emilia Internazionale Donne Elite
Bologna – San Luca, 99km

"Buongiorno e benvenuti to the Giro dell'Emilia Internazionale Donne Elite! I'm Peter Donnelly and with me today is the incredible Michaela Navarre, or should I say, Michaela Tessaro! Congratulations on your recent nuptials to Formula One driver, Amatus Tessaro."

"Why, thank you, Peter. That's very kind of you! Today's race began in the city of Bologna and winds 99 kilometers through the countryside to ascend the famed San Luca. It's on that final two-kilometer climb, with an average grade of nearly eleven percent, where we expect the big guns to come out firing."

"As we join the action at kilometer 67, the peloton has kept itself mostly intact. There have been multiple attacks by the leading teams, but World Champion Samantha Sharpe and her GoreTech teammates have been shutting down every attempt to break out."

Loren rode amidst a sea of colorful jerseys near the front of the peloton, trying to ignore the prickling on the back of her neck. They were shadowing her and Samantha Sharpe, waiting to see what they were going to do.

Riders ahead surged out of the saddle as another breakaway was attempted and two from GoreTech went after them. Loren responded, but only to increase her pace enough to keep up. She glanced over at her teammate, Elsa, who nodded. Holly was a row or two back, but Loren couldn't see her.

Hopefully, she's paying attention.

"IDC's Loren Mackenzie appears to have had enough of the close quarters and takes off, teammate Elsa Rinaldi right on her wheel."

"Riders from Orca-Roto and PZI answer the attack, with Samantha Sharpe and teammate, Polina Federov jumping on, as expected."

"And there goes IDC's Holly Parker to add to the fray!"

"Let's see if this group can work together to stay ahead of the chasers."

"Sharpe's your only threat," James said into her earpiece. "Holly is on the back to support."

Loren held back a smile. *Good. Let's get the plan going.*

"Mackenzie trades off with PZI's Ardyn Cole, who takes over the pace-keeping to hold the breakaway free and clear."

"*Even with the peloton in full cry, the gap extends to 22 seconds as they come within sight of the San Luca.*"

"*Sharpe is biding her time and letting the others battle it out. The only one who seems to be conscious of her plan is IDC's Mackenzie, who keeps glancing back at the GoreTech rider.*"

"*I'm feeling skittish, and I'm not even out there, Peter! The mountain road going up the San Luca isn't wide enough for three riders abreast, and narrower still with spectators on either side.*"

People lined the road as the small group charged up the steep strip of tarmac. Riders jostled for position, elbows jutting out to push away competitors and fans alike. A few spectators, some practically naked, ran next to the cyclists, holding signs or flags, and screaming in their faces.

Loren clenched her teeth, shouldering one body out of her way as she rose out of the saddle. Two men were running ahead of the group when something big and yellow materialized in front of her wheel.

"Fuck!" She dropped her hips over the seat, jerking the handlebars back while scooping the pedals up to hop over the tumbling man's legs.

"Did you see that? What a show of skill by Mackenzie! She bunny hops over a falling man in a banana suit!"

"*Thank goodness she has quick reactions. That would have been a terrible turn of events for IDC if she went down.*"

"Let's watch that replay again!"

As she caught up to Elsa, Loren reached down for her water bottle, but her hand met only open air.

"Shit, I lost my bottle." Elsa came in close and handed over one of hers.

"What happened? What was that?"

"Some fucking idiot in a banana suit," Loren grumbled and squirted water into her mouth. "Are you ready to end this?"

The Italian gave her a big grin. "I'm right behind you."

"The breakaway is torn asunder by Mackenzie and PZI's Ardyn Cole is the first to get shot off the back."

"*I wonder if anyone realizes her strategy.*"

"This is what burying yourself for your teammates looks like!"

Loren settled into a hard rhythm as the grade lessened by a degree, trying to stay loose and weaving through spectators. Her mind flashed back to the road race in Richmond. On Governor Street, she had glanced over her shoulder but didn't see her Team USA captain, Amber Moll behind her.

I can't look back for Elsa. She had to trust that her teammate was staying on her wheel. If Loren let up, she'd lose momentum on the climb and any hope of a podium spot for the team would be lost.

"We're within the final kilometer of the summit of the San Luca and the grade increases to sixteen percent! Oh, the agony! Mackenzie and Rinaldi are keeping to the saddle, grinding the mountain to dust!"

"Ariel Montoya is going full bore for her Orca-Roto leader, Chloe Monteith. Using a sprinter as your lead out; what a novel idea but seems to be working!"

"GoreTech's Federov is right there to mix it up for her team leader, Samantha Sharpe, inching their way past the riders from Orca-Roto."

"Mackenzie must have stolen banana-man's legs back there as she explodes out of the saddle into the last 500 meters. Rinaldi uses her teammate's incredible effort to launch ahead of the chasers."

"Samantha Sharpe jumps ahead to battle Elsa Rinaldi to the line, but it's the Italian who crosses first to win the Giro dell'Emilia!"

Loren and Holly crossed the finish line seconds after the leaders, holding each other's hand high and screaming with laughter. They caught up with Elsa, who was all smiles.

"You did it!" Loren gave her a hug.

"No, we did it," Elsa countered, and as the rest of the team gathered, she waved them closer. "We did this, together. This was our win, our season, and we should celebrate it! *Facciamo festa!*"

***

The team gathered in one of the conference rooms at the hotel and quickly tucked into the spread of salads, several pizzas and three bottles of champagne. Then, James and Ulrik walked in with huge smiles on their faces.

"Ladies, ladies! May I have your attention?" James clapped his hands, and all heads turned to him. "I have here the official team ranking for the season." He held up an envelope and ever so slowly, tore it open.

"Dad! For Pete's sake!" Holly laughed.

"Alright, alright," he chuckled and unfolded the paper. "In first, no surprise here, Orca-Roto. In second, PZI Sports." He cleared his throat, flicking the paper several times. "Now, this is a surprise. Innovative Design Cycling has officially taken third in the team ranking for the season!" Cece whooped and threw her cap in the air as the other riders cheered and hugged each other.

"Our little team is a force to be reckoned with," Ulrik told them. "You've proven yourselves under fire, and we are very proud of all of you." Somehow, the smile on James' face widened as he looked to each team member.

"I also wanted to announce I've decided to stay on as director. If you'll have me, that is." They all rushed him, nearly knocking him over with hugs. Loren was last to approach.

"I knew you wouldn't be able to leave us," she said, going in for a tight hug.

"You lot are easier to deal with," he chuckled. "Much less drama." His smile dissolved as they separated. "Darren told me of your offer to make up for the financial losses we've had. You shouldn't feel the need to do that."

"If I can help, I want to," she replied, glancing over at her teammates. "I'm investing in their future, and maybe my own." She covered a sudden yawn. "Sorry. I'm dead." He chuckled, giving her a pat on the shoulder.

"Go get some sleep. We'll see you in the morning."

Loren headed to the elevator and heard a giggling Cece come up behind her, nose to screen with her mobile.

"Have you seen the replay? The look on your face! It's priceless!" she laughed. "I'm gonna call you Guppy from now on."

"Oh god, don't remind me," Loren muttered. "I can't believe how many times they've shown that." When the doors opened, both women got on, and Loren pressed their floor button. Cece slumped against the back wall.

"I can barely even keep my eyes open," she yawned.

"I think I tweaked something," Loren groaned, stretching her back. "I haven't had to do a bunny hop that high since the Dairy Cross race last year."

"Speaking of that, are we still going?"

"Yes, of course," Loren replied as the doors opened to their floor, and they started walking down the hall. "Why would you even question that?"

"Because you got your own shite going on," Cece said. "It's not like we've had time to have a good 'ole chin wag like we use'ta."

"Yah, I know," she sighed and leaned her forehead against the door of their room. It moved under the pressure. Loren stood back, holding up the keycard in her hand, then looked at Cece. "That's not supposed to happen."

An intense tingle of adrenaline shot her heart rate up as she pushed on the door and again, it opened without her inserting the keycard. Cece shouldered the door aside and entered the room as Loren flicked the light switch. A lamp lying on the floor near the windows turned on, and their mouths dropped open.

Their duffels had been emptied and their clothing strewn across the carpet. The beds were upended. Drawers were pulled out from the dressers and smashed on the floor.

Loren clenched her fists at her sides, her lip curling into a snarl as she stalked around the room. The door to the bathroom was closed and she kicked it open, the knob slamming into the drywall behind it. Their personal items were dumped out on the vanity, and the curtain was torn off the rod.

On the mirror, written in black marker, were the words, *I see you.*

A red haze came over her vision. A small metal stool was under the sink counter, and Cece's voice faded against a high-pitched whine in her ears. Then came the echo of glass shattering.

"Loren! What have you done?" She spun around. Derek was standing in the doorway, and shards of glass littered the floor at his feet. Blood trickled down her wrist from a gash on her forearm. She was holding the stool.

"Oh my god," she moaned and dropped it. Tiny red half-moons marked her palms. Hands grabbed her shoulders. Derek was speaking to her, but she couldn't understand him. Cece took her arm and led her across the hall to Derek's room. Loren turned around in a circle, clutching handfuls of her hair at the crown.

"Oh, my god, oh, my god," she whined, and Cece pushed her toward the bed.

"Sit down, sit. It's just stuff. It doesn't matter." Loren brought her knees to her chest, rocking and trying to breathe. The bed moved as her friend sat down and grabbed Loren's arm to tend to the cut.

"Ow. That stings."

"Why did you break the mirror?"

She froze. "I broke the mirror?"

"Yah, you chucked the stool at it," Cece replied. "Frightened the bejesus outta me."

"I'm sorry." They both jumped when Loren's mobile began to play Graham's ringtone from across the room. "I can't talk to him," she choked. "Please, I can't." Cece gave her a look and walked away as she curled into a tight ball on the bed. *Let it come. Breathe.* She choked on a sob. *I can't do this.* A few seconds later, her mobile was shoved in her face.

"I'm not gonna cover for you again," she muttered. Loren took a shaky breath and accepted her mobile.

"Hi, Graham."

"Hello, love. I had a few minutes and wanted to ring you," he said. "I saw the replay. That was quite a jump." She gave a soft laugh mixed with a sob.

"Yah. It's easier going uphill." She sniffled, and the line was silent for a moment.

"Loren, what's wrong?" She pressed her lips together.

"Nothing. I just have a sniffle." Muffled voices came through the speaker.

"Dammit. I'll be there in a minute," he said, raising his voice, then coughed. "Darling, are you certain–."

"I'm good, really," she replied, forcing a lighter tone in her voice. "It's okay. Just call me again when you can."

"I love you and congratulations."

"Thanks." She squeezed her eyes shut. "I love you, too." She disconnected, then dropped the mobile to cover her face with her hands. Cece put her arm around her shoulders, but after a minute, Loren shrugged her off. "I'm fine," she muttered.

"No, you're not." They both looked up as voices came from the hallway, then a knock on the door.

"Cece, it's me. Open the door, please," came Derek's muffled voice and she rose to let him inside. "How are you two holding up?" he asked as he entered the room.

"She says we're fine," Cece retorted, while Loren wiped her nose with her sleeve. "May I go and see what's salvageable?"

"Not yet. The police are there right now," he said then sat down on the other bed to face Loren.

"Do I need to give a statement or something?" she asked.

"No, I took care of that," he replied. "You're going to stay in here tonight."

She sat up. "Where are you staying?"

"Right there." He pointed to the sofa.

"And what about me?" Cece grumbled.

"Aria is coming to take you to stay with Holly and Ashley."

Loren's mouth dropped. "But why can't I–." Derek put his hand up.

"Because it was your room, and only your room, that was ransacked, and I'm not going to sit in front of your door all night." His gaze held hers. "Why did you break the mirror?"

"I don't know." Loren closed her eyes and the words written on the mirror appeared. She put her hands over her face, and her shoulders shook with silent sobs.

***

13 October

Northaw, England

Loren woke at the barest amount of light in the room and stared at the pale blue ceiling above her. Sheer drapes covered the window wall leading to the deck and wake pool. She turned her head, and dark wood doors to the walk-in closet and the bathroom came into focus. She closed her eyes and sighed.

I don't want to be here without Graham, but I couldn't have Derek sleep on the couch another night at my house.

"And this mattress is still too damned hard," she groaned and rolled out of bed, stretching her back on the walk to the bathroom. From there, she went through the study to the kitchen. Rubbing her eyes with her knuckles, she bumped into the doorway.

"You're up early," a male voice chuckled. Her mouth dropped open at Derek standing at the kitchen sink in just a pair of joggers. Dark hair covered his muscular chest and down his taut abs in such a way that led her gaze lower.

And that's enough gawking. She ran the back of her hand over her eyes and turned when an unfamiliar raspy chuckle made her spin around. A woman was sitting on the other side of the island. Dark brows arched above hazel green eyes, and her black hair was pulled back in a loose ponytail. Derek put his hands up when Loren raised a brow at him.

"It's not what it looks like."

"I didn't say anything." She turned to the refrigerator and opened the door to grab a can of Ryzak recovery drink before facing them. He was leaning on the edge of the island, his arms folded over his chest with a smug look on his face. Loren quickly covered her eyes with her hand.

"Dude, just because you like it when the paparazzi goes nuts over your hairy chest does *not* mean you get to walk around half naked every second," she griped.

"I think I'm going to like this one," the woman laughed.

"This is my associate, Penny O'Neill," Derek chuckled as he passed. "She's going to be with you from now on." Loren did a double-take, but he had already walked down the hall. She turned to the woman.

"Wait, what does he mean?"

"Ron asked me to come on board precisely because the paps are so enamored with your new beau," Penny replied. "I suppose he reckoned that if you held *my* hand, we'd draw a different sort of attention."

Loren pressed her lips together. *Let it in. Breathe.* Derek stepped back into the kitchen wearing a white T-shirt, and she turned her glare to him.

"I don't want this," she said quietly.

"I know you don't, but we need to keep you safe," he replied, rubbing her arm. Her frown deepened as she turned back to the newcomer.

"I'm sorry for my rudeness, Penny. Thank you for helping me."

"It's alright, petal," she said, giving a warm smile. "What's on our agenda for today?"

"I need to train for a time trial next week," Loren replied. "I have a doctor's appointment later, and Graham asked if I could take the Jaguar to the dealership for an oil change. It's right next door." She gave a cheeky grin. "And, there's a Mini Cooper there I wanted to check out." She eyed Penny's leather jacket on the back of her chair. "I like your jacket. What do you ride?"

"A Ducati Monster." Penny stood up and walked around the island, motioning to her black and red leather slacks. "But I wore this just to show off for Ron."

***

Ron Hudson buried his head beneath the pillows at the rumble of motorcycle engines vibrating the windows above his head.

"Mother in heaven!" He rolled out of bed, stomping to the windows that faced the cobbled driveway and threw the curtain aside. Two motorcycles were parked near the garage, their leather-clad riders sitting on them. Loren was standing with a strange looking bicycle, talking with a dark-haired woman on a red Ducati.

Ah, that's just Penny, but who is that? His eyes narrowed at the other woman in black and pink leather on a white Suzuki. He grabbed his trousers from the chair and yanked them on, then slipped on his loafers and crossed the room to the glass slider to the patio. Loren waved to him as he rounded the corner of the house.

"Hey, sleeping beauty! Come over here!" The other two women turned to him as Ron approached. He smiled with a nod to Penny, then turned to the woman in pink.

"Hello, I'm Ron Hudson." He looked up slightly as he offered his hand to her and she grasped it firmly.

"Good to finally meet you," she said, removing her sunglasses to reveal deep brown eyes. "I'm Theresa O'Dowd."

His grin widened. "To what do we owe the pleasure of your visit, Detective Sergeant?"

"I happened to be in the neighborhood," she replied. "I pulled up to the gate at the same time they did."

"Oh, so you are just returning?" He looked at his watch. "Would you ladies like to join me for a bit of luncheon?" Loren glanced over her shoulder as she headed to the house.

"I'd love to, but Penny and I are heading out."

He turned to Theresa. "I reckon that means it's just us."

"Don't forget Derek," Penny told him as she followed Loren inside. "He was looking forward to Thai food."

"Excellent. After you," he said, motioning to the front door for O'Dowd to proceed.

***

Loren headed straight to the master, closing the door behind her and slumped against it. Around every corner, she imagined seeing the dark sedan following them, and the stress of holding back the waves of panic left her drained.

Stop it. I'm just freaking out again. Penny would have said something if she saw the car. She knocked her fist against her forehead. *Just stop it.*

Graham had sent an email while she was riding, and she took out her mobile before flopping down on the bed.

> My dearest Loren:
>
> Every day we spend apart is a day I do not feel the sun on my face. Hearing your voice and seeing your smile is as a balm to the ache in my heart. Knowing that I will soon hold you in my arms, feel your soft skin under my hands, and your tender lips against mine steels me against the longing of my soul.
>
> I'm sorry we haven't been able to connect over the last few days. I know you keep saying that you're all right, but emails aren't enough for me anymore. I need to hear your voice. I need to see your face.
>
> Ring me when you can, no matter the time. I love you.

She closed her eyes and breathed deeply, then turned over and started a video call. Graham answered on the second ring with a sleepy smile.

"Hello, darling," he murmured, stretching to turn on the bedside lamp, then snuggled into the blanket again.

"I'm sorry to wake you."

"'S alright." His smile faded as he closed his eyes. "I was dreaming of you."

"Tell me," she murmured, tilting her head.

"I was seven, and I had gotten separated from my mother at the Victoria Museum. I was watching several children running through the hall, and when I turned back, she was gone. I vividly remember that feeling of panic." He gave a slight wince. "I was back in the museum in my dream, but I was with you. You ran ahead, and I could hear you calling out for me, but the hall became longer and longer, and I couldn't reach you."

She gave a soft smile. "If you take me there, I promise not to let go of your hand."

"Thank you," he said, matching her smile. "You're in your cycling kit. I reckon you're feeling better?"

Loren shrugged. "Luckily, the sniffle didn't turn into anything. I'll have a soak for my back later, after a bit of a get-to-know-you excursion to Dr. Howell's office with my new friend."

"Ah, yes. Penelope O'Neill."

She raised a brow. "You knew?"

"Ron suggested her after The Sun alluded you've replaced me with a more handsome version." She looked down her nose at him.

"There's no replacing you, Graham, especially not with someone skinnier than you," Loren countered. "But I can't let you pay for the added expense."

He gave a half grin. "I appreciate that, but shouldn't how I spoil you be up to me?"

"Oh, I see." She squinted an eye at him. "Since you're not spoiling me with jewelry or a car like Benny did with Alejandra, you're spoiling me with security?" He drew in a breath then blew it out, pursing his lips.

"I reckon so."

She shook her head. "*Je t'adore, mon amour,*" she murmured, then rose from the bed with a groan. "I have to get cleaned up, and while I wouldn't mind you watching, you might want to go back to sleep."

"Yes, that would be rather painful to watch," he chortled. "We'll talk later."

"You bet," she replied but hesitated to disconnect. "Graham?" His brow went up in question. She took a breath to speak, but her emotions clashed with her thoughts, so she just gave him a tight smile. "I love you, you know that, right?" He nodded, but the corners of his mouth turned down.

"Talk to me, darling."

She shrugged a shoulder. "I just miss you a bit more today."

"Absence doth sharpen love; presence strengthens it," he said gently. "The one brings fuel, the other blows it till it burns clear."

She blinked at him. "That's Shakespeare, isn't it?"

"I have yet to find it in any of his writings, but it is attributed to him."

"Go back to sleep," Loren chuckled, shaking her head.

***

After Loren and Penny left, Theresa O'Dowd sat down at the kitchen island and wrapped her hands around her mug of tea. Her eyes flicked to Derek, then to Ron, who frowned at her.

"You look as if you don't have good news."

"No, I don't," she replied, taking out a folder from her pack and put it on the counter. "I've dug a bit further into Lalonde's past. Loren is not the first."

Derek nodded. "That doesn't surprise me."

She opened the file. "Three complaints were brought to the police. Two were in the US; the third was in France, in the early part of his career. None of them went beyond an initial inquiry, but the last one, in Seattle, was just after he retired from racing."

Ron sat up straighter. "You mean after Loren?" She nodded and slid a photo to him, and his eyes widened. "Other than the nose, this could be her." He passed to Derek a photograph of a young woman with shoulder length, brown hair, and aquiline features.

O'Dowd continued. "He was an Assistant Director with a men's team for about eighteen months. That young woman was a *soigneur*." She shuffled through the file and took out another sheaf of paper. "I've been in touch with her lawyer, and he was kind enough to email me the police report, redacted, of course." She handed it to Derek, who paged through it quickly.

Ron scratched his brow. "How come all this wasn't presented to the Crown Court?"

"It's inadmissible," she replied. "In each case, there was no further investigation. The complaints were withdrawn."

"Withdrawn?" Derek's voice deepened as he turned to a page in the report. "You read her statement. Do you believe she would have voluntarily done so?"

"Lalonde claimed it was consensual, and I understand there was a rather large settlement," O'Dowd answered.

"Here, let me see that." Ron wiggled his fingers, and Derek handed the papers over. He blanched after reading the page. "Mother in heaven. You can't believe she consented to be tied up." He looked back at the report. "This says there was GHB in her system," he noted, then locked eyes with O'Dowd. "If Ainsworth hadn't shown up…"

She nodded. "I think Lalonde knew her roommates weren't going to be home for some time. He didn't have any drugs on his person so, perhaps he believed he could play on their former relationship. He claims she struck him first."

Ron shook his head. "I don't doubt she did. Regardless, he still got the better of her," he grumbled. He then cleared his throat and removed his mobile from his pocket. "I reckon Graham needs to hear this. Any objections?" He glanced at both of them, and when neither dissented, he chose the contact. Graham answered on the second ring.

"You're up early," he joked.

"Hmm, funny," Ron said. "I have you on speaker with Derek and DS O'Dowd."

There was a pause. "Ah, hold on a minute." Graham's muffled voice came through, then he cleared his throat. "Sorry, Ron, I was getting coffee. Is everything alright? I spoke with Loren not an hour ago."

"Everything's fine, Graham. I'm not here in an official capacity," O'Dowd said. "I was explaining to Derek and Ron that I dug a bit more into Lalonde's past and I found three cases that were brought to the attention of the police. The most recent about four years ago, in Seattle."

Graham sucked in a breath. "That wasn't very long after she left. How come this wasn't brought before the Crown Court?"

"That's what I asked," Ron interrupted. "In each case, the complaint was withdrawn by the victim."

O'Dowd spoke then. "I believe Lalonde knew her roommates were not going to be home. It's possible he had been monitoring her activities outside of the team somehow." There was an even longer pause. "Graham? Are you still there?" He took an uneasy breath.

"Could Lalonde have something to do with whoever is following her now?"

"I'm not certain," O'Dowd replied. "We weren't able to identify the man from the Church on CCTV, but two witnesses corroborated Loren's description." She looked to Derek. "Was there security footage from the hotel in Bologna?"

"Yes, there was and–."

"What's this about Bologna?" All eyes went to the mobile on the counter, and Derek cleared his throat.

"The hotel room she shared with Charlotte was ransacked," he replied. "Footage from CCTV captured a large male with a ponytail walking up and down the hall on her floor. She didn't tell you?"

"We hadn't actually spoken until today."

"I'm sure she would have told you, Graham," Ron said.

"Right," he replied, then coughed lightly. "Does Loren know about any of this?"

"No, not yet," O'Dowd answered. "I will inform her when she returns."

"Thank you for telling me," he said, his voice tense.

"It'll be alright, Graham," Ron told him and disconnected. His eyes flicked between Derek and O'Dowd, and he made a face. "That went well."

***

When they returned, Loren followed Penny into the house to find Ron, Theresa and Derek in a kitchen smelling of Thai food. She dropped her messenger bag next to a stool and sat down, sniffing the air.

"Is there any Chu Chee left? I'm starving," she said, then straightened as all eyes turned to her. Ron put his arm around the back of her seat.

"We need to talk, dearest."

Her heart skipped. "Is Graham okay?"

"Yes, yes, he's fine," he answered, waving her off. O'Dowd cleared her throat, bringing Loren's attention to her.

"Do others have access to your calendar?"

She shrugged a shoulder. "We have a team calendar that everyone has access to, but I don't put personal stuff on it."

"You told me you made plans with Anthony and Colin the day Lalonde attacked you. How, over the phone or email?"

Loren went cold. "By text." O'Dowd nodded slowly.

"I want you to get a new mobile, with a new number, this afternoon. I'm taking this one" she said, tapping Loren's phone on the counter.

"You think he bugged my phone?" she asked, her voice tight.

"I don't know, but let's be prudent," the DS replied.

Derek turned to Penny. "Were you followed?" The agent's green eyes flicked to Loren.

"A blue saloon followed us to the doctor's office," Penny answered. "But I didn't see it when we went to the dealership." Loren jumped from her seat, her hand on her throat.

"You saw the car? I didn't imagine it?"

"Yes, I saw it. Breathe, petal."

Loren began to pace around, wringing her hands when she heard Felix whisper in her ear. *I see you. I hear you.* She stopped short and faced Theresa.

"The letters. Do you think they're from Felix?"

Derek looked up. "What letters?"

"Yah, what letters?" Ron echoed. O'Dowd removed two pieces of paper from the folder and handed them to Derek.

"They were in her mail. No return address, no postage. These are copies."

After his reading, Derek glared at the DS. "And you didn't think to share these?"

"They've been logged as evidence," she replied, shooting him a look. "I'm only sharing them now because they seem relevant."

Derek then pointed at Penny. "She does not leave your sight."

"Yea! Slumber party!" The agent put her arm around Loren's shoulders and gave her a squeeze.

"Yippie," she grumbled. O'Dowd exhaled and turned to her, grimacing. "Unfortunately, there's more."

Loren sat down heavily on the stool. "What do you mean, there's more?"

***

14 October

The dawn found Loren wide awake, her mind swirling with the wind rattling the windows. Felix haunted her dreams; visions of him standing at the foot of her bed, reaching out to touch her. He then morphed into a young woman with aquiline features and green eyes, crying out to her.

It was my fault. Why didn't I say anything? She covered her face with her hands. *Because I was afraid nobody would believe me.*

"It's all my fault!" Loren bolted out of bed, throwing open the sliding window to step outside on the patio. Cold air swept around her bare feet and legs. The seven-foot high fence blocked the landscape, but not her view of the clear night sky. Far from the light pollution of London, thousands of stars glistened overhead.

She clenched her fists, fighting the desire to scream when an unfamiliar weight on her finger tugged at her senses. She held out her hand to look at the silver ring. The garnet caught fire in the patio lights.

Do I want this? Can I live with the price? Her gaze moved to the pool, covered with the taut skin of a tarp. *He saved me, but will he want to keep saving me?* She went back inside and grabbed her mobile, then sat down on the chaise as she chose his contact.

"The party you have reached is unavailable. Please leave a message after the tone. Thank you." Her throat constricted at the beep, straining her voice.

"I don't want to text you or call you anymore. I don't want to wake up alone in the middle of the night anymore. I don't want to need you to feel safe or to tell me that everything will be alright, but I do, Graham. I need to feel your warmth when you put your arms around me. I need you to tell me it will be alright." Loren sniffled.

"And while my heart and soul are on fire for you, your house is really cold, and Ron doesn't know how to turn the heat on. Nothing smells like you anymore," she whispered then disconnected, and hot tears slid down her cheeks. A minute later, her mobile began to play his ringtone, and she took a deep breath before answering.

"Hi, Graham."

"I saw you tried to ring me. Can't sleep?"

"No," she replied, covering her mouth with her fingers. "I keep thinking of that girl Theresa told me about."

"Yes, I'm sure that would be difficult." He coughed, covering a muffled conversation in the background. Loren sat back into the chaise, her mouth in a tight line.

He's not even listening to me. "Am I bothering you?"

"What? No! I couldn't hear you clearly, and I'm a bit out of sorts," he replied. "I just left a meeting with Cortney, and I'm walking to my car."

"I see." *You were fucking Cortney is more like it.* "Why don't you call me when you're not so busy," she snarled.

"Now, hang on," he grumbled, and a car door opened and closed. "Loren, I couldn't hear you. What was it that you said?"

"Forget it," she mumbled. "It doesn't matter."

"Yes, it does matter. Are you talking about what O'Dowd found out?" She squeezed her eyes closed but didn't answer. "Please, talk to me," he said softly, and her anger and frustration boiled over.

"You don't think I know what she's been saying?"

"She, who?" Her mouth opened then snapped shut.

"Fucking Cortney Goodwin!" Loren bounced her fist against her forehead.

"Please don't do this. I've already explained–."

"I'm not supposed to get upset when she says she's fucking you?" she shouted. "You think I can just pretend that it doesn't mean anything?" She lowered her voice. "Is it true?"

"No! How could you–!"

"How could I not?" she yelled back. "I don't hear from you for six days while you were off *pretending* to fuck her, and when you finally resurface, you give me some bullshit story you're too heartbroken to even call me? I needed you, and you just left me!" She let out a sob, hugging her knees to her chest. "I'm sorry," she moaned. "I don't want to be that girlfriend that throws shit in your face."

"But you're right," he said, his voice cracking. "It is bullshit, and I've been trying to make it up to you. I was wrong to not talk to you." Loren tightened her arms around her legs and rocked as a thick silence fell between them.

"This is the opposite of being shiny, love," he murmured.

"I can't be shiny all the time, you know," she told him. "All this fucking shit just keeps piling on, and I'm freaking out, and I can't control it." She sniffled, wiping her nose on the hem of her T-shirt. "I didn't want you to see this side of me."

"But I want to see every side of you, Loren. Love is not love which alters when it alteration finds, or bends with the remover to remove. I've seen your tempest. I'm not shaken." She let out a sob mixed with a laugh.

"Now that's being shiny, Shakespeare." Graham gave a soft chuckle, but there was a weariness in it.

"It's taken me a long time not to care what they say about me, and I'm sorry if it hurts you. It's not true. None of it." A car engine started in the background. "There are some who believe holding the public's interest is worth personal compromise, but I am not one of those." The purr of the engine became louder.

"I met with Cortney tonight to try to explain the damage she was causing; not just to me, but to herself, but she didn't want to hear me. She's going to do what she wants, and I can't stop her." He let out a long breath. "Perhaps I am the self-righteous prick she called me." His voice dropped to near a whisper. "This is what it's like being with me, and I sometimes worry that I'm not enough to compensate for it."

Loren closed her eyes. "I don't dream about being with Jude Law, Graham. I dream about being with you." She could hear the smile in his voice.

"I love you, and I promise, it will be different when we're together."

"I know," she sniffled. "I love you too."

***

After yawning through a fifty-mile training ride with the team later that morning, Loren and Cece were headed to the locker room when she yawned again.

"Gawd!" Cece gave her a light shove. "Would ya stop that!"

"I'm sorry," she chuckled but ended abruptly when James came up the hallway from his office and waved to her. He wasn't smiling. "I don't like the look of this," she muttered. "What's up, James?"

He nodded to Cece. "Ah, Loren, Darren's meeting with the Ryzak people today to discuss advertising and such," he told her. "They've asked that you be there."

She heaved a sigh. "Are you kidding? When?"

"Noon-ish," he replied, grimacing. Loren glanced at her watch and tried very hard to not roll her eyes. It was almost eleven.

"Fine," she grumbled, then followed Cece into the locker room. "They better not ask me to be in a bikini." She sat down on the bench in front of her locker with her mobile in her hand.

"It's forty minutes to Harrow," she said, glancing up at Cece. "If I called Penny or Derek, they might not be here by the time I have to leave."

"We didn't see that car, and we were watching for it," she said. "What's it matter?"

"You're right. It doesn't matter." Loren dropped her mobile in her backpack and hurried to the showers.

***

The BMW motorcycle rolled to a stop at the security gate of IDC's Harrow facility and Loren looked at her watch.

Dammit, I hate being late. She pulled off her helmet and ran a hand over her braid as a guard stepped out of the security gatehouse.

"Good afternoon," the guard said, smiling. "May I help you?"

"Hi. I'm Loren Mackenzie. I have a meeting with Darren Wickersham." A high-pitched horn blared from behind them, and Loren raised her eyes to a large mirror on the corner of the gatehouse. A black Porsche 911 Carrera was behind her.

"That's a nice car, but you're still a loser, Haskins," she yelled over her shoulder. "I saw how you blew your lead in the Giro dell 'Emilia last week!"

The guard was chuckling as he stepped back into the booth. When the gate opened, Loren proceeded through and stopped on the other side. She eyed the Porsche as it rolled up next to her and Jonathan Haskins, her counterpart on IDC men's team, ducked down to see her through the passenger window.

"Good god, woman," he said, motioning up and down with his hand. "That all looks just, wow." She waved him on, her frown fighting with a smile.

"Would you just go already." He laughed and hit the accelerator as she put her helmet back on and followed. The Porsche took the right fork in the drive, heading toward a two-story glass office building, but her eyes went left. *What the hell?* A huge warehouse sat on a low hill and painted with red and white stripes. Jon was getting out of his car when she pulled up next to him.

"Honestly, I don't know how your man lets you leave the house looking like that," he said, smirking. Loren set the kickstand and removed her helmet.

"Just stop it," she chuckled and dismounted. "What are you doing here?"

"Darren told me he was meeting with the Ryzak people and said they wanted you," he replied. "I know how much you detest being in the spotlight and I reckoned you might need some hand holding." She met his gaze, pressing her lips together.

"I wouldn't mind you holding my hand." Jon walked around her bike and gathered her in a tight hug.

"Ah, lovey, I'll hold whatever you want me to."

"Get your hand off my ass, Jon," she grumbled.

***

The guard walked back to the gatehouse as the fence rolled to a close and noticed a dark blue sedan was stopped halfway to the gate. He couldn't see the driver's face, but as he approached, a camera with a long lens was poked out the driver's window.

"Hey! You can't be doing that here!" The guard held out his arms, attempting to block the view. The car backed up, but the guard quickly snapped a picture of the tag number with his mobile before it could take off. He made a notation in the log.

Dark blue saloon. Tag BD99 EMG, single occupant. Male. Large camera.

***

Jon escorted Loren though a rear entrance and IDC's cube farm, where she greeted several staff members she knew. He then led her to the large lobby.

"This place is brilliant compared to your little hovel in Enfield," he said, as they entered the two-story space.

"I like Enfield," she muttered, squinting at the white tiled floors sparkling in the sunlight coming from a giant skylight. Several stiff-looking red sofas were arranged in conversation areas around a central staircase with an enormous black and red lacquered reception desk anchoring it. "It looks like Ikea designed a hospital waiting room, in Switzerland."

"Darren does like his red and white," Jon laughed, but it was short-lived as two men dressed in IDC warm-up jackets came down the staircase. He took hold of her elbow. "Eh, Loren, maybe we should–."

"Hey, it's Oliver and Harry," she said and pulled away from him to meet them halfway across the lobby. Harry Whitman, Jon's lieutenant on the men's team, greeted her with a loose hug.

"Loren, are you alright?" He kept a hand on her elbow when they parted. His salt and pepper hair flopped over his furrowed brow and ivy green eyes.

"I'm fine," she replied, giving a tight smile. He grimaced as she slowly drew back from him.

"Lucy wanted to call you after, um, but she wasn't sure, you know…"

"It's okay. Tell her thanks for thinking of me." Loren turned to the shorter, dark-haired man who came to stand next to Harry. "Oliver Reyer, *c'est bon de te voir.*"

"*Mon cherie,*" he replied, his frown narrowing the space between his brows. He hesitated, then stepped in to kiss her on each cheek. "Had I been here and not in Spain, I would have broken his neck with my bare hands." He raised his chin. "*Je pourrais encore.*"

"*Merci.*" The tiny smile she gave faded as a heavy silence lengthened. Jon grabbed her hand.

"Gentlemen, if you'll excuse us, Darren's waiting." She had to lengthen her stride to keep up as he nearly dragged her to the offices at the rear of the building. He came to a stop before a set of oak double doors and turned to her, and his expression was a mix of regret and anger.

"You're going to get that reaction from everyone," he said, brushing her braid over her shoulder. "No one knows what to say to you. We didn't protect you, and we should have."

She nodded, glancing away. "I just want to put it all behind me."

"I understand." Jon gave her a quick hug then knocked on the door and held it open. Floor-to-ceiling windows lined the rectangular room where Darren was seated at a large black lacquer desk in the middle of it, facing a view of rolling farmlands. Low shelves bordered the window behind him. Her boot heels thumped on the acid-washed concrete, then silenced by deep green Berber carpet. He looked up and grinned.

"You're late," he said, standing up from a dark leather chair, and Loren gave him a huge grin.

"I'll get an office like this, right? Right?" She wiggled her brows as Jon laughed behind his hand.

"You only own ten percent, so, no," Darren grumbled, holding back a grin, then waved his hand toward the door. "Out, both of you!" Jon was still laughing when they crossed the hall to a large conference room where two men were seated on one side of a large table. Darren extended his hand to the younger of the pair.

"Leo, good to see you again." He then turned to Loren. "Loren Mackenzie, this is Leonardo Spada."

"Good afternoon," she greeted. The man who shook her hand with a firm grip wasn't much taller than Darren, with light olive-toned skin, cropped dark hair and smile creased chocolate eyes.

"Good to finally meet you," he said, and she blinked at his flat American accent.

"You're from the east coast."

"Is my Delaware showing?" Leo chuckled, then offered his hand to Jon. "Jon, good to see you. Loren, may I introduce Oskar Ryzak." An older man came forward and shook hands with Darren and Jon, then stepped closer to Loren. His mud brown eyes swept over her leather and Lycra moto suit to settle somewhere about her chest.

I just had *to wear this.* She gave a tight smile. "I'm pleased to meet you Mr. Ryzak." Offering her hand, she stiffened when he clasped it and raised it to his lips.

"I am honored to be near such beauty and grace," he replied in a heavy Eastern European accent. He straightened but didn't release her hand. "Please, I am Oskar to you."

"Thank you, Oskar." Her smile tightened further.

"All, please, sit." He motioned to the table and led her by the hand to a seat next to Jon, then returned to his original chair. She sat down and immediately reached for Jon's hand even as he searched for hers under the table.

"I don't like him," she whispered.

"Yep. Collywobbles," he whispered back, as Oskar cleared his throat then.

"I would like to say that we are very pleased with both team's performances this season, especially the ladies' team." He nodded to Loren. "Winning the World Championship! What an incredible comeback from your injuries in your training accident, back in August," he said, his grin dissolving into a pout. "We were disappointed not to see you at the Holland tour. I would have liked to introduce you to my son, Maksim." The shock at the reminder of the team's cover story warred with her distaste of getting to know Ryzak's offspring.

"Thank you," she said flatly, and Oskar bent his head to shuffle through some papers. She glanced at Jon and held in a snicker at his look of nausea.

"Now, we would like to discuss how we may capitalize on your success at the World Championship and, of course, how well the men's team did this season." Oskar motioned to Leo, who passed three folders across the table to them.

"We have put together an ad campaign for our new line of recovery products, featuring Loren and Jon together," he said as he sat back down. "A photo shoot has been set up for 27 October in New York, with several appearances beginning in late November."

Jon cleared his throat. "You really should have cleared the date with our PR before scheduling it," he said. "My knee surgery is scheduled for the 26th." Oskar frowned at first, but his eyes slid to Loren, and the way his thin lips curled upward turned her stomach.

"Then it will be only you and I, my dear, making the magic."

Oh god, no. She smiled politely, unable to respond but squeezed Jon's hand below the table - hard. The older man gave a chuckle as he leered at her.

"Let us share what we have planned for our stars, Leo," he chuckled.

Loren's anxiety continued to build as they reviewed the list of appearances. The photo shoot was scheduled for the day after her interview with ESPN, and the first appearance in Spain was only two weeks later, which included competing in a regional time trial.

Oh, no way is this going to happen, dammit. A hot flash of anger flowed through her, followed by a cold shot of fear as they reviewed the later dates in France and Belgium; some of which would require an extended stay.

Felix could find out where I am. He could just walk in, and there's nothing I could do to stop him. Leo saying her name brought her attention back to the conversation.

"Loren, I'll be with you in Spain for the time trial," he said. "We have a great support crew already set up with two *soigneurs* and a mechanic."

Darren chimed in then. "We already have an excellent staff for our–."

"Be that as it may–." Oskar began.

"Excuse me," Loren snapped, and all eyes turned to her with identical shocked expressions. "You're expecting me to train for an insignificant time trial in the middle of my off-season?" Leo's brows went up further.

"You're going to Chrono, what's the difference?" She clenched her fists under the table.

"My reasons for going to Chrono are personal, and have nothing to do with the team," she replied, raising her chin. "Regardless, I will have to discuss your proposal with my agent."

Jon nudged her. "Since when do you… Ah, Graham," he drawled, and she gave a tight smile.

"Yes. I have people now." Oskar stood, his mouth turning down at the corners.

"Of course. A beautiful woman such as you should have an *entourage*. Please, take your time and discuss our plan with your representative and have them contact us." He shuffled around the table, and Loren rose as he offered his hand to her. His eyes dipped to her chest. "*Děkuji*, Loren, and I hope to see you again very soon."

"I'm sure." She stayed rooted to her position as Jon and Darren escorted Oskar and Leo out of the conference room. She was trembling as she gathered the papers she was given.

Ron has to get me out of this. He has to. She leaned her hands on the table and focused on their offer of compensation. *If I gave that to the team, I wouldn't have to touch my trust.* She squeezed her eyes shut. *But I can't just sell myself like that.* She picked up her messenger bag and exited the conference room, stopping short at Jon waiting for her in the hall. His heavily-lashed brown eyes searched her face as she approached.

"I'm so sorry, love," he said, giving her a hug, then stepped back. "I had no idea they were going to set up something without clearing it with Pippa first."

"It's not your fault," she replied, sourly.

"I'm sure your *people* can get you out of it," Jon said, giving a wink.

"Yah, I'm sure." As they walked back toward the lobby, Loren spied a door marked women's locker room. "I'm going to duck in here," she said, thumbing to the entrance. He gave her a hug and a peck on the forehead.

"I'll ring you later this week. We'll have dinner, yah?"

"Sure," she said, feigning a smile. She watched him turn the corner before pushing open the door. The locker room area was twice as large as the one at the Enfield training center, with tall, dark cabinets lining pale green walls. In the center of the room were benches and seating areas of beige couches and chairs.

"This is nice," she muttered. Two open doorways were across from her. To her right appeared to lead to the showers and as she walked through the left, her brows went up further. "Damn. I want to redo my bathroom again."

Translucent green glass bowl sinks and brushed nickel swan neck faucets perched on eight feet of gold-veined marble counter. Large, gilded-framed mirrors were centered above each bowl. Glossy white tile graced the walls, accented with blue and green glass.

After washing her hands, she grimaced at her reflection in the mirror. Puffy darkness ringed her eyes, and in the subdued light, the frown lines around her mouth were more pronounced.

Why would they want me? A chorus of children's voices whispered to her. *Nobody wants you. You're broken. You're nothing.* Loren covered her ears, fighting the urge to scream back at them. *Stop it. Stop it!* Then, footsteps on the tiled floor echoed through the bathroom.

"Dammit," she muttered and turned around. A smartly dressed woman came around the partition and stopped short. Her bright pink lips curved into a surprised 'o.'

"I'm terribly sorry," she said, but then squinted at Loren. "All's well?" Her pin-straight blonde hair moved about her shoulders as she approached, and Loren pressed her hands to her cheeks.

"Yes, thanks, Pippa." She scrunched her brows. "Did you do something to your hair?" Her mouth dropped open. "Oh! You lost so much weight! I'm sorry, that was rude." The PR director's laugh was like bells tinkling.

"That's quite alright. I've lost three stone since last you saw me."

She blinked. "Three stone… that's like, forty-five pounds! Holy fuck."

Pippa laughed harder. "I can't tell you how much I'm looking forward to having more women here," she said, clapping her hands. "There's too much testosterone around, and not enough girls dropping f-bombs."

"Sorry," Loren chuckled softly, forcing her smile a little longer. "I won't keep you. You obviously came in here for a reason."

"Come and see me before you leave," she said, touching Loren's elbow. "I'm in the East wing."

Loren nodded and escaped from the locker room, but instead of heading to the lobby, she went the opposite direction. She burst through the double doors to find herself outside in the crisp fall air, facing the circus tent-like warehouse. She backed into the wall, breathing hard, and trying to quell the anxiety that gripped her.

"Pull it together," she muttered. "It's going to be fine. I'm not going to be alone." She focused on the warehouse building and the longer she stared at it, the more it helped distract her. She took a final deep breath, swiping her fingers over her cheeks and under her eyes, then pushed off the wall to head back inside.

She mustered up a smile when several IDC employees greeted her on her way through the east wing cube farm in search of Pippa. After being pointed in the right direction, she found the PR agent, tucked away at the end of a row of empty offices. She knocked on the door frame, and Pippa sat up in her chair, her brows jumping up to her hairline.

"You are a hard woman to find," Loren told her. "Why are you all the way back here?" She giggled, waving her inside.

"It's quiet, and if I need something, I have to walk there. Come in, sit, please!" Loren's smile didn't stay as she entered the office and sat down in a bright yellow swivel chair.

"Pippa, I wanted to thank you for everything you've done for me. I'm sure it hasn't been easy, with all the stuff you already have on your plate." The PR agent sat forward in her seat, her slight pout turning into a deep frown.

"Loren, what happened to you was awful," she said, her hazel eyes welling up. "The very least I can do is to keep the media at bay. I only wish I could do more." Loren glanced away as Pippa continued. "You're an inspiration." She grimaced and shook her head.

"No, I'm not."

"You are to me, and many other women I know," Pippa replied. "You've been through hell, and anyone else would have been reduced to crumbs. You came back a World Champion. I'd say that's inspiring."

She couldn't meet her gaze. *If only you knew the truth.* "Thank you."

"Cara Smith seems quite genuine in her desire to tell your side of things." Loren picked her head up.

"You spoke with her already?"

"Yes, to arrange her calls with Darren. She's also spoken with Haskins, James, and Ulrik."

Loren pursed her lips. "Did she." The intercom on her desk buzzed, interrupting them.

"Pippa? We need you in R&D."

"Yes, Paul. I'll be there directly." She pressed the speaker and stood up to wave her hand at Loren. "Come with me. R&D is brilliant!"

***

Loren sat on the steps of the deck of Graham's house, staring out at the Ridgeway, absently turning the ring on her finger. The slider opened behind her and she glanced over her shoulder as Ron walk through, then turned back to the view with a sigh.

"Please don't start with me," she grumbled. "I've already gotten an earful from Derek about not waiting for Penny." He sat down next to her and held his peace for a few minutes.

"What were you contemplating when I came out here?"

She shrugged. "What's left of my life."

"Why bother? You've already got it mapped out, yah?" Loren gave him a hard look.

"What makes you think that?"

"You don't do off the cuff." He tilted his head at her. "You're not worrying over Graham, eh?" She inhaled but closed her mouth and turned away. "You don't have to, you know," he said. "I don't see you being single for much longer."

She turned back to him. "What if I don't want to marry him?"

"Why not? He's *perfect*!" His voice rose an octave or two, then he smiled crookedly. "I get it." He motioned to the house and grounds, then to himself. "All this comes with a price, and that price fluctuates like the stock market."

"How well you know me," she muttered.

"Perhaps we're just made from the same star," he replied. "Or perhaps I've had too many clients' significant others cry on my shoulder."

She snorted. "Right, like you'd let anyone do that."

He snickered. "But that's not all you're stewing about, is it?" Loren pressed her lips together to stop her chin from trembling.

"They all think I have it together, but I'm a right fucking mess," she replied, her voice hoarse. "I can't be in the living room of my own home for more than a minute before I start to see Felix coming after me." She rubbed her palm against her chest. "I have panic attacks, and then sometimes I think, what if my father had some kind of mental illness? Like he was schizophrenic or bipolar or something. What if I–." Ron shook his head at her.

"You're not schizophrenic."

"How do you know that?"

"My sister was schizophrenic. It started in her late teens." He sighed and rubbed his finger and thumb across his eyebrows.

"How is she now?"

"She killed herself, six years and twenty days ago," he replied softly, and Loren gasped.

"Ron, I'm so sorry."

"Thanks." He leaned forward to study his hands for a moment. "I was Graham's first collector's item."

"What are you talking about?"

"You notice we all have some deep, dark secret he ferrets out somehow, yah?" Loren turned to look over her shoulder at the house.

"Derek?"

Ron cleared his throat. "He was with MI5 some years ago and received some bad intel that got his wife killed in Iraq." Her mouth snapped shut, swallowing hard.

"Bruce Carvill?"

"His three-year-old daughter almost drowned in the family pool while he was off snorting coke," he said. "Graham was visiting but had been out on a run and when he came back, he noticed she was missing. He went outside, and there she was, face down in the pool. He jumped in and saved her, then he helped Bruce get clean."

She blinked. *Is that why he freaked when I fell in the pool?* "And Benny?"

"Benny's different," he said. "They've known each other since they were boys." Loren turned away from him, pressing her lips into a firm line.

"What about that lawyer? Cecelia Lomax," she growled.

"Please, that was less than nothing," he scoffed, but then tapped his lips with his finger. "Although she didn't tell him she had a kid. I found that out, but he didn't care she had one, it's that she lied about it."

She stifled a wince. "Hannah?"

"Other than being a minger, nothing." She squeezed her eyes shut.

"And the one before that?"

"Grace," he sighed her name. "He was fairly serious about her, but there was no deep, dark secret in her past." Loren opened her eyes to glare at him.

"You said that all the women he's dated fit the damsel profile, but now you're saying–."

"I just said that to wind you up."

Her mouth popped open. "You really are an asshole."

"Yes, I am," he exhaled. "I'm the one who gets to say no to everyone. No, you can't meet with him. No, you can't interview him. No, you're not good enough." Ron raised a brow at her. "But you, you're good enough."

She barked a laugh. "Yah, since the moment he met me, my life has been one crisis after another. He'll get tired of me falling apart and–." Ron suddenly turned to face her, scowling.

"You listen here." He poked her shoulder. "If he weren't truly in love with you, you would not be in this house with those two looking after you. They're expensive," he told her. "He hasn't done anything like this before, and that minger Hannah had a stalker, or so she claimed." He sniffed. "And I certainly wouldn't be here. I'm an arsehole, remember?" She was quiet for a moment, studying him with a raised brow.

"Then why are you here? Why would you help me?" He looked down at his hands.

"Because I'm Lancelot to his Arthur."

"Lancelot was in love with Guinevere." A crooked grin spread across her face. "Ronald, are you trying to tell me something?"

"Oh, give over!" He gave her a half-hearted shove, but her laughter was short lived.

"Anyway, *Lancelot*, we have more important things to talk about than the rest of my life," she said, and he raised his brows. "That meeting with Ryzak's people today? Their proposal was a bit more involved; not to mention Oskar Ryzak is a real creeper."

***

After her talk with Ron, Loren entered the bedroom to change when her mobile pinged a video call. She checked her watch as she propped the phone up against her water bottle on the nightstand and answered as she sat down on the bed.

"Hi, sweetheart. You're up early." Her smile faded as she took in Graham's pallid skin and the dark circles around his eyes. "You're looking a bit ropey," she said.

"I'll soon be going back to bed," he muttered, his voice rough. "Benny is worse off, if that's possible." He pinched the bridge of his nose. "Alejandra put together a party for the cast and crew, to celebrate the end of filming. It was where I went after we spoke. Benny saw I was upset and kept refilling my glass, along with his own."

"Ah," she said, nodding. "You know, donuts are the best hangover cure."

His brows went up. "Any particular kind?"

"No, but I like the chocolate-frosted cake ones," Loren told him. "Or raspberry jam, sugared, not powdered."

"I'll keep that in mind." His head tilted. "How did the meeting with Darren go?"

She sighed heavily "It wasn't just with Darren. Oskar Ryzak was there, the owner of Ryzak Sports. He kissed my hand and kept staring at my chest." Graham frowned darkly as she shivered. "Ron says not to worry about it, but I can't stop worrying about it. They want me to be the face of their new recovery product line, with public appearances and photo shoots, and they scheduled one without asking me first. It's for the day after the ESPN interview." He just nodded, but she caught a hint of disappointment before he looked away. "That's around the time you think you'll be coming home, isn't it?" A slow smile formed on his lips.

"Perhaps we could extend our stay through your birthday. I did promise you a tour."

"I would love that." Her grin didn't hold up against his lengthening silence. "Graham, what's is it?" He raked his teeth over his bottom lip as his blue eyes grew watery.

"I listened to your voicemail," he said quietly. "It hurts to hear you say you don't want to need me, but I understand why, and I knew I should have sent you my washing," he muttered. She huffed and glanced away.

"I'm sorry, but it's the truth. I don't want to need you this much, but I do, and it scares me." A corner of her mouth curled up. "Maybe you can send a pillowcase?" He huffed but his humor died quickly.

"You can trust me, Loren. I wouldn't let you down." They were both quiet for a few heartbeats. "You have your last race this weekend? A time trial?" She nodded, pressing her lips together.

"Just me and Ashley. It's not a team thing."

"This is the race where your friend died, isn't it?"

"Gabi was from Les Herbiers," she answered. "We were out on a practice run the day before when she got hit by a van that ran the barricade." His mouth dropped open as he sat back in his chair.

"My god. I didn't know the circumstances. I'm so sorry." Loren nodded, unable to speak as she forced her emotions into the pink jewelry box in her mind. "Darling, don't hold it in like that," he spoke gently. "Just talk to me." Unshed tears stuffed up her nose.

"When I first came to England, Gabi was my roommate, both on and off the road. She was more than my mentor. She was my first real friend," she said. "What I didn't know was I woke her up a couple of times a week with my nightmares, and we were halfway through the season before she finally confronted me. I felt really bad, so I told her what my dreams were about. She held me and told me everything would be okay. And it was, for a little while." She sniffled, wiping her nose with the cuff of her jacket.

"I still had the nightmares, but she knew why, and I bought her a pair of earplugs." She gave a tiny smile at Graham's chuckle. "I don't think about her as much as I should, but not much of my life is the same," she told him. "I don't live in the same place, I don't have the Fiat anymore." Loren shook her head, holding in her tears.

"She said I made her carsick with my driving, and she had this laugh. She sounded like a donkey, and you couldn't help but laugh with her." Her smile dissolved. "Gabi held the team together, and I've tried very hard to emulate her."

"Darling, I reckon you're just being yourself," he told her. "I know you feel blessed by the people in your life, but perhaps it's your heart and your spirit that brings light into their world." He smiled as she met his gaze. "I know my life has become infinitely brighter because you're in it." She squeezed her eyes shut.

"I wish you were here," she told him, choking back a sob and turned away. "I'm sorry."

"My love, look at me," Graham murmured. His eyes were shining. "Unless I be by you in the night, there is no music in the nightingale. Unless I look on you in the day, there is no day for me to look upon. You are my essence. You are my heart."

"There you go, being all bright and shiny." She sniffed then scrunched her lips sideways. "I don't know how you remember all that."

He shrugged a shoulder. "I told you once before, you remember the things you love, and I love you very much." She gave more of a smile.

"I had a bit of a talk with Ron earlier. You know he's an asshole."

"Yes," he laughed. "That's what makes him good at his job."

"He told me about his sister."

He sat up and blinked. "I think I'm the only one who knew he even had a sister, let alone what happened to her." He smirked. "You've made a friend for life, you know. He's never going to leave you alone."

"That's okay," she replied. "I'm sure his powers of asshole-ery will come in handy at some point." Graham laughed but stopped suddenly as she grimaced.

"What is it?"

"He, uh, he also told me about what happened with Bruce and his daughter," she said softly. "Is that why you were so scared when I fell in the pool?"

He nodded slightly. "Yes. Addie was three at the time. I pride myself on being observant, but I had no idea Bruce was using." He gave her a bit of a glare. "Don't think harshly of him."

"I'm not about to throw stones," she replied. "*Some* people think I drink too much." Loren rolled her eyes and he huffed a chuckle.

"We come back tipsy *once* in Rochester and your aunt thinks we drink too much." They both laughed, then Graham snapped his fingers. "Oh, let me tell you how to turn the heat on." Loren clapped her hands together.

"Yes, please!"

***

Graham and Benny were out on the balcony of Graham's rented condo as the setting sun converged with the Pacific. Neither had spoken for a while when Benny cleared his throat.

"How is Loren getting on?"

"She's trying to hold it together," he replied, leaning forward with his forearms on his thighs. "The man who attacked her, Felix; the police found out he's done it before, but Loren got the worst of it, by far." He focused on taking deep inhalations and slow exhalations, but finally gave up and raked his fingers through his hair. "They reckon he'd been monitoring her somehow and knew she would be alone that day." He covered his face with his hands. *This is never going to be over for her.*

"Loren is a fighter, she'll pull through," Benny said. "You, on the other hand—."

"I'm fine," he grumbled, but his friend put a hand on his shoulder.

"No, you're not. We've been friends since we were boys, Graham. You can talk to me."

He dropped his head. "That for thy right myself will bear all wrong," he muttered. "I'm overreacting, partly because I feel guilty for being relieved that I'm not there. I can imagine what I would do."

"Sit in a corner and hide your head?" Benny jibed. He huffed, but his humor quickly dissipated.

"Yes, actually. I'm not a fighter. You were the scrapper. I just took the beatings."

"You didn't have to resort to your fists, Graham. You were always quick with the clever insults nobody understood until they looked them up. That's when they came after you." They both chuckled, then Benny continued. "Loren doesn't need you to clear the field for her. Be her rear guard. Support her." He sat back in his chair and put his feet up on the railing.

"You know, Loren and Alejandra are quite similar. There's no grey area with them. When they love, it's all in, but they need to be certain they can trust you with their heart," Benny told him. "A love like that is worth letting go of your ego and telling her you're afraid, because that's what you are, my friend. You're afraid of truly committing." Graham gave him a look. "Yah, you play the game well enough," Benny continued, "but when push comes to shove, you run. Don't run from this one."

Graham rolled his eyes. "Thanks, Benny." The two men were quiet again when one of the mobile phones on the table between them pinged an email.

Benny grabbed his. "It's not mine," he said, and Graham picked up the other one.

"It's from Ron." He checked the time and sat up. "It's three in the morning there."

"He would have rang if there were a problem, yah?" Benny asked, frowning. Graham nodded as he read, his brows furrowed.

"He says it's important, but not urgent. What the fuck does that mean?" He pressed the contact and put the mobile up to his ear and waited for the call to connect.

"You didn't have to ring me straight away," Ron grumbled.

"You said it was important."

"But not urgent," he sighed. "Anyroad, I wanted to tell you Mr. O'Connell has made contact."

Graham frowned. "Who?"

"O'Connell, Adam O'Connell. Mother in heaven, did you not look at the attachment I sent?"

"I didn't see the–." Graham opened the email again, and his mouth fell open as he read the first lines of the letter. "Have you shown this to Loren?"

"No, I haven't, and I don't know what to do. There are some photographs as well, of him and her, together. She was tiny," he breathed.

"I know," Graham sighed. "How did you get this?"

"That BBC reporter, Theo Arnold. A friend of O'Connell's gave it to him." Graham raked his fingers through his hair.

"You want to wait for me to come back, then?"

"Eh, I don't know," Ron replied. "Part of me says to wait; the other is deathly afraid she'll be right narked at me for keeping this from her."

"She's going to be furious no matter what," Graham answered. "Do what you think is best."

"You're leaving this up to me? You fucking bastard," he growled, then disconnected and Graham sat back in his chair, groaning.

"What was that all about?" Benny asked.

"It would appear that Loren's long-lost brother has resurfaced," he replied and handed Benny his mobile. His eyebrows met his hairline.

"Holy fuck. What are you going to do?"

"I don't know," Graham muttered. "I don't fucking know."

**

Loren was pacing inside the garage, wringing her hands by the time Penny arrived that morning. She flipped up her visor as she rolled to a stop on her Ducati.

"I'm sorry, petal," the agent said. "Construction has made a complete bodge of traffic."

"It's not your fault," she muttered and hit the code to lock up the house and the garage. Once out on the road, the whine of the Ducati harmonizing with the whirr of her BMW was calming but Loren's smile faded when they rolled up to the center. The team was already outside.

I hate being fucking late. She cut the engine, stifling her scowl as Cece approached.

"Hey, stranger," she called out. "I was wondering when we'd see you again."

"Ha ha, not funny," Loren grumbled, setting the stand and dismounting her moto.

"Oh, come on," she chuckled, giving her shoulder a little nudge. "How am I supposed to let you know you're missed if I can't poke at ya?" Loren glanced at Penny, who was checking her mobile and felt a twang of guilt.

"I want to go home."

"Then come back." Cece put a hand on her arm. "You're safe with us." She grimaced, her eyes flicking back to the agent.

"I feel guilty not having any extra space," she replied, and Cece heaved a sigh.

"Is the world gettin' heavy up there on your shoulders?" Loren stared at her for a second, then shook her head, her lips curling up.

"You're lucky I like you," she muttered and entered the building to change. When she came back out, James was calling the team together.

"Alright, let's get moving before the weather turns on us."

Loren approached him. "James, we're going to have a–."

"Mr. Parker?" They both turned. "Penny O'Neill." She extended her hand to him. "I'm with Lester Security."

"Hello." He stood up a bit straighter and accepted the greeting.

"It's not my intention to hinder your team's training," she said. "However, I have been charged with Loren's safety. I hope this doesn't pose an issue." Loren didn't say anything as the two stared each other down.

She might be smiling, but damn, she can be intimidating. She then looked over at James and her stomach knotted up at his dark expression.

"I don't have a problem," he replied. "Will you be following, or would you like to ride in the team car?"

"I would prefer to follow by motorcycle," Penny replied, "but being in the car with you would allow me to learn more about any situations that could arise."

"That's fine." He turned on his heel and strode to the team car. Penny turned her head to Loren, but her eyes followed him.

"What should I know about him?"

"He's a good man," Loren answered, "but don't underestimate him. You don't become a champion by hesitating to gut someone."

"Understood," she chuckled and started for the team car.

***

"They are lovely to watch." Penny nodded to the six riders stretched out in single file in front of the Volvo.

"Yes, they're working well together," he replied. "Much smoother than yesterday." At the head of the pace line, Loren jutted out her right elbow and slid off to the right, allowing the team to pass on the inside. Her new silver shoes reflected a bit of sunlight as she surged out of the saddle and tucked in behind Holly.

Penny eyed him. "She was on that bicycle the other day and tucked into my draft for a bit," she said, tilting her head. "I raced motorcycles for a few years, so I understand drafting, but this is different from what she does by herself." He glanced at her, his brows up.

"For the individual time trial, it's just you against the clock, going as hard and as fast as you can," he answered. "In a team time trial, the fourth rider across is the most important. Often the sprinters will chew themselves up at the front before sliding off, to keep the speed up." Her brows came together, still watching the team on the road.

"To put yourself through so much suffering, and for what? Money? Glory? It seems such a waste."

"There's some money to be had, but far less than the men's competitions," James told her. "There's a bit of glory, but really, why does any athlete suffer for their sport? Because we love it. We love the challenge." He took a breath. "Some have darker reasons, to use the suffering of their body to work through the pain in their lives."

"Hmm." She pursed her lips. "One fire burns out the other's burning. One pain is lessened by another's anguish."

His brows went up. "Well, well. There's a poet underneath that rough exterior," he chuckled. Penny smiled at him, and there were a few moments of silence before she spoke again.

"Most coaches wouldn't care what her emotional state was if she won consistently."

"I'm not most coaches." He glanced at her. "I want to see her succeed, and not just in competition. She's very good at anticipating what other riders might do, which I think could translate into something for her when she's ready."

"You seem to know her well," Penny said, a little smile on her lips.

"I worked with her a few years ago, when she fractured her clavicle," he replied. "She was a different person, then."

"What, loud and obnoxious?"

"Alright, perhaps not so different," he chuckled. "She's always been quite focused but lacked confidence in her abilities. Whoa!" James pulled the steering wheel sharply to the left. Penny gasped as an Audi accelerated around the team car, only to jam on the brakes at the sight of the six cyclists.

"Mother in heaven," she muttered, adjusting her seatbelt. "Other than asses like that, what do you see as a potential threat to her and the team?"

"In a race, nothing outside of the usual man-sized banana," James replied, and they both snorted a laugh. "Out here? You just saw part of it, idiots on the road. The other part has been the paparazzi." He shook his head. "The first ride after she came back to England, two motos followed her from her house. Then my daughter, Holly, told me a dark saloon tailed them from the center the next day." He peered at her. "Darren told me their security documented the driver of that same blue car had tried to take photographs of her with Jon Haskins."

"Yes, I heard about that." Penny looked over at him, her lips in a hard line. "We don't believe the man in the car is paparazzi," she told him. "Security footage from the hotel in Bologna captured a very muscular man with a ratty blond ponytail lurking around her floor. The week before, someone tried to assault her outside of the Church Pub. The police found two witnesses who saw a man fitting that description stumbling from the alley. They haven't been able to discover who he is just yet." James was quiet for several moments before he grabbed the handheld radio.

"Loren, relax. You're picking your head up again. Ashley, smooth out that stroke. Holly, you're letting a gap open." He then turned to Penny. "I don't know if there's a connection here, but I knew of a man back when I was racing who looked like what you described," he told her. "Michael Jacobson was an enforcer for one of the biggest EPO suppliers in Europe." He ran his hand over his mouth. "Rumor was Lalonde was a dealer for the same supplier, but nobody could ever prove it." She turned to him, her eyes wide.

"It can't be this easy." She chose a contact and put her mobile to her ear. "Derek, I may have an identity for our ponytail man."

Loren lagged behind Cece, Penny, and Holly as they entered the Church Pub for lunch. She stopped at the threshold, rubbing her arm when a voice came from behind her.

"Pardon me." She jumped and turned to meet the blue eyes of Officer Hamish Gilligan. "I'm sorry, Loren. I didn't mean to frighten you," he said, taking a step back.

"Oh, hi Hamish. Holly told me you were coming." She dropped her chin and moved aside. "I'm sorry, I'm in the way."

"Are ya not goin' in?" He was holding the door open for her. Her eyes flicked up to his, then to the door.

"Yah, thanks." Her gaze traveled around the Tap Room as she entered, its whitewashed brick walls accenting the dark wood paneling. *I'm not safe here, either.* Emma's voice brought her into the dining room, where she found her friend trying to clean one of the tables, but her pregnant belly kept getting in the way. Loren rushed forward and grabbed the wipe from her hand.

"What are you doing? You should be at home lying down."

"Oh, stop it," Emma chuckled and snatched the towel back to resume cleaning the table. "I'm going mad at home. I need to be doing something and the doctor thinks being on my feet will help get things moving." She straightened and pointed to her belly. "Look at me! I'm a bloody house!"

"Yes, you are a house." Loren smiled as she put her arms around her friend. "A beautiful glasshouse." She pulled back and eyed Emma's stomach. "I'd say you don't have much time left. You're carrying a bit low."

Her brows went up. "How do you even know that?"

Loren shrugged. "Maggie." They all turned at heavy footfalls approaching, and Anthony entered the dining room. He gave the young policeman a raised eyebrow.

"Officer Gilligan."

"Mr. Ainsworth." He nodded, and they shook hands. Anthony glanced at Loren, then smiled at Cece.

"Are you here to work? We're down a server."

"Heck no," Cece grumbled and wrapped her arms around his waist. "We're here to be fed!" He laughed and gave her a kiss.

"Alright then, go sit down."

As the group enjoyed their lunch, Loren picked at her sandwich instead of eating it.

"The St. Croix's won't think less of you if you don't go to Les Herbiers," Cece told her.

"I'll think less of me," Loren replied, then sighed. "It's just worse this year."

"All the fecking shite that's been happening, and your man's nine hours away, in the past!" Loren huffed, and Cece pointed her finger at her. "No

70

more of this princess in the tower shite, and don't you be giving me that look," she grumbled. "When you come back from France, you're coming home. I'll kidnap you myself if I have to."

Loren eyed her. "How are you going to do that if you can't drive?"

"Oh, give over!" Cece pushed at her shoulder, but then stayed close. "I can go with if you want. I can be in the team car again."

"That's okay," she replied. "It all snuck up on me, you know?" She took a breath and sat back in her chair. "If I'm busy focusing on other stuff, I don't think about things, much." She picked at the edge of the tablecloth. "Okay, that's a lie. I can't stop thinking about it, and that's half the problem." Loren faced her. "I want to go home, but I don't. Every time I come down the stairs–." Her head turned toward ceramic plates shattering on the cobblestone floor. Emma was doubled over holding her stomach and groaning. Colin flew out of the kitchen and helped his wife to sit down in the chair that Penny dragged over.

"Emma, what is it, love?" He brushed her hair out of her eyes.

"Oh! I don't know!" Her face went scarlet as she squeezed Colin's hand purple.

"Breathe, Emma," Loren said, keeping her voice calm as she stared at her watch. "Just breathe through it."

Colin looked up at her. "What the fuck are you doing?"

"Timing."

His mouth dropped open. "Why are you… oh right."

Emma sat up slowly, blowing out a breath. "How long was that?"

"About thirty seconds," Loren replied, "but the marker is the length between the contractions." She glanced at her watch. "It's only been about ten so far."

***

Loren put aside her tablet and rubbed her eyes. Stretching her arms over her head, she saw the time on her watch.

"Fuck," she drawled, her head lolling back. "Four hours." She righted herself to glance around the hospital waiting room. *How long were they waiting here for me?* Her gaze settled on the bank of windows facing the parking lot and pictured Graham standing there, leaning into his forearm against the glass. She smiled a little, then picked up her tablet to swipe at the screen.

Hey Stud:
   It's going on four hours now, and I'm still waiting for Baby Alice to make an appearance. Granted, I don't think she's going to just yet. Emma was low, but not that low, and her contractions were all over the place.
   I've kept myself entertained by giggling at memes of you on Pinterest. I did find a picture that I had to save, though; one of

us from Alejandra's gala. I close my eyes, and I can feel your arms around me as we danced above the lights of London. Will you dance with me like that again? I don't care where.

I wish you were here, or I was there, or we were someplace together. Like Cleveland. Or a deserted beach somewhere, just you and me.

After pressing send, Loren looked up at someone calling her name. Colin was pushing a still pregnant Emma in a wheelchair out of the double doors.

"What happened?" she asked as she met them halfway.

"The contractions were false, but Baby Alice is fine," Emma replied, rubbing her belly. "Nice and strong. The nurses were assuring me that I'll be back very soon, though."

"You've still got a week to your due date." She wagged her finger at Emma. "You better not have that baby while I'm gone!"

***

The ride back to Graham's house on her BMW seemed longer as Loren kept glancing behind her, making sure no one was following her. She was exhausted, and though Ron and Derek were in the kitchen, she went straight to the bedroom. After stripping out of her moto suit, she flopped onto his bed and curled up around the pillows to sleep, but a half hour later, her brain wouldn't shut off.

"Dammit," Loren muttered and turned over to face the windows to watch a sliver of moonlight glide over the hardwood floor. It was near midnight when Graham's ringtone from her mobile startled her. She rubbed her eyes before connecting the call.

"Hello, love."

"Hello, darling. Are you still pinning pictures of me?"

"No," she chuckled. "I just can't fall asleep."

"Mmm, I'm sorry to hear that. You're not an auntie yet?"

"Not yet. Alice still has some time in the oven, I think." Her smile dissolved, and she was silent for a moment.

"What is it, darling?"

"I don't know," she sighed, pressing the heel of her hand to her forehead. "I'm overtired, I guess."

"I reckon it's a bit more than just that, love. Talk to me." She looked up at the ceiling and let out a breath.

"There have been days I haven't wanted to wake up. Not that I would hurt myself or take too many pills like Anthony thought. He took my pain pills and all the knives. Even the butter knife," she told him, shaking her head. "He hasn't given them back, either. I need to get–."

"Loren?" The tenseness in his voice caught her attention. "Why haven't you told me this?"

"I tried to before Worlds, but you didn't get that email, remember?" She tightened her arm around her stomach. "And, because I would have to admit that I need help, and you know, I'm a little averse to doing that," she muttered. "There's so much shame to get through. It's hard to take the walls down."

"Oh, Loren," he murmured.

"Hey, it's not anybody's fault. Hello, major issues calling." She brushed an errant tear from her cheek. "I need your help, Graham, but I can't let you take me over."

He coughed softly. "So, we're back to you having to ask me nicely to save you?"

"I guess so," she huffed. "I'm sorry I'm so complicated."

"The course of true love never did run smooth, my dear," he said. "As long as we keep talking to each other, sharing our feelings, that's the important part. The rest will work itself out." Loren yawned, and Graham chuckled softly. "I'll let you get some rest."

"It's just something about you. I hear your voice, and I immediately relax," she told him. "I feel like everything will be okay, even if you don't say it."

He was quiet for a moment. "Everything will be okay, my love. I promise."

***

18 October

Les Herbiers, France

Loren and Ashley were shivering in their joggers and heavy jackets as they set up their bikes on the sidewalk near the start line.

"Where did this cold snap come from?" Ashley complained. "The weatherman said it was supposed to be much warmer." They both looked up as Aria came over with a slim wooden box in her hands.

"Did you think I wouldn't have my warming creams with me?"

"You are worth your weight in gold, Aria," Loren chuckled. The *soigneur* patted her own voluptuous curves and glanced over at Sven.

"Hear that, my love? I'm worth millions!" she laughed, then laughed harder when he blew her a kiss. After rubbing both riders' legs with warming cream, Aria stood, wiping her hands on a towel.

"Good luck and ride well." She then came in close to Loren, touching the rainbow stripes on the cuff of her jacket. "I know you are conflicted about what to do," Aria said. "I knew Gabi as well, and she would not want you to stop this time, for her sake." Loren dropped her chin and nodded.

"I understand." She watched her friend head to where Sven was set up with their time trial bikes. Her eyes slid to Ulrik, walking toward her and stuffed her emotions back into their mental box.

"Feeling good?" Both riders nodded. "Alright, then, let's get down to business. This is a fast course, with few changes in elevation," he said to Ashley, then looked at Loren. "It's your first appearance with the stripes, so there might be a bit more media attention."

"I'm counting on it," she replied, her voice hard. He nodded again, then tapped Ashley's handlebars.

"Your run is coming up shortly. Start to gather your things," he said and headed over to Sven and Aria. The younger rider dismounted her training bike and sat down to change her shoes, glancing over at Loren.

"I know you're here for Gabi, but don't you want to win?"

Loren stopped pedaling. "Sometimes it's not about winning," she replied. "Sometimes you have to do something extreme to make people notice."

"I get it." Ashley stood and patted her on the shoulder. "Whatever you decide, good luck," she said and set off after their manager. Loren thought about her question as she started pedaling again.

Shouldn't I want to win? She grimaced. *Fuck, now I don't know what to do.* She sighed and directed her thoughts back to her warmup, but memories of the accident assaulted her mind.

I saw the van coming. I tried to warn you, but you couldn't hear me. I was too far back. I couldn't do anything to save you. Ulrik had been in the team car behind them and cut her off before she could reach Gabi. *If it weren't for him, I would have quit racing that day.*

By the time Ulrik returned, Loren was off her bike and sitting in the chair adjusting her shoes.

"Are you ready?" he asked. She brushed her finger over the rainbow stripes on the cuff of her jacket.

"I can't just throw it away, can I?"

"It's your decision," Ulrik replied, putting a hand on her shoulder. "But know that we support you."

"Thanks." She scrunched her nose as he walked away. She stood and removed her jacket, revealing a pristine white skinsuit emblazoned with the World Champion stripes across her chest. As she bent to pull off her joggers, an arm slipped around her waist.

"You look damn sexy in white," a male voice murmured in her ear. Loren straightened in a flash, grabbing the arm that held her and turned with her fist raised.

"Jon, you son of a bitch! I was ready to punch you in the face," she snarled, then gave Jon Haskins a hard punch on the shoulder.

"Ow!" He backed up a step, rubbing the spot. "Why are you lookin' all kinds of spooked?"

"I'm just tired." She sat down and picked up her shoe, but it dangled from her fingers. "Bad dreams."

"Yah, me too." He bent to kiss the crown of her head. "Good luck, love." Jon turned to leave, but she stood and grabbed his arm.

"Wait. You had bad dreams? About what?"

He shrugged. "The usual sort of thing," he replied. "Failure. Bad wrecks. Why?"

"I dreamt of Gabi."

"Ah, lovie," he sighed and pulled her into a tight hug. "No wonder you're spooked." Jon released her to cup her cheeks. "You and Gabi were the best roomies I ever had. I didn't want to leave, but I fell in love, and I wanted to be closer to him." His frown deepened. "Perhaps if I had come with you instead of going to Jamaica with Darren, it might have been different."

Loren shook her head. "Don't do that to yourself." He kissed her forehead.

"Good luck and I'll see you later."

"Yep," she replied, sniffling and sat down as he walked away. She slipped into her silver bike shoes and bent to tighten the quick-release straps, but as she stood, movement across the street caught her attention. A shot of fear went through her.

A man wearing a plaid shirt lowered the long lens of his camera to reveal a face with a big nose, wide jaw, and beady eyes. Her fear morphed into a seething rage at his smirk.

"I see you," she hissed and stalked away, her hands trembling. She looked around for Derek but didn't see him in her immediate vicinity. Grumbling, she yanked her helmet on before she got to the start house where Ulrik met her at the stairs. Her time trial bike was with the stewards for the usual inspection behind him.

"You've done this course several times, so you know what to do," he said. "Will you be stopping?"

She clenched her jaw. "No. I'm not."

***

Chrono des Nations
Individual Time Trial
20km

Gabi deserves to have her name spoken on the podium, not just a passing mention in some French newspaper.

Loren stared down at the tarmac stretching out from the start house ramp, but her eyes didn't register the different textures on the surface. Nor did her ears acknowledge the announcer's voice echoing from the stage. Rage flowed into every fiber of her being.

She squeezed the slim outer handlebars and stood on the pedals, teetering a bit and glared over her shoulder at the steward holding her upright.

"*Pardon, mademoiselle,*" he said. Loren turned her scowl back on the road and gave the collar of her skinsuit a tug.

I am the fucking storm, and nothing can withstand me. She then nodded to the starter.

"*Cinq, Quatre, Trois, Deux ALLER!*"

She went out hard, pumping her legs before settling into her tucked position. The time trial bike Darren sent her adapted to her aggressive movements as she sped through the first kilometers of the course. Anger burned away any discomfort in her muscles and she put more force into the pedals. The first checkpoint was a blur when Ulrik's voice was in her ear.

"Slight rise ahead. Intersection is clear. Nineteen seconds ahead. You'll be passing Boucher shortly. Just stay out of her draft."

The wind met only a hint of resistance from the slick white Lycra suit covering her body. She shifted into a harder gear when she came upon the cyclist who started on the course before her. Loren rocketed past the young rider as Gabi's laughter echoed in her ears.

"Twenty-two seconds ahead," Ulrik said a few minutes later. "Right turn, then up the hill to the second checkpoint. Relax, Loren. Your head's popping up."

She moved her hands to the slim outer grips and feathered the brakes, bending her right knee and keeping her weight balanced as she dove into the turn. Settling her arms back into the center bar cups, Loren mashed the pedals to grind down the small hill. The bike gathered speed on the short downhill to the false flat portion of the course. She shifted again, pushing harder into the grade, but soon, a dull ache flowered in her left side with each breath.

"Third checkpoint. Thirty-two seconds ahead," Ulrik told her as she flashed under the banner.

"I am the storm!" In her mind's eye, she saw Gabi take her last breath in the middle of the road, and raw emotions propelled her through the intersection at Kilometer 16. She kept her gaze forward, holding her effort until she crossed the finish line four kilometers later.

With tears streaming down her face, Aria and Jon helped her dismount, and Ulrik and Sven soon joined their tight circle. Loren met the eyes of each, seeing her sorrow reflected there.

"For Gabi."

***

Photographer, Nick Belgrave was below the stage as Loren Mackenzie accepted the winner's medal with trembling hands. When the applause ended, she stepped to the edge, tight-lipped and pale. No one moved or spoke as she addressed the crowd in slightly accented French.

Nick struck by the rawness of her voice, and he turned to the photographer next to him.

"Rita, can you translate? My French is kind of rusty." She nodded and listened for a moment.

"She is explaining why she did not stop as she has before. She had an obligation as World Champion but also because she wanted to win for Gabriella St. Croix." The photographer listened to Loren again. "She is here to pay homage to Gabriella and to every cyclist who has died on the road. No, she said lost their life."

Loren brushed tears from her cheeks and spoke with fervor, pointing to the stage. Her storm gray eyes looked at every face below her.

"Gabriella St. Croix deserves to be honored and remembered here, on the podium, not where her life ended. *Merci*, thank you," Loren said and stepped back, to be hugged by her team's manager. A tall guy Nick recognized as Jon Haskins, and an older couple standing with him began clapping, and soon were joined by all in attendance.

"Thanks, Rita." Nick slipped through the crowd toward his car parked on a side street. He slumped in the driver's seat and skimmed through the images he captured. *They have the same scowl.* He then sent a text to his best friend, Adam O'Connell in New York.

> Dude, I'm in love with your sister.

> Fuck you. You are not.

He sniggered as he typed.

> Ok, I'm not, but holy shit, she is a force of nature.
> She smoked every female rider in the time trial
> and almost all the men, then told off the whole
> crowd saying her teammate shouldn't be
> memorialized where she died, but where she lived,
> on the podium. Fucking nuts man.
> I'm going to try and talk to her.

Adam's reply came within seconds.

> Be nice to her. She's been through a lot.
> Let me know how it goes.

***

"Your speech made international headlines, my love," Graham said when he and Loren connected by phone later that afternoon. She was in the team's hired RV, slumped in a seat with her feet up on the back of the chair in front of her.

"Yah, that's great," she muttered.

"It was a noble thing you did."

"It was a selfish thing I did," she countered. "There was some photographer in the crowd, taking pictures of me with Jon. It set me over the edge." She ground the heel of her hand into her forehead. "So many ghosts."

"Darling, you're overwhelmed, and I reckon only taking a week off after Worlds wasn't enough of a break," he said.

"Yah, maybe." She sniffled and brushed the cuff of her jacket under her nose. There was a heavy moment of silence.

"Loren, did you just use your sleeve as a tissue?"

She looked at the cuff. "I think so."

"I love you, but I'm sorry, that is manky," he chuckled. "I have some news that might cheer you up. Things are wrapping up rather quickly here, and I reckon I'll be flying home on the 21st."

Loren sat up. "Really? We could have a couple of days by ourselves."

"I hope so," he said, then let out a long breath. "I need to do nothing for a few days to get my head on straight. I'll let you know when plans are firmed up."

"Okay. Love you."

"Love you, too." Loren disconnected and slumped back into the chair. *Just us,* then grimaced. *But, it's not just us anymore.* She groaned a little as she pushed out of the chair. Stepping down from the RV, she spied a man standing on the sidewalk with a camera hung around his neck. Watching her. She recognized him immediately and glanced around for Derek.

Dammit! Where is he? She froze as the man started toward her, removing his baseball cap to reveal a carrot-red crew cut and hazel eyes.

"Hi, Loren," he said and stopped just before the curb.

"Hello."

"That was some speech," he said. "Really moving."

"Thanks," she replied and backed up a step. He moved with her, his hand outstretched.

"Wait, could I have of couple minutes?" She shied away, and he pulled his hand back. "Sorry, I didn't mean to frighten you." Her surprise turned into a scowl.

"I'm not afraid of you." The man sighed and ran his hand over his hair.

"I am totally fucking this up. I'm sorry." He glanced over her shoulder, his eyes widening a trifle. "My name is Nick Belgrave," he said quickly as footsteps approached from behind her. "We have a mutual friend and–."

"Get away from her," Derek growled, pointing to the photographer, but Loren put a hand on his arm.

"It's okay," she said, then turned to Nick. "Mutual friend?" He nodded, his gaze fixed on the security agent and reached into his jacket to slowly remove a white envelope. She jumped back as Derek leaped forward, his hand on his Taser.

"Watch it!" Nick put both hands up.

"Whoa! It's just a letter!"

"Yah, well, I've gotten some real interesting letters of late," she hissed, hiding behind Derek. "You'd better start talking, buddy." Nick's gaze flicked between the two of them.

"My friend, Adam, asked me to give this to you, but this is the first chance I could get anywhere near you," he replied. "I gave Theo Arnold a copy but–." Loren came nearer, glaring at him.

"You gave a copy of what to Theo?"

"This." He offered up the envelope, and she snagged it then turned her back to him. "Can I put my hands down now?" Nick asked.

"Yah, yah, whatever." She waved her hand then tore open the envelope. It took her a few seconds to read the letter and a few more to process it, then a few more to try and tamp down her reaction. It wasn't working, and Loren turned on him, clenching her fists.

"My brother is your friend?" she snarled, and Nick backed up a step. "You've been at every race almost since the season started! Did he ask you to do that?"

"No, um, well, yes, but–."

"And you've been taking pictures of me! Have you been selling them too?" Derek grabbed her arm before she could get too close. "Let go of me," she snapped and tried to pull her arm away.

"Hey, I'm just doing my job," Nick replied, standing his ground.

"Your job? Derek, let go! I'm not going to hurt him." Loren faced the photographer again, waving the letter in his face. "You gave Theo a copy of this? Why would you do that?"

His brows went up. "I thought he was your friend."

"It doesn't matter if he's a friend, he's a fucking reporter!" She turned around, raking her hand through her hair, then stared at the letter crumpled in her hand. "Is he really my brother?"

Nick huffed. "You've got the same scowl. It's kind of scary." She eyed him over her shoulder.

"Obviously he knows where I am, so why ask you to do this?"

"He didn't ask. I offered." He shrugged. "Emails get lost. Phone messages don't get returned. You want his number?"

She shook her head. "He says he gave his card to Graham, but maybe you can give me his email?"

"Yeah, sure." Nick took out a business card from his pocket and wrote on the back, then handed it to her. "I'll leave you alone now."

"Wait," she said as he turned. "What's he like? What's he really like?"

He smiled at her. "What can I say? He's my best friend. He saved my life."

***

Enfield, England

Loren was silent as Derek drove his Audi Q7 through the quiet streets of town, but her thoughts whipped through her mind as fast as the lights going by the window. She eyed the driver a few times, trying to gather the courage to speak.

"I want to go back to my house," she said finally.

"Damn. I owe Penny twenty quid," he muttered. She scrunched her lips together as he continued. "She said you've been moping around and reckoned it was because you wanted to go home." She crossed her arms over her chest.

"Twenty quid, huh? That's all?"

He chuckled softly. "Loren, now that we are apart from your team, that photographer who approached you. Do you believe him?"

"There was a photograph in the envelope that I've seen before, in a photo album my aunt showed me. That would be hard to fake," she replied. "Anyway, why would anyone want to con me? I'm not worth anything." He gave her a quick glance.

"I beg to differ. However, I would advise proceeding with caution. Let me run a check on him." Loren tried very hard not to roll her eyes.

"Fine." Silence enveloped the vehicle for the remainder of the drive. After pulling into the parking area of her house on Essex, Derek turned to her.

"Why did you break the mirror in Bologna?" She sat back into the seat and focused on her folded hands in her lap.

"I lost control."

"There was something written on it, wasn't there?"

She closed her eyes. "I see you."

***

London, England

"Now, leave me alone," Felix Lalonde muttered and slammed the door on the sneering faces of the two hospital orderlies. He'd given them fifty pounds each to leave him alone for thirty minutes, but he wasn't going to spend his time getting drunk. He quickly made his way to the bedroom and his computer.

I just need to see her. The program had just started a reboot when there was a hard rap on the door of his apartment. *It's only been five minutes!* He strode through the main room to the front door and yanked it open. Fear froze his, but Felix recovered quickly to glare at the large, ponytailed man standing in the hall.

"Why are you here?"

"Where've you been, man?" Michael Jacobson pushed Felix out of the way and entered the apartment. "You've been out of contact for weeks."

"That is of no concern to you," he grumbled. Jacobson turned around, his beady eyes narrowing as he held up a thick legal-sized envelope.

"I got another offer for your little picture show and wouldn't you know, she's worth a whole lot more than you're supposed to be paying me," he sneered. "This batch netted me fifteen, with another twenty if I catch her doing something embarrassing." Felix clenched his fists.

"You have no right to–." Jacobson took a step closer.

"You think you can order me to do your shit work, then disappear without paying me?" A cold smile formed on his face. "I don't blame you for trying to hit that ass, though." He held out his big hand. "Fit right in my palm and man, it was tight." Felix lunged at him, his rage overwhelming his sense, but Jacobson easily pushed him out of the way, laughing.

"You're gonna get yourself hurt, Lalonde." Felix shoved him again.

"What have you done!" Jacobson's beefy hand grabbed him by the neck and squeezed.

"I left her a couple of love notes," he breathed in his face. "And that necklace my buddy at the prison found in your pocket when you were booked? I left it right where she could find it. Her face was priceless." Felix stumbled as Jacobson shoved him away. "Then I caught her in the alley behind that pub she works at sometimes. I would have fucked her right there, but she got in a lucky kick."

"A mere woman got the better of you?" Felix scoffed.

"You think that's funny?" Jacobson snarled, stepping closer to point a finger in his face. "When I catch that little cunt by herself again, she ain't gonna be so pretty."

"You will not touch her again," Felix bristled, clenching his fists.

"Like you can stop me." Jacobson shoved him backward and walked toward the door, slamming it on his way out.

Felix ran a shaking hand through his hair. *He's going to hurt her. I can't allow that.* But every idea he had only led to incriminating himself. He picked up the envelope Jacobson had left and slid the glossy photographs out on the table.

Her face was everywhere, but the photos he was most interested in were at the bottom of the pile. Several were of her on the trainer, warming up or chatting with Ashley Hargrove and Aria Rabicchi. Another grouping was of her with Jonathan Haskins.

"That fucking *pédé*," he muttered, tossing away the image of Haskins kissing her on the forehead. Felix then picked up one of her looking directly at the camera. Her eyes were almost black, her posture threatening, and the corner of his mouth curved down.

Hatred is a dark emotion for you, mon tresor. Is that why you did not stop at Chrono? He shuffled the images around and found the group of her on the podium, accepting her medallion. Many more were of her on the edge of the stage with tears in her eyes.

This is the face I fell in love with, when you told me what your father did to you. Courage mixed with vulnerability. How I wish I could be as strong as you. Felix picked up another picture, a close-up, and he brushed her cheek with his fingertips. *We understand each other, Loren. We were meant to be together.*

20 October

Loren groaned and rolled over for what seemed like the thousandth time to stare at the angry red 1:22 on the clock next to her bed. Adam's letter weighed heavily on her mind, along with the guilt for not telling Graham about it. She sat up and glared at her messenger bag propped up on the floor next to her desk.

You had to do this to me now! Her eyes welled up. *But I wanted to find him, and there he is.* She got out of bed and rummaged through her bag for his letter then sat down at her desk to read it again.

Loren:

I've wanted to find you since we were separated, but for my survival, I had to move on from it. Mom and Amy were gone, and I knew you were safe with Aunt Maggie. That's all that mattered to me.

Should I tell you about my life? Should I try and explain why it's taken me this long to contact you? To be honest with you, with myself, I was scared. I'm still scared, of what you might think of me, of what you might say. What if you don't know me? What if you won't forgive me?

I saw you in Philadelphia in June. You were standing right in front of me, and I said your name. I had no idea you would hear me. You turned and looked right at me, but I hid behind my camera. What could I say to you? I'm sorry? Even I know that's not enough.

Like you, I have a different name now. Adam T. O'Connell. The 'T' is for Tiberius. Yes, I'm still a Trekkie. Don't judge, Shadow. I remember you would run home to watch Rainbow Brite for the thousandth time.

I want to see you, but I'll leave that up to you. I'll meet you anywhere in the world, just tell me when and where, and I'll be there.

Always,

Adam

P.S. I've run into your boyfriend, Graham a few times in LaGuardia. I gave him my business card, so he would know how to contact me. If not, my friend Nick, the guy who gave you this letter - he can give you my number.

My brother. Loren sat back in her chair. *He gave Graham a business card, but Nick gave me his email address.* She sighed, and her eyes slid to her messenger bag slouched on the floor. The large envelope filled with pictures and papers from the box her aunt had given her was in there, as well as the background report Graham's father had commissioned. She avoided even touching them, putting them in a separate compartment of her bag that stayed zipped shut.

He asked me not to look at this stuff by myself. She looked down at her bag again, then picked up her mobile to send a text to Graham.

I don't know what's worse;
not being able to sleep because
I'm thinking about you,
or falling asleep to dream of you,
only to not want to wake up.
I miss you. I love you.

She glanced at the clock again, gathered up her bag and peeked out into the hall. Light brushed the carpet under Cece's door at the end of the hallway. Loren bit her lip and crept to the door, only to stand there.

Knock on the fucking door. Do it. You need help. Do it. Do it now. She lifted her arm to put her knuckle on the door when it opened on a startled Cece.

"I was going to the loo." She cocked her head. "Are you alright? You're looking a mite lurgy." Loren ducked her chin, gripping her messenger bag tightly in her arms.

"I need your help," she whispered, and Cece's brows went up.

"Okay. With what?"

"Can we go downstairs? I don't want to wake up Holly," Loren replied. "And I'm probably going to need a drink."

"Yah, sure, but I still have to go to the loo."

"Right." They quietly headed downstairs where Loren sat down at the table while Cece ducked into the half lav. When she came out, she stopped at the pantry.

"Eh, there's no whisky left," she said, poking her head out. "But there's marshmallow vodka."

"That Holly's," Loren told her.

"So what? You'll get her another one," Cece said, coming out with the bottle. "And you know what would be perfect with marshmallow vodka." She pulled out a container. "Oreos."

Loren sighed. "But those are–."

"You'll buy her more," she chuckled. "You're loaded now."

"I'm not loaded," Loren countered. "Do you have any idea how much tax I have to pay on a distribution from the trust? Like, more than half, and it's got to last me five years."

"Oh. I didn't know that," her friend replied, making a face as she sat down. She poured out the vodka into two shot glasses and handed Loren the cookies.

"Not that I'll see most of what's left anyway," she grumbled, twisting apart a cookie and eating the top half. "I invested in the team."

Cece's brows knotted. "Why would you do that?"

"Some of our sponsors didn't renew," Loren said, her frown deepening. "Ulrik thinks it's because they supported Felix."

"The feck you say."

Loren shook her head. "It doesn't matter, but that's not why I need your help." She knocked back a shot. "This is good stuff." She refilled the glass and had another, then took a big breath and looked at Cece straight on.

"I didn't lose my family in an accident," she said, quietly. "My father killed my mother and my sister, and my brother shot him before he could kill me." She pointed to her shoulder. "That's what this scar is from."

Cece gasped. "Oh my god. And the one on your back?"

"That went through here." She touched her upper stomach area. Cece quickly downed two shots of vodka, then munched on an Oreo before she spoke again.

"Does Anthony know about this?"

Loren nodded. "I told him in September, while you guys were in Holland." Cece slid her eyes away, pursing her lips.

"Your brother's still alive then?"

"Yah," Loren sighed and slid a piece of paper to her. "At Chrono, some photographer claiming he was my brother's friend gave this to me." Her mouth fell open as she read it.

"It's no bloody wonder you've been going right mad," Cece said, her brows pinching. "Have ya told Graham what happened to you?"

She nodded. "Because I had to." She slid the folder across the table. "His father had someone run a background check on me, and Graham confronted me with it the day before the time trial." Cece nodded slowly, grimacing.

"So, that's what happened in Richmond," she said, and Loren's brows went up. "I wasn't earwinging! My nose was twitching." Her frown deepened, and she dropped her volume. "Your father hurt you, didn't he?" Loren nodded and turned away.

"My Da thought so," Cece continued. "That's why he keeps his distance. It's pretty much why the boys don't tease ya none, either. They don't want to spook ya." She reached over and grasped Loren's hand. "When Jamie was telling how they stuffed me in the cupboard when I was little and forgot about me, you left all sudden like. You had a nightmare that night, and Jamie was beside himself 'cause he heard you screaming."

"I was in a foster home for a while after my parents died," Loren said quietly. "They locked me in a closet for two days because I ran away." She breathed deeply, avoiding looking at her friend. "I'm sorry I never told you. I was afraid if you knew, you would think there was something wrong with me."

"You see this?" Cece held up her left hand and pointed to the thin white line on her palm. "I can't stop being your sister any more than Alfie can stop smelling so manky." Loren burst a laugh through her tears.

"It's finally gotten to you, huh."

"It's not the house, thank god, it's the bloody Rover and the cloth seats." Their chuckles died out over two more shots and some Oreos. Loren smiled a little, watching her friend twist a cookie apart, scrape the filling off with the top half and eat it.

"You're just as good at distracting me with shiny things as Graham is," she said.

"Oh bother," Cece muttered then pushed her chin toward the large envelope. "What's all that, then?"

"Some stuff Maggie found," Loren replied as she emptied the envelope out on the table. "Pictures, my school records, letters from Family Services, that kind of stuff. We just mostly talked about my mom." Her lips pressed together. "That was fucking hard. I didn't want to remember her, and I still don't."

"I can't imagine even trying," Cece answered as Loren picked up a folded piece of paper. She spread it out and felt the blood drain from her face.

"What is it?" She tore her eyes from the page and looked up at Cece, then handed it to her.

"I dreamt of this, but I wasn't sure if it was real." On the paper was a crayon drawing, obviously done by a child, but it fairly accurately depicted a black horse, with a rider wearing yellow clothes and curly brown hair. Cece turned the paper over, frowning.

"Who's LoriAnn?"

"That's me. That was my name," Loren told her. "He was my knight. He was supposed to save me, but he never came back."

"Wait, I don't understand," Cece said, reaching her hand over the table. "Why would he have to save you?" Loren spread the photographs out, picked up the one she wanted and handed it over.

"The woman in blue is my aunt. The other one is my mother."

"Holy Mother in heaven, that's fecking bonkers." Cece grabbed another shot of vodka and knocked it back. "But you knew they were twins, right?"

"I did, and for a long time, I couldn't even look at Maggie," Loren answered picking through the other pictures. She recognized her younger self in several of them, but not the people she was with until she turned one over and almost dropped it. The image was of her, with her arms around the waist of a man with curly brown hair. *He kind of looks like Graham.* Then her eyes went wider.

"Oh my god, it's him. This is my knight! The one I drew," she choked, handing the photo to Cece.

"No way! There can't be two of 'em!" She pushed the photo back. Loren picked it up and flipped it over to scrutinize his face.

"Martin Garrett. No, Graham's eyes aren't as round, and his lips are fuller." She pointed to the picture. "And this guy looks like he's got a really bad perm. Graham's hair is wavy, not curly."

"But at first glance, that could be your smarmy pirate."

"Smarmy pirate," Loren huffed and shook her head. "You know, he loves it when you poke at him."

Cece giggled. "It is fun." She picked up a few more photos. "Who's this?" She pointed to an image of a girl sandwiched between two dark-haired boys, both several inches taller.

"That's me." Loren held back a laugh at her friend's shocked expression.

"You were tiny! What the hell happened?"

"I don't know. It wasn't because of drinking milk." She tapped the photo of Martin Garrett. "I lived with him and his family for almost a year, but I barely remember anything about them." She pressed her lips together. There was so much more, but the memories were fractured; holding glimpses of things she didn't understand enough to explain to Cece.

"I have to talk to Aaron. I mean, Adam. Whatever the fuck his name is." Loren downed another shot of vodka and broke open an Oreo to lick the center.

"Have you contacted him, your brother, I mean."

"No, not yet," she replied, popping the rest of the cookie in her mouth.

"What are you waiting for, then?"

"I don't know. I'm scared?"

"What are you afraid of? That he won't answer?" Cece shook her head. "He wrote to you."

She grimaced. "Alright, alright." Loren took another shot then grabbed her tablet from her bag. As she typed, Cece leafed through the pictures, every so often pointing and asking questions or just to laugh at what Loren was wearing.

"Stop it," she chuckled, tossing a handful of snapshots at her friend. "I don't doubt that if I asked, your Mum would pull out several hundred pictures of you in nasty plaid dresses and pigtails no less!"

"Aw, I know!" Cece laughed, covering her face. "It's bloody awful what mums do to their kids." Their chuckles died out to companionable silence as Loren finished writing her email to Adam. She pressed send and was about to say something when Cece jumped out of her seat and shoved a photo across the table.

"Oh my god! Oh my god!" She backed up toward the door with her hand clamped over her mouth.

"What? What is it?"

"No! Don't look at it!" Cece lunged to grab the photo, but Loren picked it up first, only to drop it and topple her chair to get away from it.

"Oh god! Amy!"

"I'm sorry! I'm sorry!" She flipped the crime scene photograph over. Loren stood in the doorway, her arms tight around her stomach.

"Graham said he got rid of them!"

"Yah, well, he missed that one!" Cece started toward her, then stopped. "What do I do with it?"

"Burn it," Loren groaned. "Fucking burn it."

The two women stood before the fireplace and watched the edges of the picture curl in the heat of the flames. Neither moved until the image was no longer visible.

"I'm sorry I didn't tell you before, Charlotte."

"I don't blame you at all." She let go and looked up at Loren. "I don't know how you've stayed sane with all that."

"I've been very good at compartmentalizing, but now, it's all been shoved in my face," Loren replied, grimly. "But I can't let my fear rule me anymore. I have to fight back."

***

Los Angeles, California

Graham was writing out a reply to Loren's note when there was a knock on his office door.

"Karen! Come in." He stood as his former production assistant came into his office. "How's the new position working out?"

She grinned. "I know it's only been a couple of days but working with Benny is a dream come true." She tucked her lip between her teeth. "Not that it wasn't a dream working for you."

He waved her off, chuckling. "Don't thank me. I only recommended you for the associate position. You're the one who dazzled him."

"It's all smoke and mirrors." Her smile softened as she looked down at an envelope in her hand and her head popped back up. "I almost forgot. The cleaners found this under the bench seat in your trailer."

"Thank you," he said, and came around his desk to accept the envelope. "I have no doubt we'll be seeing each other again, but you know a handshake just won't do." She laughed and gave him a quick hug. With a wave, Karen closed the door as she exited his office.

His smile vanished as he recognized the handwriting on the envelope.

My dear Son:

I am truly sorry for bringing all of this terrible knowledge out into the open. My only wish was to protect you, but I have violated your privacy and abused your trust. I never meant to hurt you, or Loren, and I deeply regret my actions.

I was horrified and furious over what has happened to such a gracious young woman. It is staggering that she has to carry this burden, yet she is extraordinarily courageous for holding up under such incredible strain. I know your heart breaks for her, and you will love her gently.

It is my wish that one day, you will have a child of your own and I know that they will be as precious to you as you are to me. Then you will realize that a parent will do anything within their power to protect their children, out of love.

Love always, Dad

Frederick, you son of a bitch. Graham closed his eyes, crushing the paper in his hands. *You cannot apologize your way out this time.*

***

21 October

It was after 8 pm when Graham disembarked his flight from New York, more than an hour later than scheduled. The additional delay getting through customs only increased his frustration, and his long strides outdistanced the other passengers as he made his way toward baggage claim. When he exited with his bags, his driver, Jim Reading, was waiting for him and the older man's face split into a grin.

"Mary will be glad to know you don't look like you're starvin'," he said, and extended his hand to Graham.

"Good to see you too, Jim," he chuckled and accepted the handshake. "Tell your lovely wife not to worry." The driver put the bags on a trolley, and as they made their way to the exit, Jim nodded toward the throng of photographers.

"Excellent, they're occupied." The paparazzi swarmed around a pop star that had been on the same flight as Graham as she stopped to sign an autograph for a fan. When they reached the Mercedes parked in the taxi zone, Jim put the bags in the trunk and Graham took out his mobile as he went around to the front passenger side. The older man poked his head around the trunk hood.

"Wouldn't you rather sit in the back?"

"No, it's alright," Graham replied, waiting for the call to connect and opened the door. He frowned when his ringtone from Loren's mobile came from inside the car. He leaned in to find her smiling at him.

"You sure you wouldn't rather sit in the back?" she purred. Graham straightened and shook his head at his driver.

"You cheeky bastard," he chuckled. Jim barked a laugh as he came around the car.

"Loren rang this morning and had a nice chat with Mary. You know women."

The opaque privacy glass that separated the driver's area from the passengers was up as Graham slid into the seat. Her long, bare legs were crossed. The bright pink color of her high heel shoes caught his eye. She wore a short beige trench coat over a cobalt blue skirt. Her hair cascaded in loose waves past her shoulders, softening her features, but her smile faded slightly as the silence grew longer between them.

"You're staring at me."

"If it be thus to dream, still let me sleep," he murmured, tracing her bottom lip with his thumb. His skin tingled when she touched the tip of her tongue to his finger. His rumbling groan was her only warning before he took possession of her mouth, and both were breathless when he parted from her. His gaze moved over her face, and he touched her hair.

"It's gotten so long, and darker."

"Moira did it." She frowned, running her fingers through the ends. "You don't like it?"

"I love it," he breathed. "It makes you look mysterious." He kissed her again, his hand gliding up her thigh and under her skirt. He moaned at finding no resistance to his questing fingers. "You are just full of surprises." His breath mixed with her sigh as she shifted, allowing him better access.

"I want to be full of you," Loren murmured, reaching down to caress him.

"Mmm, not here," he groaned and moved away from her. "As much as I want you, I respect Jim too much." Adjusting her clothes, she retreated to the other side of the seat.

"No, you're right," she said, breathing deeply. "Unfortunately, I'm the only good surprise." He knotted his brows. "It's been requested that we're seen together in public, tonight," she told him.

"Are you serious?" Graham rolled his eyes. "I just want to go home and do all that again, naked, to fruition."

"Hmm," she pouted. "So do I, but *they* knew you were flying home and I don't want to be hounded every time I leave the house."

"Where are Derek and Ron?"

"They'll meet us later." She came in close and pressed her lips against his neck. "Our evening starts off someplace special."

"Oh?" He gathered her into his arms. "Where's that?"

"You'll see."

A half-hour later, the Mercedes pulled into the circular drive at the entrance of the Park Plaza, near the London Eye. Graham assisted her out of the car, hooking her arm under his and they walked into the lobby, with a valet trailed behind them with their bags. The concierge greeted them with a bright smile as they headed toward the elevators. The valet stood at the other side of the car, politely ignoring the couple and pressed the button for their floor. Graham leaned closer, his lips to her ear.

"It's unfortunate that we have company," he whispered. Loren chuckled softly, and when the doors opened to the 29th floor, she led him to the left and proceeded to the end of the hall. He tapped the suite number when they arrived.

"Is this the same suite?" She flashed him a smile and inserted the keycard, opening the door to a view of the London Eye and the Thames beyond, framed by floor-to-ceiling windows. Graham stood aside for the valet but stopped the younger man before he went too far into the suite.

"You can just leave the bags here, thank you." He offered his hand to the valet with a hundred-pound note. "Please make certain we aren't disturbed."

"Of course, sir. Thank you, sir. Have a good evening," the valet stammered. Graham closed the door after him and locked it before turning back to the room.

The living area was illuminated by tiny pinpoint lights from the ceiling, highlighting the dark oak floors and colorful abstract art on the walls. Low white couches were arranged in an 'L' shape, one facing the flat screen TV above the fireplace, the other looking to the view, with a knee-high glass table taking up space in the middle. Loren was on her mobile, watching him.

"Hey, we're here." Her silvery eyes met his briefly, then moved downward. She had removed her trench, revealing a low-cut black top that showed some cleavage. His gaze followed the lines of her hips and as she turned, the tight fabric of her skirt only accentuated her curves. His lips parted to take a deep breath but remained where he stood as she continued her conversation.

"Hmm. Neither of us is happy about this, but if we give them what they want now, perhaps they'll leave us alone." She sighed. "Fine, we'll meet you down there. In a bit," she grumbled then dropped her mobile in her bag and pitched it to the couch as she approached him. Loren brushed her fingers along his cheek.

"How could I have forgotten how blue your eyes are." She slid her hand around the back of his neck to draw him in for a kiss. She teased him with the tip of her tongue, then, suddenly pushed him away.

"Take your clothes off," she purred. He narrowed his gaze but didn't move, and she dropped her chin slightly. "Go on, take your clothes off."

"Alright," he drawled but took his time removing his jacket as she crossed the room to the windows. Loren pressed the button that closed the shades then turned back to him as he pitched his jacket to the back of the sofa.

"What are you waiting for?" A slow smile spread across his lips.

"I'm not sure."

"You need to get cleaned up, and you can't wear that suit," she said. "It's too small now."

His smile broadened. "Will you be joining me in the shower?"

She pointed to her hair. "Do you have any idea how long it took to do this?" In three strides, he was standing before her, his fingers raking through the back of her hair.

"It looks lovely, but it will look even better, after." He hungrily dominated her lips, sliding his hand down her back to unzip her skirt and push it down her hips where it fell to the floor. She pulled away to start on the buttons of his shirt.

"This is gonna be quick," she muttered. Graham nodded, breathing hard and interrupting her by tugging her shirt over her head.

"We can go slower, the second time, and the third."

"Right. Damn buttons," Loren chuckled huskily. She yanked his shirt open, popping off the last few, and he shivered at her cool hands sliding up his chest, followed by the heat of her mouth. He then backed her toward the bedroom, her pink heels clicking on the hardwood, but he missed the doorway and she bumped into the wall next to it.

"Ow," she giggled against his neck. Her fingers tickled his skin unfastening his belt buckle and trousers, then released him from his garments. He growled, nipping at her neck and pressing her tight against the wall with his hips as he slid his hands up her sides. He dragged the straps of her bra over her shoulders, his mouth leaving a trail of heat down her chest. She breathed his name as he teased the sensitive areas of her breasts.

His hand went further down, catching the back of her knee and lifting her leg over his hip, bracing her against the wall. Her arms came around his neck and shoulders, raising her body a little higher, but Graham hesitated, drawing back to meet her gaze.

"I don't want to hurt you, love." Loren tightened her arms, pulling him closer and curled her leg higher on his hip.

"Are you not good?" she breathed, her lips brushing his ear.

"Oh, I hope so," he groaned as she sucked on the lobe of his ear.

"Why then, can one desire too much of a good thing?" she whispered and pulled him into a deep kiss. He shifted his hips, and a soft gasp passed her lips as he entered her. The heel of her shoe dug into the back of his leg as she met each thrust, but he didn't care. Her body pressed tight against him, her short nails digging into his shoulder blades, the silky heat of her core pushed him closer and closer to the edge, and as their desire overwhelmed them, their voices joined in their release. Graham leaned his forehead against her shoulder, his arms and legs trembling.

"My god, woman," he huffed. "You'll be the death of me." Loren gave a husky laugh that turned into a groan when she released the vice grip on his hip and put her foot down.

"I'm going to feel that later, or now," she muttered and slowly slid down to the floor. She rolled her head to look at him as he crumpled next to her. "Wow." Graham caressed her cheek.

"Did I hurt you?"

"Oh, goodness, no," she replied, moving closer to give him a long kiss. "Let's do that again."

"Oh, yes," he hummed as their lips met. Loren pushed him down to the floor, pressing her glorious body to his, but the pinging of three text messages in a row from her mobile had her pick her head up.

"Dammit, Ron! Go away!" she whined.

"He's not going to stop," he muttered. "How do the paparazzi even know we're here?" She waved her hand around.

"You tell one person, they tell someone else, and suddenly you have tents popping up on your front yard. Like literally." Her brows went up. "There was a pup tent at the park entrance next to my house yesterday." She adjusted her bra straps before slowly getting up off the floor, then offered her hand to him. "I brought your favorite blue suit." Graham didn't let her go after he stood up and drew her in closer, wrapping his arms around her.

"How do you know it's my favorite?"

"Oh, I think I read that somewhere." Her smile faded, touching his cheek. "Is this real? Are you really here?"

"I'm here." He kissed her then drew back. "And while I've dreamt of making love to you like that, my fantasy pales in comparison." They both groaned when her mobile pinged another barrage of text messages.

***

Loren caught a glimpse of Ron and Derek in the bar as she and Graham followed the maître d' to their table in the hotel's restaurant. It wasn't private, but the table was at the rear of the dining room, away from the two-story windows.

"Would you care for a bottle of wine, sir? Madam?" the host inquired as they took seats next to each other.

"Let's start with champagne," Graham replied. "I apologize for being particular, but if you would, please bring an unopened bottle."

"Of course, sir." The man nodded and retreated. Graham moved closer to Loren and kissed her shoulder.

"Thank you again for surprising me," he said. "It was perfect."

She smiled at him. "I like surprising you."

"Did you say you met with Dr. Howell the other day?" Her smile faded as she sat back into her chair.

"Yes. Neither of us is sure the anxiety is part of my personality or a symptom, but at least I'm not having headaches as often. Then he suggested talk therapy." Loren rolled her eyes. "Been there, done that."

"Are you still having night terrors?"

She shrugged. "Not every night, maybe four out of seven, but it's an improvement." She gave a small smile to the waitress who brought a basket of warm rolls to their table, waiting until she left before resuming their conversation.

"Dr. Howell got the approval letter from the UCI, and I started on a low dose of Zoloft. It's probably a good idea until I get myself under control again." He leaned in closer, tucking a lock of her hair behind her ear.

"You have seemed calmer."

"Yah, no. I'm just good at covering it, remember?" She broke open a crusty roll, taking her time buttering both halves, but still got the spread on her fingers. Loren put half on his plate when Graham caught her hand, raising it to his lips to draw her finger into his mouth. She was tingling all over when he released her.

"You are an evil man to tease me in such a way." He gave a toothy grin and leaned in to kiss her when the waiter returned with their champagne. The man coughed lightly as he placed the bottle on the table.

"If you're ready, I can take your dinner orders."

"Ah, yes." Graham quickly reviewed the menu then glanced at Loren. "Salmon?" She nodded. "The lady will have the salmon, and I'll have the roast *poussin*, thank you."

"Excellent choice, sir. Madam." After the waiter left, Graham unwrapped the cork and deftly opened the bottle of champagne with only a small *poof*.

She pouted. "Aw, where's the big pop?"

"You only open champagne like that on the podium," he laughed, pouring her a glass.

"Yah, and that's the best part!"

He rolled his eyes. "I'll open the next one like that." She chuckled as he resumed his seat, slipping his arm around her waist to pull her closer. "I can't keep my hands from you," he murmured, leaning in to kiss her but she drew away.

"I greatly dislike being a zoo exhibit," she muttered, jutting her chin at a table to their right. The couple sitting there wasn't even trying to hide their gawking. He tightened his lips.

"So what? You let Haskins grab your ass in public." She stiffened, her ears burning as she turned her glare to him. "I'm sorry," he said softly. "I didn't mean that."

"Yes, you did."

He sighed. "I'm sorry. I'm exhausted, and I didn't want to do this."

"Then save your attitude for Ron, not me."

"I am truly sorry," he murmured, kissing her neck, but she pulled away again. Two of the service staff appeared with their meals.

Both were in better spirits after they had eaten and enjoyed most of the bottle of champagne. Loren giggled, trying to keep him from stealing her caramel ice cream even as she reached over to nick some his *semifreddo* chocolate mousse.

"I don't want to stop touching you," he murmured in her ear as his hand skimmed up her thigh, "but I must beg your pardon. I'll be back directly." He kissed her cheek then slid out from his seat.

"You'd better," she replied, smiling up at him. He stood there for a moment, studying her. "What?"

"With the dark hair, you do resemble Athena."

"Just go." She held in her grin and shook her head. Graham left her with a bright smile and a wink.

I'm home. I'm finally home. His smile widened as his thoughts going back to seeing her in the back of Jim's Mercedes. *No one's done anything like that for me.* He headed toward the restroom, noting Ron and Derek watching him in the mirror behind the bar. *I'm back now. We're not going to need them anymore.*

Upon exiting the lavatory, he headed to the lounge area sinks, nodding to the attendant standing near the door when it opened. A large man entered, and Graham glanced at him as they passed each other, noting the man's ill-fitting suit jacket. After washing his hands, he reached for a paper towel to dry off, his eyes flicking to the mirror when a hot flash of fear shot through him.

A broad-chested man with a ratty blond ponytail stepped up to the sink next to him. The lopsided mouth curled into a smirk.

"Nice night out, isn't it."

You fucking son of a bitch. "Yes, it is," he replied, turning to glare down at the man. "You should enjoy it while it lasts. There's a storm coming." He tightened his fists, but he was dismissed with a sniff, and the man faced the sink. Graham backed up a step, then turned and exited the restroom. He strode to the bar, his scowl deepening with each step, a mix of emotions churning in his gut.

I'm no knight. He'd take me down with one punch. Derek was standing next to Ron at the bar as he approached, but both were watching the dining room in the mirror.

"What can I get for you?" the bartender asked as Graham took out his billfold.

"Teeling whisky, straight. Thanks," he replied and dropped a fifty on the bar. He didn't look at Derek when he spoke but kept his eyes pinned on the door to the men's room in the mirror. "Coming out of the lav now, is that your man?"

"Did he speak to you?"

"Just said that it was a nice night out." He gave a tight smile to the bartender when he returned with his drink. "Keep the change," Graham said then knocked it back, grimacing as the liquid burned down his throat. Derek dropped his chin slightly to speak into the mic hidden in his jacket lapel.

"Eyes up, my dear."

"I'm getting Loren out of here," Graham muttered, then walked away. When he returned to the table, Loren was looking at her mobile and giggling.

"Is something funny?"

"Just Cece keeping me grounded," she said as he sat down. "What took you so long? I was getting lonely." She lay her hand on his shoulder and leaned close, her other hand on his thigh, edging higher. "I have dangerous plans for you, Mr. Atherton." He grabbed her wrist tightly.

"Stop."

"What's the–. You're hurting me." He let go, looking at the entrance to the restaurant, then to the bar area, where Derek nodded to him. Graham turned back to her frown. "Are you going to tell me what all that was about?"

"Yes, but let's get out of here first." He stood and extended his hand to her.

"Okay, but, where are we going?"

"Home."

Loren held a tight rein on her mouth when Graham all but dragged her through the restaurant to the hotel lobby. But, when the doors of the elevator closed, she shoved him up against the wall, her forearm pressing into his throat.

"No more of this cloak and dagger shit," she snarled. "You're gonna tell me what the fuck is going on." His larynx jumped as he swallowed, and she moved her arm down to his chest.

"When I went to the loo, I recognized a man that came in after me. That fucking ponytail," he muttered. "He's the one who's been following you. That's why we're leaving."

"What?" She stepped back, a shot of panic shooting through her. "No," she growled, clenching her fists. "No. We are not leaving."

"Yes, we are," he snapped, moving toward her.

"I've had enough of this bullshit." Loren turned and smacked the emergency stop button, wincing at the harsh buzzing of the alarm. She let out a growl and pushed him up against the wall again. "I will not let some fucking ponytailed reject from the grunge era intimidate me! He hasn't done anything but take fucking pictures, and he's probably making a good dollar on 'em, too!" She poked him in the chest with her finger, hard.

"I had the whole fucking night planned out! Granted, I didn't plan for what happened earlier, which was a very, very nice surprise, but I am done being scared! We're going dancing, and you will not say no, goddammit!" He blinked at her, then reached over and reset the elevator.

"Did you drink the rest of the champagne?"

"Maybe." She crossed her arms over her chest and raised her chin. "But I really did have the whole night planned."

"You are amazing," he said, a little smirk on his face.

"Why?"

"You told me off and poked me in the chest. That hurt, mind you." He rubbed the spot. "You even said fucking four times." His smirk grew larger as he took her hand. "My warrior goddess has returned."

"Yah, well, I'm fucking pissed off." The elevator dinged and the doors opened revealing the hotel manager, concierge, and three security officers standing there, concern written on their faces. Loren quickly put her hands up.

"I'm sorry! I backed into the button!"

**

22 October

Loren woke laying on her back with sunlight hitting her in the face and her head throbbing. She groaned and started to roll to her side but was held fast by a man's arm and shoulder over her chest.

"Holy sh-!" She pushed at the body covering her, then froze. Graham didn't open his eyes, nor did he let go of her, even with her struggling. She studied him as her breathing and heart rate came back to normal.

"How many nights have I longed for this, and yet I almost punched him in the face because I thought last night was a dream."

"I'm glad you didn't punch me," he muttered, his voice raspy. "That would have hurt."

"I'm sorry. I didn't mean to say that out loud." He groaned, moving to his back.

"Come back, *mon Coeur*." She hummed, stretching out against him.

"It's almost eight."

He cracked an eye. "So?"

"I only booked the suite for one night."

A smile slowly began to appear. "I guess we'll just have to–." His mobile started to ring, and both of his eyes popped open, only to roll closed again. "I want to ignore it, but he'll just keep ringing back," he grumbled and answered on speaker. "What do you want, Ron?"

"And here I thought you two were those annoying morning people."

"That's her, not me. Hey!" Loren poked him in the ticklish spot under his arm and he squirmed away laughing.

"There's been some news we need to discuss," Ron said. "We'll be up in fifteen."

"Dammit," Graham mumbled, putting the phone back down on the nightstand.

"I'm starving," Loren said, snuggling up with him. "Do you think room service can get donuts?"

***

Graham and Loren were seated at the kitchen island with their meager breakfast when Ron and Derek walked into the suite. Ron set his briefcase down and reached for the cover of one of the dishes on the counter.

"They didn't have any donuts," she pouted, adjusting the collar of her fluffy white robe.

"Aw, poor you," Ron pouted back, then turned to Derek. "Perhaps we should have worn our robes. I might have to go back and nick mine."

"What's this news you have, Mr. Hudson?" Graham chuckled.

Derek answered. "Penny and I followed our man to an apartment building in Peckham." Loren shot a glance at Graham. "We're watching him, and if he goes anywhere near Lalonde, we'll inform DS O'Dowd."

"Good job," Graham said, then turned to Ron, who was buttering a bagel. "Is that all?"

"No, it's not," he answered, licking his fingers. "A wonderfully handsome couple made the front page." He brought out several tabloid papers from his briefcase and slapped them down on the counter next to Loren. She looked down at the image and snarled. The photograph wasn't of Graham and Loren. It was of Jon Haskins kissing her on the cheek.

"Fucking son of a bitch." She started to turn away. "Wait. Is it just this photo or are there more?" Ron picked up the other papers and opened each one to photos of Loren and Jon from the time trial in France and at IDC's main campus. Graham picked up the one of Jon grabbing her ass.

"And two seconds later I punched him for it," she told him.

"Did you?" He transferred his glare to Ron. "This is ridiculous."

"I agree," he said. "Which is why I've arranged for–."

"No. No more games!" Graham stood, toppling his chair to throw the paper at Ron. "What does it fucking matter anymore?" He stormed off to the bedroom, slamming the door behind him to pace around the room, clenching his hands at his sides.

What did she expect? Now the whole world thinks she's fucking Haskins! He sat down on the bed to yank on his jeans, then went around the room, collecting his things and throwing them into his suitcase on the bed. *She goes off on me, yet she's the one keeping secrets! She has no idea how it makes me appear.* He balled up his trousers and was about to pitch them into the case when he froze.

What am I doing? He sat down heavily on the bed. "None of this is her fault, or Ron's." He stood up and his foot knocked over her dragonhide messenger bag. Two pill bottles and a small wooden box came out. Graham picked up the bottles and opened the Zoloft, counting twenty-two pills. He then opened the Xanax, and all fifteen were still there. Closing the top, he put both bottles back in her bag, then picked up the box. Turning it over, a bicycle wheel was etched on the top.

"Neat little box," he muttered and slid the top open. Inside was a cuff bracelet made of strips of leather woven through the links of a bicycle chain. It appeared large enough for his wrist.

"I made that for you." He looked up at her voice, the box still in his hands. "Holly showed Cece and me how, and we made a bunch to sell at the Cycle Expo," she said, her eyes flicking to his suitcase on the bed.

"It's brilliant," he told her, examining the bracelet again. "I'm sure they'll sell out quickly."

"You don't have to wear it if you don't like it," she said flatly. He took the cuff out and slipped it on his wrist.

"It fits perfectly. Thank you." His hands fell to his sides. "Loren, I'm sorry."

"Why are you being like this?" Her voice broke over the words. "What did I do?"

"You didn't do anything." Graham looked away from her, rolling his eyes. "I just feel restless, agitated. I don't know. I don't feel quite myself yet." He came near and reached out to touch her shoulder. She flinched. "I'm sorry, darling. It's not you; it's me." She stepped away from his touch, giving a humorless laugh.

"It's not you, it's me," she parroted, snidely. "I'm still a joke, huh? Some bad rom-com?"

"Why would you think–?"

"What do I know. I can't read your mind. All I feel is your anger," she shot back, pressing her clenched fist to her chest. He walked to her, placing his hand over hers.

"I'm sorry, love. I'm tired and stressed, and I open my mouth without thinking," he murmured, then took a breath. "Let's go do something together, alone. We have the entire city of London before us."

"Sounds like fun," she said, pulling her hands away, then reached into her back pocket to hand him a key fob. "Derek left the Jag in the parking garage." Graham bent down a bit to see her face, but she turned her head.

"Darling, I'm truly sorry. Please, forgive me."

"There's nothing to forgive." She headed to the bathroom, closing the door firmly behind her.

"Dammit," he mumbled, bumping his fist into his forehead.

***

Loren's chilliness thawed a little by the time they headed down to the lobby of the hotel. They stopped at the concierge desk and picked up tickets to one of the river cruises.

"I would suggest taking the side exit," the young woman said, winking. "We have a bit of an issue with *pigeons* milling about out the front."

Graham nodded slowly. "How inconvenient. Thank you." Once outside, he held a large umbrella aloft and offered his arm to Loren.

"Pigeons?" she asked, hooking her arm under his. They peeked around one of the columns and saw several people with cameras standing to the sides of the entrance. "Ah. I get it." They walked quickly in the rain the few blocks to a small tea shop near the river, where he chose a table by the large window in front.

Graham watched her sip her tea while she read the river cruise brochure spread out in front of her. The light coming from the window caught the red highlights in her hair and brightened the blue of her thermal top. Her silvery eyes flicked up to him.

"I can feel you staring at me."

His smile widened. "Full many a glorious morning have I seen flatter the mountain tops with sovereign eye; none compares to the beauty I see before me." Her mouth twitched as she put her cup down.

"Now what do I say to that?" Her smile faded as she reached over and touched his arm. "I'm sorry about earlier. I just–." Loren began to move away but Graham caught her hand.

"Please don't pull away from me," he murmured. Tears sprang to her eyes.

"When we were together before, it felt so perfect," she said, touching just above her heart. "I could almost feel you, here, but now…" Her expression changed in a flash, focusing on something over his shoulder and she yanked her hand back. Three teenage girls came pushing through the tables behind him, squealing with excitement. A brunette got to him first.

"You really are Graham Atherton! Could we get a picture with you?" He glanced at Loren, who was scowling with her arms crossed over her chest. He sighed and gave the teens a tight smile.

"Ladies…" He sighed again at their hopeful expressions. "Alright, quickly please." The brunette shrieked, then faced Loren, holding out her mobile.

"Would you mind?"

Her mouth popped open. "*I don't fucking believe this*," she muttered, shaking her head but took the girl's mobile. They draped themselves over Graham's shoulders and just as Loren pressed the button, they all kissed him on the cheeks. The girl grabbed her phone back and the trio bounded away without even a thank you.

"Hmm." Loren flipped her hair over her shoulder and went back to her tea.

"I'm sorry about that," he said, reaching to touch her hand but she moved it to look at her watch.

"Mmm hmm. We'd better get going if we want to make the boat."

"I thought perhaps we might walk across the bridge," he said, raising his brows.

"Westminster Bridge?" She blinked at him. "In the rain?"

"There's a spot in the middle where everyone takes selfies with the London Eye in the background," he said. "I reckoned we could get one like that."

She gave him a tiny smile. "Sure."

The rain had slackened, but the weather still kept most tourists off the bridge. Graham tucked her arm under his and held the umbrella over their heads as they strolled along the walkway. He caught her glancing at him a few times before she spoke.

"I read something about you the other day." He raised a brow in a silent question. "You said in an interview that you went to a boarding school, but I thought you lived in London," she said.

"I was seven when my parents divorced," he replied. "My mother moved us from Falkirk to London to be near her sister. That's when I met Benny." His expression darkened. "I was eleven when my father insisted that I go to Fettes College in Edinburgh, where he went. My mother fought him on it, but in the end, I still had to go. It was there I became interested in theater." They separated as a large group of young students moved past them on the sidewalk, a few looking up at Graham in surprise and recognition. When they came back together, he slid his hand down hers to interlace their fingers.

"You didn't tell me about that." She was frowning when he met her gaze.

"My childhood was idyllic compared to what you went through," he said, bringing her hand to his lips. "I got to see my mother and sister whenever I felt like it."

"They weren't in London?"

"They were, for about a month," he answered. "Mum hated I was at Fettes by myself, so she packed up our flat and moved." A slow grin spread across his lips. "It was decreed by the Fates because if she hadn't, she wouldn't have met a rather gentlemanly taxi driver."

She sucked in a breath. "You're kidding!"

He shook his head. "If Frederick hadn't been so adamant, my mother would never have met Gerald, and I wouldn't have become an actor."

"I bet he regrets that," she huffed.

"Yah, I reckon he does." He stopped and glanced around them. "I think this is the spot." Behind them, the London Eye oversaw the expanse of the River Thames. He brought her in close and swiped his thumb over the button of his mobile to change the selection to burst, then extended his arm.

"Do I have anything in my teeth?" She brushed her finger over her front teeth.

"Hmm, let me." He moved his arm up her back to hold her in a dip, then kissed her. She was laughing when they straightened. "I love you," he murmured, "and I'm sorry about those girls." Loren touched his cheek and kissed him again.

"I love you, too, and I'm sorry about Haskins grabbing my ass."

"I can't much blame him. It is perfect," he said, squeezing her bum and making her laugh. They continued across the bridge, arms around each other.

"I have to go home tonight," she said finally, and he stopped walking to face her.

"Why's that?"

"I'm leading a Breeze ride tomorrow morning," she replied, not looking at him. "And I have a lot to do before we leave for New York." She pulled a face. "And Anthony asked me to watch Alfie." His mouth compressed into a hard line. "It's just for Saturday night," she continued. "He's taking Cece on a weekend trip."

"Why can't Colin take–."

"Because Emma is going to drop any minute." She sighed. "Is it such a big deal?"

"I reckon not." He rolled his eyes as he turned to start walking again. The rain stopped by the time they reached the other side where he closed the umbrella. Their boat was loading at Westminster Pier, and they jumped aboard just in time.

"Come on, let's go up top." Loren grabbed his hand and led him up to the covered observation deck but stopped at the top of the stairs. "Um, where do you want to sit?"

"Oh, well, it's just so crowded," he chuckled, sweeping his arm toward the empty upper deck.

"How about right here, in the front?" She side stepped to the seat near the end where the deck went out another foot beyond the railing. "It's like sitting in the front of a rollercoaster. I love roller coasters!"

"Why doesn't that surprise me," Graham muttered, keeping his eyes on his feet as he followed her.

"Oh, that's right. You don't like heights," she said, patting the seat next to her. "Come here. I'll keep you safe." He stopped to frown at her.

"Who says I'm afraid of heights?"

"You said, when what's-her-face made you take that helicopter ride," she replied, smirking up at him.

"You mean Hannah."

"Yah, what's-her-face." She patted the seat again, and with a sigh, he settled onto the slightly damp plastic. "What happened between you?" she asked. "Was it really just the house?"

He squinted at her. "You're being quite nosey today."

"I suppose. I don't know. It seems like everything I know about you is from an interview or the gossip columns."

His brows went up again. "You don't honestly feel that way, do you?"

"Well, kind of," she answered, mirroring his frown. "I mean, there's a lot of stuff I know because I read it." Her gray eyes reflected the clouded sky touching her fingers to his lips. "But then I look at you, touch you, and I think I can feel you in my soul. Am I crazy?"

He moved closer to her. "Love is merely a madness." A chill ran through him as they kissed, and he cupped her cheek to deepen it when the cruise boat lurched away from the pier. Graham pulled away to clutch at the railing. "Bloody hell!"

"Relax," she laughed and pulled him back into his seat. She slipped her hand into his, linking their fingers and snuggled close. "Now tell me what happened with what's-her-face."

He exhaled sharply. "We were rarely alone. She had to have at least three people with her at all times, not including me," he said. "She was constantly running out of money because of her so-called friends, and I stupidly financed half of them through her." He shook his head. "They weren't all her friends, really. I reckon some might have been at one point, but most of them were fairly useless."

"Like vultures waiting for scraps."

Graham huffed. "Exactly." He sat up to look into her eyes. "I liked her, but it wasn't enough. She was fun and spontaneous, but neurotic. She needed me; that's what I liked." Loren brushed her fingers through his hair and a little smile formed on her lips.

"You like to be needed."

"Who doesn't," he replied sourly. "She only needed me for what I could do *for* her and who I knew, and I grew tired of being a part of her entourage."

She kissed him. "I need you, but not for what you can do for me. You can't change a light bulb."

"Yes, I can," he retorted, holding back his chuckle. "It's when you want the whole fixture changed. That I can't do."

"That's okay. I can." Her smile faded a little. "I need you for how you make me feel, even when you're not around." Her eyes seemed to darken the longer she held his gaze. "Sometimes you lead, sometimes you follow, and sometimes, I need you to save me, but only if I ask nicely." Graham could only stare at her, overwhelmed by too many emotions.

"I have never felt like this," he whispered. "It was strong before, and it's only gotten stronger and it scares me a little bit."

"I know." Her eyes lit up with her smile. "But isn't love supposed to scare you a little bit?"

"I reckon so." He kissed her tenderly, then tucked her under his arm with a contented sigh. "Hannah would never have gone roaming with me, especially not in the rain," he said. "She probably would have melted."

"Like the wicked witch," she chuckled. "I could spend the whole day wandering around a flea market in any kind of weather." Graham sat back from her, his eyes wide.

"You're joking."

"No," she replied. "Where do you think half the stuff in my house came from?"

"There's one not far from Butler's Wharf. You want to go?"

Loren jumped in her seat. "Yes!"

***

24 October

"You've got to be fucking kidding me," Loren muttered, turning her BMW down the alley next to her house on Essex. Anthony's Rover was in the parking area, and two photographers were attempting to hide in the bushes. She came to a stop at the rear gate and flicked up the visor on her helmet, rolling her eyes at the click of camera shutters behind her. As she dismounted, the gate opened, and Anthony stepped out. He glanced pointedly down the alley.

"Where's Graham?"

"He'll be here later, maybe," she muttered, removing her helmet.

"Maybe?" She shrugged, pushing her moto through the gate and toward the shed. Once there, Anthony had to unlock it for her.

"I thought you were going to take Cece on a motorcycle trip?" she asked, guiding her moto through the open door. She smirked at his heaved sigh.

"You were right," he grumbled. "She was none too thrilled when I suggested it, so I can't leave you the Rover. I reckoned you'd have the Jaguar anyway."

Her smirk dissolved. "You think Graham is going to let me put Alfie in the Jag? It has leather seats."

"Put a cover over them," he countered.

"Yah, that'd go over like a ton of bricks." Loren leaned into the Harley to shove the BMW into the stand next to it. When she turned to leave, Anthony was blocking her.

"Trouble in paradise?" She rubbed at a spot on the seat of the Harley, avoiding his gaze.

"I don't know. He's just…" She took a breath. "One minute, things are great, but then he gets all huffy like he's mad at me for something, but he won't talk about it. He just storms off. I had that Breeze ride with Cece yesterday, and when I got back, he was all snippy with me." Her volume rose as she spoke.

"And then, he storms out of the house because Haskins called me. He was inviting us to dinner!" She raked her fingers through her hair, yanking out the ponytail elastic. "Like anyone could compare to him!" Anthony leaned against the workbench smirking.

"I'll try not to take that as an insult." Loren spun around to point at him.

"Oh, and then he starts in on Derek and Penny, that if it weren't for them, we'd be able to pick up and go anywhere we wanted. He fucking hired them!" She pressed her hand to her chest, gasping at the sudden pain.

"Hey, steady on," he said, holding shoulders. "You're getting all wound up." She looked up at him, desperately trying to hold it together.

"I don't understand. While we were together in the States, we…" She held out her hands to him. "You know those couples you hate because they finish each other's sentences and they're constantly touching and rarely say I love you because they don't have to. They just feel it," she whined. "That's what it was like. It was perfect. But now, it's like he doesn't want to be with me anymore. What did I do? What did I do wrong?"

"You didn't do anything," he said, patting her arm. She stepped back, sniffling and brushed her sleeve under her nose.

"I'm scared. This isn't how it's supposed to be. I'm walking on eggshells around him all the time." She took a shaky breath. "I don't know what to do to fix it."

"Hey, no more tears," he said, rubbing her arms. "I'm going to let you in on a little secret. Men are afraid to admit we're afraid, and it comes off as being angry."

She snorted. "That's not a secret."

"Fine then," he retorted, then took a breath. "Graham's afraid and perhaps he doesn't know why, exactly, and he's frustrated with himself, like I was." He raised his brows. "You recall what I was like a few days before I, uh, I took those pills."

"You were a real dick," she replied, and he looked down his nose at her.

"Yes, but you realize you do the same thing," he countered. "When you get scared, you go all aggro."

"Yah, I know," she grumbled, eyeing him. "But only with you."

He huffed. "It's going to take time to discover how you fit into each other's lives." Anthony tweaked her nose. "Have some patience."

"I'll try." Loren squinted at him. "Why can I talk to you like this, but I can't with him?"

"Because you know you can say anything to me and I'm not going to leave you." Loren dropped her chin, her throat tightening. He touched her cheek. "It's going to be alright. Give him some space and let him work through it."

"But I want to help him," she whined, and Anthony stooped down to get in her face.

"You try so hard to be everything to everyone, but you're the only one who feels it when you fail." His eyes flicked away. "I love you, and you know I'm always here for you, but right now I have to go gather up Cece. We have a bit of a drive." She gave a breathy chuckle.

"Thanks for the brotherly advice." He put his arm around her shoulders as they headed to the house.

"Anytime, little sister."

***

Graham parked the Jaguar in front the house on Essex later that afternoon, glaring at the paparazzi on the other side of the bushes.

They can't leave us the hell alone. His annoyance only increased each time he had to ring the bell.

"Where the hell is she?" he muttered then took out his mobile to call her when the door finally opened.

"I'm sorry, I forgot to give you the code," Loren said when Alfie began barking and tried to jump out of her grip. "Christ, dog!" She yanked back on his collar. "Come in before he pulls my arm off." Graham stepped through and closed the door behind him.

"I was in the basement," she said. "He wouldn't let me up the stairs." Graham looked her up and down, his brows going up.

"Is that what happened to you? You're filthy," he chuckled. Her hair was back in a dusty ponytail, and a dirt streak marked her forehead. Dark smudges ran up the sleeves of her red T-shirt, and the knees of her jeans were black.

"I went down to start some laundry when I saw a box with my handwriting on it, but I didn't remember what was in it." She sneezed into her elbow several times in a row. "Uh, so much dust," she groaned.

"Bless you." He grabbed a box of tissues on the side table and handed it to her.

"Thanks." She grabbed a wad, held it to her nose and blew as she went back into the kitchen. "Then I saw more boxes, and I couldn't just leave it alone."

"Do you need help?" he asked, following her.

"Thanks, but there's no use in both of us getting dirty." Graham came up behind her and put his arms around her waist.

"I don't mind getting dirty, so long as we can get cleaned up together," he murmured, nuzzling her neck. She hummed, holding his arms to her.

"My shower isn't big enough for the two of us."

"We could always go back to my house." He kissed her just under her ear and felt her shiver. She looked down at the Mastiff, his big brown eyes gazing at them.

"I can't leave him here," she said, turning around to put her hands on his chest. "And I'm afraid of what he'll do to your car, and your house. He can get a little nuts."

He frowned at the dog. "You're not going to give us trouble, are you?" Alfie flattened his ears and lowered his head, but kept his eyes locked on Loren. "I'm sure he'll be fine," Graham said.

"Right," she drawled. "You'll both be good boys and get along." She pulled out of his arms. "Let's go get busy." He caught her wrist and brought her into his arms.

"I do like the way you think," he said, his voice low and rumbly as he backed her to the counter. He kissed her then, tightening his arms around her waist to lift her to sit on the cool bluestone. Loren hummed and deepened their kiss, wrapping her long legs around his hips as his hands found their way under her shirt. She dropped her head back for him to nibble down her neck, then stiffened.

"Uh, Graham?"

He brought his head up. "Huh?" Her eyes directed him to Alfie sitting next to them, his tongue hanging out. Panting. "Is he going to sit there and watch?"

She made a face. "Ew."

"Agreed." He pulled down her shirt and gave a long sigh. "Let's go get busy," he muttered and helped her off the counter.

With Graham's help, Loren quickly went through the rest of the boxes in the basement and separated out hers from the Ainsworth family's items. Alfie stayed upstairs, supervising, but when they finally came up, the dog was at her heels as she carried two boxes into the front room. As she bent to put them down, Alfie knocked her out of the way to stuff his head into one.

"Dog," she chuckled and pushed him away. She went back into the kitchen to wash her hands in the sink, peeking over her shoulder. "I'm starving. You want to get take-away and watch a movie?"

"I like that idea," he answered, and a loud thud came from behind her. "Goddammit!" She turned around, and Graham was gesturing angrily to the dog, who was trying to scuttle under the table. "He tripped me!"

She heaved a sigh. "Alfie, come." She patted her thigh as she opened the door to the back garden. "You don't need to get so worked up." Loren shooed the dog outside, but he went straight to the fence, barking and digging under it. "What are you bothering with now?"

"There were photographers on the other side of the bushes when I got here," Graham answered from the patio. Her brows knotted as she looked back at him.

"More? How many?"

"I don't know," he retorted. "I didn't count them."

Loren rolled her eyes. "Alfie, down. Down!" She pulled at the dog, but he wouldn't budge. Graham came over and reached for Alfie's collar.

"Here, let me–." The Mastiff snarled and spun around, snapping at his arm. Loren hip-checked the dog away from Graham and pointed to the house.

"Alfie! Place!" He whimpered but obeyed, slinking back into the kitchen. She turned to touch Graham's arm. "Are you alright? He's never done that before."

"I'm fine," he grumbled, pulling away. She reached for him again, but he pushed her hand away. "I said I'm fine." She flinched, then her expression hardened.

"I've had enough of you scowling at me." She lunged at him with curled fingers, poking him in the ribs at his most ticklish spots. Graham writhed away, checking his indignation and caught both her wrists in one hand. She relaxed with a slight smile on her lips.

"Your hands are rather large to be able to hold me like this. You know what they say about men with big hands."

His lips twitched. "That I have big feet?"

"I was thinking a little higher than that," she said, tilting her head back, eyes smoldering.

"That I have long legs?"

"Something else entirely," Loren purred, her gaze dropping to his mouth. Graham drew closer, lowering her hands to his waist. She brushed her fingers against him, her brow twitching at his involuntary reaction.

"You deserve a bit of punishment for that," he said.

"Do I?"

"Aye, you do." His lips skimmed across hers as he released her wrists. She settled her arms about his neck, pulling him to the patio table where he leaned her backward on the tiled surface. His hand slid under the back of her shirt as her leg curled around his hip. Their passion was soon interrupted when Alfie tore back outside to the fence, snarling and barking Shouts came from the other side as the Mastiff dug under the fence.

"Shit! Alfie! Stop!" Loren pushed Graham off her and ran over, grabbing the dog's collar to haul him away from the fence. A large camera lens lay in the dirt near a break in the boards.

"Serves them right," Graham muttered. His irritation turned to concern at the drops of blood congealing in the soil. "Check his mouth, Loren. He might be bleeding." The Mastiff whined as she gently opened his mouth.

"Oh, Alfie," she groaned. "He's lost a tooth. Come on, dummy." She stood up and dragged the dog back inside the house. "God, Anthony's going to shoot me!"

"Surely he can't blame you for this," he scoffed from behind her.

"Doesn't change how guilty I feel."

"Loren, it's a dog." She faced him, glowering.

"Yah, *he's* a dog, but if it weren't for him—. Forget it." She waved him off and turned back to Alfie.

"No, please, finish your thought," Graham snapped. "I want to hear how much you owe to a dog." She jumped to her feet to poke him in the chest with a finger.

"He was here when you weren't! He got me out of bed when I didn't want to!"

"You sure that wasn't his master?"

She winced. "Fuck you." His scowl deepened looking down his nose at her, then he turned on his heel and strode out of the room.

"Graham!" She lunged to the doorway to find him at the threshold of the front door with his hand on the handle. "Please, don't leave again," Loren said, her voice shaking. He let go and the door slowly closed.

"I'm sorry," he murmured and in two strides, she was in his arms, holding tightly. "I'm sorry. I don't know what's wrong with me. I didn't mean to insinuate–."

"Stop." Loren drew back to search his face, fear swirling in her gut. "I'm sorry, too."

***

Graham tried to lighten the mood by ordering dinner from her favorite pizza place around the corner. He chose an action comedy film to watch and while she laughed, Loren was still a prickly jumble when they headed upstairs to bed. Alfie pushed his way into her room to jump up on the bed and sprawled out on his back.

"Oh, no," she drawled. "You get the rest of the house." She dragged him out the door, then listened for Alfie's nails on the hardwood steps as he went downstairs. She turned and burst a laugh at Graham on the bed, his arms and legs in the air and his tongue hanging out. He moved to his side for her to lay down next to him, but her humor was gone.

"Please tell me what's bothering you," she said. He sighed and turned over to his back.

"Nothing's bothering me."

"Then why do you keep pushing me away?"

"*I* keep push–." He ran his hand down his face. "Right," he drawled, his volume rising. "So, it's my fault, now. All the shit happening, it's all my fault."

"I did not say–." Loren sat up to glare at him. "Stop it. We're like a fucking tennis match. You get angry, I get angry, and then we both blow up. Why can't you just talk to me?" It took a minute of them staring at each other for his scowl to soften.

"I wanted to take you away and go lie on a beach somewhere, alone," he answered. "I need to reconnect with my own emotions, and you are at the core of that." He squeezed his eyes shut. "So much of what happened to you and what I was feeling, is wrapped up in the character and I'm having trouble letting it go." She leaned over to put her hands on his cheeks.

"Why couldn't you just tell me that?"

"I reckon because it sounds mad and selfish." He put his hands over hers. "I loved waking up next to you every morning. It was like you said, we felt connected, but then we parted, and I didn't realize how much it would hurt," he told her, his eyes welling. "I need you, and I don't want you to be apart from me again." His words set off an alarm in her mind, but she forced the thought away and kissed him.

"I'm here, right now," she whispered. His fingers tangled in her hair as he kissed her again then pushed her down onto the bed. He released her to be quick at removing his clothes as she pulled her shirt over her head. Loren arched her back as his lips and tongue slid down her neck, removing her bra while kissing his way along her body as his nimble fingers unfastened her jeans. His mouth touched newly exposed skin, making her tremble with desire.

Then Alfie began to whine and scratch at the door.

Graham dropped his head to her stomach. "It's like he knows," he moaned. Loren cupped his face, breathing heavy.

"Make like we're doing a sex scene in your movie and ignore him." He stared at her for a second.

"But that's not what it's like!" He sat back on his heels with his hand over his forehead. "I'm not actually doing what it looks like I'm doing. It's a suggestion. I didn't even take off her clothes. The camera pans to her face, and she's writhing on the bed in a bodysuit, alone." She gaped at him, holding in her laughter.

"You're lying."

"No, I'm not," he sighed, rolling over to sit on the edge of the bed. "Kissing, yes. Touching, it depends, but there's nothing sexual about it for me."

"Then why did you say you felt like you were cheating?"

He hung his head. "Because I felt… I *feel* guilty that I wasn't here for you when I should have been," he said, softly, then gestured to the door. "Like he was." Graham looked over his shoulder at her. "I ruined the mood, didn't I?"

"Yah, a little bit," she said. Alfie scratched at the door again.

"You can let him in," he grumbled.

"Are you sure?"

"It's one night, right?" Loren moved to her knees and kissed him.

"Yes, just one night. I love you." She got up and grabbed a T-shirt to pull it over her head as she walked to the door. As soon as she opened it, Alfie burst in and jumped up on the bed as Graham moved off to put on his boxers. When they all settled down, Alfie was whining and thumping his tail on the mattress between them.

"Don't be so joyful, dog," Graham muttered.

***

Light filtered through the curtains to reveal Graham staring at the ceiling, agitated and exhausted.

How could she sleep through that dog snoring like that? Loren was curled up next to him and he lay his hand on her hip. The warmth of love and desire mixed with the bitter pang of his plans ruined, but a slight smile formed on his lips at the snore coming from the floor.

Man's best friend indeed. He sniffed. *Who won that battle, eh?* He moved to spoon her and brushed a lock of her hair away from her neck.

"I love you," he whispered against her skin.

"I can tell," she sighed, wiggling her bum against his growing hardness. She turned her sleepy smile to meet his lips. He slipped his hand under her shirt to cup her breast, but when she started to roll over, the bed shook, and they looked down at their feet. Alfie had his paws on the bed, panting.

"Alfie, down," she croaked. "Down." The Mastiff obeyed with a groan and a snort. "You, come back," she whispered and met Graham's kiss again, but as soon as she made a sound of pleasure, the dog was back up on the bed.

"That's it! I'm done!" Graham threw the blanket off and rolled away from her to grab his clothes from the floor.

"Wait, what?" Loren sat up as he yanked on his jeans. "Where are you going?"

"I'm leaving," he snapped, sitting down in the chair to put on his boots. "I've had enough of *him.*" He gestured to the Mastiff, who was watching him, ears up, head tilted.

"What the hell are you getting so angry about?" He stood and threw his hand in the air.

"Him! All this! I don't know!" Graham turned around in a full circle, then stopped to clench his fists. "You've been lying to me again," he snarled, taking a step closer to her. Loren held perfectly still, her eyes wide but he ignored the fear he saw there. "Why didn't you tell me someone broke into your hotel room? And what of the notes you found in your mail? The necklace I gave you? How could you not tell me a man tried to assault you?" He leaned his hands on the bed to get in her face.

"Why did I have to find out from some fucking report my father gave me that Felix raped you?"

The naked disgust on his face left her too stunned to even breathe. Loren could only watch as he snatched his jacket from the arm of the chair and his boots from the floor, then stormed out of her room. Alfie's whine spurred her into action.

"Graham, stop!" She launched from the bed and ran down the stairs with the dog at her heels, but he was already out the door. Loren halted at the end of the walkway and grabbed Alfie's collar before he could bolt after the three photographers standing at the park entrance. When she turned back, the Jaguar was backing out of the space and with a squeal of tires, it was gone.

"Please don't leave me," she choked. One of the photographers took a few steps toward them, causing Alfie to bark and jump at him, pulling Loren off balance. She just stared at them, then walked back into the house with the dog by her side and slammed the door shut. She paced the front room, wringing her hands and gasping for breath.

He left me. I let him in, and he left me. The room spun. Her knees buckled and she collapsed to the floor.

***

A wet nose snuffled at her ear and she pushed it away.

"Stop, dog." She had been on the floor long enough for the tile to leach all the warmth from her body, leaving her stiff and shivering. Loren slowly got up to lumber into the kitchen where Alfie was scratching at the back door.

"Alright, I get it." She opened the door to let the dog out but left it wide open, then headed upstairs to her room. The sheets still smelled of him, which spurred her to call Graham but only got his voicemail. She left a string of messages, sent multiple texts and emails, pleading, then begging him to call her, but he didn't reply.

Late afternoon found her curled up with Alfie, who whoofed at a knock on the door.

"Jim's here, Loren," came Holly's muffled voice.

"Okay, thanks." She dragged herself off the bed and went into her bathroom. Alfie sat the doorway watching her gather her toiletries together. The bottle of Xanax was on the shelf. A tear slid down her cheek.

I can't do this. With a shaking hand, she grabbed the bottle and opened it, dumping several pills in her hand. *If I could just sleep, maybe all this would be a dream.* She popped all of them into her mouth, choking on them as she reached for a cup of water and she spit out the pills into the toilet.

"What the fuck am I doing?" She then took out one pill and with a gulp of water, swallowed it. The rectangle pill scraped against her raw throat. The garnet ring on her finger caught her attention, glowing a dull red in the pinpoint lights in the ceiling.

"I ruined it. I couldn't tell him the truth. Why can't I trust him? Why can't I trust anybody!" Alfie whined and jumped up, his big paws on her shoulders and licked the tears from her face. "Okay, okay! That's enough." She shoved him off, then gave him a pat on the head. "Thanks, Alfie."

After applying some makeup and a change of clothes, Loren picked up her orange duffle and messenger bag, then walked out of her room. Jim took her duffle when she came down the steps.

"No Graham?" His frown deepened at the slight shake of her head. "Alright, then. Ron and Penny will meet us at the airport." She held her messenger bag tightly to her chest following him around the house and almost back at seeing the Rover in the space next to the Mercedes. Loren ignored Anthony calling her name as Jim opened the car door for her.

"Loren, stop." Anthony caught her arm as she was lowering herself into the seat. "Where's Graham? What's happened?"

"It's over," she replied hoarsely, pulling out of his grip and shut the door.

***

Shoreditch, London

The doorbell rang as Claire Atherton was sitting down with a cup of tea. She glanced at the clock on the kitchen wall and let out a groan.

For fuck's sake, Dad. Just once, can't you ring before popping by? She didn't move though, hoping he'd think she wasn't home, but the bell rang again.

Dammit. She pushed away from the table. Trudging down the steps from her second-floor walk-up, she opened the door and her brows flew to her hairline. Graham was on the stoop, disheveled, pale and haggard. She reached for his arm.

"Are you alright? Were you jumped?" He shook his head and spoke quietly.

"I'm sorry to bother you so early, but I didn't know where else to go."

"Come in, come in!" Her frown deepened at his slow climb up the stairs. He then stood in the front room with his hands shoved in his pockets and shoulders hunched.

"Would you like some tea?" she asked.

"Yes, thank you," he replied, barely audible.

"Come sit down, then." She motioned for him to follow her to the kitchen area. Claire poured another cup and set it in front of him, then sat down on the chair next to him.

"Isn't Jared home?" he asked, his voice hoarse.

"No, he's working today," she replied. "Darling, what's happened?" He took a deep breath and stared his fingers, loose around his cup.

"I've tried very hard not to be like Dad. I wanted to be a better man." He lifted his head, unshed tears welling in his blue eyes. "But I failed. I failed her, Claire. We had a–." He shook his head. "No, it wasn't even an argument. It was just me being a fucking prat." He sniffled and wiped his nose on his jacket cuff. Claire curled her nose then pushed a box of tissues at him. He took one but just held it, twisting and ripping it to pieces. "I said terrible things. Horrible, hurtful things and I walked out. Just like Dad." He covered his mouth with his hand.

"Dad would leave when things were good as well, but you don't recall that," she countered. "What did you say to her?"

"I threw everything back in her face," he choked. "She didn't tell me someone's been stalking her or that she was attacked, or that the same man broke into her hotel room. And then the fucking Yank corners me in the lav of a restaurant in London." He ran a trembling hand through his hair.

"But it's not her fault. None of it," he insisted and sniffled again. "How could I have said those things? She's everything I've ever wanted, and I ruined it." Graham put his head down on the table, quiet sobs shaking shoulders. Claire reached out and brushed his arm.

"Come on, little brother. It runs deeper than that."

He sat up a bit, sniffling. "I'm scared. I feel helpless, and I'm ashamed of it." A tear hit the table in front of him. "I'm no knight in shining armor. I can't protect her," he said, his voice breaking. "I love her, but my pride pushed her away. I've ruined the best thing that's ever happened to me." Claire squeezed his hand, then sat back in her chair with a long exhale.

"You've always been a dreamer, darling," she said. "You weave yourself into a cocoon of infatuation. You don't want to think about the past or the future. You can just be with her, and fuck like rabbits." She gave a half-smile at his snort. "The world fades away and everything feels perfect, and you call it love." His injured frown told her words hit home and she tilted her head.

"And then reality comes rushing back ten-fold, and you can't breathe. Every minuscule fear is amplified, and you can't tell them your true feelings. You can't argue with them, even if you know you're right. You can't let them see past the glamour, because you're terrified that they will see you as you see yourself, and they'll reject you. So, you push them away, bit by bit, because it's easier to be alone than to face your fear of being abandoned by someone you love. Just like Dad did to us."

"That's right. That's exactly right," he whispered, his chin trembling. "But I do love her, Claire. It's not infatuation. It's real. I know it is. It hurts to much not to be real." His frown reappeared. "How do you know of all that?"

"Many years of therapy," she replied, giving him a tiny smile. "Why do you reckon it's taken me three years to marry Jared? Or Mum marrying Gerald? Moira's the lucky one, Gerald's never run out on her or Mum." She sighed and patted his hand. "Love is merely a madness." He sniffled, catching her hand and squeezing it.

"Love's reason's without reason."

"To say the truth, reason and love keep little company now-a-days," she replied, and Graham pressed his lips together.

"For aught that I ever could read, could ever hear by tale or history, the course of true love never did run smooth."

"True that," Claire laughed softly but it died out as he met her gaze with pleading eyes.

"How do I fix this?"

"I'm sorry, love, but you can't. Where is she now?"

"On her way to New York." His face scrunched up. "I was to go with her."

"Oh, Graham, this is massive." She winced, biting her lip. "If you want her, you have to go, now, but know this might be the end of it." Claire took a breath to steel herself from his reaction. "Loren is a very nice girl, but with all that's happened and everything in her past, are you certain she's worth it?" His hands curled into tight fists.

"What do you know of it?" he snarled.

"Dad told me what he did," she replied and held her hand up before he could speak. "Yes, I know, you're very angry and he shouldn't have done that, but think about your career. How much can all that getting out damage you?"

"I don't care, do you understand that? *She* is not her past," he yelled, smacking his palm on the table. "Loren is not Hannah. She doesn't want me for what I have; she just wants me." His eyes slid away as he sat back, covering his mouth with his hand. "She just wants me. What have I done?"

Claire was silent as he collected himself. *He's been upset over breakups before, but not like this. And he's never come to me.* That alone told her he meant what he said.

"Love is not love if it wanes as the other person grows, or if it disappears when you are apart," she said. "Absence will only deepen its roots in your heart. If she is who you want, you do whatever it takes."

"Whatever it takes," he repeated, then leaned in to give his sister a tight hug. "I'm sorry to just show up like this. I know Dad does it to you all the time."

"It's alright," she said, holding him tighter. "I don't mind when you do it."

He drew back from her. "I love you, Claire-Bear."

"You haven't called me that in ages," she giggled, her eyes watering. "I love you, too, Graham-Cracker." They both laughed. "Now go and do right by her. Ring me when you return?"

He nodded and kissed her cheek. "I will."

As Graham pulled the Jaguar into the long-term car park at Heathrow, his mobile pinged a voicemail. His stomach sank when he saw who it was from. "Ron," he sighed and pressed play.

> *You fucking son of a bitch. You had better be dead 'cause I'll kill you myself if you don't fucking ring her and explain yourself. Do you have any idea what you've done? She's a walking zombie from taking that shit the doctor gave her and she hasn't needed it through everything she's been through until now, all because you've got your fucking panties in a wad and walked out. Get the fuck over yourself, you fucking wanker and get your arse on the goddamn plane to New York. Your ticket is waiting for you at the counter. I will not play Lancelot to your Arthur, Graham. You don't fucking deserve her.*

Graham turned to his reflection in the rearview mirror. *He's right. I don't deserve her,* then shook his head. *I have to make this right.* He parked the Jag and got out to retrieve his bags from the boot, then headed toward the terminals.

After receiving his boarding pass and slipping past the paparazzi, his long legs made short work of the trip to the International Terminals. Once at his departure gate, he chose a spot near the windows overlooking the runway and pulled out his tablet. Closing his eyes, she was before him, sitting on her bed only a few hours ago. His throat constricted at the fear in her eyes, knowing he put it there.

I'm so sorry, my love. I have to make this right. I can't lose you.

My Dearest,

I am deeply ashamed for what I've done, and it's killing me to think I've broken your heart. I was wrong to say those things. I was wrong to blame you because none of it has been your fault, but I can't undo what I've done, nor can I take back what I've said.

I see it in your eyes. You need me to be your champion, your knight in shining amour, but I fear I will fail you. I'm afraid I'm not strong enough for you and in my shame, I push you away.

But I cannot stop my heart from loving you and I only hope it's not too late. I need your help, Loren. Lend to me your courage. Bless me with your forgiveness, and grace me with your love again.

I want to be a better man for you.

***

26 October

"There is no way in hell I'm letting you take another one of those fucking things," Ron bellowed as he stuffed Loren into the back of the Escalade. "Do you even remember who the fuck I am?" She rubbed her eyes and squinted out the window as the SUV pulled away from the airport terminal.

We're in New York? I remember getting to Heathrow. Her brain felt coated in wool and her mouth was dry.

"I know who you are, Ron," she mumbled pressing her forehead against the cool glass.

"Well, that's just fucking peachy, because you didn't remember who *you* were on the plane!" She turned wide-eyed to Penny O'Neill, sitting next to her, who nodded.

"You kept insisting you were Xena and if we didn't tell you where Apollo was, you would crash the plane," Penny told her. "It was quite funny until you stopped talking altogether. Then we were a bit concerned."

"I'm sorry." Loren pressed her forehead onto the glass again. *No way am I taking another one of... oh, pretty.* The kaleidoscope of passing lights was hypnotic and suddenly, the vehicle was pulling up to a building in the city. She pushed her nose against the glass and stared up at the enormous high rise.

"This isn't a hotel."

"That's right, it's Benny Wallace's flat," Ron answered, and she turned to watch him hand Penny a keycard. "Show that to the doorman and he'll sign you in. Go and get some sleep, ladies. I'll be back tomorrow, 'round ten." Penny assisted Loren out of the car, then the agent bent to poke her head back into the car.

"You had better not be going out to have fun without me," she quipped. He leaned on the seat to frown up at her.

"I'm going home. Why? You want to come with?"

"Perhaps another time." She gave him a wink then followed the doorman, dragging Loren with her. She showed the keycard to the concierge, and after he documented their names, the doorman pushed the trolley to the elevator for them. Alone in the elevator, Loren rounded on Penny, teetering a little bit.

"What was all that about?" she slurred, clutching the chrome handrail. "You like him or something?"

"He doesn't see me in that way, so it's of no consequence."

Loren snorted. "Well, I think you're pretty fucking awesome and he's a stupid-head if he doesn't see that." Her head lolled back as she leaned into

120

the wall. "He's a little short for me, but you'd be perfect. You're like, the same height." She blinked up at the lights. "Are we going down? It feels like we're going down." She started to slide to the floor, but Penny stepped over to prop her up.

"I think you're pretty fucking awesome yourself, and if Graham can't see past all this, he isn't worthy of you."

"But I did this," Loren cried. "I couldn't let him in and now he's gone. I hate myself. No one can ever–." She wiped her nose with her sleeve. "He speaks in Shakespeare, Penny! And the way I feel when he looks at me. Oh, god, it's over and I ruined the best thing that's ever happened to me!" She flopped her head back against the wall of the elevator and sobbed.

"It's going to be alright, petal." Penny's mobile pinged in her pocket. She glanced at her watch to read a text from Ron.

The fucking wanker picked up his ticket.

A tiny smile formed on her lips. "It's all going to work out. I promise."

***

When the Xanax wore off completely, Loren was wide awake, standing before floor-to-ceiling windows that framed a picturesque view of Central Park at midnight.

"I'm heading to bed, petal. You'll be alright?" She turned when Penny spoke.

"Yah, I'm fine," she said, then bit her lip. "I'm sorry about earlier. I don't get emotional like that, normally." The agent approached her with a deep frown.

"It's not always a good thing to hold it in," she said. "I won't tell anyone you cry ugly." Loren snorted a laugh even as her eyes welled up.

"Thanks. Um, Penny?" She turned back with her brows up. Loren squinted at her. "Petal?"

"I don't mean it as condescending, like how the kids use it these days. You remind me quite a bit of my friend, Rosemary. I called her petal. Goodnight." She then headed to the stairs, leaving Loren to stare at her retreating form.

Okay then. She turned back to street lamps flickering through the leaves of the trees forty stories below. *The glass is so weird. I can't see myself.* She touched the solid pane in front of her. *And now I'm officially freaked out.* Backing away from the view, she then gawked at the interior of the living space.

"This place is five thousand square feet of fucking awesome," she muttered and pinched her arm. "Nope. Not dreaming. It all happened. Every little bit." She blew out a breath and looked up to stop from crying again. Tiny pinpoint lights were embedded in the twenty-foot high ceiling of the living room, providing enough light to see as she roamed. Warm taupe walls and large colorful pieces of furniture made the cavernous living space seem cozy. An open dining area and adjacent galley kitchen took up one side of the main level of the duplex, and a natural stone fireplace separated the living room from the study. A spiral staircase led to the second floor and provided a barrier from the noisy elevator vestibule.

Loren wandered from window to window, not noticing the time passing until fatigue finally caught up with her. She settled in a chaise in front of the fireplace and after finding the remote, it whooshed to life. The gray-gold sky outside held her attention briefly and her eyes soon fluttered closed when her tablet pinged an email. She looked at it, then snatched it up at seeing Graham's name. Hot tears slipped down her cheeks as she read his words.

"Damn you." She sat up to hug her knees to her chest. *But I love him. With every breath, I love him.* Her fingers few over the screen's keypad.

> We could have fixed it right then, but you just left. You didn't call me or respond at all. You didn't come back for me, and that hurts worse than you walking out the door.

***

The *snap* of the deadbolt from the vestibule door jolted her awake. She sat up, clutching the blanket to her chest as Graham walked into the apartment, pulling his carry-on behind him and stopped short.

"Hi," his hoarse voice echoed across to her. She stared at him, her lips parted.

"What are you doing here?"

He took a step closer. "I came back for you." Tears sprang to her eyes and she covered a harsh sob with her hand. He dropped his bag and rushed to her side.

"Please, please forgive me," he said, his voice cracking. "I was stubborn and selfish and–." Loren gave him a shove but kept a tight hold on the silky Nylon of his jacket.

"You say these things to me, you give me this ring," she growled, punctuating her words with a little shake, "and you have the fucking–." She held her breath for a second. "You let me get on that fucking plane without even a word!"

Tears spilled down his cheeks. "I'm sorry. I'm so sorry," he choked. "I know just saying it isn't enough but–."

"It's bullshit, Graham!" She gave him another jolt. "You're fucking scared. You don't think I'm scared? You hurt me and part of me wants to make you feel that." Loren searched his face, taking in his pallor, the darkness circling his red-rimmed eyes and his wrinkled clothes.

"You look like shit," she said. He grimaced but didn't look away from her, his chin trembling.

"I haven't slept. I've read your texts and emails and listened to your messages over and over. I'm so sor–." She placed her fingers on his lips.

"I'm cold." He rose off the chaise to lie down and gather her in his arms. His scent was intoxicating, emotional and primitive, but did nothing to quell the deep ache in her chest. She closed her eyes, clutching at his jacket. The stubble on his jaw grazed her skin.

"Where did you go?" she whispered.

"I started toward home, but I found myself at the corner where we first met," he said, softly. "I sat on the stone wall and thought of every word I said to you that day and yesterday." He adjusted his position to be able to look at her, and the corners of his mouth turned down low.

"I was angry with you for not telling me the truth, but really, I was angry at myself for blaming you." A tear slid down his cheek to get lost in his scruff. "When Jacobson confronted me in the lav at the hotel, I felt like I was eleven years old again, being threatened by the neighborhood bully. I was afraid, and I didn't know what to do, and the hamster wheel in my brain began spinning. I couldn't stop it and then I started to take it out on you, Derek, and Penny." Graham averted his gaze. "I'm not as strong as you are, Loren. I ran away like a petulant child," he said. "I'm not good enough for you." She cupped his cheek to make him see her.

"But if you're not good enough for me, and I'm not good enough for you…" She squinted. "I'm not sure where I was going with that." He huffed but she turned solemn. "I couldn't tell you because I've thought what happened to me was my fault." Graham inhaled sharply, and she put her fingers to his lips. "I know it's not, here," she touched her forehead, then put her hand over her heart, "but here is filled with so much shame."

He put his hand over hers. "And I've proven myself unworthy to even help you carry it."

"I can carry my own baggage, Graham. Most of them have wheels." He chuckled even as another tear slid down his cheek and she brushed it away. "We're both scared of the same thing, you know. But we're just going to keep hurting each other unless we do something now to change it because I don't want just a couple of months with you. I want–." He cupped her cheeks and kissed her.

"I want you," he told her, then kissed her again. "I want to fight with you. I want to love you. I want to make you smile; I want to let you in. I only hope you can forgive me." Loren tucked her head under his chin and cuddled close, fighting tears.

"I will, but I'm gonna need a few days."

"Loren? Are you– Oh!"

Graham woke with a start. "Huh? What? Oh, Penny, hello," he coughed as he turned over on the bed in Loren's room. Her arms were crossed over her chest and scowling at him.

"And when did you arrive?"

"Around four or so," he replied, glancing at the bathroom door and the faint sound of falling water. "She's having a wash."

Penny narrowed her eyes. "I don't make a habit of getting involved in my client's personal lives, but in her case, I've made an exception." She took a threatening step closer to the bed. "If this happens again, I'll be holding you down so Ron can cut your bollocks off."

He sat up a bit more. "That is, uh, truly frightening." His gaze slid to the door as the water turned off and he cleared his throat. "My behavior towards you and Derek this past week was unacceptable. I'm sorry." He grimaced. "I'll speak with Ron when he arrives."

"Fair enough," she said, lifting her chin. "He'll be here 'round ten." She turned on her heel and closed the door behind her. Loren came out of the bathroom then, wrapped in a robe with her hair in a towel turban.

"Was someone here? I thought I heard you talking."

He nodded. "Penny wanted to be sure you were alright."

"Ah." She then came to sit on the corner of the bed, and Graham moved to lie on his back next to her.

"You've got your thinking face on," he said.

"Yah," she huffed, but her frown returned. "I have something to show you." She grabbed her messenger bag from the floor and dug around to pull a piece of paper out then handed it to him. "At Chrono, a photographer approached me and gave me that." He pressed his lips together as soon as he read the first line. "You've seen it before," she stated.

"Ron was given a copy by Theo Arnold." He held up his hand as she took a breath. "Don't be angry with him. I asked him not to say anything to you until I returned."

"I'm not mad at him," she replied, looking away. "And that was not what I was going to say."

He closed his eyes. "I'm sorry. It was wrong of me not to tell you, but I was concerned for your reaction when you read it."

"Right, which has been my reason for everything, but whatever. It doesn't matter anymore," she muttered. Graham winced at the jab, and they were silent for a few moments.

"Have you contacted your brother?" he asked.

"Last week," she said, pulling the towel from her head. "I sent an email, but I haven't gotten a reply yet. I was too scared to call."

"I understand." Graham began to rake his fingers through her damp hair. "Just give it time. He'll respond."

"Yah, like I don't have enough to worry about." Loren hummed, leaning closer to him. "You sure do make a good kept man."

***

Graham was waiting for him in the elevator vestibule when Ron arrived later that morning.

"So good of you to show up, Highness," he snarled, and Graham put his hands up.

"You're absolutely right. I owe you an apology."

"You owe me more than an apology, you son of a bitch!" Ron took a swing, but Graham dodged the punch.

"Whoa! What the hell!"

"How could you do that to me!" He shoved Graham in the chest. "She was begging me to find you, and it was all I could do not to tear the whole fucking plane apart. You have no idea what you have, and you just threw her away!"

"I'm here aren't I?" he snapped back. "I made a mistake. We both have, and we're trying to work it out." The two men stared each other down when Graham dropped his chin. "I might know Benny longer, but you know me better," he said. "I never meant to put you in this situation, and I'm sorry." His eyes welled up as he faced Ron again. "I love her more than I ever thought I could love anyone, and it scares the shit out of me."

"Yah, s'alright. I get it," he drawled. "You're both fucking mental, you know that, but I'll tell ya this." Ron clasped his shoulder, making him wince as he dug his fingers into the joint. "You do something like that again, I'm gonna hold you down so Penny can cut your bollocks off." Graham moved back, rubbing his shoulder.

"Did you two spend the whole flight coming up with that?"

***

Loren paced the length of the windows, dreading the interview with Cara Smith. Fear and shame chased each other around her mind, sending her into a full-on panic.

I can't breathe. She looked up at the ceiling, gasping when Graham appeared at her side.

"Easy, love. Sit down. Breathe," he murmured, guiding her to the sofa. "It's going to be alright."

"Please don't make me go." She took short, shallow breaths, gripping his hand tightly but looked to Ron as he sat down next to her. "Please, I can't."

"You have nothing to worry about, dearest," he said. "I trust her, but I promise, you say the word, and it all ends right then. Alright?"

She sniffed. "You promise?"

"I promise." He crossed his heart, then picked up her backpack. "Let's go. We're already running a tad late."

Graham held her hand as they walked to the elevator and once inside, Loren kept her eyes on the chipped corner of the mirrored doors. She envisioned the pink jewelry box in her mind and stuffed every emotion she had into it.

"*I am the storm,*" she mumbled. "*I am the storm.*" Graham squeezed her hand.

"You can do this," he whispered. Loren nodded and took a deep breath. When the elevator reached the ground floor, she straightened her shoulders, set her expression on neutral and walked out, her neon green trainers squeaking on the marble tile.

"This is all my fault," Graham murmured, watching her.

"Yes, it is," Ron snapped, pushing past him to greet the ESPN reporter, Cara Smith as she entered the lobby. The attractive blonde was dressed in a blue cycling kit with a stylized cat design on the front. He extended his hand as he walked toward her.

"Cara! How nice to see you again." She smiled and met his greeting.

"And by nice, you Brits really mean that it's not."

"Oh, bollocks," he muttered. "She's onto us, Graham." Cara laughed and patted his shoulder.

"I sent Loren outside to look at the bikes we brought. She seems a little nervous."

"You have no idea," Graham told her as they exited the building. Loren was standing on the ramp of the production trailer wearing a familiar pinched expression.

"It's a great bike, but they're a competitor of my sponsor," she told the production assistant, pointing to the white lettering on the bicycle frame.

The man nodded. "Not a problem. I can put gaffer tape over the brand on the tubes," he said. She thanked him then jumped down to street level, giving a tight smile.

Cara frowned. "Is everything alright?"

"Uh, sure," she said, glancing back at the trailer. "I can't be seen on a competitor's bike, is all. Everything I use is sponsored, right down to my socks." She kicked out a shoe when a perky brunette production assistant stepped in front of her.

"Hi, I'm Kate," she said, reaching for the zipper on Loren's jersey. "I just need to get you mic'd–." Loren backed off a step with her hands up.

"I'm sorry, you what?" Cara took the mic pack from Kate.

"I won't remember everything we talk about, and this way we can just ride and let the conversation come," she said. "They also want to get some action shots."

Loren rolled her eyes. "Whatever."

***

The afternoon found Loren scowling up at the nondescript high rise on West 28th Street. "What the fuck else do we have to talk about?" she grumbled to Graham as she took his hand to get out of the Escalade. "She didn't get enough in the two hours we were riding around?" He gave a tight smile and squeezed her hand.

"I'm sor–." She pulled out of his grasp.

"I don't want to hear you're sorry again." Loren stormed off and shoved open the glass doors to the building. Ron patted Graham's shoulder.

"Just keep supporting her like you're doing," he said. "I'll try and draw some heat."

Graham eyed him. "Why are you being nice to me all of a sudden?"

"Because I'm feeling a wee bit sorry for you," he replied, then headed inside the building. Loren was already in the elevator.

"I'm shocked you even waited for us," Ron quipped. Her answer was to glare at his reflection in the brass doors as they closed. "Smith asked a lot of puff questions, eh?" he asked, pressing the button for their floor. Her storm gray eyes narrowed further, but again, she didn't reply. "I reckon somebody needs a bit of chocolate," he muttered.

"Fuck you, dwarf," she snarled, folding her arms across her chest tightly.

"Oh! I'm mortally wounded," he laughed, putting a hand on his chest. "Sorry, dearest, but you'll have to be more creative if you want to insult me."

"Shut up!" Loren barked as the doors opened then stepped out. A woman with bright purple hair was waiting in the lobby, surrounded by a small troop of people.

"Loren! There you are!"

"What the…?" She backed up a step. "Who are you?" The woman smiled brightly.

"I'm Tiffany with the RH Group. I'm the coordinator for your wardrobe and styling team." She glanced at Ron. "We're good?" He nodded, and Loren turned to scowl at him as Tiffany took her hand.

"You fucking son of a–."

"Love you too! Have fun!" He waved as she was pulled down the hall. Graham couldn't hold in his laughter when she gave them the finger.

"You didn't tell her she was going to be on camera?"

Ron sucked in a breath. "I reckoned she'd balk."

"She's not going to like you very much later on."

"I'll just tell her it was your idea," he shot back, patting him on the shoulder.

"So much for drawing heat," Graham said under his breath.

***

Loren was in better spirits when she was escorted down the hall to the waiting room. Ron and Graham stood up as she entered, and she gave a hesitant smile, running her fingers through her dark auburn waves.

"Hi." Their silent stares made her more uncomfortable and she brushed her hands over the pearl leather jacket she wore. "I think I need to keep the whole outfit. These are so kick-ass." She lifted the leg of her navy slacks to show off her brown suede stiletto boots. Graham held out his hand as he moved closer.

"One fairer than my love? The all-seeing sun ne'er saw her match since first the world begun," he murmured then kissed the palm of her hand. "I'm not certain I like the boots so much." She giggled as he stood up straighter to look down at her again.

"Ahem!" She peeked around him at Ron, who was frowning with his arms were crossed over his chest. "You clean up rather nice," he said and stepped forward.

"Thanks." She took a breath, her eyes flicking between them. "I'm sorry about earlier. I'm freaking out, and I'm taking it out on both of you, and that's not fair." Graham bobbed his head toward Ron.

"He deserves it."

"No, he doesn't," she countered and put her arms around Ron, who gently patted her back and stepped away.

"S'alright, dearest." He cleared his throat. "Let's put our game-faces on, yah? We've reviewed her questions, so you have an idea of what you'll say," he said, brushing non-existent fuzz off her shoulder. "I have no doubt she'll spring something on you but if it makes you uncomfortable, just give her *the look*." Ron gave an angry face, making her smile.

"Yes, sir," she said and tugged at the bottom of the jacket. "I'm ready to get this over with." She held Graham's hand tightly as they walked down the hall, but she stopped just before the door to the studio space.

"Please don't leave me," she whispered. Graham stopped and glanced at Ron.

"Go in, we'll be right there," he said, then led her back to a window alcove. "You don't want to hear me say I'm sorry, but I can't think of anything else to say."

She gave a weary smile. "All that Shakespeare clogging up your brain, and you can't think of anything?"

"Well, I could recite the entire St. Crispin's Day speech from Henry V for encouragement, but it's rather long."

"No, that's okay." She brushed her fingers along his bearded jaw then traced the line of his mouth. "How about I say I'm sorry, and I love you. And I need you, and I'm sorry, again."

Graham kissed her forehead. "You've spent two hours riding around on bikes with her. Perhaps even trusted her a wee bit not to send you to the tarmac?" Loren grimaced, nodding her head. "I don't think she'll do that now," he said. "Besides, Ron likes her, and he's a much better judge of character than I am."

She pursed her lips. "That was better than the St. Crispin's Day speech," she said and kissed him. "Thank you." He led her back into the studio where a production assistant met them. Graham squeezed Loren's hand and let go.

"We'll be right over there," he said, pointing to the white couch on the other side of the room. Tight-lipped, she nodded and followed the assistant through the wall of lightboxes.

Loren was shown to a stiff leather armchair, then frowned at the large video camera aimed at her from ten feet away. She turned, and sure enough there was another one, sitting a few feet behind her.

Damn you, Ron. You didn't tell me this was going to be on camera! She stifled her annoyance as Cara Smith sat down in the chair across from her. The reporter gave a smile then shuffled through her notes, sending her long blonde hair over her shoulder with a flick of her hand. Loren admired the sleek beige suit and orange blouse Cara wore, then noticed her bright turquoise heels.

"I really like your shoes."

"Thanks." She kicked out her foot. "They're pretty comfortable too." Cara tapped her papers against the side table to get them straight, then glanced over her shoulder to a man standing behind the camera.

"We good?" He nodded, and she faced Loren again. "We're just going to start where we left off earlier, okay? You seemed comfortable dashing between cars this morning. Do motorists steer clear of you at home or do you get harassed?" Loren glanced up at the camera then cleared her throat softly before answering.

"The majority of people are accepting of us blocking the road briefly, especially around Enfield," she replied. "We get comments sometimes, but the more of us there are, the fewer are made."

"Are you concerned about getting hit by a car?"

"That's already happened twice this year. Sideswiped, really," she said, squinting an eye. "One was a bunch of teenagers; the other was an older woman. She was texting. I try not to think about it though. I mean, I could step outside and get hit by a bus full of tourists." She glanced to her right at Graham's chuckle.

Cara smiled. "What do you think was your worst wreck?"

"This year, definitely the Giro prologue," Loren said, nodding slightly. "I crashed in Flanders too, but coughing up blood is way worse than just a busted-up pinky finger."

"Oh, right," the reporter winced. "Do you recall what was going through your mind in the prologue?"

She shook her head. "Everything happened so fast."

"I understand you had a concussion and a fractured nose," Cara said. "Why did you continue?"

"I didn't want to let my team down," Loren responded, then raised a brow. "Granted, the first two stages I almost got dropped, but by the end, I came back."

Cara nodded. "That you did. How did you feel about setting the course record?"

She huffed. "I didn't find out until later what my time was, and it's just two seconds. Somebody will best that soon enough."

"Do you think there will be a women's Tour de France?"

"There used to be, you know," Loren retorted, then looked away. "I hope La Course can be turned into a stage race again, sharing some of the routes the men ride. The infrastructure is already there, and we've been able to show the world how exciting women's cycling can be. It's up to the world to start demanding more."

Cara glanced at her notes. "Who do you feel is the most respected rider in the peloton?"

"Chloe Monteith," Loren said. "Mary Laws, as well."

"Some would say it's you," Cara said, and Loren blinked at her. "What was it like when you put on your first team kit?" the reporter asked.

That wasn't on the list. She raised a brow and considered how honest she wanted to be, then straightened her shoulders.

"When I put on my Bucknell skinsuit for the first time, I stared at myself in the mirror for a good half hour. I went back and forth between being mortified at how tight it was, to thinking how amazing and strong I looked. I was often underestimated because of my body type, and I used that to my advantage." She raised her chin just a touch. "I would rather be disliked for kicking ass in a race, not for how big my tits are." She smirked at the guffaws from around the studio. Cara hid her grin, then cleared her throat.

"Your first pro signing was with GTS' continental team. What was that like?"

"I was in awe," Loren replied with a slight grimace. "I had people telling me they would do anything for me, which made me uncomfortable. I didn't feel like I earned that kind of treatment, and I didn't ask for help, even when I should have."

"Did that change when you went to IDC?"

"No. It was worse at first," she answered. "I felt I had to prove myself and if I asked for help, it would make me seem weak. But, after the spring classics, Jack Thompson, our former DS knew I was drowning, and I couldn't hide it anymore."

"Do you feel that training and racing interfere with having a normal life?" the reporter asked. Loren blinked at the abrupt change in topic.

"I have a normal life for a professional cyclist," she blurted. Graham cleared his throat, and she pressed her lips together. "Mostly." Cara's gaze slid toward where he and Ron were seated.

"I'm sure being featured on the sports page is different than being the headline on the entertainment section."

"Very." Loren dropped her chin. "It's a package deal, you know, but it doesn't mean I have to like it."

"Graham's joined you on the podium a few times."

"Yah, that's been special." She cast a wistful glance in his direction when the reporter's next question brought her back.

"On the San Luca, you had to do some quick maneuvering around some guy in a banana costume. Was that the first time something like that's happened?"

"To me, yes," Loren replied, smiling. "It was a bit frightening, seeing this big yellow thing fall in front of me. I didn't think about what I was doing, I just leaned back and popped up over his legs. And now, somebody keeps putting a banana in my locker," she grumbled, and Graham and Ron laughed behind the lights. Cara chuckled, but it rapidly faded.

"Your speech in Les Herbiers was very emotional for you," she said, and Loren focused on her folded hands in her lap. "Who was Gabriella to you?"

"Gabi was more than just my teammate. She was my mentor and a close friend." She blinked at the sting in her eyes. "It's not fair, what happened to her."

"The man who hit her, do you know what happened to him?"

Loren stiffly nodded. "He killed himself last year. On her birthday." She swallowed hard. "That's not fair, either." She took a deep breath, forcing her feelings back into the pink jewelry box while twisting the ring on her finger.

"Other athletes I've interviewed have mentioned they sometimes use their emotions in competition," Cara said. "Donnelly and Navarre have made comments to that effect about you, especially during La Route this past July. Were they correct?"

Loren met her gaze. "I think we've all done that at one point or another." The reporter nodded and glanced at her notes.

"What would you like to see done differently in women's cycling?"

Loren hesitated. *Another abrupt change. What are you trying to get me to say?* "I'd like to see greater media exposure for our sport. Most of the races have live feeds that could be streamed online," she answered. "I understand there are licensing issues and such, but if one organizer did it, worldwide, the others would follow. The fans are there, we just need to be able to reach them consistently." The reporter nodded then returned to her notes.

"There's a big difference between the men's and women's pelotons–."

"What, other than our races being shorter?" Loren tilted her head.

"Not just that," Cara chuckled. "It seems the women's peloton is a lot younger. There aren't many who stay beyond perhaps their early thirties. What do you think is the reason for that?"

Loren crossed her legs as her smile dissolved, recalling what Theo asked after the Women's Tour. She took a breath before replying.

"The male riders are guaranteed a base salary and don't have to work a second job, or a third, just to be able to do what they do," she replied. "So many young women have to try and balance earning an income with training, or they have to rely on family or a spouse to put a roof over their head and food on the table."

Her tone hardened. "But, it's the nature of the sexes, really. Men can't have children, but if a woman chooses an athletic career, or any career, over having a family, she's often looked at as selfish. That's not right, in my opinion." Loren blinked then grabbed the glass of water from the table between them. *Whoa. Where'd that come from?* She took a drink as the reporter continued.

"What were your thoughts when Marcia McMichel first called you about being on Team USA?" Loren held in a grimace as she put her glass down.

"I was excited at first, but I started to wonder, why now," she said. "Don't get me wrong, I'm incredibly grateful for the opportunities I've been given, but I didn't have the greatest season. While I won the Aviva Tour, La Course, and a few stages here and there, and *maybe* I would have had enough points to be in contention for the World Cup, there were other Americans Marcia could have chosen. *Should have chosen,*" Loren muttered, looking away.

"But you have a World Championship."

"Yah, for proving I can suffer more than anyone else," she bit back, then pressed her lips together. "I'm sorry. That came out harsher than I intended."

Cara gave a small smile. "The time trial is often referred to as the race of truth. What does that phrase mean to you?"

"You learn the truth of yourself when you suffer," she replied, her gaze flicking to the camera over Cara's shoulder. "Do you roll over and give up when it hurts, or can you overcome the pain to give everything you have to win." Her attention wavered. *When I'm a hundred leagues under, I would learn the truth of myself.* She bit her lip. *I'm relying on Cece's Gaelic translation of what her grandmother said, but maybe she didn't mean water.* Loren shuddered when the reporter coughed softly. "Sorry."

Cara nodded. "In Richmond, there seemed to be some tension between you and the other riders on Team USA, specifically Heather–."

Loren shook her head. "I'm sorry, Cara. I'm not going to comment."

"Alright," she drawled, tapping her pen on her thigh. "What happened in the road race?" Loren shifted in her seat, again wondering where Cara was leading.

"The plan was for me to support Amber and go all out into the turn at Governor Street on the final lap," she said. "But, when the time came, she wasn't with me, so I executed Plan B. I tried to win."

"What was the team's reaction to you taking fourth?"

"No comment," she said quickly. Cara glanced over her shoulder at her cameraman, then picked up a red folder from a side table. As she opened it, she gave a long sigh.

"You met Felix Lalonde when you were with GTS and began a relationship with him, is that correct?"

"That was *not* on your list," Loren hissed.

"You've been able to avoid the media to this point, but Sylvia Montgomery's accusations kicked open the door," she said, then softened her tone. "If you tell your side now before they really start digging, you are in control."

"I don't have anything to say." She sat back into the chair and looked away, but she could feel the weight of Cara's gaze on her.

"Five women have accused him of assault in his career," she said softly. "In each case, the charges were dropped because he claimed it was consensual."

"F-five?" she choked, covering her mouth with a trembling hand. The reporter leaned closer.

"What happened between you in Colorado?"

Loren held her breath, desperately trying to stifle her reaction when she saw Graham, standing just beyond the lights.

"I love you," he mouthed. She brushed a tear from her cheek and turned back to the reporter.

"He told me he loved me," she said, her voice strained. "I didn't believe him at first, but then he told me his mother abandoned him as a child, and a man who was supposed to protect him, abused him. He was broken, like me. I fell for him, but I was also terrified of him." Loren clenched her fists. "He tried to get me drunk and force me to sleep with him, but I wouldn't.

Not like that. He hit me, and I ran away. I never told anyone; even when he came to IDC, I didn't say anything."

"What happened in August?"

Shame burned deep in her belly. "I was stupid and naïve to think it was in the past, but it wasn't. He wouldn't leave me alone." Loren gnashed her teeth, holding back her tears. "He showed up at my house, drunk and I told him to leave, but he hit me, and he kept hitting me and then he tried to rape me," she whispered.

The silence that followed was deafening, broken only by soft footfalls. Graham was pacing the floor beyond the lights. She met Cara's gaze and her resolve hardened at the reporter's expression of sympathy.

"I don't want your pity," she hissed. "He'll pay for what he's done."

"Loren," Cara began, then took a breath. "A packet of information was delivered to my office last week. In it were details about the death of your parents and your sister."

"Oh my god, no," she groaned, clamping her hand over her mouth. Ron and Graham started yelling over each other.

"Gentlemen, please," Cara barked, then turned to Loren again. "I know how painful this is, I do, but you're not unique. I've talked to many women in sports who have lost their families tragically." She moved to the edge of her seat. "The fact you have achieved so much in spite of what happened to you, then and now, is an inspiration. You are an amazing and formidable woman and your story could help other survivors of domestic violence. Please, let me tell that part your story." Cara sat back in her chair, her large blue eyes imploring. "I'll give you a few minutes to decide."

Loren held it together until the reporter and her cameraman disappeared behind the lights, then collapsed forward and covered her face with her hands. Graham was with her then, holding her as she cried.

"It's too much," she sobbed. "I can't."

"My love, you are everything she says you are," he whispered. "You are amazing, formidable, and inspiring." She sniffled and he gently brushed her hair away from her eyes. "We'll support whatever your decision, but darling, what if your story can help someone else? Wouldn't it be worth it?"

"But everyone would–." She breathed deeply. "It's bad enough with everything that's happened. You don't need this, too." Graham kissed her forehead, then looked into her eyes.

"Your baggage has wheels, right? So do mine. We'll pull them together."

***

When Cara returned to the studio, she didn't bat an eye at the additional guest seated with Loren. She took to her chair and smiled at the couple.

"Are you alright, Loren?"

She nodded. "Who sent you that packet?"

"I don't know. It was delivered by courier," she replied.

"What else was in it?"

"Police and coroners' reports. I had the photographs destroyed immediately," Cara said, grimacing. "There was a copy of your adoption records, along with a criminal complaint for your brother and one for your father." Loren glanced at Graham. "You didn't know your father was in jail?" the reporter asked.

"I wasn't sure," she replied. "My memories aren't clear." Cara looked to her cameraman, who nodded and left his post.

"How about we don't video this part," the reporter said, turning back to her. "I still have that digital recorder. We can just talk." Loren held Graham's hand tightly and nodded.

"Then let's talk."

***

Ron and Penny sat quietly together on a leather sofa in the green room, waiting for Loren and Graham. He took a breath to speak when Penny beat him to it.

"These are all your people?" she asked, motioning to the open door across from them.

"They are but a small part of The RH Group."

She huffed. "You seem more like Graham's manager, not so much a publicist."

"My role has evolved, mostly because he trusts me," he answered. "He's the only client I work with personally at this point. How can I let someone else take care of my best mate?"

"I get that." She nodded, pursing her lips. "I'm concerned for Loren. She's been under so much pressure, I fear she'll break."

"She's already broken," he muttered. Penny turned to him, her brows knotted. "What Lalonde did to her was nothing," he said, and she gaped at him.

"Ron, he raped her."

"So did her father," he replied, grimacing. "Then he killed her mother, her sister and tried to kill her as well."

"Oh my god." Her eyes slid away. "Why didn't I know this?"

"That's a question for your brother."

"Derek is not my brother," Penny retorted. "He's my uncle." It was Ron's turn to gape.

"But you're nearly the same age."

"My mother is the oldest of fourteen. Derek is the youngest." She then fell silent for a moment. "Her tenacity and her smile remind me of Rosemary." He frowned for a second, then his brows went up.

"You mean Derek's girl? The one that–."

"Yes," she answered quickly. "She was my best mate."

"I'm sorry, Penny."

She let out a breath. "It was a long time ago." They went back to watching the comings and goings of people in the hall. After a few minutes, Ron gave her a sidelong glance.

"What do you do when you're not protecting people?"

"I train," she replied. "I have to keep in practice, you know."

"Well, yes, but I meant for fun."

"I read," she told him. "I like poetry."

He rolled his eyes. "If you say Shakespeare, I'm very likely going to be sick."

She chuckled. "Shakespeare is rather long-winded. I like things short and sweet." The corner of his mouth curled up.

"I'm not that short."

Her grin widened. "You're not that sweet, either."

"I can be."

"I rather like an intelligent man," she said, leaning back into the sofa. "All I've seen that's smart about you is your mouth."

"I like you, Penny O'Neill," he laughed.

"What does that mean, exactly?"

"You're a strong woman," he replied. "I find that attractive." She moved closer to him, her green eyes closing slightly.

"You like to be dominated?"

"I wouldn't go that far."

"Good," she said, drawing back. "I don't mind being a bitch to get the job done, but that's not my personality."

"Well, I am an arsehole," he scoffed.

"I don't think that at all," she said. They stared at each other until Ron glanced away. He stifled a flinch when she slid her hand down his forearm to link their fingers. "What do you reckon we should do about this?"

"I'm not sure," he replied, shifting to face her. "We both have jobs to do."

"Perhaps we can find some time to explore our options."

"I do rather like that idea." His eyes flicked to her mouth, but he didn't move. Penny raised a brow.

"This is the part where you kiss me, Ronald."

***

27 October

Graham sat up, breathing hard with his scream echoing in his brain. He brushed his hands over his chest and stomach.

I was burning. I can still feel it. He turned his head toward a soft whimper. Loren was curled up next to him, held captive by her dream. He touched her hip.

"Darling?" She shuddered and let out a yelp. "Easy, love, it's just me," he said. She put her hand over her face and took a shaky breath.

"I'm sorry I woke you."

"You didn't," he said. "But I'll tell you mine if you tell me yours." She stared open-mouthed at him.

"You had a nightmare?"

"Yah. I thought I was awake. You were calling for me and this snake creature had you. I tried to fight it, but I was losing when this blinding light came out of me. I was burning." Graham laid back on the pillows, squeezing his eyes shut. "I woke up just now with my skin tingling. It felt so real."

"It must have been the Chinese food," she said, putting her hand on his shoulder. "Goodness, you're shivering. Come here." She gathered him into her arms with his head on her chest and he kissed her collarbone.

"Will you tell me of your dream?"

"It's been just about the same dream for the past week or so," she murmured. "Sometimes I'm on my bike, sometimes I'm running, and I see this dark storm cloud coming. It gets closer every time."

Enjoy it while it lasts. There's a storm coming, he had said to Michael Jacobson. Graham closed his eyes to focus on quelling his anxiety. The beat of her heart was soothing, and as her breathing slowed, he relaxed further, and they both began to fall back to sleep when the alarm on her mobile phone chirped. Loren reached over to turn it off.

"I didn't want today to come," she said, and he propped up on an elbow to see her.

"I know, love, but getting all dressed up and having people fawn all over you is fun."

She gave a little smile. "They did let me keep the boots yesterday."

"See that?" he chuckled. "You even get to keep stuff. You'll have a blast." He gave her a kiss and rolled out of bed.

"I'm sure I will." Her smile faded as her eyes followed him across the room. *I don't have a good feeling about this.*

***

The Escalade pulled up to a loft building on West 36th at 7th Avenue later that morning, and Loren was once again accosted by makeup and wardrobe people. This group, however, was not as pleasant as the staff from the RH Group.

The four women spoke to each other in a language that Loren recognized, but couldn't translate. Their tone and disapproving looks, however, were enough to decipher their meaning. They didn't like her for whatever reason and no matter how appreciative she was, the atmosphere didn't change. She was soon delivered to the Green Room dressed in her white World Champion skinsuit, and her mood soured further.

"Ah, there you are!" She stood stiffly as Oskar Ryzak crossed the room to grab her shoulders and kiss both her cheeks. His hands slid down her arms to stretch them out for his eyes to rake over her figure.

"*Velkolepý*! You are magnificent!" Graham was standing behind Ryzak with Ron and Leo Spada. All were frowning darkly.

"Thank you," she said and moved out of his reach. "Leo, good to see you again." He met her halfway with an outstretched hand, and her smile turned a bit more genuine.

"Likewise," he replied, shaking her hand.

"I see you've met my people." She looked to Ron, who gave her a wink.

"Yes. I'm impressed and a little intimidated by Mr. Hudson's reputation," he said, grinning. "If you're ready, the photographer is almost set." Leo motioned to the door, and Loren picked up her messenger bag to follow when Graham blocked her path. His mouth was in a hard line.

"I'm a bit torn," he said, his voice low. "I don't want to make you more nervous by standing around watching you, but *that* one raises my hackles." He nodded slightly to Oskar Ryzak standing in the doorway, chatting with Leo.

She drew closer. "I don't like him either, but he's the one signing the check, and I'm not doing this for me." He drew back a bit, his eyebrows pinched. "We lost some sponsors that supported Felix," she told him. "I'm trying to close the budget gap without my account taking a major hit." He half snarled and shook his head.

"I can have Penny take care of him."

Loren kissed him. "I love you."

"I know, and you look amazing," he said. She grinned at him, then followed Ron out to the hall. Oskar sidled up next to her, taking her arm and tucking it under his.

"Come, *můj krásný*! Let us go make the magic," he laughed and led her into the studio where the photographer and his assistants were waiting. "Roman! Come and meet *naše bohyně!*" The photographer made no effort to hide his leer as he approached, with the stench of his cologne preceding him.

"Oskar, you were not exaggerating. She is a goddess," he drawled. "Hello, beautiful. I'm Roman Mayer." He extended his hand and Loren had to force herself to shake it. What little hair the man had on his head was slicked back from his wide forehead, while an overabundance of chest hair flowered out from his unbuttoned shirt. She tried to keep her eyes averted from the prominence in his unnaturally tight jeans when Roman raised his arm and snapped his fingers.

"Lanie! Show our star where to stand." A young woman materialized next to her as Loren glared at the photographer's departing back.

"You let him treat you like that?"

"He pays really well," Lanie muttered. She showed Loren to her mark on the floor, then disappeared behind the light wall. Ron came to her side, and she clutched at the arm of his jacket.

"I might joke that Graham is a smarmy pirate, but that guy is the very definition of smarmy." They watched the photographer sucking up to Ryzak in the corner. She cringed when both men turned to smile at her.

"Let me know when you've had enough," Ron replied.

"I've had enough already, but thank you, Lancelot."

"I regret telling Penny to sleep in," he grumbled.

"What's that supposed to mean?" she asked but he slipped back behind the box lights. Lanie emerged with a bottle of mineral oil and covered Loren's arms and legs with it, while another assistant fluffed her hair and touched up her makeup. A large reflector was placed near her, making her slightly claustrophobic when another assistant rolled in a prototype IDC time trial bike.

"How did you get this? It's not in production yet." Oscar's voice came from behind the lights.

"Darren had it shipped in just for you, *můj krásný.*" Then Roman stuck his head out from behind a light.

"Alright, just lean into your elbows on the seat there. Right, but unzip your top a little." She stifled a scowl but pulled the zipper down an inch. "Yeah, that's great, but how about a little more," he called out.

Loren shook her head slightly. *I cannot believe I'm doing this.* She took the zipper down another half inch, and the lights flashed several times.

"Great! Can you get up on the bike and give me a sexy pout?" She clipped her shoe into the pedal and swung her leg over to settle on the seat, but Loren didn't give a pout. She glared at him, and crossed her arms under her chest, not realizing she was widening the neckline of her jersey and pushing up her cleavage.

"Oh yeah, that's perfect," Roman cooed. "Drop your chin more. Make those eyes burn. That's perfect! How about standing in the pedals?" After she adjusted position, the lights flashed a few more times, then he handed his camera to an assistant.

"Alright, you can get down, babe." Roman came over as she dismounted and stood with her as one of the crew took the bike away. She stiffened when his hand pressed into the small of her back.

"You're doing great, but you need to relax a little," he said, sliding his hand over the curve of her hip. "I can get you whatever you want. Beer, vodka, a little weed. Whatever you need, baby." His removed his hand to snap his fingers. "Lanie! Take her back to wardrobe and put her in the next outfit." An aisle appeared between the lights and Loren mechanically followed the assistant to the dressing room where Ron caught up with them.

"How are you holding up?" She stopped and looked at him, wanting to tell him what just happened, but couldn't find the right words.

"I'm fine," she muttered and turned to keep going, but grasped her arm. She yanked away. "Please don't touch me."

"Loren–."

"I said I'm fine." She left him in the hall.

***

Loren felt a little better when she headed back to the studio. The clothing stylist and makeup artist were nicer to her and gave their directions in English this time, and she wondered if Lanie had something to do with the abrupt change in attitude. She stopped at the Green Room to find Graham lying on the couch with his arm over his eyes, still wearing his quilted jacket. His dark denim-encased legs traveled the length of the sofa for his brown boots to hang off the other end.

"Hey," she said, bumping his leg with her knee, and he almost fell off in his haste to get up. She stepped back and motioned to the midnight blue silk goddess gown she wore, holding in a smirk at his mouth hanging open.

"You shouldn't stare, you know," she said, raising her chin. "It's not polite."

He blinked. "I can't let you go back in there looking like that." She pouted and placed her hand over her cleavage.

"What? The neckline's a bit deeper than I'm used to, but–." Graham drew close and held her hand.

"I'm sor–." He blew out a breath. "I didn't mean to make you uncomfortable," he said. "You are absolutely stunning, and I regret I have nowhere to take you tonight."

Her smile was half-hearted. "I don't mind when you look at me like that," she replied, trying to project everything she felt but couldn't voice. "I guess I'd better get it over with." She moved to leave but he didn't let go of her hand.

"I'm no longer torn," he told, his voice deepening. "I can see it in your eyes. What aren't you saying?"

"Mon chevalier," she murmured, cupping his cheek. "Think of someplace to take me." His answering kiss kept her smiling until she entered the studio, only to disappear as all eyes were focused on her. Roman licked his lips and whistled as he approached.

"Your body is magnificent," he said, his eyes hovering at her cleavage. He snapped his fingers again. "Lanie!" The young woman showed Loren to her mark in front of a chaise lounge and once again, she was surrounded by lights and reflectors.

"I'm going to take a quick test of the lights," Roman said, and the flash went off. "I love that dress on you, baby. So sexy. Let's get some music going and have some fun!" House music began to play out of hidden speakers, and from somewhere behind the lights, a fan circulated air around her.

"Amazing! My god, you look so freakin' hot. Turn your shoulders a little, just stay on the mark there. Yeah, put your hand on your hip. Just like that," he purred. "Sit on the edge of the lounger there. Perfect." Loren tried not to glower as she did as he asked, but at the same time, she found herself liking the approval, which made not scowling even more difficult.

"Arch your back, yeah, that's it," the photographer directed. "Chin down a bit. Roll a bit more on your hip, yeah. Oh yeah. Straight on to me, that's right, baby. Drop your chin a tiny bit more, perfect. Look off to the side, just your eyes. So sexy. Back to me, just those eyes. Damn!" The lights flashed a few more times, then he handed the camera off to the assistant.

"Okay, let's take a minute to change things up." Roman came around the lightbox and pointed to the chaise. "Lie back on the other side there," he said, patting the cushion. "Lean into the arm, yeah, just like that. Shoulders back." He dragged his fingers along the velour as he leaned over her. "Put your hand over your head, just like that, good." Roman bent further, blocking her view of the outer room. His hand slid from the couch to cup her breast, rubbing his thumb across the silk. She flinched at the heat of his touch through the thin fabric. "You're making me want to fuck you." Rage primed her muscles to fight.

"Get your dirty hands off me," Loren hissed, swiftly standing up to shove him away.

"Hey, baby, it's cool," he sneered, his hands up. "I was just gonna help you relax." She clenched her fists, her voice deepening as she took a step toward him.

"Touch me again, and I'll break every fucking bone in your body." Ron slipped through the space between the lights to stand between her and the photographer.

"I would suggest you step back, lest she follows through with her threat."

"Hey, whatever, little man," Roman sneered. "No piece of ass is sweet enough to deal with that kind of drama." Scowling darkly, Ron stepped over to stand nose to nose with the photographer.

"You know who I am, boy-o?" he snarled, and Roman's eyes widened. "Be very grateful you don't work for me, because you wouldn't work ever again, anywhere." Ron turned and escorted a trembling Loren from the studio. Neither spoke until they were back in the dressing room where she barreled through the door for the knob to be imbedded into the drywall behind it. He pulled the knob free to shut the door and turned just in time to duck away from her flying shoe.

"He doesn't get to touch me like that!"

"That's right," Ron said calmly. "The man's a fucking pig, but we need cool heads now, dearest. Diplomacy before violence." Shaking badly, Loren collapsed into the chair, clutching her arms over her chest.

"I'm sorry. I don't mean to be a problem. I just... He touched me," she sobbed, and he knelt before her.

"I know. I saw," he said and offered her a packet of tissues. "Do you want me to call the police?"

She choked. "What? Oh my god, no!"

"Dearest, that's sexual assault. He shouldn't be able to get away with it."

"I can't." Her hand went to her throat. "I just can't." He sighed, shaking his head.

"Now I really wish Penny were here," he muttered and stood up.

"Where is she? Where's Graham?"

"She wasn't feeling well, and I didn't think we would need her. I told *him* to go for a coffee a bit ago," he replied. "Why don't you get changed and when you're ready, we'll go get a drink. I think we both need it." Loren peered up at him, her chin trembling.

"I knew your powers of asshole-ry would come in handy someday." Ron gave her a look that was half shocked, half amused.

"Powers of asshole-ry. That's good. I'll be right outside the door," he said and closed it behind him. His grin dissolved instantly. "Motherfucking goddamn nonce."

***

Hoboken, New Jersey

"Home at last," Adam O'Connell groaned and flopped down on the dark leather couch in his living room. His eyes closed as his head fell back.

All I want to do is sleep. His client was a hot-headed high-profile politician in town from DC who didn't shy away from run-ins with protesters. The two

142

weeks of stress with little sleep had taken a heavier toll than Adam wanted to admit.

His phone buzzing in his pocket roused him. Taking it out, a text from Nick was on screen.

Have you heard from her?

No, she hasn't called, but I've been working.

Are you an idiot? Did you check your email?

"Email," he muttered, smacking his forehead. "I am an idiot." He checked his account with the Associates and found her reply. "Shit, this came last week." He sat back into the sofa and opened the email.

Adam:
I want to know you, but I'm also afraid of what seeing you could do to me. To say the last few months have been difficult for me is an understatement.
Concussions are funny things, and I had two in quick succession. The effects have forced me to deal with memories I buried because they were too painful and too filled with shame. And now here you are, the embodiment of everything I left behind with my name.
Why now? Why did you wait so long? What were you afraid of? That I wouldn't know you? That I would reject you? You're my big brother. Everything I am, everything I've done, is because you saved my life. How could I ever forget that?
And that's literally the conflict I'm stuck with.
Are you married? Kids? Pets? Do you live in New York? How were you able to run into Graham so many times?
And I did NOT run home for Rainbow Brite. I ran to beat you there.

He shook his head. *My little Shadow.* He then began his reply.

Loren:
Why did I wait? You said it yourself. Our past is too filled with shame and loss, and it's very hard to look back. And yes, I thought you might hate me, but here I am anyway so I get your conflict.
Why now? I don't need money, and I'm pretty sure I'm not going to die anytime soon. I saw your picture from the ESPY awards a couple of years ago and I thought I was looking at a ghost. You look so much like Mom, but I needed to be sure. I was in Afghanistan with the Army Rangers then so I couldn't do anything to find you until I was discharged.
I was in Philly in June. I saw you before the race. You walked right by me and I said your name. I didn't think you heard me, but you turned around. I was an ass and hid behind my camera. I'm sorry if I freaked you out.
I know what Felix did to you, and I can't express how sorry I am. I'm sure there's a line of people waiting for a phone call from you to

have him taken out, so I won't make the offer. But, just in case the Hell's Angels are in England, I might know a guy.

I'm not married, but I was engaged once. No kids. I did have a cat for a while. I like cats but not so much dogs. I live in a brownstone in Hoboken. It's an artsy neighborhood and I like the vibe, even though I don't have an artistic bone in my body. I have a motorcycle, a Triumph Thruxton. I heard you have a BMW. It would be cool to ride with you.

As for how I ran into Graham, when Nick saw you kissing him on the podium, he figured I'd want to do the older brother schtick and he told me when Graham was flying out of England or New York. The first time I caught him was dumb luck. I was dropping off a client when I saw him.

I've attached a couple more photos of me, and of you and me when we were kids, and one of Nick and me, just in case you didn't believe him that we were friends. He's been my best friend since basic, and he'll tell you a long story about how I saved his life a couple of times, but that's not exactly true.

I wish you a happy birthday every year, in my head, but I can do it now for real. Kind of.

Happy birthday, Shadow.

***

"He did what?" Graham snarled after Ron told him what happened with the photographer. Loren was next to him, and the heat of his anger radiated from him. Ron moved nearer to the door as the Escalade pulled up at The RH Group offices on West 55th Street.

"You can just drop me here," he told the driver, then turned to Graham. "You should be proud of her. She didn't kill him." Ron gave her a little smirk and got out of the SUV. Silence filled the interior as their driver then continued the slow crawl toward West 63rd.

Loren pressed her forehead to the cool glass, but it did nothing to relieve the ache. The photographer's greasy voice echoed in her mind, mixing with her conflicted emotions to dredge up shame-filled memories of her father.

Come to daddy, little girl, he cooed to her. *I got a present for you.* She slid her hand over the seat to Graham, and he grasped it.

"I'm here, love."

"Please don't be angry with me," she said, choking on unshed tears.

"Darling, no." He grasped her shoulders, and she leaned into his waiting arms. "I'm not angry with you. Not in the least."

She let out a sob. "I can still feel his hand on me."

"It's going to be alright," he murmured, gently raking his fingers through the back of her hair and over her neck. His attentions relaxed her, and it was a few moments before he spoke again. "I'm glad you didn't kill him. That gives me a chance."

Loren huffed. "Penny might beat you to it." She sat up a little to see him. "I think she and Ron hooked up last night."

He nodded. "Hmm. From what Derek has told me, she's been after him for a while," he replied and kissed her forehead. "You okay?"

"I'm getting there," she replied and settled into his arms again. "Just don't let go of me."

"I won't let go," he said. "Never again."

When her mobile pinged an email a few minutes later, she took it out of her pocket to glance at it and went rigid. Graham rubbed her arm.

"Darling, what is it?" Her hand shook as she showed him her mobile screen.

"He replied," she groaned. "But I can't deal with this right now."

"Easy, love." He put his arms around her, drawing her close. "Just breathe. It's alright."

Loren focused on outside the window. Her brother's laughter echoed in her ears. She saw the look of horror on his face when he pulled the bloodied bat from her hands after she used it on their father. He was screaming for her to not die and leave him alone. She was paralyzed yet her whole body trembled.

"Graham," she gasped. "I can't breathe." He quickly reached over and hit the button to open the window. She covered her eyes and took a long inhale the crisp autumn air, tinged with exhaust, decaying leaves, and the smell of baking pretzels. Her stomach growling threw a wrench into her panic response.

"Can we get pretzels?" she blurted, her voice still shaky. "But not right now."

He snorted a laugh. "Of course, we can. Anything you want." She pressed the button to close the window then leaned into him.

"Why? Why is all this happening to me?"

"I don't know love. Just let it be for now," he murmured, holding her closer. "We'll deal with it later."

When they reached their destination on West 63rd, Loren was silent walking through the lobby. She stood away from Graham, keeping her focus on the tiny chip in the mirrored door of the elevator and tried to stuff her emotions back into their pink jewelry box when his voice cut through the noise in her head.

"It's going to be alright, love."

"No, it's not!" She rounded on him, her fingers clutching at her hair. "You don't fucking get it! Everything's piling on, and I feel like I'm drowning," she cried. "I don't want to be here anymore. I just want to go home!"

"I do understand." Graham came to her and placed his hands over hers. "Please, let me help you." She closed her eyes and buried her face against his neck, savoring the warmth of his arms around her.

She bit her lip. *How can you help me when you hurt me too?* The elevator chimed their floor then, and as the doors opened, he inhaled sharply.

"Uh, Loren–."

"There you are!" ginger-haired Benny Wallace laughed as he walked into the vestibule. His statuesque wife, Alejandra was with him. "We were wondering what time you would be getting back. Where's Ron?"

"I, uh, I didn't think we'd see you," Graham replied as he left the elevator, and went in for a handshake and bro hug. "Ron had to check in at his office."

"Ah, the poor thing. Always working," Alejandra pouted, then gave Loren a tight hug. "We wanted to be here for your birthday." She mustered up a true smile.

"Thank you for letting us stay here. Your home is beautiful."

"Lorina, you are welcome anytime, whether we are here or not. Come with me," she said as they entered the apartment, and pulled Loren toward the kitchen. The white marble, dark oak, and stainless steel of the galley-style kitchen showcased the north facing view out the windows. Loren turned, pointing to the windows, but Alejandra was leaning against the counter, frowning.

"What happened on Sunday?"

Loren swallowed hard. "There are pictures, aren't there?"

"Yes, of Graham leaving your house and of you, standing on the pavement watching him drive away, looking as if your heart had been ripped from your bosom."

"Of course," she muttered and shrugged a shoulder. "He's here, so that means something, doesn't it?" Loren shook her head. "But it wasn't all his fault. I said things, too. I kept things from him."

Her friend's frown deepened. "Regardless of who said what, it pains me he did that knowing–." She stopped and took Loren's hand. "I'm sorry. I should not be reproaching of your relationship," she said and gave her hand a squeeze. "I did not see through the act before, but I see it now."

"What do you mean, act?"

"His insecurity," she replied. "Benny was the same at the beginning. He felt inadequate to be with me."

"Well, duh," Loren drawled. "Look at you." Alejandra pursed her lips and Loren dropped her chin. "I'm not like you. I'm not beautiful. I'm too athletic. I'm not smart enough," she said. "I'm not enough for him."

"That's right," Alejandra replied, brushing her hair away from her face. "You are *more* than enough and never forget that." She tilted Loren's chin higher and gave a slight grimace. "Who did this to your face? There are makeup remover wipes under the sink in your bath. You should have a soak while you're there."

"I'll do that," she huffed. "My face is starting to itch." They exchanged another embrace, then Loren headed upstairs to the bedroom, closing the door to lean against it. Hot tears spilled down her cheeks.

Oh god, there are pictures of me! She pushed off and went into the bathroom to scrub her face raw. Felix's words came back to her. *He's an actor, Loren! He pretends at love!* She put her hands over her ears.

"Stop it. He's here. That's what matters." She left the bath to cross the room to the enormous plush beanbag situated before the floor-to-ceiling windows. Focused on the orange glow of the city skyline, Loren maneuvered herself into a position where every muscle was supported.

Don't think. Just breathe. It was barely a minute before she groaned and took out her mobile to find all the pictures Alejandra told her about, and then some. Loren set her phone on the floor next to her.

Why did I do that? It took a few more minutes of focused breathing before she could pick up her phone again. She read Adam's reply, studying the image of a serious-looking man with auburn hair, dressed in a dark green military dress uniform and tan beret. She swiped to another photo, the one of him and Nick laughing, and her eyes welled up.

I remember that smile. He had tiny creases around his mouth and at the corners of his eyes, with a deep line between his brows. His jaw was wider than hers, but they shared the same chin and nose shape. Loren brushed her nose and giggled.

He's got my freckles. She then focused on his eyes. They were a bit more gray-brown because of the touch of gold around the iris. She closed the email and settled back into the plush.

What do I do? She ground the heel of her hand into her forehead. *Band-Aid theory. Just do it quick. Call him. Do it now.* She typed in his number, her finger hovering over the call icon for a second before she pressed it. *Go to voicemail, go to voicemail, go to—.*

"O'Connell."

Oh shit! She took a breath to speak, but nothing came out.

"Hello?" His voice was deeper than she expected.

She coughed. "Um, you could always wish me happy birthday in person?"

There was a moment of hesitation. "Loren?"

"Hi, big brother." She bit her lip. "Is this a bad time?"

"No, no. It's fine. Where are you?"

She looked out the window. "I have one of the best views of Central Park at the moment."

"You're in New York?"

She huffed. "I'm surprised you didn't know that."

"Nick was upset he frightened you, so he's kept his distance."

"I meant it was in the tabloids," she said, frowning. "And I wasn't afraid of him."

"I told him you weren't. You've always been fearless." They were quiet for a few seconds. "Happy birthday, Shadow."

"Shadow," she murmured, then squeezed her eyes shut, the tears beginning anew. "I'm sorry. I'm not having the best week."

"I'm sorry to hear that."

She shrugged a shoulder. "What can you do, you know? Life sucks sometimes." Loren blew out a breath. "So, what do we do now?"

"I don't know. Talk, I guess." Adam paused. "Do you like cats?"

***

A little while later, she heard the door open softly behind her, but Loren still shuddered when Graham spoke her name.

"Sorry, I didn't mean to startle you," he said, crossing the room.

"It's okay."

"May I join you?"

She smiled and scooted over to make room. He eased himself down onto the plushness, but it took a few minutes of them smooshing and chuckling to find a comfortable position together. Graham ended up on his back with his legs stretched out. Loren curved around him with her head in the crook of his shoulder.

"We need to get one of these," he said, cuddling her closer.

"Mmm, but it would have to be bigger," she murmured, fiddling with the pearl buttons on his striped dress shirt. She brushed her lips against his neck, slipping her fingers through the opening to touch his skin. "I need more of just being alone with you." His warmth seeped into her skin to relax her enough for her eyes to flutter closed. Sleep began to drag her down when he roused with an inhale.

"You're going to put me to sleep," he muttered. Loren huffed, then picked up her mobile to show him the photo of her brother in his uniform.

"The background Derek ran said Adam was an expert sharpshooter with the Army Rangers. That's what the tan beret and the medals mean." She swiped through the photos to the one of two children together. "I look at these and I can hear him screaming for me not to die." She took a breath. "I called him."

"Just now?" Graham struggled to sit up on the beanbag but gave up with a huff. "What did you say? What did he say?"

"We talked about cats and motorcycles, but there was a lot of silence in between," she answered. "I told him we were in New York and we're going to meet up tomorrow sometime."

"That's great," he said, then moved to face her with knotted brows. "We, meaning you and him." Her stomach flipped over.

"You wouldn't come with me?"

"Yes, of course. I just... I'm sor–." Loren put her fingers to his lips.

"No more I'm sorry, remember?" She gave a half-smile. "You're not perfect, Graham. You have ugly feet, and lopsided eyebrows and you can be a dick sometimes, but what I feel for you has pretty much ruined me for anyone else." Loren scrunched her brows. "You speak in Shakespeare. Who else is gonna fucking do that for me? Jude Law? I don't think so." He laughed, brushing his fingers against her cheek.

"You swear like a pirate, and you're a right hot mess, but I wouldn't love you as much as I do if you were average," he said, then lifted her left hand to touch the Claddagh on her finger. "This holds the same promise that my great-grandfather gave. I want to marry you, Loren Mackenzie. Someday. If you'll have me."

"Someday," she repeated. "I think can manage that." She kissed him, sliding her hands underneath his shirt to touch his skin. His fingers entwined in her hair, deepening their kiss as he rolled her beneath him when someone cleared their throat from across the room. Graham pulled away, and they both looked up at Ron, standing in the doorway with his arms crossed over his chest.

Loren grinned. "You're back!"

"Ah, yes. The door was open, but I did knock," he said, smirking. "Penny and I are going to go out for a bite and a drink. The old married couple is staying in and by the looks of this," he waved his hand at them, "shall I assume you'll be staying in as well?" She looked to Graham, and he licked his lips.

"Um, we'll join you," he replied and gave a toothy grin. "But, can you give us a few minutes?"

His smirk grew. "Are you certain that's all you'll need?"

***

Adam O'Connell tailed the two couples into McGee's on West 55th Street, careful not to attract attention. He adjusted his Toledo Mud Hens ball cap while observing the group in the bar.

He already knew the tall, well-dressed man with his arm around Loren was Graham Atherton. After edging nearer to them, he overheard her call the shorter guy Ron and the dark-haired woman he was with, Penny.

The two couples were laughing and talking when Loren poked Ron in the shoulder then called the bartender over. Adam covered his frown with his glass of water when the bartender returned with a tray of shots. He noted Graham's disapproving look, as did Loren.

"I'm done being the dancing monkey." She brushed off his hand on her shoulder. "It's my birthday, dammit and I'll do what I want!" She grabbed a shot and drank it in one gulp, then turned the glass over on the counter to glare at Ron. "You're turn, little man." Adam shook his head, watching the two try to out-drink each other.

That's not going to solve your problems, Loren.

It was almost two in the morning when he followed them out of the bar, where they crossed 8th Avenue at 56th and stopped at a courtyard. He ducked into an alcove to observe as Loren pulled Graham into the open space and placed her hand in his with the other on his shoulder. The Englishman then led her through a waltz across the square, her rich laughter echoing through the empty intersection.

Movement across the street caught his eye and Adam took out his phone, holding it to his ear and looked. A large man was pointing a long lens camera at the group from the opposite corner. Penny appeared to notice and corralled the other three into moving again.

He narrowed his eyes. *She's not a friend. She's a security agent.* When she put her hand out to stop a cab, the photographer lifted the camera to his face, and the click of the shutter rang across the quiet street.

Once the group got into the taxi, the man started off around the corner, heading west on 57th. Adam followed, ducking into doorways when he thought the guy might turn around, but he never did. Then his mark turned onto Amsterdam.

Wallace's penthouse is on 63rd. Is that where you're headed, pal? I don't think so.

***

Michael Jacobson woke sprawled out on the steps of a brownstone on Amsterdam Avenue, with a bottle in a brown paper bag in his hand. He sat up slowly when a bright light was flashed in his face.

"Hey, buddy, you can't be sitting there." The light was moved slightly, and the faces of two uniformed New York City policemen were visible. "What are you doing here?" Jacobson raised his hand to block the light from his eyes.

"I was walking down the street and the next thing I know, I'm sitting here." The second officer relocated his beam to the bag in Jacobson's hand.

"And what do we have here? An open container?"

"I don't know anything about this." Jacobson stood up and dropped the bottle. It shattered on the pavement, splashing the two officers' shoes.

"Yeah, right, buddy," the cop said. "You'd best be stepping down now." Jacobson glanced around at his feet and started to panic.

"Where's my camera bag? I had a bag with me." He reached around to his back pocket, and his eyes went wide. "My wallet! My wallet's gone!"

Adam looked down at the Michigan driver's license and US passport in his hand as the photographer continued to argue with the policemen.

You're a long way from home, Mr. Jacobson. The sound of electrical currents came to his ears, and he lifted his head. A body with a ratty ponytail was quivering on the sidewalk. *What an asshole.*

***

London, England

Felix Lalonde woke slowly to a throbbing head. He rolled onto his back and stared at the ceiling.

Another day I am not dead. He was no stranger to pain, being accustomed to physical suffering in one form or another. Rehabilitation, however, was physical, mental, and emotional suffering, and the combination broke his will. His only comfort was being in his own bed, alone.

The intensive program was twelve steps. For steps one through three, he was able to fabricate the emotions and prostrate himself enough for others to believe he was sincere.

I am powerless over my addiction. I believe in a higher power, and I will turn over my will to that higher power. He chuckled softly. *Fools, every one of them.* Steps four and five, however, proved to be his undoing.

To take a moral inventory of myself, then admit to God, and another person, the exact nature of my wrongdoings. He let out a breath. *It was hard enough to tell Loren what happened to me as a child when I was drunk. To tell a stranger, stone sober, was more mental pain than I could stand.*

And so, he told the lie he had been telling through his entire career, but Alan, his sponsor, saw through him. Over the course of a week, the older man pushed and needled, prodded and cajoled, then ultimately threatened Felix with jail. For the second time in his life, he admitted the abuse he suffered, revealing to Alan that his mother abandoned him to die on the streets and his supposed benefactor turned him into a prostitute. Then, he told what he had done to Joanna and Simone; to Iris, Caterina, and Marie. And to Loren.

Felix admitted to seducing, coercing, then drugging the five women to get what he wanted from them. He wanted them to be addicted to him and abuse them as he was abused. Shame burned his gut and he covered his eyes with his hand.

I wanted them to beg for me, yet in the end, I was the one begging. He pleaded with his sponsor to release him from his guilt, but Alan could only recommend his release from the hospital.

"I must find forgiveness within myself," he muttered. He began to laugh but dissolved quickly. "I remember all now. I hurt her. I forced her. How can I ask for her forgiveness when I cannot forgive myself for what I've done? How can I make amends if I cannot speak to her?" He squeezed his eyes closed. *If I can't love her, I don't want to live anymore. I don't want to live without her.*

A mobile phone ringing from the other room brought him back to reality.

"*Merde,*" he muttered and stumbled out of bed to answer it. "I told you not to telephone me anymore," he snarled when the call connected.

"That fucking cunt cost me twenty thousand dollars!"

"What are you talking about?" Felix flopped down onto the armchair and covered his eyes.

"Montgomery was gonna pay me a lot for pictures of her drunk ass stumbling all over the place, but somebody hit me from behind. They got my camera, the memory cards, and my wallet! I had to call my ex-wife to bail me out of jail."

"You had a–?" Felix cleared his throat. "You were in jail?" Jacobson swore under his breath.

"I told you! Somebody hit me from behind. When I came to, I was arrested for fucking disorderly conduct."

Vous imbécile. He smothered a laugh, but his humor quickly ended. "What do you mean, they? Who was with her?"

"Atherton, his agent and some other woman."

"Atherton? He left her. I saw it myself," Felix shot back. "I saw her face."

"He showed up Monday and they've been holed up in his buddy's penthouse ever since," Jacobson grumbled. "They damn well better make an appearance somewhere 'cause if they don't, that twenty thousand is coming out of her ass. I swear it, Lalonde."

Felix curled his lip. "You will not touch her," he snarled but the line was already dead. He sat back in his chair, shaking his head. *I heard what he said to her. I saw him leave.* He sniffed. *No, he is mistaken. She would not have taken him back after such a betrayal. Or would she?*

***

28 October

Loren woke with her heart pounding in her ears. Every muscle complained as she turned over to burrow deeper into the blankets. With a few deep breaths, the tension eased, and she was drifting off to sleep when the bedroom door opened.

"Happy birthday, darling!" She sat up too fast, then fell back into the pillows with a moan.

"Dude! Not nice," she whined.

Graham chuckled. "I'm sorry, love. It's after nine. I thought you'd be awake by now." She opened one eye to see him standing over her, balancing a covered metal tray in one hand and a small tea kettle in the other. She propped up on an elbow, nodding her chin at him.

"What's all that?"

"It's your birthday breakfast in bed." Graham set the tray and kettle down then removed the cover with a flourish. "*Voila!* We have chocolate covered donuts, your sports drink, coffee for me, bagels with that berry Philadelphia soft cheese you like, and a couple of hard-boiled eggs for good measure."

"Oh god, that's so much food," she whined, reaching for the Ryzak can. His smile faded a little.

"Darling, you've barely eaten anything in the past two days, including last night," he said, moving the tray to sit next to her on the bed.

"Food hasn't been agreeing with me lately. I keep forgetting to take the Lactaid." She rubbed her eye with a knuckle. "What did we do last night? It's kind of foggy." Graham reached over to the nightstand, retrieving the box of lactase tablets and handed them to her.

"I'm not surprised you don't remember." He picked up half a bagel and a knife to cut into the cream cheese. "You recall we went to a bar with Penny and Ron?"

"Yah, McGee's." Loren chewed the chalky tablets as Graham deftly applied the pink spread without getting any on his fingers. "How do you do that?" she grumbled, and he raised a brow at her. "You didn't get any on your fingers." Graham held up his pinky to her.

"But I did. Do you want to lick it off?" Holding his gaze, she brought his hand nearer, drawing the tip of his finger into her mouth then slowly removed it. He didn't speak; she didn't think he even took a breath for a full minute after.

"What else did we do last night?" she asked huskily, and he cleared his throat.

"You challenged Ron to a drinking contest. He lost, by the way," he answered. "You then wanted to go dancing and we tried to convince you it wasn't a good idea, but you disagreed." He got up from the bed to retrieve his mobile from the desk and sat back down. Loren took a bite of her bagel and leaned closer to him to see video of them waltzing around the courtyard of an office building.

"Can we do that again?" She looked up at him. "The dancing part, I mean, not the drinking."

"It's your birthday," he replied and kissed her nose. "We can do anything you want." She laid her head on his shoulder and immediately sat back up, wiping the side of her face.

"Ew! Why are you wet?"

"It was raining when I went for a run," he laughed. "I'm going to have a wash, then we can talk about where we're going to meet your brother." She went to put the bagel down. "Finish that, please," he said, and Loren rolled her eyes.

"Fine," she muttered. Her gaze followed him as he walked to the bathroom as he removed an article of clothing every few steps. She sighed, then checked her email while eating the rest of her bagel then two of the eggs. Several messages were from her teammates, wishing her a happy birthday, to which she replied with 'Thank you. I miss you guys!'

She then moved on to Cece's email.

Hey you.
    I gave you a few days to get through whatever the hell Sunday was all about, but it's time to fess up. I can't be waiting until you get back. Those pictures were awful, I tell you! My twitching nose tells me you're all right, but I need to know for sure, so ring me or reply. Whichever, but do something because Anthony keeps bugging me about it. I don't know why he doesn't just ring you himself.
    Holly went to Australia with Ashley, so the house is too empty without you. You're still working the booth at the expo with me on Sunday, right?
    Get this, Anthony showed me there was a loose floorboard in the corner under my desk where he used to hide things. It was adorbs watching him play with old Army men, making battle noises and such. I had a wee laughing so hard.
    I'd better hear from you soon.

Loren sighed. *Do I sugarcoat it, or do I lay it out?*

Hey yourself.
    I can't even imagine him playing with tiny green men, and I'd probably pee my pants, too. Yes, I'll be with you in the booth. Jon and Oliver will be there for part of the day as well.
    Graham and I had been arguing since he came back, so it wasn't just Sunday. You know I haven't been completely truthful with him. I didn't tell him about the notes, or the break-in, or the guy who jumped me behind the Church. We both said some not so nice things, and if we were at his house, it would have been me storming out.

154

When you two got home, I hadn't heard from him, and I didn't know if that was it or not. Graham showed up here around 4 in the morning on Monday, begging me to forgive him.

All he had to do was come back, and it wouldn't have been that big of a deal, but he didn't. He let me leave the country without so much as a text. That hurt more than anything he said. And yes, I saw the pictures.

I need time, and we need time, together. I wish you guys were here though.

She pressed send as Graham came out of the bathroom with a white towel wrapped low around his hips. She stared at his naked back as he rummaged through his garment bag.

He's definitely put on muscle. The corner of her lips curled up. "You shouldn't walk around like that, you know. It's distracting." He turned, smiling as he let the towel drop to the floor.

"I like distracting you."

She gave a husky chuckle. "Well, then come here, you incredibly sexy distraction." Loren moved to her knees on the edge of the bed as he approached, drawing her hands up his taut stomach. He cupped her jaw, brushing her cheek with his thumb.

"My heart's core, aye, my heart of heart, belongs to you," he murmured. Even as he spoke, Felix whispered to her.

He deceives you with his pretty words. Her mouth tightened into a line.

"Make me believe it." Graham dropped his gaze, raking his teeth over his lower lip.

"Bid me do anything for thee, and I would gladly do it," he said, his voice tight. "But there are no more dragons to slay, and I can't bring you the heads of your enemies. It's against the law."

She gave a tiny smile. "Kissing me would be a good start."

"It's my favorite thing to do." He brushed his thumb over her lips before his mouth took its place. His arms skimmed along her waist and under her T-shirt, moving up her back to pull her closer. Her hands slid around his hips, encountering the smooth skin of his bum and gave him a pinch. He chuckled softly and pushed her down on the bed, bracing himself on his hands over her. His blue eyes traveled over her face when he suddenly reared back, grabbed the hem of her shirt and pulled it over his head to blow raspberries on her belly.

"Stop it!" she giggled, squirming against him.

"There's got to be a ticklish spot around here somewhere," came his muffled reply. Loren held still as his lips brush against her skin.

"You're wasting your time. I'm not ticklish," she told him, closing her eyes to better concentrate on not responding. His mouth moved over her left side, and she couldn't control the shiver that ran through her at his tongue teasing her breast.

"Ah, a reaction," he murmured, continuing his attentions, and drawing a soft moan from her. He moved lower, his hips parting her legs further. Loren clumsily pulled her shirt over her head while he relieved her of her remaining garment. He then resumed his inspection for a ticklish spot, kissing and tasting his way up her right side. Meeting her lips in a passionate kiss, he added to her torture by raking his hardness against her. Growling low in her throat, she broke away.

"I want to watch you," she whispered, shifting to adjust him, and his eyes nearly closed as he slid inside her. He held still at first, trembling slightly, his pupils dilating with his slow, deliberate withdrawal. A crooked grin crossed his face at her groan as he executed his reentry at the same leisurely speed.

They rocked together, sharing their pleasure through sight and touch, but she wanted more. She grasped his buttocks, urging him deeper, tightening her legs around him to meet each thrust; stroking their fire into an inferno neither could withstand, with their cries of fulfillment muted by each other's lips.

They remained entwined while their breathing eased. Loren traced lazy circles across his back, then slid her hand lower to caress his bum.

"It's such a cute little thing," she said. Graham laughed softly, raising up on his elbows.

"It's the only thing that hasn't gotten larger, and I've tried."

"You might not have the genetics for it." She gave him a pinch. "The English are renowned for their beanpole-ishness."

He laughed harder. "Is that even a word?"

"It's a word," she chuckled.

"I often admired yours when you're not looking. So dangerously curved," he purred.

"*Je suis a vous,*" she murmured and kissed him. Graham moved to his back with a long exhale and covered his eyes with his forearm. Loren propped up on her elbow next to him. "Are ya gettin' sleepy?" She slowly trailed her fingers down his chest, her touch following the ridges and valleys of his stomach where the thin line of hair escorted her gaze lower.

"What are you doing?" His question brought her attention back to his face, and a slow smile spread across her lips.

"You are a fascinating specimen," she said, drawing her fingers down his stomach to fondle him.

"I'm not responsible for what happens if you keep doing that."

She raised a brow. "You wanna go again?"

"It'll take a few minutes, as you well know," he replied, his voice cracking at her ministrations, but then turned his head toward the door at the echoing voices from the other side. "And not having people waiting to wish you a happy birthday would help." Loren leaned in and kissed him.

"Hmm, true, and I need to call Maggie, but after a shower," she said. "Would you stay with me when I talk to her?"

"Of course." He touched her cheek, then raised a brow at her half-eaten donut on the side table. "I'll start the shower while you finish your hangover cure."

"You already gave me the best hangover cure," she breathed and kissed him again.

***

Loren got dressed after her shower with her thoughts on what to tell Maggie. Glancing at her watch, she heaved a sigh and sat down on the bed.

Band-Aid theory. You can do it. She reached for her mobile and began a video call, then moved to the desk near the windows.

"There's my birthday girl!" Maggie sang when the video connected, but her expression changed to a deep frown. "Are you alright? You don't look so good." Loren patted her cheek.

"I'm fine. Nothing a bit of tea and a soak can't cure." Her aunt's frown didn't budge.

"The girls at work showed me pictures of you from Sunday. Are you still going to insist it's just the tabloids trying to spin something?" Loren glanced away, shrugging.

"Graham and I had an argument. That's all. Looks worse than it was." Maggie raised a brow, and Loren rolled her eyes. "Leave it alone, Mags."

"Uh huh," she muttered. "What do you have planned for today?"

"Honestly, I just want to sit here and stare out the window." She turned the screen to the misty view.

"Wow. Is that Central Park?"

"That it is." She turned the camera back to her. "Fortieth floor penthouse on West 63rd, courtesy of Benny Wallace."

"Damn. Maybe I should find myself an actor." They both chuckled, but Loren's didn't last long. "There's something else, isn't there," Maggie noted. "You're got your thinking face on."

She huffed a laugh. "I got an early birthday present. A letter from Aaron." Loren scrunched her nose. "His name is Adam, now." Her aunt's mouth popped open.

"You're joking."

"I'm sending you a copy of his letter now." She grabbed her tablet and pulled up her email. After she pressed send, Maggie's tablet pinged almost immediately. Her aunt's brows knotted as she read and when she was done, she looked up with tears in her eyes.

"Holy fuck."

"Maggie!" She put a hand over her ear. "My virgin ears!"

"Oh, stop it," she laughed but let it die away. "He was in Philadelphia. Do you know what he's talking about?"

Loren nodded. "Yes, and I was a little freaked out, but I had to focus on the race." She bit her lip as she opened her email again. "I emailed him back the other day. I just sent you his reply." She turned when Graham came back into the bedroom, and he leaned down to see the screen.

"Hi, Maggie."

"Hey." She gave a distracted wave as she was reading, then looked back to Loren. "O'Connell is my maiden name."

"He said that's why he chose it." She sat back to gloat at Maggie's open-mouthed stare.

"You talked to him?"

"Last night." Her eyes slid away and swallowed. "Mags, I've started to remember more and none of it is good." She glanced at Graham. "We were going to meet up today, but the more I dwell about it, the more I'm freaking out." He put his hands on her shoulder.

"You have to do what's best for you, love," he told her. "You can't think about hurting his feelings, but I'm certain he'll understand." Loren worried at her fingernail before looking to her aunt again.

"I need to know what's real and he's the only one who can tell me."

"I know, kitten, and I'm sorry I can't help you more," Maggie told her, then glanced at her watch. "Poop. I have to go, but call back later, okay? The kiddos will be happy to hear from you."

"I will." Loren sat back in her chair after disconnecting and stared out the window. Graham touched the back of her neck.

"You've got your thinking face on." She gave a soft smile, then pressed her lips together.

"I need to be in control, and I'm not."

"Loren, you can't control everything."

She shot him a look. "I know I can't, but I should be able to control my reactions. With everything that's happened…" She sighed, and Graham put his arm over her shoulders.

"Darling, you've spent years winding yourself up so tightly," he said. "You've been able to function, but I don't think you've actually lived."

She raised a brow. "And then you came along, and my whole world started to unravel."

"You make it seem like that's a bad thing," he said, his mouth somewhere between a frown and a smirk.

"In some ways it is, but I think my remembering was only a matter of time," she replied, then ran her hand over her face. "James told me I had to stop looking down into the hole I dug, because if I looked up, I would see how many hands were reaching for me, to help pull me out." She turned to him. "I'm holding onto yours the tightest." Graham put his hand out to her.

"I've got strong hands, you know. I can change out a bike tire."

***

When Loren and Graham made their way down to the main living area, she stopped at the edge of the dining room were several boxes of donuts were set out on the table, and a dozen pink Mylar balloons floated above a bouquet of roses as a centerpiece.

"What's all—."

"Surprise!" Loren jumped at the chorus from behind her.

"Oh my god!" She glared at Benny and Alejandra as they came out of the kitchen, followed by Penny and Ron. "You didn't have to do this," she said, frowning darkly.

"You only turn thirty once, *cara*," Alejandra said and kissed Loren's cheeks. "Happy birthday."

"Thank you. Did you guys buy out the bakery or something?"

"I told them about your donut hangover cure," Graham laughed as they sat down. Ron held up a half-eaten cruller.

"These are the best donuts I've ever tasted," he moaned, then playfully swatted at Penny's hand as she attempted to grab the box from him. "Unhand my crullers, woman!"

Loren's chuckles ended abruptly when Graham slid over a white box tied with red and white-striped string with sticker from Amy's Bakery in Chelsea on the top. He was smirking when she met his gaze.

"I already gave you a ring," he said. "Open it." Inside, she found a black and white cookie the size of a dinner plate with *Happy Birthday Loren* written in red and white frosting on it.

"How did you get them to make this?" she laughed.

Graham shrugged. "I ordered it yesterday, but that's not the real gift. Take it out." She raised a brow then took hold of the wax paper and lifted the cookie. Underneath was a picture frame with a three-photo collage of them kissing on Westminster Bridge.

She gave him a teary grin. "I love it, thank you." Alejandra then pushed a colorful gift bag across the table to her.

"Just something small," she said, wrinkling her nose. Loren burst out a laugh when she opened it.

"It's a bag of socks! That's so awesome."

"We made sure they were from your team sponsor," Benny added.

"Thank you," she giggled, holding up several pairs of rainbow-striped socks. "I don't have any of these yet." Ron cleared his throat and slid a small package to Loren.

"My turn."

"You didn't have to do that," she told him as she brushed her fingers under her eyes. When she opened the package, she burst into laughing tears again. "It's Guitar Hero Live! I don't have this one." She sniffled. "Thank you so much."

"So!" Alejandra sang, patting her hands together. "What do you have planned for today?" Loren glanced around the table.

"I'm going to meet my brother," she said softly. "I haven't seen him since I was nine. He lives in Hoboken."

"Goodness!" Alejandra covered her mouth with her fingers. "That certainly takes precedence over what I was going to suggest."

"I'm sure there's a story behind that," Benny remarked, and Loren gave him a tight-lipped smile while Alejandra shushed him.

Ron cleared his throat. "If I may suggest, don't meet in public."

"Hmm." Loren eyed Graham. "That makes sense."

"You could invite him here," Benny told her.

"I can't ask you–."

"What about Ron's office," Penny interjected. "Neutral territory, and we can control who comes and goes."

"I like the way you think," Ron told her, then smiled at Loren. "Go do some touristy things and give me a few hours to adjust my schedule."

"Yes!" Alejandra clapped her hands again. "We can go shopping for something new to wear to the gallery party tomorrow night!"

Loren gave a faux smile. "Gallery party?" She looked to Graham.

"Rex White is having a thing at an art gallery," he said. "We were invited, but I hadn't replied as to whether we would be attending."

She blinked. "Rex White, the late-night TV host?"

He nodded. "I've known him since University."

"Of course you have," she replied, pressing her lips together. "I guess we can do that. How does four o'clock sound?" She looked to Ron, who glanced at his watch.

"Perfect. It's just past eleven," he replied, then stood. He frowned as Penny stood with him. "Um, what are you–."

"I'd like to check out the building and offices if that's acceptable," she said to Loren.

"That's fine with me," she replied, hiding her smile behind the rim of her teacup.

***

Ron studied the woman standing next to him in the mirrored doors of the elevator. Penny was dressed as she usually was, in a fitted black button-down shirt over slim dark denim. Her black ankle boots had a bit of a heel, which made her slightly taller than him, but he didn't mind one bit.

Evens out when we're lying down. Her green eyes sparkled as she looked to him, making him stand a bit straighter. *How did this even happen?*

"Did I assume too much?" She turned to adjust the collar of his gray jacket, and his neck tingled where she touched him.

"Well, er, no…"

"If you rather I didn't…" Her mouth twitched as she brushed her fingers over his shoulder.

"No, no. Please do. You keep surprising me, is all." His heart skipped at the smile she gave him.

"I like surprising you."

The offices of The RH Group were buzzing when the elevator doors opened. Penny clasped his hand as Ron led her through reception and the cube farm beyond. Heads turned toward the couple striding down the aisle to the corner office where he came to a stop at the desk of a young woman with bright blue streaks in her hair.

"Ron!" She stood up quickly. "We didn't expect you until later."

"Good morning Haley," he replied. "Were you all going to be partying without me?"

"Never!" she laughed. "The party doesn't start until you arrive."

"That's right," he chuckled. "Do you have anything for me?" Haley's eyes slid over to Penny then back to him.

"Ah, just a few things that need your signature." Penny released his hand for him to take the file and he motioned for her to precede him into his office.

"The view isn't anything to write home about," he said as the agent walked to the windows.

"I like the furniture," she commented, testing out the sofa at the far end of the room. "Very IKEA."

"That's where I got it," he answered and leaned on the corner of his desk to review the paperwork. Penny settled in the beige leather chair before him and put her feet up on the desk next to him.

He glanced at his assistant. "Haley, please reschedule the staff meeting for one o'clock and request Alex from Lester Security to join us in ten minutes," he said and handed her the file. "I need to brief him about a high-level client arriving at four." She nodded, but her attention was on Penny. Ron cleared his throat. "Thank you."

"Of course," Haley stuttered, backing out of the door to close it behind her.

"You didn't introduce me," Penny said.

"How am I supposed to introduce you if I don't know how to refer to you," he replied. "Are you the liaison from Lester's UK office or are we friends?"

Her smirk grew. "I reckon we're a bit more than friends now, Ron."

He frowned. "Would I be jumping the gun to say girlfriend?" Penny tapped her lips with a finger.

"Hmm, perhaps not quite that far."

"What's in between friend and girlfriend?"

"Seeing each other?" Her smile widened as his frown deepened.

"We're not dating?"

She leaned back in her chair. "We haven't actually been on a date."

"You are making this entirely too complicated," he said, shaking his head.

"I'm a complicated woman," Penny replied, her husky voice even raspier, sending warmth flowing through his veins.

"I bet you are."

***

Adam O'Connell exited the elevator promptly at four o'clock but stopped before the black lacquer door of The RH Group to take a calming breath. Trepidation mixed with a generous portion of guilt tightened his throat.

"Relax. She doesn't hate me." He rubbed his hand over his jaw and encountered the unfamiliar texture of a beard. He hadn't shaved since he gave Nick his letter in the hopes it would mask the resemblance to his father. Even he was sometimes jarred by the likeness and he didn't want to cause Loren any more anxiety.

After a final stiff breath, he grasped the nickel handle of the door and opened it to enter a high-ceilinged reception area. A striking woman with dark hair and deep green eyes sat at the desk and met his gaze with a polite smile.

"Good afternoon. How may I assist you?" Her husky voice held a hint of a British accent. She looked familiar but he couldn't place her. The lapse put him on guard.

"Good afternoon. I'm Adam O'Connell. I'm here for a four o'clock meeting."

Her smile widened further. "If you will follow me, please." She rose and led him through an open office area where several employees were working at large quad desks. Her movements were measured, and she kept her head ever so slightly turned toward him.

He slowed his stride. *She's the agent from last night.* "How long have you worked here?" he asked. The woman stopped before a solid oak door flanked by frosted glass panels.

"Not very long," she replied, then knocked and opened the door for him.

The office was spacious, with a wall of windows bracketed by a desk at one end and a seating area at the other. Movement from the windows caught his attention. A couple standing there turned to face him, but it was the woman's silvery eyes that captured him.

Too many emotions swirled in their depths. She was taller than he expected, with her long legs encased in dark denim and brown knee-high boots. The deep blue of her tunic complimented her creamy complexion. Her hair was darker than he remembered, and cascaded past her shoulders, softening the angles of her face.

She then raised her chin and any apprehension he thought he saw was replaced by a cool façade. She was Loren Mackenzie, professional cyclist. The Ice Queen.

"Nick was right," Adam said. "You can be a little intimidating."

"Well, he was being a bit stalker-ish." Her voice had a deeper pitch in person than over the phone.

"God, look at you, all grown up." He took a few steps toward her but her widening eyes stopped him.

"Please, don't." She stiffened and held up her hand.

"It's okay. I understand."

"Do you?" she snapped, then turned away, gripping the man's arm. "Please, I can't do this."

"It's alright, love," Graham Atherton murmured, then moved forward with his hand extended to Adam. "It's good to see you again."

"You, too," he replied, accepting the greeting, and the actor motioned to the couch.

"Please, have a seat." Adam chose one of the chairs while the couple sat close together on the sofa across from him. Her heel started tapping as she clenched and unclenched her hands.

"I didn't mean to frighten you," Adam said.

"I'm not afraid of you," she replied, glaring at him, but her expression softened when Graham shifted to put his arm over her shoulders. "I'm sorry but my brain is overwhelmed by fragments of memories I don't understand." Her eyes were like quicksilver. "There are so many ghosts."

"I see them too," Adam replied.

"You do?" She hesitated, then reached out her hand to him. "I'm not dreaming? You're really here?" Her palm was cool, but dry against his skin and as she pulled, he pulled, and they both stood. She let out a sob and stepped into his arms.

"I'm here, Shadow," he whispered. Their embrace was short-lived, and she moved away, sniffling.

"You look different than your pictures. I like the beard," she told him, and he brushed his knuckles against his jaw.

"I wasn't sure how it would turn out." He dropped his chin. "And I didn't want to make you uncomfortable by looking too much like Dad." Her expression hardened but she didn't look away from him.

"I know you're not him, and what I see in my dreams is not a man. He's a monster." Loren glanced at Graham, then she cleared her throat. "Would you like some coffee, or something? I would suggest going out someplace, but–."

"I know the drill," Adam replied as they regained their seats. "I've worked with other A-list talents. There's no such thing as spontaneity."

"No kidding," she muttered and gave a small smile when Graham nudged her shoulder. Adam took out an envelope from his jacket pocket.

"I brought more pictures," he said. "You remembered Sherbet was a cow." He handed her a picture, and Loren's eyes widened.

"She was brown. I didn't remember that." He nodded, then handed over two more pictures. "We had chickens," she said and met his gaze. "Daffy's the black one, right?"

"Bugs was white," he said, and she narrowed her gaze.

"Is that why you live in Hoboken? Because of Bugs Bunny?"

"Pretty much," he chuckled. "Hoboken!" they said in unison and laughed. Adam slid over a few pictures to Graham.

"She was quiet, and never missed anything. Always in motion."

"Some things haven't changed," he answered, and Adam handed her another picture.

"That's Mom."

Loren placed the photo on the table. Anger and resentment burned in the back of her throat. At first glance, the woman resembled Maggie, but Alison's eyes and mouth turned down further at the corners. Her blonde hair fell in lank sections about her shoulders and she was much thinner than her sister.

Fragile is what I remembered. "That woman is not my mother," she said shoving the picture back to him. "She didn't take care of me. You did. You made me feel loved and protected me as best you could." She turned away, squeezing her eyes closed. Images and emotions washed over her, and she grasped Graham's hand tightly.

"The things I see are half-remembered nightmares," she choked. "I don't know what's real and you're the only one who can tell me." He sat back, his eyes wide, and Loren put up her hand.

"I don't mean right now! God, I-I couldn't handle it, but maybe we could spend time together," she said, looking at Graham. "I don't know, like,

164

maybe we could go to Rochester for Christmas. I know Maggie would love to see you."

"Yeah, sure. I'd like that." Adam glanced away, licking his lips.

Your tell is showing, big brother. "You don't have to, you know." His gray eyes turned to granite. "I get you don't want to see her," she said.

"It's not that…" He let out a stiff breath. "Fine. You're right. That's a bridge I don't know if I can cross. I'm sorry."

Her attitude softened. "Don't be sorry. I'm still working through my own issues with her." His tight smile mirrored hers, and Graham let out a smothered laugh.

"You are definitely her brother," he said. Adam's smile widened and he handed Loren a photo of an older couple in matching overalls.

"Do you remember them? Jeb and his wife, Martha?" She squinted and shrugged a shoulder. "They were our neighbors," he said. "They made sure we were fed and had clothes and shoes. When the farm was sold, Maggie sent them a letter to let them know you were fine. She included a few pictures of you on a bicycle, and that was my first clue on how to find you.

"She also sent a letter for me, in case I ever showed up." Adam reached out his hand, and she grasped it. "I have never stopped thinking about you, and I'm sorry it's taken me so long." Loren nodded and let go, not trusting her voice. She looked to Graham with pleading eyes, and he picked up on her silent cue.

"What happened to you, after?" Adam ran his hand over his bearded chin before replying.

"I was arrested. They thought I shot all of you." Loren gasped, but he gave her a half-smile. "Obviously, they figured it out. At the arraignment, several people came forward saying Dad had been going around town that day threatening to shoot people." He grimaced. "I was sent to a foster home on the other side of the state. I don't know why they didn't keep us together. Maybe they thought I was a danger to you." He looked to her with tears in his eyes.

"They let me see you in the hospital before I left, but you were unconscious," he said. "That was the last time I saw Maggie, too. We were all in rough shape, and I told her I thought you would be better off not knowing me." Loren couldn't breathe around the awful pain in her stomach.

"Why would you think that?" she gasped. "I wasn't better off. She went back to Germany. She didn't come back for me for over a year."

Adam blinked. "But I thought…" His mouth shut with an audible click. "She left you? Why?"

"She did what she thought was best for her, just like you did," Loren replied, acidly. "She couldn't deal with my pain, because she was so wrapped up in her own guilt. I was fostered with the veterinarian who saved me."

His mouth popped open again. "Fucking Martin Garrett. I should have known. He started sniffing around Mom just after Dad went to jail for beating her." The room began to pitch, and Loren focused on the table between them.

"What are you talking about?" she croaked. "We knew him?"

"Yeah, he and Mom were having an affair." It was her turn to stare at him, open-mouthed. Adam let out a long exhale. "I would've been happy for her if he was serious about leaving his wife, but when Mom told him she was pregnant, he disappeared."

Her vision narrowed. "Amy was his?" she choked, leaning closer to Graham. "But I don't understand. They were going to adopt me."

"How do you know that?" he asked. Graham bent and grabbed her messenger bag for her.

"Because of this," she answered and placed a thick folder on the table. Adam opened it, spread the papers on the table and blanched.

"There's not just information about you in here," he said. "Who else knows about all this?" Graham pulled a face and rubbed a finger over his brow.

"My father, my sister, the man he hired to do it, who quite possibly sold it."

"What!" Adam jumped to the edge of the chair. "Your father sold it?"

"No! His father didn't sell it," Loren replied, glaring at him. "All we know is a reporter from ESPN was given a copy recently, and not by us." She took out her mobile and showed him the screen. "We think she got it from this man." His eyes narrowed then flicked up to her.

"I saw that guy last night. He was following you."

"Wait, what? He's in New York?" Graham cupped her cheek for her to look at him.

"He will not come anywhere near you." The set of his jaw and the force of his voice lent her strength. She nodded, licking her lips, and they both turned back to Adam. "You followed him," Graham stated. "Then what?"

"He was taking pictures, and then your girl out there corralled you into a cab." He brought out a camera card from his pocket and put it on the table. "After that, he was headed toward Wallace's apartment. I wanted to find out who he was, so I took him down."

She blinked at him. "You did what?"

"I knocked him out, went through his pockets. I took his camera bag, wallet, and passport, but I gave all that to my buddy at the City Intelligence Bureau. I imagine he has them back by now, minus this," Adam replied, tapping the data card. "I propped him up on somebody's stoop with a bottle of vodka in a bag I found in the trash, and the police picked him up. He didn't exactly cooperate, so he got zapped." His grin evaporated as they stared at him. "What's the matter?"

"We think he's been following me for Felix, but we can't prove it," she told him. Adam ran his hand over his mouth.

"Now I understand why you have Lester."

"They're part of The RH Group and Derek Graves is a good friend," Graham told him. His mobile pinged a text message then, and he pulled it out of his jacket pocket. "Speaking of friends, it would appear you have been invited to dinner." He held up his hand as Adam took a breath to speak. "Alejandra Wallace does not take kindly to people telling her no."

***

Penny studied the newcomer as Ron and Alejandra peppered Adam with questions about himself over dinner. The resemblance between brother and sister was pronounced, but it was his eyes that spoke to her.

Haunted. Tragic. She glanced at Loren. *Like hers.*

"Were you sent to a foster family as well?" Alejandra questioned.

"Yes," he said. "I lived in Anderson, South Carolina, that's about three hours from Charleston."

"You were in the military?" Ron asked, and Adam nodded.

"I joined the Army after high school and went on to the Rangers," he replied. "I was discharged two years ago." Penny narrowed her eyes at him.

Someone's being humble. During her call to Derek while she and Ron waited in his office, she discovered Adam had served several tours in Iraq and Afghanistan and received a Medal of Honor.

She tapped a finger on her lips. *What kind of web are you weaving little spider?*

"That's a long time to be out of the world," Alejandra commented. "And now you're a security agent, like Penny and Derek? How did that happen?"

"I wanted to go into law enforcement, but I don't have full range of my shoulder," he replied. "Too much scar tissue from shrapnel. I can predict the weather now, so that's useful." His brows went up and he pushed his chin to the kitchen. "The powder room's through there?"

"Yes," Alejandra said. "Through the kitchen." Adam stood and left the room, and Ron leaned closer to Penny.

"Well, go on then, 007," he murmured, and she frowned at him. "You reckon I was questioning him because I wanted to get to know him? I'm not that nice."

She pressed her cheek to his. "Ask if anyone wants a drink and follow him," she whispered. As they rose, he cleared his throat.

"Would anyone like a refill?" A chorus of no thank you followed them out. Upon entering the kitchen, Penny grabbed him by his lapel and pushed him against the refrigerator.

"Now who's surprising who," she murmured, low and husky. She gave him passionate kiss, then released him and straightened his jacket. "Thank you, love."

"A-any time," he answered as she sauntered around the corner. Penny stood outside the half bath with her arms crossed over her chest, mulling over her next actions.

Go aggro or play nice? When the door opened, Adam was quick to cover his surprise.

"You didn't have to wait," he said, a familiar pinched smile on his lips. "I'm told there are five other bathrooms."

She tilted her head. "Why were you following us last night?" An expression flashed across his face as he licked his lips, and she almost laughed outright. "You are definitely her brother," she said, taking a step closer. "The slight backward movement of the ears, a twitch of the mouth just before you moisten your lips. That's her face when she's about to lie to me." His eyes hardened to granite, then motioned for her to follow him into the half bath and closed the door.

"I wanted to see her, the real Loren, but I wasn't the only one following her."

"Yes, I know," she replied, serenely. "Burly, six-foot bloke with a ratty blond ponytail." He nodded, a slight curl to his lip.

"I tailed him after you all got into the cab, and when he turned down Amsterdam, I figured he was headed here. I knocked him out and went through his pockets," he said. "He had a burn phone on him, and I jotted down the numbers he's been calling, but I haven't had the chance to run them." Adam took a slip of paper out of his pocket and gave it to her.

"My buddy at City Intelligence was very interested when I turned in a license and passport belonging to one Michael Jacobson of Wilmot, Michigan. Outstanding parking tickets."

"Isn't that always how they catch the bad guy," she said with a husky chuckle. He smiled, but it wasn't friendly.

"What do you want to do to him?"

Penny raised a brow. "To him? Nothing, but now we have confirmation of his identity. I do know he was enforcer for a drug dealer in Italy, and a marginally successful boxer who took one too many hits to the noggin." She looked at the numbers on the paper and pursed her lips.

"Both of these are UK exchanges. When we tracked him 'round London, it struck me as odd he wasn't evasive. Even sharks turn to see what's behind them, but he didn't, not once."

"I noticed that, too," he replied, his smile showing up again. "Either he doesn't think anyone's marked him or he can't physically turn his head." She huffed but then grew thoughtful.

"Your colleagues at the Associates speak highly of you, as do your clients," she said. "Perhaps it's because of your military background, yet you downplay your role in Afghanistan. Do you keep that Medal of Honor in your sock drawer?" He took a step back and dropped his chin, and again she was struck by the resemblance between brother and sister.

"Don't be cross, Adam. You had to know we were going to inquire," she said, her lips curling up at the corners. "It's quite odd, really. I've seen photographs of Loren with her aunt, and they appear so similar, and yet I see you, and there's no aunt at all. Perhaps it's merely her femininity."

"Maybe." His brow went up. "I've done my own digging, you know," he replied. "Your brother was MI5, but you were MI6. You served in Iraq for over three years, but then you disappeared. Four years later, here you are. What happened?" She pursed her lips, studying him for a moment.

"Perhaps I'll tell you someday."

"Right," he drawled. "We should get back. Your boyfriend might get worried."

She scoffed. "You wish."

The gathering had moved to the living room when they returned, and she took a seat on the arm of Ron's chair. Adam resumed his place across from Loren and Graham, and when there was a lull in the conversation, Penny cleared her throat.

"Might I assume you're in for the evening?" she asked Loren. "I have a few things to arrange if you're to attend the gallery event tomorrow." Loren nodded and gave a little smile as Ron shot to his feet.

"I, uh, I have a few things to do myself," he said. "A mountain of post to sort, you know."

"Uh huh," Graham chuckled as he and Loren rose from the sofa. "We'll walk you out." She nudged Ron with her shoulder as they went with them to the elevator.

"Have fun you two."

"To what you are referring?" he muttered, hiding a smile as she hugged him. "Ring me when you get back to England," he said. "We'll chat about how to salvage the whole Ryzak thing." He then shook hands with Graham, then he and Penny entered the elevator.

"See you later." Loren's smile faded as the doors closed. "It'll be weird, not having him around."

Graham huffed. "He's a slob though."

She turned, grimacing. "Oh, I know!" They were both chuckling when they returned to the living room and reclaimed their seats, but the silence went on too long for Alejandra.

"Adam, what was Loren like as a little girl?" Loren groaned, covering her eyes with her hand.

"She was a lot like she is now," he replied, smirking at her. "Loud and obnoxious." Everyone chuckled as he took out a large envelope. "I have pictures, if you'd like to see them."

"Oh! Yes! I want to see!" Alejandra jumped from her seat to trade places with her husband. Pictures were passed around and as they came to her, Loren placed them on the table, taking her time in studying them. The photos with her mother in them she put furthest away, then Graham handed her an image of her six-year-old self, laughing at several chickens pecking the feed out of her hand.

She reached for the small pile on the table in front of Adam and turned over another photo with writing on the back. Her nine-year-old self stood before a blank wall in a stained school uniform that was several sizes too large, and without shoes. Her hair was matted in places and beneath the familiar scowl, dark circles shaded her eyes. There was a faint bruise on her right cheek. Loren closed her eyes, forcing back the memories of gnawing hunger, tightly controlled anger, and deep shame.

"I don't want to remember anymore," she choked, shrugging off Graham's arm to head to the sideboard in the dining room. She grabbed the bottle of Highland Park whisky, poured herself a double and knocked it back. Her glass made a loud *tink* on the marble counter as the whisky burned her already raw throat. She was glad for it; the pain gave her something concrete to focus her rage. After pouring another drink, she returned to her seat. Graham placed his hand on the back of her neck.

"Loren–." She pushed him away.

"You're not in my head," she hissed, then raised her eyes to her brother. "And neither are you." Adam's gaze flicked to the glass in her hand.

"You have a high tolerance for that, don't you?" His disapproving tone set her off, and she downed the whisky in one swig.

"And?" she snarled and plonked the glass on the table.

"Alcoholism runs in our family."

Her mouth popped open. "I don't... Who are you to–." She jumped to her feet and punctuated her words with a jab of her finger in his direction. "Fuck you, *Adam O'Connell,* or whatever the fuck your name is! You don't know a fucking thing about me!" She stormed off to stomp up the stairs to the guest room, not quite slamming the door.

Adam took a deep breath. "And that's my cue." He gave the others a pained smile and stood. Benny glanced at Graham, then back to Adam.

"It's a lot to take in, for certain," he said. "We can't imagine it's been easy, for any of you." Alejandra affixed her dark eyes on him.

"You're quite fortunate she didn't hit you, Adam. I understand she has a rather nasty right hook."

Graham raised his brows at her. "How do you… Ron," he muttered, shaking his head. Adam shook hands with Benny, then offered it to Alejandra.

"Thank you for your hospitality."

"You are most welcome," she replied, ignoring his hand and rose to give him a brief hug. "We'll see you tomorrow, at luncheon." He took a breath to decline but just nodded.

"I'll walk you out," Graham told him, rising from the sofa. When they reached the vestibule, he closed the door to the apartment and Adam folded his arms over his chest.

"How much did you tell them about her? About my family?"

"I said nothing of her childhood, but because of Cara Smith, all that's going to come out sooner or later," Graham replied, mirroring his posture. They stared at each other silently until Adam glanced away.

"She's right," he said. "I don't know her anymore."

"The last few months have left her shattered," Graham said. "She needs time to put the pieces back." Adam pressed the call button and put his hands in his pockets before facing him with a hard glare.

"What happened on Sunday?"

"I don't owe you an explanation." Graham took a breath and looked down at his shoes. "We said things in anger, and I made the terrible mistake of walking out." There was a short silence, then Adam patted him on the shoulder.

"She still looks to you for support. Take heart in that." The elevator doors opened, and he took a step, but stopped. "But I feel a little better knowing I'm not alone in pissing her off."

***

Benny and Alejandra were not in the living room when Graham returned, so he headed upstairs. He listened at the door to the guest room before knocking softly and entered.

The lights were off, and the shades were up, bathing the room in a dusky yellow hue. Loren was on the bed, facing away from the door, but she didn't turn over as he closed it. Graham walked to the chair across from her and sat down. Her expression remained neutral, even as she spoke.

"You make a better door than a window."

"All the better that you have to pay attention to me," he replied. "What use would I be if I were transparent?"

"What use are you now?" Graham flinched. "That was harsh," she said softly. "But I'm not sorry."

"You have every right to be angry," he said, and she turned over to her back.

"I am so done. I'm overdone. I am a fucking hamburger hockey puck."

He held in a smile. "Are you hungry? We could–."

"Shut up."

"Okay," he drawled, and she quickly rolled to her knees.

"Where the fuck does he get off telling me what to do? Where has he been my whole fucking life!" She threw her arm out, pointing to the door. "He waits until now, when I'm in a fucking death spiral, to show up and push me over the edge!"

"Death spiral?" he scoffed. "Now who's being overly dramatic?" She sat back on her heels and glared at him.

"Why would he think I was better off without him?"

"That would have been a question to ask, instead of storming off."

"Yah, I guess," she said, curling her lip. "Look at you, being all adult over there."

"We did agree one of us has to stay sane while the other goes off the rocker." She huffed a laugh which broke into a sob.

"If you don't want to be with me, please tell me now," she cried, and he moved swiftly to gather her in his arms.

"I'm sorry. I'm sorry I hurt you," he said, kissing her forehead, her cheeks, her lips. "I do want you. I do love you. I was wrong." He held her close as she cried, and when her tears subsided, Loren sniffled.

"And here we are again. I'm upset, and we're lying down."

Graham kissed her forehead. "I told you before, I'm lazy."

***

29 October

The dawn found Loren staring up at the ceiling with her stomach burning and her head spinning. Her anxieties played out in her dreams leaving her exhausted.

I'm out of control, and I don't know what to do. She sighed and turned over for what seemed like the thousandth time to find Graham's bright blue eyes watching her.

"Is being thirty weighing heavily on you?"

She huffed. "I almost forgot it was my birthday yesterday."

"I can see how that could happen," he said, then kissed her.

"I'm sorry if I embarrassed you in front of your friends," she said, closing her eyes.

"Please, I've embarrassed myself much worse, and they're your friends as well. I reckon they like you more than me right now." Loren opened her eyes to his grimace. "Alejandra gave me quite a dressing down the other day then showed me a picture of you outside your house. I knew the photographers were there and how it would look and I'm sor–." Loren pressed her finger to his lips and spoke around the knot in her throat.

"We've said that enough, okay? We're trying to go forward, not back."

Graham nodded. "Right." Silence stretched too long for her and she let out a breath.

"Still, I acted like a spoiled brat," she sighed and ran her hands over her face.

"You acted like someone pushed far beyond their endurance, my love," he countered, propping up on an elbow. "Tell me of the battles your heart is fighting."

"I want to cry, laugh, and run away all at the same time," she answered. "It feels like nothing's real, but it hurts too much for it not to be." He gathered her in his arms, not speaking, not demanding or enticing; he just held her. His warmth seeped into her, relaxing her. Her eyes grew heavy and she would have gone back to sleep if not for the static in her brain.

"What did you think of Adam?"

"I was able to decipher some of his expressions, which are much like yours, and Maggie's," he replied. "He was nervous and trying to hide it."

She sniffed. "He was doing a better job of hiding it than I was."

"You might think that, but you have a very good poker face." He brushed her hair out of her eyes. "I do wish I could pluck from the memory a rooted sorrow, but that's not what you need." She shook her head, and a crooked smile began to form.

"You're ripping off of Shakespeare now?"

He shrugged, chuckling. "I can't help it."

"I love you," she sighed, snuggling up with him again. "Do we have to go to the gallery thing tonight?"

"*We* don't, but I do, sadly. Rex is expecting me, and I can't back out now," his voice rumbled under her ear. "I would like you to go with me, but I understand if you aren't up for it."

"Well, it would be a shame not to wear the dress I bought yesterday," she said, popping up to look at him. "I look pretty hot in it."

He grinned. "You could always put it on now."

***

After a late breakfast at a diner on West 60th, and a side trip to Brooks Brothers for a new suit for Graham, he, Loren, and Penny returned to the penthouse to find Adam leaning against a pillar in front of the building. He pushed off to greet them, and Graham got to him first.

"Good to see she didn't frighten you off," he said, switching the garment bag to his other shoulder to shake hands.

"I remember her temper," Adam replied, giving a wink to Loren.

"Well, come on then," Graham said and led the party through the doors of the building. Loren trailed behind, her eyes focused on the marble tile floor to cover the sting at Adam's comment. Penny stood next to her in the elevator as the two men chatted about the suit Graham purchased.

"Something tells me there are unspoken words between you and your brother," she murmured. "Kick him in the shin if he steps out of line." Loren huffed a laugh as the doors of the elevator opened, and Penny walked out first. Graham touched Loren's arm as they entered the penthouse.

"I'm just going to take this upstairs." He kissed her cheek and headed for the steps to the second floor. Her eyes followed him to avoid looking in Adam's direction, then she went to stand at the windows overlooking Central Park. She couldn't see his reflection in the windows but sensed his presence when he came up behind her.

"I really can't stay for lunch," he said.

"It's okay. I'm sorry for what I said last night."

"I should be the one apologizing," he replied, and she turned to him. "You're right. You're not my little shadow anymore, but I hope you'll let me get to know you again."

"I'd like that." She turned back to the view. "It's freaking me out I can't see myself in the glass." Adam leaned in close to the pane and bumped his nose.

"That is freaky," he chuckled, and Loren laughed as he rubbed his nose.

"What's freaky?" They both turned to find Graham standing near the sofa.

"How you can't see your reflection in the windows," she answered, walking over and taking a seat next to him. Adam chose the sofa across from them.

"There's a special coating on them," Graham explained. "Benny didn't tell me about it when they first moved in, and they had quite a laugh when I tried to put my hand through it." Their chuckles soon died out to silence, and Loren raised her eyes to Adam.

"What was your foster family like? Were there other kids?"

"Kelly and Frank have a daughter, three years older than me," he replied. "Before I got there, they adopted brothers, Michael and Desmond. They're a couple of years younger."

"But they didn't adopt you," she said. "Why?"

"They wanted to, but I said no," he answered and dropped his chin. "I had parents, and they were gone."

"You didn't want to compare them," she stated. Adam met her gaze and nodded. "That's how I feel about Maggie and Randall. I've never been able to call them Mom and Dad, but I didn't want the Miller name anymore, and the only way to change it was to be adopted."

"Or by petition," Adam said. "That's what I did when I turned eighteen."

"But you had to tell them why," she countered, shaking her head. "I couldn't tell…" She turned away, trying to force her emotions back into their box. Graham then took up the conversation.

"Do you keep in touch with your foster family?"

Adam nodded. "I see Desmond most often. He's a lawyer in Florham Park, New Jersey. Michael is a high school science teacher in Atlanta, and Rachel lives in Orlando. She works at Disney World as a Princess."

Graham's brows went up. "She's an actress?"

"Which princess?" Loren asked at the same time.

"Jasmine or Pocahontas," he replied, smiling. "Depends on the day."

"Now that's got to be a dream job," she said.

"Eh, she and Michael have the same complaints. It's not the kids that make the job hard, it's the parents."

"And you went from the Army to be a bodyguard instead of a police officer," Graham said, and Adam smiled back.

"I fell into it, I suppose. I got to know the owner of the gym where I was rehabbing my shoulder. He mentioned his daughter was a musician, and she was getting some unwanted attention at shows. I offered to work security for a couple of her local gigs, and when she went on tour, her manager asked me to go with her. The Associates came knocking after she was signed to a major deal a year later." He shrugged. "I only work with her now when she goes on tour."

"What led you to the Army in the first place?" Loren asked.

"Frank. He was retired Navy and encouraged me to join ROTC in high school," Adam replied. "When the Sergeant saw my rifle skills, he got me into more intensive training. I was good at it, so why not."

Loren sat back on the sofa, pressing her lips together. Memories of her father and brother coming back from hunting hit her in a wave.

They never came back without something they killed. She blinked. *If he wanted me dead quick, he would have shot me in the head.* The thought turned her stomach, and she swallowed hard. *That's why there was so much blood on the floor. He made her suffer.*

"What's that look for?" Adam's question derailed her train of thought.

She shook her head. "It's nothing," she replied quickly and held Graham's hand tighter. "My stomach's bothering me. I'm eating things I normally wouldn't," Loren rolled her eyes, "and I keep forgetting to take my Lactaid tablets."

His brows went up. "You're lactose intolerant?"

"For as long as I can remember."

"Me too, but the Army doctors called it irritable bowel."

She huffed. "If only they knew." She put her head on Graham's shoulder. "*Je t'aime,*" she whispered.

"*Je connais.*"

Adam cleared his throat. "My friends used to tease me about Loren following me everywhere, like a shadow. I remember she would come tearing after us on her little bicycle." The memory was a slap to the face, and she sat up.

"And you would laugh at me when I couldn't keep up," she snapped, and his mouth popped open.

"Loren, I was thirteen," he countered, his shoulders up. "I didn't want my little sister hanging around." Graham squeezed her hand.

"Is that why you always held back for Kevin?"

She glared at her brother. "I don't drop my teammates."

"I didn't know you took it so seriously," Adam huffed, shaking his head.

"You left me behind," she choked, then took a few deep breaths. "How could you think I'd be better off without you? You were the only one who loved me, and you just left me! Did you even care about what would happen to me?" She squeezed her eyes shut and leaned into Graham's shoulder. "

"I did care. That's why I left. I thought you safe."

"I wasn't safe," she hissed. "They abused me at the foster home. They locked me in a closet when I didn't do what I was told. I ran away to try and find you." Two tears slid down her cheeks. "They beat me for it, then threw me away like I was trash." Adam covered his mouth with his hand, collapsing back into the sofa.

176

"Oh my god," he muttered, his eyes turning to quicksilver. "I didn't know. I swear, if I had, I would have come for you."

"I know you would have," she rasped. "I don't want to remember anymore." She ducked her head into his chest when a soft *tink* came from the coffee table. A palm sized piece of pale blue sea glass glowed in the spotlights. Loren gasped and picked it up, turning it over in her fingers.

"Do you remember when we found that?"

"It was the last time we went to the beach," she replied. Their eyes met, and Adam nodded. "I wanted to dig a hole to China." She handed the piece to Graham. "We kept finding little pockets of sea glass in all kinds of colors and shapes. That's the biggest one." She turned back to her brother. "You kept it?"

"It's been to Iraq, Afghanistan, India, Japan," he answered. "You've been with me all over the world." She wiped her cheek with her knuckles.

"Damn you, and your shiny things!" Adam huffed a laugh, then gave a soft smile.

"I think that's enough of memory lane for now," he said. "I'd like to tag along tonight, if that's alright with you." She and Graham looked to each other.

"Well, Penny's going to–." he began, but Adam put his hand out.

"I won't get in her way," he said. "I'll watch from the sidelines, in case our friend decides to show his face."

"We would appreciate that," Graham answered. "We'll be heading there around six."

"Okay," he said and stood, taking a step away. "I'll see you–." Loren jumped up and caught his arm.

"I don't hate you, I just…" She looked down at her hand on his arm, "I've never dealt with any of this. I was always too afraid to look back. I can't close the door again, but I can't face it alone." Adam touched her shoulder to draw her into his arms.

"You don't have to, Shadow." Her resolve crumbled against his gentle embrace and dissolved into body-wracking sobs. "I love you, Loren," came his tearful whisper. "I'm sorry for leaving you behind. I promise, I won't do it again." She slowly pulled away, bringing her tears to a sniffling end, and was about to brush her sleeve under her nose when a tissue appeared in front of her. She gave a weepy laugh.

"Thanks, love," she said to Graham, then faced Adam. "We'll see you later, right?"

He winked. "If you see me, I'm not doing my job." Watching him disappear into the elevator gave her a little pang, and she sat down next to Graham on the sofa. The warmth of his hand on her back spread through her.

"I keep saying it's going to be alright, because it will be," he said, "but I imagine you're getting tired of hearing it." Loren gave a tearful chuckle and turned into his embrace.

"A little bit, but I still need you to tell me."

***

Michael Jacobson stood outside the Midtown Gallery on West 57th, scowling and scratching at his chest.

Everything was riding on that twenty thousand! His eyes darted around to the faces of the other paparazzi on the sidewalk. *This is fucking stupid. They complain about wanting privacy, but somebody in their camp tipped off the paps that they were going to be here.* A black Cadillac SUV pulled up to the building, and he sneered as a dark-haired woman who got out of the front passenger door.

Maybe I can recover something. Atherton exited the vehicle next, turning to take Mackenzie's hand as she stepped onto the sidewalk. Jacobson took a moment to leer at her tight pink dress and long bare legs before raising the camera to his face. Photographers pushed against the makeshift barrier leading to the entrance of the gallery, yelling their names or shouting questions. They were ignored as the couple headed into the building, followed by their bodyguard. He lowered his camera to check his shots on the 2x2 screen, and satisfied, he glanced at his watch, then up at the building.

I'm not going to walk in and find Atherton in the john like in London. That time, he wasn't sure who was more surprised, the actor or himself. *And the fucking pussy thought he could intimidate me.* He scoffed and leaned up against the wall of the building, envisioning how he'd rip the pink dress off the cyclist.

Three hours later, he was on the curb at the bumper of the Escalade when Mackenzie and Atherton exited the building. Camera flashes lit up the block. He lowered his camera to show his face at their approach, expecting the scared rabbit look when she saw him. She stopped, but the glare she gave him was lethal.

"*I see you,*" she mouthed and climbed into the vehicle. Atherton followed and gave him a similarly deadly scowl.

What the…? Jacobson stepped onto the sidewalk as the SUV drove away. He glanced around at the other photographers milling about on the sidewalk, noting many dark looks thrown in his direction. He didn't care. His prey had flown, and he started toward 6th Avenue. Noise besieged him from all directions.

"I hate this fucking city." He winced at a taxi horn screaming by the intersection. The commotion made him anxious; he couldn't tell where sounds were coming from until they were right next to him. The doctors told him he was going deaf.

"Fucking assholes don't know everything." His mood improved patting the camera around his neck. *I'm going to bleed every red cent out of that SkyNews reporter.* His thoughts went back six years as he walked, when he received a message from Felix Lalonde. He remembered the Frenchman from when they were both working for Tomaso Maestri, and he initially refused Lalonde's proposal. He changed his mind after the Frenchman said how much he was willing to pay.

"You will follow her to England. I want to know where she goes and who she's with at all times. I will pay you ten thousand for this."

For five years, Lalonde paid him ten thousand every six months for photographs and information, but not just about her. He wanted to know about those around her as well. Photographs of IDC's owner shaking up with his lead rider made Lalonde very happy.

Then, she met Atherton, and the frog went off the deep end, but he didn't want to wait for the actor to hang himself with his co-star. Jacobson dug up photos of Atherton and some blonde lawyer, and Sylvia Montgomery did the rest.

What a fucking snake. He rubbed his chin as the reporter came to mind again. *What her investigator found, damn. Those crime photos ruined my sleep for a week.*

His musings came to an end when he spied a Starbucks on the corner and entered. After retrieving his coffee, he sat down at a table to get a better look at the images he shot when he caught a glimpse of a dark-haired woman stop and look in the window.

That's the security agent. His annoyance increased each time her ponytail bopped past the window. Jacobson remained seated until she went by again, then quickly rose to leave the shop. He picked up his pace to join with a group of tourists going in the opposite direction, then ducked into a darkened doorway to wait.

Her nose was to her phone screen when she passed, and he stepped out to follow, biding his time for the people ahead of her to thin out. One block later, he slipped a hulking arm around her chest with his other hand covering her mouth and dragged her down a narrow alley. He shoved her face first into the wall, assuming he'd pinned her with his bulk.

"You think you can follow–." The woman tried duck out of his hold, surprising him, then reached back to claw at his face. "You fucking bitch!"

She moved fast, grasping the base of his thumb and yanked downward, rolling his wrist in a direction it wasn't meant to turn. A line of fire shot up his arm and he let go of her, roaring in pain.

The woman didn't release him; she pivoted, and her balled fist made rapid and repeated contact with his groin, dropping Jacobson to his knees. She stepped around him, holding his arm out at an awkward and painful angle.

"I'm terribly sorry, does that hurt?" she purred in his ear. He growled and raised his other fist to take a swing at her, but he couldn't reach. His wrist and arm bent back further, drawing a groan from him.

"You accost a young woman in a dark alley, and you think there's no price to pay?" she snarled, and his anger overcame his sense.

"You little cunt. I'm gonna fucking kill you." A wet snap came from his wrist, sending a shock of intense pain up his arm, but his howl was again cut off by a delicately placed boot to his testicles. The woman then released his arm to grab his hair and expose his jugular to a cold, sharp blade pressed against it.

"Touch her again, and I promise, you'll not see your death coming," she whispered. There was a millisecond of blinding pain in the back of his head, then blackness.

"What have you done?"

Penny O'Neill looked up from the body crumpled at her feet.

"Mr. O'Connell. What a surprise," she drawled. Adam stood off a few yards with a familiar scowl directed at her.

"What the hell are you doing?"

She raised her chin. "I gave a first and final warning. If he's smarter than he appears, he will heed it." Penny dropped a small mobile phone at her feet and crushed it with her boot heel. "I'm starving. Fancy some nosh? There's a diner just down the street." He gaped at her, pointing to the body of Michael Jacobson.

"You can't just leave–."

"He assaulted your sister," she hissed. "Do you really give a fuck what happens to the bastard?" Adam's frown deepened, looking down at the prone man, then followed her out of the alley.

***

Loren paced in front of the windows of the living room when the elevator clanged to a halt in the vestibule.

"You didn't have to wait up, petal," Penny said as she entered the penthouse.

"I wasn't," she replied, tucking her lip in her teeth. "I got a phone call from my friend, Colin. His wife had a baby girl about an hour ago." Her brows went up as Adam came into view. "You came back?"

"Uh, yeah, I forgot my, uh," he peered around her at the coffee table, "ah, there it is." He went over and picked up a cell phone battery charger. "I can't live without this. Bye."

Her mouth dropped open. "Wait a minute!" He turned, giving her a crooked grin.

"I'm kidding," he chuckled, walking back to her. "I wanted to say goodbye to you."

"That's not funny," she muttered, crossing her arms over her chest. Penny coughed lightly.

"I'm absolutely knackered, and we have an early flight." She shook hands with Adam, grinning. "I'm sure we'll see each other again soon."

"I'm sure we will," he replied, and Loren narrowed her eyes at their flirtatious tone. She waited until Penny's door closed upstairs before rounding on him.

"She has a boyfriend."

His brows went up. "What, we just rode up in the elevator together." Loren dropped her chin and flopped down on the sofa.

"I'm sorry, I…" She licked her lips. "I'm out of sorts. My friends, Colin and Emma, they're like family. Emma had an emergency C-section and I feel bad not being there for her." She took a breath, clutching at the hem of her shirt. "Then, I got an email from Randall about my trust."

Adam squinted at her. "Your what?" She motioned to the sofa.

"Sit down, please." She waited until he did so before speaking. "When the farm was sold, Maggie put the money into a trust for me, but it should have been in both our names. Randall made the first distribution to my brokerage account today."

He shook his head. "And you're telling me this, why?"

"Because it's six hundred thousand dollars and half of it is yours." Adam reared back and put his hands up.

"No, it's not," he said. "I told you, I don't want your money."

"It's not *my* money," Loren countered, her frown deepening. "It's for both of us."

"I don't want anything to do with it," he responded, and she glared at him until he dropped his chin and sighed. "That farm was his legacy, and Dad told me many times he was keeping it for me." Adam gave a hard smile. "I hope the fucking bastard is rolling over in hell knowing it was turned into a golf course." Her expression didn't change, and he sighed again.

"After what he did to you, to Mom and Amy, it should be yours," he said. "Do something good with it. Be happy." Her chin began to tremble.

"Why did you wait so long?" she whined, and he took hold of her hand.

"I wanted to find you, I did, but I wasn't in a good place when I came back from Afghanistan the last time," he said, quietly. "I was in a lot of pain, and everything I had was gone. My fiancée left me, and she took the cat." He sniffled. "I loved that cat." She gave a little smile as he continued.

"I thought my life was over and I went on a bender. About a week later, I woke up in our neighbor Jeb's barn in South Carolina, with no memory of how I got there and that scared the fuck out of me." Adam glanced down at their clasped hands. "Jeb helped me sober up, and he took me to my first AA meeting. It's been two years and one hundred and forty-two days."

"I didn't know," she whispered, and he squeezed her hand.

"Hey, I don't feel alone anymore. I have my sister back, and there's no way I'm leaving you behind again."

"You better not," Loren answered, her eyes shining. "I know where you live now."

***

30 October

Northaw, England

It was late afternoon when Loren and Graham stumbled through the front door of the house on Vineyards.

"I'll go turn the heat on," he said and took their bags into the laundry as she headed to the great room.

"I'll get a fire started." Glancing around, Loren started moving pillows and sofa cushions. "Where's the damned clicker-thing?" Spying it on the side table, she grabbed the remote, and the gas lit with a *whoosh*. Groaning, she flopped down on the plush floor pillows arranged in front of the fireplace.

"I just want to lie down and never get up again."

"If you sleep now, you won't later," he called from the kitchen.

"I didn't sleep as much as you did on the plane," she grumbled. "I don't know how you can just pass out like that." His chuckle opened her eyes. He was standing over her with a mug in each hand.

"You look like the Cheshire cat," he said and handed her one. She hummed, inhaling the sweet scent of chocolate and passionfruit. The crackle of the fire and the gentle tapping of rain on the deck outside joined with his warmth to relax her body, but her mind buzzed around in circles. Graham rubbed his cheek against the top of her head.

"I don't even need to see your face to know you're wool gathering."

"You don't, huh?"

"I can hear the gears moving in your head," he replied. She huffed, dropping her chin.

"We've been home for less than an hour and it already feels like last week was a dream." He moved back to see her face, his brows tight together, then took her mug and placed it with his on the table behind them.

"You've been on an emotional rollercoaster for months now, and not just with what I've put you through. I reckon it's time to talk to someone."

Loren shook her head. "I told you, I went to therapy when I was a kid and in college. It didn't help."

"Suppressing your pain hasn't worked either," he replied. "It's coming out in your dreams. That gathering storm? You feel threatened, and as much as I want to, I can't help you fight it. You need more expert help, and I'll go with you."

Her eyes went wide. "You would do that?" His fingers moved deeper into her hair to gently pull her toward him.

"Know me not by now? I would move heaven and earth for you." Their breath mingled just as her mobile pinged a text on the table behind them.

"Ignore it," he whispered, moving closer to deepen their kiss when her mobile began to ring. Loren groaned, moving back to see the caller ID.

"Shit. It's Colin." She pressed the icon to answer the call on speaker. "Hey, what's up?"

"Emma saw you on the telly. Are you back for real?"

"Well, yah, but we just got–."

"She wants you to visit," he said, and Loren looked to Graham with raised brows. "She said it's important you come tonight, before her mother gets here in the morning."

"Uh, okay then," she replied, glancing at her watch. "We'll be there as soon as we can." She disconnected and met his gaze. "Um…"

"You want me to go with you?"

"Yes, but they're probably going to say something to you," she said.

"I have little doubt of that, but you're worth it." Graham kissed her. "Besides, I love babies."

***

When they entered the waiting room of the Maternity Ward, Cece launched from the yellow pleather sofa.

"You're a bit late to the party," she said and gave Loren a rib-crushing hug.

"I needed a shower. I smelled like airplane." Cece passed her into Anthony's embrace.

"You okay?" he murmured.

"Yah, I'm okay," she whispered, then released him.

"She's in room five." He pushed his chin toward the hallway. Loren took a step away, but frowned at Cece, then turned back to Graham. He kissed her forehead.

"Go. I'll wait here." She narrowed her eyes at her friends again, then headed down the hall.

Graham let out a groan and lowered to the stiff couch. He leaned forward, his forearms resting on his thighs and linked his fingers between his knees.

"So," he addressed the couple glaring at him from across the coffee table. "Let's have at it, then."

"You fecking, selfish son of a bitch," Cece growled, jabbing her finger at him. "How could you do that her? You had to have known the photographers were there!"

"Charlotte." Anthony gently grasped her hand, then looked to Graham. "You don't have to explain anything to us. You're here with her, that's all that matters." Cece pulled her hand away.

"You get this straight, you used caravan salesman," she snarled, pointing at him again. "She might say she's forgiven ya, but she hasn't, not really."

"I know," he said, dropping his chin. "I promised you I wouldn't hurt her, but I broke that promise."

"Twice," she said, holding up two fingers.

Graham nodded. "We've both made mistakes, and we're trying to heal and grow, together. I hope you will support and respect that." She sat back from him, crossing her arms.

"Yah, well, she's not perfect, neither. She didn't lie, exactly, but she didn't tell you everything that was going on. I did get on her about that, I'll have you know." Cece eyed him with a little curl of her lip. "She was a wobbly stool before, and he'd have broken her if you hadn't come along, and I couldn't have done anything to stop it." His eyes welled up before he could stop them.

"Felix merely widened the crack that was already there," Graham said softly. "She's going to need us more than ever. She found her brother, and what she's remembering is tearing her apart."

***

Loren knocked on the door marked Room 5 and slowly pushed it open. Machines beeped in their stands around the room. The curtains were drawn on the windows, and the lights were dimmed, but the woman and child in the hospital bed were bathed in a halo of golden light.

"Knock, knock," she murmured, crossing the room to the sink to wash her hands.

"You're here," Emma called hoarsely. "Happy birthday! Look what I did!" The proud mother shifted the swaddled infant in her arms. Colin squinted at his wife.

"What you did? I reckon I had a bit in that." Loren gave him a look.

"No, you didn't," she retorted, and her attention went right back to the smallest person in the room. "She's perfect, Em." Emma uncovered the baby's face.

"Alice, dear?" The infant stirred at her voice. "This is Auntie Loren. She's going to be one of the most important people in your life. She's your godmother."

"Godmother?" Loren pulled her hands back, her tear-filled eyes wide.

"Yes, silly. We wouldn't have anyone else," Emma said and handed over the child. Loren sniffled, gazing into the tiny face attached to the little body in her arms. Tears welled up again as Emma continued.

"That's why I wanted you here tonight. You were the first to hold Laurence when he was born, and I wanted you to be the second person to hold Alice." Loren blinked at her. "Colin was the first. I don't count," Emma chuckled. "I've been holding her for the last nine months."

"She wouldn't let Anthony hold her either," Colin added. Alice yawned and opened her eyes, and Loren stopped breathing. Another baby girl's face appeared in her mind; a little older, but just as sweet, and she brushed her nose against the tiny pink cheek.

"Hello, baby," she whispered. Alice's steel gray eyes fluttered open, only to close again. "You are so gonna be spoiled." Tears slipped from her eyes. "Okay, that's enough." She carefully handed the baby back to her mother. "I'm sorry. This week's been really hard, and you just sent me over the edge." She choked back a sob and covered her mouth.

"Oh darling, I'm sorry!" Emma cried softly. "Graham's with you, so everything's alright, yah?"

"It will be," she replied, sniffling. "We both have a lot to work through, but we'll do it together."

"I'm glad. I really like him, and I like you with him." Then, Emma frowned at her. "But there's something else, isn't there?" Loren nodded and took a big breath.

"I found my brother."

***

The night sky flowered with stars as Graham drove the Jaguar back to Northaw. He glanced over at Loren in the passenger seat, her head resting on the window with her eyes closed.

His heart melted when he held Alice, and then, seeing Loren with the baby, smiling at him with tears in her eyes, a deep pang of love mixed with regret hit his chest. He touched her hand resting in her lap, and she linked her fingers with his tightly.

"It's quite an honor, being godmother," he said. Loren nodded but didn't open her eyes.

"Yah. That was a shocker," she said. "Luckily I don't have to convert. The Church of England is a little more lenient about me being Catholic."

"You'll have to start going to church, you know."

Her head rolled back. "Fuck."

"You'll have to stop swearing, as well."

"Fuck," she drawled, but their chuckles faded into silence as the Jaguar slipped passed the fields of the Ridgeway.

"I've been wondering something," Graham said, quickly eyeing her. "How did you know what was happening to Emma, the first time?" She sat up, and he was surprised to see tears in her eyes. "What is it?" She licked her lips and took a deep breath.

"When Emma started bleeding out, I was just as terrified as she was, because I knew what was happening," she said. "It was the same with

186

Maggie, about a month before I left for Colorado. I happened to be home that day, but if I wasn't, she could have died."

"Oh my god," he said softly.

Loren sniffled. "I had nightmares for a long time after that and it was just another reason for me to run away." A heavy silence came between them until he pulled the Jag into the garage of the house on Vineyards. He turned off the engine, but neither moved to get out of the car.

"Loren, might I ask–."

"You don't have to ask to ask a question."

He smiled and nodded. "Alice is so tiny and perfect, and seeing you holding her…" He began speaking quickly. "I know we touched on the subject of children previously, and with all that's happened between us this might not be the best time to broach the subject, and by the look on your face I'm right, but I'm finding the words are just tumbling out of my mouth! Please stop me," he tittered. She squeezed his hand.

"I love you, Graham. Can that be enough for now?"

He nodded slowly. "Yes. Yes, it can."

***

31 October

"It was really nice of Claire to invite us to dinner," Loren told Graham as he maneuvered the Jaguar into a parking spot across from a brick three-story. "But I would have thought they had plans. I mean, it's Halloween."

"No, they're homebodies," he replied. "We'll probably watch a horror film though." He leaned over and kissed her wrinkled forehead. "Never fear, my love. I won't let the Bogeyman get you."

"Hmm, Bogeyman," she muttered and got out of the car. He tucked her in close as they crossed the street as she eyed the corners, searching for a blue sedan when Graham suddenly halted.

"I don't fucking believe this," he snarled, and she turned around.

"What's wro– Oh." Frederick Atherton's silver BMW was parked at the curb.

"We're going somewhere else," he hissed and grabbed her hand to pull her along, but she resisted.

"Wait. Why don't you want to see your dad?" He grimaced, raking his fingers through his hair.

"I haven't seen him since September, and I don't want to now, and neither should you after what he did!" He walked off a short distance, running his hand over his mouth, then started back to her, but turned around again. His agitation was boiling over and all he wanted to do was run away, but when he headed for the car, Loren stepped in front of him, catching his wrists.

"Easy. Breathe." He licked his lips, looking everywhere else but at her. "*Mon amour* talk to me," she murmured, giving his arms a little tug.

"He… my father wrote me a letter," he croaked and pulled away to remove his billfold from his jacket pocket. He withdrew a folded piece of paper and gave it to her.

The letter was on the film studio's letterhead, and when Loren smoothed it out, the ink was smudged in places. As she read, her brows inched higher up her forehead, then looked up. Graham had moved a few feet away, clinging to a light pole like a drowning man. She went to him and touched his shoulder.

"It hurts, I know, but he's apologizing and using some pretty big words. Isn't that a good thing?" He yanked away from her, his mouth pressed into a thin line.

"Can you honestly say you've forgiven Maggie for abandoning you in that hell of a foster home, merely because she apologized?"

Loren held her hands up. "Whoa! That's apples to oranges."

"How? How is it any different?" he countered, stepping closer to her. "She thought she was doing the right thing, just like your brother. Has that knowledge made the pain any easier to bear?"

She raised her chin. "No, it hasn't, but it makes it easier to put the anger aside," she replied. "They're my family, and while he might be an asshole, Frederick is your father." He took a breath to voice his opinion, but she put her hand up. "I know you're upset, but it was my life he dug into, not so much yours."

"Are you not cross about that?" She looked away, breathing deeply.

"I feel sorry for him. I can imagine he feels threatened." Loren pressed her lips together. "I knew I should have gotten that gold digger T-shirt," she muttered. He groaned, pushing his hair back with his hands.

"How can I be righteous in my anger when you're being all adult about this?"

She batted her eyes at him. "We did agree one of us has to stay sane when the other goes off the rocker. Now it's your turn." His trembling alarmed her when he pulled her in for a tight hug. "Graham, love, it's okay."

"I need you just as much, you realize that, right?" he whispered against her neck. "There's no going back now." Loren brought her hands to his face to make him look at her.

"That's not really a choice, remember? You've ruined me for anyone else." She kissed his forehead. "We can still want to go somewhere else, if you want."

"Yes, I want to, but no. You're right. I have to face him," he grumbled, then took her hand to lead her to the stoop of the townhome. He rang the bell and soon, there were footfalls on the stairs. The door opened to reveal Graham's slightly harried, but grinning, soon-to-be brother-in-law, Jared Abernathy.

"We didn't expect you for another half hour," he chuckled, shaking Graham's hand. He then turned to give Loren a hug. "You must have some influence to hurry him along."

"Not really," she replied, stepping back. "We didn't hit much traffic on the way."

"Well, come in then!" Jared's athletic form bounded up the stairs where Claire met them at the top. The stairwell opened into a spacious living and dining area with natural pine flooring that flowed into a large, artisan kitchen. The rooms were decorated in cream and pale yellow, red and orange, highlighting the gold and bronze of the acid-washed concrete island and countertops. Loren's eyes widened as she looked around, then turned to Claire to give her a hug.

"Your place is incredible. I wish my house looked this put together."

"I can't take credit," Claire replied. "It's Jared's superpower, the decorating thing." Graham moved over to give his sister a hug.

"All's well?" she whispered.

"We're working on it," he murmured, then pulled away, frowning. "Did you invite him?"

Claire gave him a hard look. "You know he just shows up, but I am rather glad he did. You all need to talk." She nodded her chin to a door off the kitchen. "They're out on the roof deck but do get a drink first. Jared's quite proud of his concoction," she said, holding back a grin. Her fiancé was waving them over to the island counter while pointing to a steaming cauldron. Loren already had a smoking chalice, and her eyes lit up when she took a sip.

"Jared, this is amazing!"

Gilded plastic chalices in hand, Graham opened the rear door for Loren and followed her out to the deck where Serena Harris and Frederick Atherton were quietly arguing in the far corner.

"I told you we shouldn't have barged in on them, Frederick," she said, but their posture changed quickly, and Serena clapped her hands. "Oh! Loren! Graham! How wonderful! We saw your car when we came out here." She gave both a hug and a kiss on the cheek.

"Good to see you as well, Serena." Graham gave a tight smile, but his humor dissolved as his father came forth. "You're looking well, sir," he said, holding out his hand. Frederick hesitated but accepted the gesture.

"Yes, as are you." His dull blue eyes flicked to Loren. "I'm happy to see the presenters were incorrect in their reporting the relationship had ended." She gave only a tight smile as a reply, and the heavy silence that followed went on too long for Serena.

"I see you have some of Jared's spirits," she commented, holding up her ornamented chalice. "It's quite delicious, but I fear I've had far too much, and it's become a tad chilly out here." Serena put her hand on Graham's arm. "Would you be so kind as to open the door? It's a bit stiff."

"Of course." He gave a hard tug on the knob and held the door open for the older couple to enter the flat but caught Loren's elbow before she followed. He let the door close, and when he faced her, his lips were white.

"I can't do it," Graham choked, his fingers curling into tight fists. "I want to scream at him. I want to hurt him."

She gripped his shoulders. "Easy. Breathe. You're going to pass out."

"I'm sorry." He swallowed between breaths. "I'm sorry."

"Don't apologize, love," Loren said, holding back a smirk. "It's just your turn for your trolley to get derailed." He stared at her for a second.

"It's off your trolley," he muttered. "Thank you for distracting me with your shininess."

***

Loren covertly studied the older man seated across from her, noting Frederick had gained a little weight since she saw him last. His hair was more salt-and-pepper than black and trimmed in a shorter style similar to Graham. He didn't speak to her, other than to request an additional napkin or the salt. Her brow twitched when his faded blue eyes flicked up to meet her gaze, then slid away.

It's killing you to sit there and stare at me, knowing what you did to me. She glanced at Graham next to her. He was still pale but animated in his discussion with Jared about possibly renovating his study. She leaned over his shoulder.

"Do you think we can enclose the hallway somehow and make it all a giant closet?" They both turned to stare at her, then Graham sighed.

"You're envying Maggie's closet, but I'll think about it."

When dinner finished, there was a lapse in conversation as Claire and Jared began clearing the table. Loren took a long drink from her chalice and regarded Frederick Atherton over the rim.

Band-Aid theory. She put her glass down and took a breath, forcing all her emotions into her mental box before she spoke.

"I read your letter, Mr. Atherton." He raised his sullen gaze to her. "I understand you only wanted to protect him, but what your man found was never meant to be public. I didn't want Graham to know about my family because I was afraid he would reject me. I was wrong to think that, but you were wrong in your assumptions about me." Loren narrowed her eyes at the older man. "You hurt him, and you hurt me and my family. I just needed you to know that." Graham found her hand under the table and held it tightly.

"Do you understand what damage you have wrought?" he said to his father. "A reporter in New York confronted her with it. It's not confined, Frederick." His father blanched but didn't look away from them.

"I had to protect my son," he said, his eyes flicking to Jared and Claire standing at the other end of the table. "I have to protect my children, but I deeply regret what happened. I had no idea what they would do with the information, and Graham, Loren, I'm sorry. Jared and Claire, I apologize to you as well." Frederick then faced Graham. "I would understand if you did not wish me to be a part of–."

"That's not..." Graham pinched the bridge of his nose and exhaled. "You are my father. I look at you, and I see myself, the good and the bad," he said, his voice hard. "Perhaps, once things have settled down, my feelings might change, but right now, we need time. I need time." Frederick looked to Serena, who patted his shoulder.

"I understand," he replied. Another heavy silence ensued, where the older adults found their plates very interesting. Loren glanced over at Graham's sister, who was paler than new milk, and Claire coughed softly.

"Dad, it might be helpful if you could tell them the name of your investigator," she said. "If they knew, their security agent could track this man down."

"Of course," he said, glancing at Serena. "I contacted uh, an old friend at The Sun, but a few days later a different chap rang me up." He removed a small notebook from his jacket pocket. "I make notes, you see. I have trouble recalling things occasionally." He flicked through a few pages. "Here it is. He was an American. Michael Jacobson." Graham stood up, knocking over his chair while Loren sat in shocked silence. Claire half-rose from her seat.

"Graham? What's the matter?"

"That man has been following Loren for months!"

Frederick blinked. "You're saying you know who this man is?"

"He's been taking pictures of me, the people I'm with," she replied, her voice shaking. "He tried to hurt me."

"My god," he muttered. "I had no idea."

"How could you know," she retorted. "We didn't know who he was for sure until last week." Loren raised her glare to Frederick. "Who is your friend at The Sun?"

He blanched, his gaze looking to Serena. "Ah, well, she, ah–."

"Sylvia Montgomery," she said, with a curl of her lip. "That woman is a vile serpent. I told you, Frederick. Nothing good would come of this." Loren stood and moved closer to Graham.

"We need to call Derek."

***

1 November

Graham stared at the ceiling, unable to sleep with the Napalm his father dropped burning in his gut.

Sylvia Montgomery. He clenched his fists. As soon as they left his sister's, he was on the phone with Derek and Ron. *We can't touch her, at least not yet, but I know Ron won't let it go unpunished.* He turned to Loren, asleep on her side with a foot touching his ankle. He wanted to curl up with her again, but his need for information was greater and he eased out of bed to go into the library.

Lalonde is connected somehow, but how do I prove it? He paced the length of the room, rubbing his hands together as his thoughts swirled, then stopped abruptly.

"I know where he lives." Graham hustled around his desk to search through the reports from Lester Security he received via email.

When the Frenchman was first released from jail in mid-September, he was frequently tailed from his home to several bars in his neighborhood, a mid-scale hotel, and a nearby cafe. At the beginning of October, however, there was an indication Lalonde had checked into a rehab hospital. Graham still found that absurd and read the report again. He then reviewed the most recent email, which said Lalonde had returned home while they were in New York.

I still don't believe it. He skimmed through the past ledgers to find the notation of Lalonde's address, and sat back in his chair, scowling at the screen. A soft footfall came from the hall, and he swiveled around.

"You're up early," Loren said, leaning against the door frame.

"Did I wake you?"

"Your absence woke me," she replied, and Graham held his arms out to her.

"Come here," he said, but she raised her chin.

"No. You come back to bed."

"Oh, alright," he sighed, giving her a smile as he clicked the icon to activate the screen lock. Once back in bed and snuggled up against her, fatigue caught up to him with a yawn.

"Did you find what you were looking for?"

He froze. "What do you mean?"

"You looked like you made a decision." Relieved, Graham nuzzled her neck, inhaling her scent of roses and lavender.

"I was looking at motorcycles. There aren't many made for beanpoles like myself, but I reckon I found one I liked."

She chuckled. "You fit on the Harley, but Anthony would know better than me." Loren turned her head to see him. "Why not call him later? The

Church is closed today and with Cece and me at the expo, and Colin and Emma busy with her family, he probably has nothing to do."

He yawned again. "I might do that."

The shower running was the next thing Graham heard and he glanced at the glowing red 7:45 on the clock. He groaned and rolled over to focus on going back to sleep when Loren's mobile rang on the other side of the bed. He propped up on his elbow to see the screen.

Adam? He pursed his lips, considering whether to answer it, but when he finally moved to pick up her mobile, the call went to voicemail. She came out of the bath then, wrapped in her robe and smiling as she headed to the walk-in closet.

"Hey, sleepy." She stopped, tilting her head. "What's up?"

"Uh, your mobile was ringing," he said. "It was Adam." Her brows went up and pointed at the clock.

"This early?"

"It's almost 3 in the morning in New York," he replied. "He might be just getting home."

"You talked to him?"

"No. It went to voicemail." He handed her the mobile as she sat down next to him. "I didn't know if I should answer it."

"You could have," she said and gave him a kiss on the forehead as she listened to Adam's message. "He wants to pass something by me. Hmm." She then pressed his contact. "Hey yourself. Did you just get home?" She paused to listen to a muffled male voice. "Working? It's almost three in the morning. Oh, right, a concert. So, what's up?" She paused again, and her brows went to her hairline. "You want to come here? I'd love that! When?" Another brief silence. "Wednesday's perfect," she laughed. "Okay, I'll look for it." She disconnected and turned to Graham. "He's coming here."

"On Wednesday." His gaze slid away. *Will we never be alone?*

"Graham, this is important to me," she said, bringing his attention back to her. "He can stay at my house. He could have my room, and I'll stay in Holly's. She's in Australia anyway." He pinched the bridge of his nose, pushing away his annoyance.

"I'm not sleeping with you in Holly's room. Adam can stay here."

"Are you sure?" She came to stand between his knees and put her hands on his shoulders. A pang of regret hit him at her hopeful smile.

"I told you a long time ago, this is your home as well." Her smile became more seductive as she moved her hands to his neck, caressing his jaw with her thumbs.

"Maybe tomorrow we can bring some of my stuff over," her voice husky. "You know, like some warmer clothes and my cross bike, 'cause you know, I have to ride the trail back there."

His brows went straight up. "You'd move in with me?"

She squinted. "I didn't say that." His stomach sank to the floor. "Graham?" He raised his head, and she kissed him. "I love you very much, but I've never lived with a boyfriend before. I don't use a coaster all the time, and I track mud on the floor. I hang my kits up to dry all over the place. It's going to take some getting used to, for both of us, and I don't want to fuck it up."

"I don't either," he replied, then glanced at the clock on the nightstand. "Although it doesn't bode well for you that my habit for tardiness has already rubbed off." She looked at the clock too.

"Aw, fuck," Loren grumbled, pushing him off to head back to the closet.

***

"How did I let you talk me into this?" Anthony muttered, turning to Graham standing on the other side of the red telephone booth. He held back a grimace at the haunted look on the actor's face. "What am I supposed to say to him?"

"I want to know why," he croaked, and Anthony heaved a sigh.

"How do you even know where he lives?"

"I've had him followed since he was released from jail," he replied, staring at the cafe across the street. Anthony felt his mouth open slightly and shut it.

"Even if he tells me what you want to hear, how is that supposed to help Loren?"

"It doesn't." He ran a hand down his face. "I don't know what I'm doing, and now I've pulled you into this mess."

"We haven't done anything, yet," Anthony glowered. "And I didn't say I wouldn't talk to him." He winced at the naked gratitude in Graham's blue eyes.

"Thank you, Anthony." He gave a tight smile and headed to the café across the street.

I can't believe I'm doing this. He sat down at in a chair along the windows, eyeing the gaunt and slightly disheveled man at the next table. Anthony ordered a large coffee from the waitress who appeared at his side, and when the drink materialized, he took his time with the cream and sugar.

Two months ago, he would have pounded the Frenchman into a bloody stain on the pavement if he saw him on the street. But there he was, Felix Lalonde, casually sipping his coffee under an awning in front of a tiny coffee shop in London's Soho.

And I feel nothing but pity. Anthony clenched his fists and turned to speak when another man sat down at the Frenchman's table.

"Atherton?" Lalonde rose a few inches from his seat, glancing around the patio. "You cannot be here!"

"That court order doesn't apply to me, just my house," Graham snapped, pointing at the table. "Sit the fuck down." Felix glared at him but didn't argue and took to his chair.

"What do you want?"

"I want answers," he growled.

"What does it matter now?" Lalonde replied, acidly. "I am guilty. I've lost every–."

"You haven't lost everything," Graham hissed, his fists curling on the table. "You're still alive." A thick silence spanned a few moments as the two men glared at each other. "I want to know why."

"You want to know why," Felix repeated, averting his gaze, then spoke quietly. "I wanted her from the first moment I saw her, but then something changed." He raised half-closed eyes. "She cried for me. She wanted to save me, and I fell in–."

"Don't try to bullshit me," Graham shot back. "I know what you did to those other women. You would not be a free man if any of that were revealed."

Anthony's mouth dropped open. *Other women?*

"I am not free." Felix bent and pulled up his trouser leg to show the ankle monitor. "They know where I am at all times."

"Don't even." Graham shook his head. "You're not somebody's Sally, which I reckon you should experience. Perhaps then you would understand what you've done to her."

Felix clenched his jaw. "You dare lecture me?" He leaned closer, his thin lips stretching into a hard smile. "You and your little blonde whore. I have seen the photographs, but I suspect Loren hasn't, else you would not be so arrogant."

"You fucking bastard," he snarled and started to rise.

"Graham…" Anthony warned. Felix sat back in his chair, a sneer on his lips.

"She loved me. She trembled at my touch. She still does, and that is why you are here, is it not?" His smile widened. "The demon is eating you from the inside, and you think hurting me will soothe it, but it won't. It will always be whispering in your ear," he leaned closer, "I had her first." Graham jumped from his chair, shoving the table aside to reach Felix, but Anthony was faster and blocked his advance.

"That's enough!" They grappled for a few seconds until Anthony caught Graham's arm and bent it behind his back. "Stop it! It's not worth it." He gave the actor a shove toward the corner. "Go on!"

196

Graham stared blankly out the window of the Rover on the ride out of London.

How could I be such a fucking idiot? His stomach burned worse than before with the confrontation replaying in his mind. Anthony's voice startled him.

"You alright?"

"No, I'm not." He ran a hand over his stubbled chin. "I knew he was baiting me, but it was as if I were outside of my body. I couldn't stop myself."

"Just let it go. He's not worth it."

"I can't just let it go," he groaned. "The man who attacked her outside the Church is the same man that confronted me in the fucking loo at our hotel in London. Lalonde has something to do with it, and I wanted him to admit it. I wanted him to be repentant." He banged his clenched fists against his forehead. "What was I thinking? I'm no knight," he muttered.

"He's not a small man, Graham, but he showed true fear when you sat down at his table. If he weren't somewhat concerned of what you might do, that would not have been his reaction."

"Perhaps," he said and dropped his hands to his lap, hunching his shoulders. "But he's right. The demon has been eating at me for weeks. I've had dreams of her dying in my arms time and time again, and all the while he's laughing. I can't get it out of my head." Silence returned to the vehicle for another kilometer before Anthony spoke.

"I've had dreams like that. It's post-traumatic stress. What happened to Loren resonates with everyone she's touched, and we all feel we failed to protect her, but you feel it most because you're in love with her."

"And you're not?" he retorted, and Anthony gave him a hard look.

"I'm not in love with her," he answered. "I've wanted to hate you for hurting her, but I've never seen her smile like she does when she looks at you." He gripped the steering wheel tighter. "From the very beginning, you knew she was fragile, despite the front she puts up. You give her strength, so I can't hate you. Charlotte can, but I can't."

Graham huffed. "And yet you left me that threatening voicemail message."

"Yes, she needed you and you were being a fucking wanker."

"Yah, I was." He rubbed his forehead. "I don't know how to thank you."

"You don't have–." Both of their mobiles pinged text messages, and Graham picked his up.

"It's from Loren. They're going to The Kings Head near Palmers Green tonight, around nine."

Anthony eyed him. "What are you going to tell her?" Graham closed his eyes and banged his head against the headrest.

"How can I?"

"How can you not?" he shot back. "She's going to be right narked anyway, but I reckon because you got a swing at him first."

***

It was late when Penny settled in front of her laptop to write her report to Derek. She sat back into her chair and ran her hands through her long dark hair.

I thought I saw Lalonde at the pub but can't be certain it was him. Do I report that? She shook her head and her thoughts turned to how Jon Haskins' antics at the Expo left Loren unnerved.

"I'm going to hurt him if he doesn't stop manhandling her," Penny muttered, then heaved a sigh. *I'm letting it in, but I can't help it.* Her mobile rang then, and she glanced at it before picking it up.

"Hello, Uncle. I was just about to draft my report."

He huffed. "Hello, Niece. I'll look for it later. I received a message from Ramesh earlier. It appears Mr. Atherton had a rather intense conversation with Mr. Lalonde today."

Her eyes slid away. "That would explain his agitation this evening," she said. "Did Ramesh say what they spoke about?"

"He wanted to know why," he replied, and she dropped her chin.

"He wants to know why," she said, a tiny sneer forming on her lips. "I could tell him why." There was a moment of silence.

"Penny, you're too close to this."

"You're right," she replied, her composure crumbling. "I provoked Jacobson in New York. I let him think he got the drop on me because I wanted to hurt him. All I could hear was Loren screaming from behind the Church, and I was right back in Mosul, hearing Rosemary crying out in the cell next to me."

"I knew I shouldn't have let you see that," he muttered. "I'll be there in the morn–."

"Please don't take me off," she said, sniffling. "If anything were to happen to Loren and I wasn't there, I couldn't live with myself." She took a deep breath. "O'Connell is flying in on Wednesday. He'll work with me. We'll keep her safe until O'Dowd tracks down Jacobson."

"Fine," Derek grumbled. "But I'll still be there in the morning." He disconnected abruptly, and Penny covered her mouth with her hand.

What have I done?

***

198

3 November

What have I done?

The bedroom was draped in darkness, soothing to both the ache in his head and body as Felix dried out once again. His dreams since the confrontation with Graham Atherton were vivid and disturbing. Her sighs of pleasure, her skin like silk under his hands, but then he would be outside himself, watching helplessly as he repeatedly struck her, ripped her clothes and forced her over the back of the sofa. The turmoil had him scurrying to the corner bar to drink through his fear and disgust instead of calling on his AA sponsor.

How could I tell anyone? Felix rolled over onto his back, and a faint beep from his computer drew him from his bed. He touched the mouse, and the screen flared to life.

She was on her mobile, pacing across the floor. He couldn't hear her clearly at first; she was keeping her voice down, but she stopped suddenly and looked up.

"Why can't you just tell me what's really bothering you, because it's not about me stopping at my own house." She covered her eyes with her hand but not before Felix saw her tears. *"Right, it's nothing. You're just picking a fight with me for no reason."* Loren held the phone away from her as a male voice bellowed from the speaker.

"I'll talk to you tomorrow, Graham." She pressed the screen then dropped her mobile on her bed. Slumping down to the floor, she covered her face with her hands, but Felix wasn't surprised when she got up a minute later, wiping her fingers over her cheeks.

That's right. He is not worth your tears, mon trésor. The buzzing of his mobile interrupted his thoughts, and he reached over to pick it up. He had to hold the phone away from his ear as a male voice began yelling as soon as the call connected.

"Where have you been?" It was Michael Jacobson. "I've been trying to reach you for two days!"

"Why would I want to speak with you? I told you not to—."

"Fuckin' Montgomery backed out of our deal," he snarled. "I told you I was gonna get my money one way or the other, Lalonde. Your little whore's gonna pay me fifty grand if she doesn't want what I have to get out." Felix barked a laugh.

"You believe me a fool? If Montgomery backed out, you have nothing." His humor dissolved as Jacobson lowered his voice to a hiss.

"I'm gonna hurt her. I swear, I'm gonna break her fucking neck."

"You will do no such thing," he bit back. "You will stay away from her or I will—."

"You think you can stop me, you fucking pussy? Get in my way, and I'll kill you." The line went dead. Felix sat back in his chair, his heart racing and touched his fingers to her image on the screen.

"What do I do?" He squeezed his eyes shut. *I have to keep you safe, but how?*

***

4 November

Adam O'Connell exited baggage claim at Heathrow and almost burst out laughing at the sight before him. Loren, Penny and Graham stood in the middle of the concourse dressed in black suits, white dress shirts with skinny black ties and dark sunglasses. Penny was holding a sign with his last name on it. He smothered his grin and approached them.

"I believe you're looking for me?" Graham quickly took his bag as Loren put a hand on his elbow. Her heavy Yorkshire accent had him doubt who she was for a second.

"Of carse, sirah. 'Dis wa, plehse." She and Penny flanked him while Graham brought up the rear as they passed a group of photographers. Two heads followed them, with one nudging another and soon, the intruding lenses were pointed at *him*, not his escorts. Airport security blocked the photographers from following, and the foursome made their way toward the private parking garage.

"You guys are having too much fun with this," Adam muttered as Loren and Penny walked next to him. The agent just chuckled.

"Did you see their faces?" Loren giggled, removing her sunglasses. "They didn't know what to do!" She stopped and gave him a tight hug. "I'm glad you're here." She skipped ahead to catch Graham's hand.

"Her mood has improved immensely," Penny told him.

"I noticed," Adam said, then raised a brow. "Has our friend made an appearance?" Her smile tightened, and she slowed her pace.

"Jacobson, no, but our man covering Lalonde said Graham had a very intense conversation with him on Sunday." His brows went up further as she explained what her associate told her.

"Does Loren know?" he asked.

"No, but Derek will be having a rather pointed discussion with our employer soon enough."

Once at the car, Adam surveyed the parking garage until Loren and Graham were in their seats. Then he realized Penny was doing the same thing.

"Never take a day off, huh?"

"Takes one to know one," she retorted, shooting him a bright smile over her shoulder then disappeared into the back seat of the Jaguar. Loren glanced at him when Adam got in and closed his door. She ducked her chin and her gaze flicked to Graham in the driver's seat, then back to him. The tightness of her mouth sent a brow up.

"Um, I didn't plan anything to do today," she said. "I wasn't sure what you'd feel up to when you got here."

"That's cool," Adam replied. "I was going to head over to Nick's later on to get settled."

Her brows went up. "Nick's? I thought you would stay with me, I mean, with us." She quickly glanced at Graham.

"I don't want to put you out, either of you," he said.

"Oh, it's no bother, Adam," Graham countered with just a hint of disdain. "The house isn't completely full." Loren gave him a dark look, and Adam cleared his throat.

"Am I miss–?" She held her hand up but spoke to Graham.

"If you have a problem–."

"I don't have a problem with him," he bit back.

"Then why are you–."

Adam spoke louder. "Guys, I can stay at Nick's."

"No," she snapped, pinning him to his seat with her glare. "We will stay at my house." The Jaguar swerved in the lane as Graham turned to her.

"Did I not just say he can stay at mine?"

"Why are you being… You know what? Cleveland!" She crossed her arms tightly over her chest and turned away. Graham mumbled something and focused on the road, but a minute later, he placed his hand on her thigh, palm up.

"I'm being a knob," he muttered. She hesitated for a breath, then interlaced their fingers but kept her focus out the window. Adam glanced at Penny, who just rolled her eyes and waved him off. He cleared his throat again.

"How about we go get something to eat?"

"What an excellent idea," Penny chimed. "I'm famished."

***

After dinner at the Two Brothers, Adam followed Graham, Penny, and Loren into the house where she motioned to the hallway off the foyer.

"Come on, let's get you settled." Loren escorted him to the first door and opened it, revealing a large bedroom, decorated with modern furnishings accented with pale yellow and green.

"Penny's at the end of the hall, but you have separate bathrooms," she said as he flopped his suitcase on the bed.

"This is much nicer than Nick's hole of an apartment." He went over and poked his head into the large ensuite bath, his eyes widening at the multi-head stall shower. "Oh, I know what I'm doing first."

"It's a steam shower and the tub is jetted," she told him. "Maggie fell asleep in it." He chuckled and turned around to have his humor evaporate. Loren was standing in the middle of the room, her hands tightly clenched together.

"I'm sorry for earlier, in the car," she said. "We're still working on the communication thing, you know?" She took a deep breath. "That's what happened last week. We both said things, and it all blew up in our faces." She turned and took a few steps toward the windows.

"He wants so much to be the knight in shining armor that it's smothering sometimes, and yet for so long, that's exactly what I've dreamed about." She raked her fingers through her hair. "It's a fucking frustrating mess." Adam gave a slight grimace as he drew nearer.

"Wanting the thing and having the thing are two different things." She huffed and dropped her chin as he approached. "It doesn't mean there's something wrong with either of you, or that your relationship won't work out," he said, giving her chin a nudge with his knuckle. "Hell, you're light years away from most people. You've figured it out before you fucked it up."

"It still hurts."

"Of course it does," he said, touching her arm. "If it didn't hurt, you wouldn't love him." She eyed his hand on her, then raised a brow at him.

"I thought you said you didn't know much about relationships."

"I said I don't understand women," he replied, leaning toward her with a tiny smile. "I've ruined enough relationships to have pretty good hindsight." Her expression was neutral, but he could sense the current of emotions beneath.

"How easily we've fallen into these roles," she murmured finally.

"Like it was meant to be," he answered with a smirk.

She huffed. "Why don't you get settled and have a wash, as they say here, then we'll give Maggie a call." She glanced at her watch. "It's a little after two there."

"Sounds like a plan," Adam said as she turned to leave. "Uh, about tomorrow." She faced him, her brows up. "I have a meeting at the London office in the morning, and I was going to meet up with Nick after," he said, giving a tight smile. "I'm going to need a ride to the train."

"Graham has a meeting as well, but we can talk about it later," she said, then gave a little smile. "Enjoy your shower."

Loren closed the door and walked out into the kitchen where her mood soured. Graham was out on the deck without a jacket, a hand on his hip while the other dragged through his hair. He then stomped down the steps to the grass and turned to scowl at the house.

What did I do now? Her gaze scanned the great room. No glasses were left on the coffee table, and the sink was empty. She sighed, put on her sweatshirt, grabbed a jacket for him and went outside.

"Hey," she called as she closed the slider. "All's well?" He glared at her, then returned to the view. Loren hopped off the deck to the spongy earth, grimacing at her trainers squelching in the mud and walked over to drape his jacket over his shoulders.

"This isn't working," he grumbled, shoving his arms into the sleeves. Her stomach bottomed out as she licked her lips.

"W-what's not working?" He half turned to her, extending his arm to the yard. There was a white remote in his hand.

"The floodlight sensor," he replied sharply. "It's not fucking working." When she could breathe again, she spoke.

"The floodlight sensor. Right." She jogged halfway to the rear of the property and started jumping up and down, waving her arms in the air. The floodlights came on, blinding her.

"Aw fuck," she muttered, covering her eyes with her hand and headed back to him. "They're working now."

"Thank you for that brilliant deduction, Watson." She stopped short, her brows up, and Graham winced. "That was uncalled for," he said, coming nearer. "I'm sor… I don't mean to take my frustration out on you." She put her hand on the side of his neck.

"How about you just talk to me." He gave a long exhale and dropped arms to his sides.

"I did something, and I don't want to tell you because it was stupid and egotistical, but I can't let it go, and it's burning me up." His blue eyes welled up when they reached hers. "I confronted Felix."

"You did what?" She took a step back. "When?"

"Sunday, when you were at the bike expo," he replied quietly. "I wanted him to be penitent, but he wasn't, and I let him get into my head. I wanted to hurt him, and if it weren't for Anthony–."

"You dragged Anthony into it? Graham!" She turned around in a circle, clutching at her hair. "What were you thinking?"

"I wasn't thinking!" he cried, holding his hands out to her. "I wasn't rational, but I had to do something. It's been building and building!" She gaped at him for a second.

"Did you think he was just going to roll over and let you beat him up? He's a fucking sick, narcissistic bastard and he infects everyone he touches!" Loren clenched her teeth. "What did he tell you? That I let him? That I enjoyed it? What did he say?" She shoved him in the chest. "Tell me what he said!"

Graham didn't look at her. "He said he had you first." Her eyes traveled over his hunched shoulders, his arms limp at his sides, and her anger abated, but only a little.

"It bothers you that I wasn't a virgin?" His head came up and gave an incredulous snort.

"No. I don't see how–."

"You're not upset that I was with Philippe or Ted or Edward before you. You're just upset because *Felix* said he had me."

He blew out a breath. "I know it's irrational but I–." Loren stepped closer.

"Sex for Felix is not about love, or sharing yourself, or any emotion at all. It's about domination," she said, her voice hard. "He wanted to own me. He wanted to get inside my head and make me a slave. That's what parasites like him do." She grasped his hands tightly, tears filling her eyes. "I know how hard all this is for you. You had no idea what you were getting into when you stopped to help me, and I'm sorry for that. I wouldn't blame you if you–." Graham abruptly gathered her in his arms.

"You're the best thing that's ever happened to me," he whispered. "You see me like no one ever has and you still love me."

"Yes, I do. Very much." Loren held him another minute, then drew back. "This is what we need to keep doing; telling each other how we feel, no matter what."

He gave a little smile. "I like how I was feeling when I was holding you just then." She shivered at a sudden gust of cold wind.

"How about you hold me inside. It's a little chilly out here." He huffed and took her hand to lead her into the house, but her thoughts swirled with the leaves on the deck. When she slid the door closed, she turned to him as he started into the kitchen.

"How did you know where he would be?" He stopped but didn't turn all the way around.

"I, ah, I've had him followed."

Her anger reignited. "Is that what Derek's been doing? Is that the *real* reason why Penny came on?" Graham opened his mouth to reply, but no sound came out. She smacked her forehead. "Oh my god! And he agreed to do that?"

"Up until perhaps the middle of the month, Derek felt Felix was still a credible threat."

"And what happened to change his mind?" Graham raked his fingers through his hair.

"They found out Felix was admitted to a rehab hospital." Her eyes narrowed, and she moved closer to him.

"And you know that how, exactly?" He still wouldn't look at her.

"They send me weekly reports."

"I want to see these reports," she snarled. He nodded and slowly walked toward his study, then sat down at his desk and called up the files on his computer. The reports detailed an agent following Felix to various locations within a ten-mile parameter of his apartment for about a month, then on 5 October, the agent relayed about the hospital admission.

She tapped the screen. "This confirms he went to rehab."

"If you believe what the agent was told," Graham scoffed.

"Why wouldn't you? Theresa said treatment was part of his plea bargain," she answered. "If outpatient wasn't working, he would have to go inpatient or go back to jail." She looked at the screen again. "But this means he wasn't in contact with Jacobson the entire time that fucker was harassing me." Her eyes slid away, her thoughts rolling. "What if he was really trying to change?"

"Loren, this doesn't say he wants to change," he retorted. "He's playing the system."

"You couldn't give him the–."

"Hey, guys." They both looked up at Adam standing in the doorway. "You want to call Maggie now?" Loren pointed her thumb at Graham.

"Do you know what he did? He confronted Felix on Sunday." Her brother's eyes flicked from her to Graham, and back.

"Well, that's unexpected." He nodded slowly. "I'm equally shocked and impressed."

She gaped at him. "Do not encourage him!"

***

5 November

His book went flying from his hands at the pounding on the apartment door.

"Lalonde! Open up!"

"*Merde*," he muttered, picking up his book, but didn't otherwise move. A fist hit the door again.

"I know you're in there, you fucking son of a bitch!" Felix got up and slowly went to the foyer.

"Go away before someone calls the police!" Michael Jacobson hammered on the door.

"Open up, or I'll break it down!"

"Fine," he grumbled. At the snap of the deadbolt, the door burst open and he was slammed into the wall with a casted forearm pressing into his throat.

"I warned you. If you got in my way, I'd kill you," Jacobson spat. "Tell me where she is."

"I don't know," Felix wheezed.

"Bullshit. You know every move she makes." Jacobson leaned further into his throat. "Tell me where she is, or you're fucking dead."

"Harrow…" he choked. "She's gone… Harrow."

"There now," Jacobson cooed. "That wasn't so hard, was it?"

Felix brought an arm up to block the cast coming for his head, then blackness.

***

Music echoed up the hall and into the garage of IDC's training center. Penny drew the roll of packing tape over the top of a box of training manuals while humming and moving her hips with the beat. Her mobile pinged a text then and she put the roll down to reach for it when a breath of cold air licked the back of her neck.

That came from the lobby. She glanced at her watch. *Aria and Sven only just left.* Senses on high alert, she eyed a box cutter lying within easy reach. Penny flicked her long dark hair over her shoulder, pretending to read the screen of her mobile when a familiar ringtone cut off the music. Her ears then confirmed what she sensed: heavy footsteps on concrete, coming toward her.

Come closer, said the spider. She moved fast, stepping around the stack of boxes to grab the cutter to hold it behind her. She then turned to face the intruder and forced her expression to stay neutral, even as her heart rate spiked at the man continuing across the garage.

"Do you not learn from your mistakes?" she said, and Michael Jacobson held up his casted hand.

"You're gonna pay for this, bitch." He lunged and caught her forearm, but she easily broke the hold and swiped at his arm with the cutter as she moved out of his range. He came at her again, only to receive another slice on his arm.

"I'm gonna kill you," he snarled.

"You can try," she replied and kicked a wheeled cart at him. He tossed it out of the way, swinging his casted fist at her head, but she weaved to avoid it. He jabbed, she evaded. He threw punches, she countered, bloodying his nose and drawing him further away from the lobby door.

Jacobson came at her again with an overhand swing, but instead of dodging as he expected, she stepped into it, blocking with her raised left arm and jabbing his throat with her pointed right knuckles at the same time. He stumbled away from her, coughing and holding his neck.

A screech echoed up the hallway, drawing Penny's attention for a half-second, when searing pain knocked her backward, stealing her breath. Taser electrodes stuck out from her chest. Blue fire snaked up the wire to the bolts, sending lightning coursing through her muscles.

"Who's laughing now, bitch," Jacobson sneered, wiping the blood from his mouth. He hit the button again and sent another jolt through the quivering woman on the floor.

***

Loren was in Aria's office, packing a box when the music playing on her mobile was interrupted by Graham's ringtone.

"Hey you," she purred when the call connected. "Did you have a good meeting?"

"I did. I'm excited about the opportunity to do voiceover work. It's not something I've done before," his reply was hollow-sounding through the speaker. "The best thing is I get to stay home."

She grinned. "You mean I can come home after a hard day of training, and you'll have dinner and a bath ready for me?"

"I could do that, once or twice," he laughed. "In other news, the meeting ended in time for me to catch Adam and Nick for lunch."

Her brother chimed in then. "Your boyfriend's a funny guy. I barely got in a word with the two of them riffing off each other."

"I'm not surprised," she laughed, and Graham spoke again.

"Anyroad, I wanted to let you know we are almost to you. There's a bit of construction on the 401, but I reckon we'll arrive in fifteen minutes or so. Is anyone there with you?"

"Penny's in the garage, sealing up boxes," she replied. "Aria and Sven left for Harrow already, but we should be done by the time you get here."

"Alright, love. See you in a bit."

"Bye, sweetheart!" Adam laughed, and the call disconnected. Chuckling, Loren placed her mobile on the desk and turned the music back on, but a minute later, she hit pause and turned to the door.

Was that a crash? She moved to stand in the doorway and listened. Not hearing anything else, she turned back to the room when a hand went over her mouth. An arm slid around her throat, jerking her backward and off her feet and she was dragged kicking and screaming into the darkened adjacent room then thrown face first to the floor. A body pressed heavily on her upper back.

"I will let you up, but you must remain silent," he growled in her ear. "Do not make me harm you any further." She nodded and he moved off. Loren pushed up from the floor and lurched away, her nails biting into her palms.

"Felix, you fucking son of a bitch!" A right cross, followed immediately by a left, connected with his face before he could shove her away.

"Stop it! I don't want to hurt you."

"You don't want to hurt me?" She went at him again, and her punch connected with his cheek. Blocking his counter, she went to strike at his nose with the heel of her hand when his fist met her stomach, and Loren dropped to her knees, coughing. His fingers dug into her hair and her head back.

"Why do you make me do this?" Felix hissed. "There is a man here who means to do you harm. Now get up." He shoved her away. She put her hands out to stop her momentum, then lumbered to her feet.

"He's here?" she squeaked. "Jacobson is here?"

Felix scowled at her. "You know his name."

"I know he's working for you."

"No," he said, shaking his head. "I did not order him to harm you, but I did set us on this path, long ago. I promise, I will put it right." Her breath caught in her throat when he turned fully to her. His left eye was swollen to a slit, his face blotted with bruises.

"I didn't do that to you," she said, moving closer and extending her hand to touch his cheek. He closed his eyes and leaned into her caress. "Jacobson did this?"

"I wouldn't tell him where you were."

"Why would you do that?" His dark eyes burned as he looked to her.

"To protect you. All I have done is for you," he whispered, closing the distance between them. "I should have stopped him. *Je suis désolé, mon amour. J'avais peur.*" His eyes flicked to her mouth. "I love you, Loren. I always have." He pressed his lips against hers and their heat melted her resistance.

His arms slipped around her, drawing her against him, but Loren came to her senses and pushed him away.

"No," she said. "This isn't right."

"Yes, it is. You were meant to be with me." He held her face in his hands. "Come with me. I will make certain you are safe." She rocked back, shaking her head.

"I'm not alone here."

"It matters not," he said, taking a small pistol out of his pocket. Her mouth dropped open.

"What are you going to do with that?" Her hand reached to her back pocket to touch the titanium ASP she carried.

"I'm going to keep you safe. Now, let's go." He grabbed her arm, but she got out of his grip.

"I'm not going anywhere with you. Pen–!" His slap cut off her shriek. She stumbled, then glared at him, her hand to her cheek. With a flick of her wrist, the baton was extended. "You fucking bastard."

"*Tais-toi!* I tell you, he is here to hurt you!" Felix clutched at her arm and dragged her into the hall.

"Let go!" Loren twisted her wrist out of his grip and swung at him. A hollow *twang* came from titanium hitting wood. She missed, and Felix shoved her against the wall, pressing her own forearm to her throat.

"Drop it." He leaned into her. "I said drop it." She opened her hand and the baton clanked to the floor. "Good girl. Now, do as I say, or you will not survive. Do you understand? He will not hesitate to kill you, or me. Now, go!" He forced her through the door and toward the rear exit. She grappled with him, getting in a good punch to his bruised cheek and he let go. Loren dove for the ASP but he caught her ponytail and yanked her backward, then shoved her into the conference room. She stumbled into the chairs, sending them in all directions.

"I am trying to keep you safe!" he screamed.

"She's not safe anywhere, Lalonde," Jacobson said, shouldering past Felix, his squinty gaze on Loren. "You owe me fifty grand bitch and I'm taking it out of your sweet ass." She backed up a step, fear and fury mixing. The baton was in her hand, and with a flick of her arm, the shaft snapped open.

"You can leave now, La–." She threw all her weight into her swing, hitting him as he turned back to her. Jacobson lurched sideways, and she went for the backhand strike, but he caught her wrist.

"Whoa, that tickled," he laughed, squeezing hard and forcing her to drop the weapon. His eyes flicked to follow it, and Loren jabbed at his bloody nose with her other fist, but Jacobson dodged it and seized her by the throat to pull her in close.

"That's right, baby. Fight me. It's turning me on." He lifted her off her feet and slammed her onto the table, pinning her right arm beneath her. Dazed and struggling for breath, she feebly fought against him forcing her thighs apart. He leaned heavily onto her, still squeezing her throat, and sniffed at her chest.

"You smell so good, baby," he muttered. "I get why you can't leave her alone, Lalonde." His big hand cupped her breast and his fingers caught the neck of her shirt and jerked it down, exposing her bra.

"No," she choked, struggling to push him away with one arm. Her eyes locked on Felix, standing behind Jacobson. "Felix, help me."

"Don't bother, baby," Jacobson muttered. "He wants to watch." He drew his tongue over her skin, hooking his finger under the edge of her bra cup and pulled it down, revealing her naked breast. "I bet you taste real sweet." Loren screeched as he bit her.

"Stop!" Felix shouted behind them. "You will let her be, or I will shoot!" Jacobson pressed onto her more to look over his shoulder, forcing any remaining air out of her lungs, but his shifting weight gave her the chance to pull her arm free.

"You gonna shoot me with that little pop gun there?" he laughed. "I don't think so." He turned back into her strike to his nose, and the bones crunched under her knuckles. Howling, he retreated, and Loren rolled over to fall to the floor, gasping. A sharp pop had her diving under the table and covering her ears.

"You shot me! You little faggot!"

The impact of shattering glass brought Loren out from under the table. Large, razor-edged pieces stuck out from the frame of the glass wall that separated the conference room from the hall and hand-sized shards glittered on the carpet. Felix was struggling to get up on the other side of the opening, bleeding from cuts on his arms and face. He raised his arm and pointed the gun at Jacobson again.

"Stay back!"

"I warned you, Lalonde. You get in my way, and I'll kill you." He stepped through the now empty frame while reaching into his back pocket. With a metallic click, a switchblade snapped out from the handle. Felix fired again, and Loren jumped back under the table as a bullet sizzled through the air to hit the wall behind her.

"You little..." He rushed at Felix, but the smaller man couldn't block the thrust aimed for his midsection, and his face contorting in a silent scream. Jacobson seized him by his jacket and threw him against the wall, punching at his head and sides, and Felix collapsed to the floor.

"No!" Loren scuttled out from under the table, her palms scraping on the twinkling pieces covering the carpet. Her gaze lit on ASP she dropped and grabbed it as she got to her feet and slammed the titanium shaft into the side of Jacobson's head. He pitched with her strike, then spun around with his arm out. She evaded his reach and hit him again, the force turning his head.

"It's your turn, bitch," he laughed then lunged, both arms extended, forcing Loren to shuffle backward. His long reach overcame her defense, and he caught her by the throat. She scratched at his burly forearms and kicked hard at his midsection, but Jacobson just laughed again, then rammed her against the wall, cracking the drywall.

She clutched at his hands, her vision clouding, fighting for each tiny breath when someone screamed her name. The hands holding her let go, and she crumpled to her knees, coughing and wheezing. Two sets of feet entered her field of vision, and one was wearing brown boots.

Loren looked up. "*Graham! No!*"

Jacobson backed away from the onslaught of jabs and uppercuts to his face and midsection. A well-placed strike with a solid boot heel to the outside of his knee brought Jacobson low, and a sharp right cross snapped his head back. He staggered a bit, then retaliated with an upward swing but missed. Graham hit him again, bloodying his knuckles on Jacobson's face when he stepped into a casted backhand hit him on the chin.

Loren screamed as he lurched backward and went down to the floor in a heap. She heaved to her feet, fists clenched and ready to fight, but his attention was focused on a new foe.

"You should have stayed in New York, pal," Adam taunted, waving Loren off. She snarled at him, then turned and sprinted to Graham's side. Blood trickled from the corner of his mouth, and the left side of his jaw was already beginning to swell beneath his beard. She pressed her fingers to his jugular and let out a sob of relief at his steady heartbeat. Gently, she pulled his eyes open to check for pupil dilation. Both were splotched with broken vessels but reacted to the light. He moaned and rolled his head away.

A grunt from directly behind them had her glance over her shoulder in time to see Jacobson reel toward them. She shoved her hands under Graham's arms and dragged him further down the hall.

"Graham, please, wake up. Please." He groaned as she eased him down to the floor. Felix was slumped against the wall across the hall from them, struggling to breathe. Her chin trembled as she kissed Graham's forehead.

"I'll be right back," she whispered and got up, but Adam and Jacobson barred her way. Her brother was the epitome of calm and cool facing the much larger man.

"You have a choice here," he said. "You can get down on your knees, put your hands on your head and wait for the police, or I'm going to hurt you."

212

"Yeah, right," Jacobson scoffed, then went after him. Adam ducked the incoming casted fist, pivoted into the attack and slammed his elbow into Jacobson's face. Loren's jaw dropped as he fell like a tree.

"Holy shit." A groan pierced her stupor, and she rushed to kneel next to Felix and touched his shoulder. "Felix," she whispered. Both of his eyes were swollen shut. He coughed, and his bloody hand fell away from his chest, revealing the hilt of a knife protruding from his stomach.

"Oh, god. Adam!" Loren ripped off the hem of her shirt and pressed the cloth to his wound, but the strip was soaked with dark blood in seconds.

"I already called Emergency Services," he replied from behind her.

"Felix?" She touched his cheek. "You're going to be alright. Just stay with me."

"*Mon tresor*," he choked. "I'm sorry. I tried to change for you."

"Shhh, don't talk now." She started to split another strip of cloth from her shirt when he touched her hand.

"Please, forgive me," he whispered. "Please." His breathing became labored and his eyes closed. "I love you."

"No, no, Felix. Please, stay awake!" She pressed her fingers against his neck and felt for his pulse but there was none. "No!" she wailed. "You don't get to do this to me!" Loren pushed him over to his back, intent on starting CPR, but the full extent of his injuries stopped her. The wound was deep, and the skin of his abdomen stained a deep purple. She flinched away from the smell, pressing the back of her hand over her mouth.

Oh god, he's dead. She licked her lips and tasted blood. Then she saw her hands. Loren staggered away to clutch the doorjam of the conference room and retch. The glint of steel caught her attention. Her gaze flicked to Adam, who had a woozy Jacobson on his knees with his arm pinned behind him at an odd angle. Rage bubbled to the surface of her mind, tightening every muscle in her body. She picked up the gun and approached, her hands steady, and pointed the barrel at Jacobson's head. She cocked the hammer, keeping her finger on the trigger.

"Jesus! Would you put the fucking thing down," Adam barked, nudging her with his elbow.

"He needs to pay for what he's done."

"Dammit, Loren. You don't want to do that. Believe me." Sirens echoed through the building. "The police are here. Put the gun down. Now!" She jumped when he stomped on her foot.

"Ow! Fine!" She then uncocked the hammer, reversed her hold on the gun and applied the grip to the back of Jacobson's head, hard. Adam let go as the large man went limp, then grabbed the gun from her.

"What did you do that for?"

"He killed Felix," she replied, scowling at the unconscious body at her feet.

"Snap out of it." Adam gave her a shove. "Go back to Graham. I have to check on Penny. I left her in the lobby." Loren nodded once, then kicked Jacobson in the side before limping off, swearing under her breath. Graham's eyes fluttered when she knelt behind his head.

"Don't move, love," she murmured, sliding her hands under his neck to steady him. "The ambulance is here. You're going to be okay."

"I'm fine," he mumbled and began to move his arms and legs.

"No, you're not." She kissed his forehead. "Please, just stay still." His bloodshot eyes focused on her face.

"Are you okay?" he croaked, and her gaze went to the body across the hall.

"No, I'm not."

***

After giving her statement to a detective, Loren stayed with Graham as the EMS team packed him up, then walked with them to the lobby. He tried to turn his head against the neck brace when she let go of his hand.

"No, Loren, please don't leave me."

"You're going to be okay. I'm right behind you." She swallowed her tears as the tech pushed his gurney through the doors, then turned to see Penny on another stretcher nearby. She approached, noticing wires tangled around the agent that connected to a small machine at her feet. Penny struggled to sit up, but Loren stopped her.

"Hey, don't do that. You already look like hell."

"Have you seen a mirror?" Penny said. "It's just a wee bump on the head. I'll be fine."

"Bump on the head, huh? Is that why there's a charged defibrillator attached to you?"

"I'll be fine," the agent replied flatly.

"Adam said he left you up here."

"I made him help you first," she replied, her voice even raspier. A paramedic came between them. Loren squeezed Penny's hand, then let go to move out of the way. She twisted the hem of her warmup jacket watching them push the gurney out the double doors and jumped at a light touch on her shoulder.

"I'm sorry, I didn't mean to startle you," said a woman paramedic. "Come and sit down so I can assess you."

"I'm okay. I'm just a little sore in places," Loren told, but followed the medic to one of the couches in the lobby and sat down.

"Head up, please." Loren winced at the penlight in her eyes, and the medic nodded. "Alright, remove your jacket." Reluctantly, she unzipped her jacket, revealing her tattered shirt and turned her head away. "Your neck is a bit red, but I'm concerned–."

"It's fine," Loren countered, flinching when the medic moved her shirt away from her chest, exposing her upper breast. She pushed the medic's hand away. "I said I'm fine."

"Have you had a tetanus shot?"

She clenched her jaw. "Yes. Last year."

The medic put her hand out. "Your hands, please." She raised a brow at her bloody knuckles, then pulled out a packet of antiseptic wipes from her bag to clean the abrasions and a cut on Loren's cheek, then covered it with a small wing bandage. She pulled out another packet of wet wipes and handed them over.

"If you feel light-headed, nauseous, or your pain increases, go to the clinic immediately." She then gave her a business card. "This is in case you need to talk." Loren held back a cringe at Dr. Pallas' name on it.

"Thanks," she muttered, zipping up her jacket again. She waited until the woman walked away before shoving the card in her back pocket. Movement caught her eye as DI Gordon Carson entered the lobby with Adam, in handcuffs. Loren jumped off the couch to cut them off from the exit.

"Where are you taking him?"

Adam sighed. "Loren, don't–."

"You listen here, Gordon Carson," she growled, poking the DI in the chest. "You have no reason to put my brother in cuffs."

"Take him to Gilligan's car, please," Carson said and handed Adam off to a uniformed officer. "Settle down, Loren. It's procedure."

"Bullshit it's procedure!" She shoved her wrists in his face. "Then I should be in handcuffs, too!"

"Did you beat somebody up? Did you kill someone?" She opened her mouth to answer but dropped her arms to glower at him. Carson bent slightly to meet her eyes. "Is there somewhere we can go and talk?" Loren glanced around the lobby, quickly averted her eyes from the two men pushing a gurney with a long black bag on it.

"Yah, outside," she muttered. Clutching at the neck of her jacket, she led Carson down the hall. The smell hit her then, and Loren slapped her hand over her mouth and nose and bolted passed the dark stain on the carpet. She burst through the rear door to a small grassy area and stumbled over to the trash bin to throw up.

"Easy, there," Gordon cooed, patting her back. When she straightened, he helped her to a bench then gave her a few moments to pull herself together but became increasingly alarmed when she hadn't moved from her slumped position. He placed a hand on her arm.

"Loren, are you al–." She was trembling, and Carson knelt next to her. Her pupils were dilated, and she was gasping for breath.

"Fuck," he muttered and grabbed his radio from his jacket pocket. "Neuland? If there's a medic still on scene, send them out back. Loren's gone into shock."

***

Adam O'Connell avoided his reflection in the two-way mirror on the wall of the interview room, choosing instead to focus on the steam from the cup of coffee between his hands. Officer Gilligan stood at the open door.

"You're not being held on any charges, but DS O'Dowd wants to speak with you," he said. "She won't be long, I suspect."

"I'll be right here," Adam replied, and shook his head at Gilligan's cackle. "*I'm not that funny*," he muttered under his breath.

His coffee was cold by the time the door opened, and a statuesque woman entered, reading a file in her hands. She didn't speak as she sat down and placed the folder on the table before her. Adam noted a quickly suppressed look of surprise when she finally looked at him.

"I apologize for the delay. I'm Detective Sergeant Theresa O'Dowd," she said and offered her hand to him. She was striking, with dark hair and eyes set against ivory skin, and dressed in a well-tailored suit jacket.

"Nice to meet you." Her hand was warm and dry, and he felt a little zing at her touch. She let go, then pulled in her chair further, and removed a small tablet from her jacket pocket. A crease appeared between her brows as she swiped at the screen.

He coughed softly. "So, you're keeping me here because…" he drawled, and she shook her head.

"I'm sorry, I was waiting for my partner to send me Loren's statement." Her deep brown eyes meeting his gaze again.

"Is she alright?"

"Quite shaken, as I'm sure you can imagine," she answered, and glanced down at the screen. "Mr. O'Connell, I've read your statement, but I'd like to review a few points with you, if you don't mind."

"Of course, and please, call me Adam." He sat up in his seat, his palms flat on the table.

"As you wish, Adam." He liked the way the corners of her mouth curled up as she said his name. "When you and Graham arrived at IDC's training center, what did you observe?"

"We had just gotten out of the car when I heard a gunshot," he said. "I told Graham to go around the back while I took the front. I figured he'd be safer if I went in first, but he runs faster than I thought, and I didn't anticipate finding Penny O'Neill lying on the floor in the lobby."

He pursed his lips. "Graham tried to be a hero, which only got him hurt. Lalonde was on the floor and didn't look good, so I didn't bother. Jacobson was the real threat."

"Mr. Jacobson has stated that Loren pistol-whipped him."

Adam met her gaze directly. "No. I had the gun, and when he took a swipe at me with his cast, I knocked him out."

Her frown appeared again. "Felix Lalonde is dead."

"Yeah, I assumed so," he muttered, shaking his head. "How's Graham?"

"I'm not certain. He was taken to hospital with Ms. O'Neill."

"She had a heart attack, didn't she?"

The DS slid her eyes away. "Again, I'm not certain. I do know she's in the ICU." O'Dowd swiped at the screen of her tablet. "You are former Army?"

"Yes, 75th Ranger Regiment. Discharged two years ago."

"You're a security agent, like O'Neill and Derek Graves, but you're not with Lester?"

"That's right. I'm with a different firm." She typed something on her pad.

"How long will you be in England?"

"Probably no more than a week, but that depends on my sister," he replied. She tilted her head, and that tiny smile returned her lips.

"I've known Loren for a few years now, but I wasn't aware she had a brother. Well, other than Anthony and Colin Ainsworth." The reminder of his failure was a kick in the shin, and felt he needed to explain.

"When our parents died, we were placed in separate foster homes," he said. "We only just reconnected." There were questions in her eyes, but she didn't ask them.

"That's good, for both of you," she said. "Loren is a survivor, and I admire her for that." His smile mirrored hers and neither looked away for several moments when his stomach decided to make itself known.

Adam gave a cringing grin. "Lunch was a long time ago."

"Come on, then," O'Dowd gave a deep chuckle. "I know a good pub not far from here. My partner will keep us updated."

***

Loren had quickly shaken off her stupor when another medic tried to check her over at the training center. She then pestered Carson to drive her to University Hospital where Graham was taken, unshed tears giving her plea added power. Once there, he escorted her to a consultation room where she told him what happened without holding back anything, even holding the gun to Jacobson's head. They stared at each other across the table after she finished.

"Felix was trying to change, Gordon," she croaked. "He asked me to forgive him, but I don't know how to do that. He's done so much, and not just to me. Five other women won't get justice."

He touched her hand. "But, it's over now. He can't touch you or them, ever again." She nodded, sitting back in her chair when there was a knock on the door and a man in blue scrubs entered.

"DS Carson? Ms. Mackenzie? I'm Simon Marcum. I've been taking care of Mr. Atherton."

Loren jumped to her feet. "How is he?"

"He's been taken to CT, but I can take you to his room," Simon replied and opened door. Loren and Carson followed him out to the long hallway and through the steel doors of the Emergency Department. Her brain was slow to process what the nurse told them.

"He's having a CT? Does he have a concussion?"

"We were concerned about the possibility, along with other injuries," Simon answered. "He lost a molar and has eight or nine stitches in his mouth along with quite a bit of bruising and swelling, so we'll be watching him for a few more hours." Loren threw an anxious glance at Carson when they halted at Room 12.

"Here we are." The nurse slid the door open. "He'll be back soon."

"Thank you," Loren said and entered the meager quarters, fiddling with the zipper pull at the neck of her jacket. The bed was missing, but Graham's boots and a large plastic bag marked 'patient's clothing' were sitting on the chair next to the window. She darted over and opened it.

"Just his jeans and sweater," she said, looking up at Carson. "At least he's not running around bare-assed." He snickered and patted her on the shoulder.

"I'm sure he'll be fine."

"You don't have to stay. I'll be okay."

His frown returned. "Are you certain? I can faff about for a bit."

"No, I'm alright. Just don't rough up Adam too much, okay?" A corner of his mouth went up.

"Not any more than he already has been," he said. "O'Dowd's taking him to the Church for some nosh."

"Oh jeez," Loren huffed and shook her head but as the door closed behind him, her humor vanished. The walls began to close in, backing her to the chair. She picked up the bag with Graham's belongings, hugging them to her chest and curled up on the cold vinyl.

It's all my fault. She shook her head. "Stop it. I have to keep it together." Launching from the chair, she took the bag and his boots with her to the bathroom. She took out the sweater to inspect it, brushing her fingers over the soft brown wool, then cried as she scrubbed the few spots of his blood from it. After hanging it up to dry, she checked his boots. She sniffled and wiped her sleeve under her nose.

I better leave them alone. I don't want to ruin them. Loren went back into the room and curled up on the chair again, clutching his boots and stared out the window. It looked windy; the bare branches of the trees were swaying outside. Dark thoughts swirled with the clouds in the sky.

What if he were hurt worse? He could have died. She squeezed her eyes shut. *Stop it! He's going to be fine. He has to be. I can't lose him.* Tears slid down her cheeks to the leather of his boots.

An hour passed when the door slid open, and Simon entered, walking backward to maneuver a bed through the doorway. Loren stood, biting her lip as they went by her. Graham's eyes were closed, and he was whiter than the blankets covering him, save for the purple-black bruising on his cheek and jaw. The nurses murmured to each other as they reattached his leads, bringing the machines that lined the wall behind the bed back to life.

Simon smiled at her as he followed his co-workers from the room. Loren watched Graham for a few moments, trying to hold in the despair when he grumbled and turned over but became tangled up in the wires and IV tubes.

"Dammit," he mumbled, then hissed, putting a hand on his cheek.

"I guess a good snog is out of the question?" His eyes popped open and she moved to sit on the bed next to him. "No, no, lay back down," she told him, laying her hands on his chest.

"You'll just have to be gentle with me," he mumbled, and she burst out a laugh that eroded into soft sobs. She leaned closer, hesitating to touch his unbruised cheek when he pulled her in and kissed her as best as he could. Loren brushed her lips across his mouth, his cheek, his nose and eyes to gently press her forehead to his.

"What were you thinking? He could have killed you!"

"I wasn't thinking," he croaked, caressing her face. The pulse monitor began to alarm. "He had you by the throat, and all I could see were my nightmares coming true. I had to do something."

"Don't you ever do anything like that again," she sniffled and lay her head down on his chest. She closed her eyes, tucking her arms under him and holding him tight. "I can't lose you, Graham."

"You won't lose me," his voice rumbled in her ear. "Are you alright? You have a plaster on your cheek."

"I have a what?" Loren drew back and touched her face. "Oh, a Band-Aid." She sniffled again. "No, I'm not okay. Felix is dead." She closed her eyes and saw his lifeless body on the floor in the hallway.

"What? How?"

"Jacobson stabbed him," she answered quietly. "Felix had a gun and shot him to try and get him away from me, but that just pissed him off." She held her breath for a second, but her tears overwhelmed her. "It didn't have to end this way. He didn't have to die. It's all my fault."

"No, it's not," he whispered, drawing her into his arms and holding her close. "It's over now, love. It's finally over."

***

Manhattan, New York

Ron Hudson's mobile buzzed on the other side of his desk. He glanced at the ID, then quickly reached for it with a smirk on his face.

"Penny," he drawled. "You can't be missing me already." There was a brief pause, and when she spoke, her words were stilted.

"They tell me I'm not supposed to be using the telephone, but I'm finding I need to hear your voice."

"What do you mean you're not supposed to–." He sat up straight in his chair. "Penny, what's happened?"

"Derek says Lalonde is dead and Michael Jacobson has been arrested for his murder," she said, weakly. "Adam was involved, as I'm fairly certain he picked me up off the floor. Am I slurring?"

"Picked you up off the… Dearest, you're not making sense."

"I made a mistake, love. Loren and Graham were hurt because of me. I got too close. What happened to her, happened to me, too." She took a deep breath, but it came out as a sob. "We were in Mosul, but something went horribly wrong and we were taken. The guards, they assaulted us. Rosemary fought them, and they killed her. I heard her screaming!"

His mouth dropped open. "Oh, god, Penny. My dearest, I–." Her tears stopped abruptly.

"Ron, they need you here. The police will have to question them again." He swallowed hard, then checked his watch. He reached over to grab his tablet and logged into the British Airways app.

"The next flight is at 5:30. I'll make sure I'm on it."

"Good." She paused for a moment. "And Ron?"

"Yes, love?"

"I think I might need you, as well," she whispered.

"I'll take care of you, I promise."

"I just might let you."

***

Northaw, England

220

Lights from the house flickered through the darkened trees as a Skoda sedan pulled up to the gate on Vineyards. Theresa glanced at Adam in the passenger seat.

"Do you know the code?" He leaned forward to look at the keypad.

"Ah, no."

"Do you reckon they're still awake?" she asked. "Shall I press the intercom?" Before he could reply, the keypad buzzed, and the gate slowly swung open. "And there's my answer," she chuckled, releasing the parking brake and proceeded down the driveway to turn around before the garage. She turned off the engine, and they were both quiet for several moments before Adam turned to face her.

"Thank you, Theresa, for everything."

"I wish I could do more, other than feed you," she replied, placing her hand on the center console. Before he realized it, they were touching and linking their fingers together. Her skin was warm and as they moved closer, the gold flecks in her brown eyes caught fire in the lights from the house.

"Adam–."

"I'm not sure either, but I feel–." Their lips met, and for a tender moment, nothing else existed. "I should go," he said, but didn't move away.

"I reckon you're right." She kissed him again, passionately this time, their bodies drawn together like magnets and both were breathless when they parted.

"You know where I'll be," he murmured against her lips.

"Indeed, I do."

Adam got out of the car and watched the sedan slowly roll down the driveway. He sighed heavily and ran his hand over his mouth.

Oh man, what am I doing? He closed his eyes and let his mind race through the possibilities but soon came to a screeching halt. He saw Loren pointing the gun at Jacobson's head, then her as a child, beating their father with a baseball bat.

I need to be here for her. He turned to climb the steps and enter the house, locking the door behind him. Whitewashed brick led him to a vaulted ceiling great room where Graham and Loren were on the sofa sectional, facing him. Graham's head was in her lap with his hand covering his eyes. The picturesque view out the window wall was obscured by frosted glass.

"I didn't know the windows did that," he said, pointing at wall behind them.

"I didn't either at first," Loren answered.

"I'm sorry you guys had to wait up for me," Adam said.

"It's okay. He can't go to sleep anyway." She brushed her fingers through Graham's hair.

"My head feels like it's about to explode," he muttered and slowly moved off her legs to settle on the yellow accent pillow. She kissed his forehead and got up, then walked toward Adam, nodding her head toward his room.

"Let's talk, yah?"

"Carson told you I was with O'Dowd?" he asked, then grimaced when she entered his bedroom. "Oh, jez, lemme get all that." He jumped ahead to snatch up a T-shirt, pair of jeans and a random sock off the floor.

She huffed a laugh. "Yah, he did. She's really great." Loren turned to face him, her eyes shining. "I'm sorry I got you involved in all this," she said, her voice raising an octave.

"Hey, it's okay." He quickly skirted the bed to grab her hands. "I'm just glad you're safe." She nodded and stepped back from him, sniffling and wiping her nose on her cuff.

"They didn't rough you up too much, did they?"

"No, Colin and Anthony didn't hate on me," he chuckled softly.

"That's good. I'd have to yell at them if they did." Her eyes teared up again. "I can't even begin to thank you. He would have killed Graham if it weren't for you."

No, he would have killed you. "It's going to be alright," he said and gave her tight hug.

Loren sniffled. "You're gonna teach Graham and me how to fight like that, right? 'Cause that was fucking cool."

***

6 November

Loren opened her eyes when a mobile chimed from across the room. The stone fireplace on the far wall came into focus, along with the large colorful pillows clustered into a nest on the floor before it. A tiny smile crossed her lips when her gaze came to three glasses on the coffee table. Only one had a coaster beneath it.

He didn't even get mad that Adam and I forgot to use the coasters.

Graham lay beside her on the sofa, his long body covering half of her and his unbruised cheek pressing into her shoulder. His hair was a mix of blonde ends and brown roots, and she loved how it stuck out in random places. Her gaze moved over his profile, following his straight nose down to his expressive mouth, but her frown returned at the blot of bruises beneath the scruff along his swollen jaw.

She kissed his forehead and closed her eyes. Visions came unbidden: Jacobson swinging his cast, Graham lying on the floor unconscious; a dark stain stretching across the carpet. Felix's blood staining her hands. Loren held Graham a little bit tighter.

I could have lost him. Then he started snoring in her ear and she adjusted her shoulder to move his head to a less constricted position. She closed her eyes again, but they fluttered open at shuffling feet and Adam flopped down on the other side of the L-shaped sofa.

"You're still out here?" His voice was rough with sleep.

"Yah. My back hurts, and the couch is softer than the bed." He nodded, then closed his eyes. Her gaze moved over his sharp cheekbones and tapered nose and smiled at the faint line between his brows. Broad shoulders and developed chest stretched the black T-shirt he wore. His lower half was covered by a ratty pair of sweat pants that his knee was poking through.

"Dude, how old are those sweats?"

"Pro'lly as old as you are."

Her stomach growled then, reminding her that she hadn't eaten since lunch the previous day.

"Adam, do you want–." A loud banging came from the front door, and Graham woke with a shudder. He sat up, breathing hard, then groaned in pain, holding his cheek.

"Easy, love. Lay back down," she cooed to him. "I think somebody's at the front door, but I didn't hear the gate." Adam pointed to her as she slid off the couch to her feet.

"You stay there."

"I will not," she snapped, jumping around the couch to speed passed and into the hall. She peeked out the side window. "Well, this is unexpected." Loren unlocked the deadbolt and opened the door to reveal Cece standing on the top step with her bike leaning against the retaining wall. "What are you doing here?"

"Anthony told me what happened." She stepped into the front hall and grabbed Loren in a tight hug, then pushed her away to glare at her. "I've been ringing and texting, but you're not answering!"

"I don't know where my phone is," she replied, her eyes welling up. "I'm sorry to worry you."

"Ah, Loren," Cece muttered and gave her another hug. "It's gonna be okay." They were both sniffling when they separated, and she glanced around the foyer. "Show me around, then?" Loren gave a soft chuckle and started toward the great room with Cece's cycling shoes clicking on the bamboo floor following her.

"I reckoned his house would be bigger," she said in a loud whisper.

"I heard that," Graham said hoarsely from the other side of the room. "And you're scuffing up my floors, dammit!" He started to get up as they approached, but Cece waved him off.

"Don't you get up, and I put the covers on so don't you worry about your precious… What is this? Knobby pine?" She pointed down at the bamboo flooring, then sat on the coffee table in front of him. "You could've gotten yourself killed, taking that bastard on like that. Don't you ever do anything like that again."

Graham raised a brow. "After the dressing down you gave me the other night, I swear, it almost seems like you care about me."

"Yah, well, what am I supposed to do with her if something happens to you, eh?" Her chin began to tremble. "Giraffe."

He scrunched his lips a little. "Pug."

"Stork," Cece muttered.

Graham sniggered. "That's a new one."

She huffed. "You look like shite. Both of ya." She turned around, and her eyes went wide at Adam on the couch. She looked up at Loren standing behind him, back to Adam, then turned back to Graham. "Damn, that's scary-clone-like."

He leaned toward her. "You know he can hear you."

"Still," she said, turning back to Adam. "Where'd you come from?"

"I flew in from New York on Wednesday," he replied. Cece pointed at him, looking at Graham.

"Gawd, he even has that little grin she's got."

Adam chuckled. "You must be Charlotte."

"That I am." She got to her feet, and they shook hands. "I hate to greet and ride off, but my Breeze ladies are waiting for me at the gate," she said, patting Graham on the knee. "They needed a break, and we were passing by.

Apparently, I'm workin' them too hard." Loren walked with her to the front door where Cece grabbed both her hands. "You sure you're okay?"

"No, I'm not, but what am I supposed to do? I can't fall apart." She glanced back at Graham on the sofa, his beard not hiding the gauntness of his face. "He needs me."

"You're just gonna bash on, then? You're a right stubborn bird, you know that, yah?"

She huffed. "Yah. I know. Thanks for coming to check on us." Cece gave her another hug and Loren watched her friend ride her bike through the grass, leaving behind a tire trail.

"She did that on purpose," she muttered, chuckling softly as she closed the door, only to cover her mouth with her hand to hold in her sobs.

"Shadow?" Adam's voice made her jump, and she turned around, wiping her fingers under her eyes.

"I'm fine," she sniffled, forcing a smile. "Do you want something for breakfast? I make a mean scrambled egg." He walked over and put his hands on her shoulders, but it was his intense stare that held her still.

"You're stuffing everything down in your gut, but it's not going to stay there."

She pulled away from him. "What am I supposed to do? I relive it every time I close my eyes," she choked, clutching at her shirt. "Jacobson on top of me; Graham lying on the floor. Felix's blood on my hands. The smell!" She wiped her hands on her leggings. "I can't get rid of it."

"You can't keep running away either. Believe me," he said, grabbing her shoulders again. "Drinking, drugs, sex, none of it has taken the memories of everything Dad did to me. I still see you bleeding out in my arms. I remember all the lives I've taken." He licked his lips. "I see the ghosts too, and I've let them ruin every relationship I've had." Adam cupped her cheek.

"But then I got help." He kissed her forehead. "I love you, Shadow. Please, let me help you."

* * *

The distress in Loren's voice roused Graham enough to fight against the painkillers and crack an eye. He listened to her talk with Adam, and quickly realized he shouldn't interrupt.

Good. She's unloading on someone. He grew unfocused and soon, sleep dragged him down. When he opened his eyes again, the late afternoon sun hit him in the face. Loren was curled up against him with her head in the crook of his shoulder. A surge of anger and love mixed with heavy regret came as he gazed at her.

A bruise covered her cheek, with an angry-looking cut in the middle of it. Red-brown marks crossed her neck. When she helped him shower last night, there were similar spots on her breast, and what he thought might be a bite mark, but he didn't need to ask what happened. The look on her face was answer enough. He held her and shared tears of pain and sadness, but also of relief, and in that moment, he fell more in love, and more in awe of her strength.

Murmuring voices floating from the kitchen disrupted his thoughts. He slowly shifted to look over the back of the couch without waking Loren and was surprised to see Ron Hudson sitting at the island with Adam. Graham sighed and closed his eyes again, soaking in the feeling of her in his arms when the reason he woke prodded him again.

He started to slip out from under her when she opened her eyes and sat up.

"Do you need anything?" she asked in a hoarse whisper. "Can I get–."

"You can't go to the loo for me, love. Just rest." She nodded and curled back up as he draped the blanket over her.

Graham then swayed his way across the great room toward the half bath, mumbling a hello to the two men as he passed the kitchen. He steadied himself on the wall of the foyer, breathing heavy when Ron appeared at his side.

"Do you need help?"

He shook his head. "I'm fairly certain I can hold my own knob, thanks."

"Gotcha," Ron laughed and walked away.

After his relieving and several splashes of cold water on his face, he exited the bath feeling a bit more refreshed but still as weak. Again, he slid his hand against the wall and slowly shuffled into the kitchen. Loren caught his elbow to help him sit down on one of the high stools.

"I thought you were sleeping," he said.

"I heard his voice," she replied, nodding at Ron, then turned to him. "We didn't know you were coming."

He rubbed his forehead. "Penny rang me yesterday. I flew in this morning."

She put a hand on his arm. "Have you seen her? The nurses wouldn't let me."

"No, but I spoke with Derek when I landed, and they're releasing her tomorrow," Ron replied. "I'm going to stay with her for the time being." Graham nodded, and Adam cleared his throat.

"I talked with O'Dowd a little while ago," he said. "She and Carson will be here tomorrow morning, but she assured me we didn't need a lawyer."

"Wonderful," Graham muttered.

Loren's eyes narrowed. "You must've made quite an impression."

"I guess so." Adam shrugged and glanced away.

226

Ron coughed. "Anyroad, the biggest issue now is the media. My office has received inquiries, and I've spoken with Pippa from your team." He nodded to Loren. "They're issuing a statement later today since it was their property where all this happened. She's determined to be as vague as possible." He grimaced. "The police report, however, is another matter. Since there was no, ahem, sexual assault, there's no mandate to withhold your identity." Loren clenched her hands in her lap.

"What do you think we should do?" His eyes flicked from her to Graham.

"I reckon we should wait to see what O'Dowd and Carson have to say and make a decision from there."

***

"Why did you have to come back? Why couldn't you leave me alone?" she screamed at the blonde woman standing before her. *"I hate you! I hate you!"* Her hand stung where it connected with the woman's face - a face so much like her dead mother's she was terrified to even look at her.

She ran up the stairs and slammed the door to her room, only to then kick and beat her fists against the hollow wood. She flew into a rage, ripping the covers off her bed, knocking over her dresser and desk, and spreading the contents of each on the floor. Anything solid she could get her hands on she threw across the room or smashed on the hardwood under her feet.

Soon, there was nothing left to break. She paced around, clutching at her shirt, desperately trying to contain the monster still clawing at her insides when a rainbow of sunlight glinted off glass and hit her in the face. She jumped on her bed to reach the shelf and her fingers closed around the figurine of a rearing horse. She turned it over in her fingers for the facets to catch the light, spreading prisms around her.

A cruel smile formed, and she flung it across the room where it hit the wall and disintegrated. Two more followed in quick succession and she was about to throw a fourth when the crystal horse in her hand began to glow like a star. The light brought her back to herself and the realization of what she had done stole her breath.

With trembling hands, she placed the horse back on the shelf and jumped off the bed. Tiny shards sparkled on the floor. She tried to sweep them up into her hand, but the glass sliced her skin.

There was no bringing them back.

Her knight would never come to save her again.

The wail began deep within her and came out of her mouth as a howl of pain and suffering.

Loren woke with a strangled cry and sat up.

"Oh, god, why?" She doubled over, covering her mouth with her hands. She peered over at Graham, sprawled out on the other side of the bed.

How do I even explain? She eased off the bed, picked up her sweatshirt from the bench and left the room. She walked through the study and into the kitchen, stopping short. Adam was there, with his head stuck in the refrigerator.

"Hey, I thought you went out," she said. He popped up with a can of Ryzak recovery drink in hand and a carrot stick hanging from his lip.

"Uh, hey." He removed the stick and glanced at his watch. "It's two in the morning. I just got back."

"Oh." She nodded and moved over to the counter. Adam came to sit across from her.

"Are you okay? You look spooked."

She rubbed her eyes. "I'm fine." His narrowed further and she snorted a laugh at the familiar expression. "You really are my brother."

"You doubted that?"

"No, not really." Her smile faded. "I had a nightmare."

"You have them a lot?"

She nodded. "Almost every night. Graham's a heavy sleeper so at least I don't wake him up all the time."

"Do you want to talk–."

"No, I don't," she said, getting up to go to the pantry and grab the bag of bagels, feeling his gaze on her when she came out. "Fine," Loren sighed, rolling her eyes. "Do you remember the crystal horses Maggie gave me?"

"Yeah, for your seventh birthday." Adam opened the paper bag and took out a blueberry bagel. "Got any cream cheese?" She nodded and opened the refrigerator as he went through a few drawers in the island to find the utensils. She placed the block of berry Philadelphia cream cheese next to him on the counter.

"Sit," he said, pointing to the stool. She watched him cut open the bagel unevenly and apply the spread, smiling a little when he got some of it on his fingers. "You want half or a whole?" he asked.

"Just half." Adam raised his brows and waved his hand for her to continue. "Fine," Loren sighed. "Maggie flat out refused call me Loren. She said it wasn't the name my mother gave me, and that made me hate her more." She followed the swirls in the concrete counter with her finger to shove her emotions back into their box.

"I wanted her to hurt as much as I did, and I lost it. I slapped her and ran to my room and tore it apart. I saw the horses on a shelf over my bed and I threw one against the wall. I felt a little bit of relief, and before I realized what I was doing, I broke two more." A dark splotch appeared on the counter. "That was the day I stopped believing my knight would come and save me."

"Your knight?"

Loren brushed her fingers over her cheek, then rose from her seat to pick up her messenger bag from under the corner table next to the sofa. She opened the zipper compartment and took out a thick, legal sized envelope. From that, she removed a yellowed piece of construction paper and a photograph and handed them to him. Adam unfolded the paper, his brows narrowing at the drawing of a knight on horseback, then looked at the photo. His jaw dropped as he pointed to the drawing

"You're telling me *this* is Martin Garrett? *He's* your knight?" She winced at his bitter tone.

"You have to understand. I dreamed of someone to protect me. A father who loved me." She looked away. "That day, I knew I was dying. I could feel myself floating away, but then I heard a voice calling my name. I looked up, and there was a knight in golden armor with bright blue eyes," Loren said, her voice soft. "He said he was there to save me, and I would never be alone again. I've held on to that ever since." It hurt to see his closed expression, but she pushed on.

"Thing is, it wasn't until I came to England that I realized I already had a mother and a father who loved me, but I kept pushing them away because of a childish dream." She sniffled and wiped her nose on the cuff of her sweatshirt, then gave him a sidelong glance. "I knew you wouldn't understand," she muttered. Her brother got up and surprised her with a tight hug.

"I do understand," he whispered. She gave him a squeeze, and Adam sat back down. She scrunched her nose, weighing telling him something else.

"You're going to think I'm crazy, but the first time I saw Graham as Apollo in *Crusade of the Gods*, I had dreams for weeks that he was my knight. And then by fate or random chance, and I was right. He did save me." Adam blinked, giving her a funny grimace.

"Yeah, I think you're nuts." His smirk appeared, curving into a smile, and they both broke out in tearful laughter.

"Yah, maybe I am," she chuckled, then focused on eating her bagel for a few minutes. Her thoughts slid along different strings until it met a knot and she raised her gaze to him again.

"So, you went to see Theresa?"

"I don't know what I'm doing," he groaned, looking down at his hands. "I like her. I like being with her, but we both know the timing is way off. It's just... I can't stay away." His shoulders hunched as he picked at the remains of his bagel.

"I know what that's like," she said. "It feels like a joint popped back into place and the pain you didn't realize was there, is suddenly gone." Adam gaped at her and let out a long breath.

"But yours turned into something. That doesn't happen for me. I can't let people get close." It was her turn to give the funny grimace.

"What's all this then?" She motioned with her hand between them.

He shrugged. "You're my sister." She gave a little smile, recalling what her other brother told her.

"Because you know you can say anything to me, and I'm not going to leave you," she murmured. "That's what Anthony told me."

Adam curled his lip. "Yeah," he drawled. "I'm really going to end up hating that guy."

She chuckled softly. "Why did you come here, Adam?" His gray eyes darkened as he leaned toward her.

"For a long time, I was able to put the guilt aside and focus on building my life," he said, his tone heavy. "But when I saw that picture of you, it just about killed me. I could see how much pain you were in, and I was responsible for it." She sat back from him, her brows scrunching.

"What picture?" He pulled out his phone, swiped at the screen, then handed it to her. She glanced at an image of herself, hysterical on the side of the road in Les Herbiers as Ulrik tried to calm her.

"Ah." She grimaced. "Right. Time Magazine picked up that one." Loren shook her head. "How could you think you were responsible for that?"

"You said it yourself," he told her. "Everything you are, everything you've done is because of what I did."

"You are not responsible for *my* life," she countered, jabbing her finger on the counter. "I'm here because of choices *I've* made, nothing else." He didn't reply right away; he just put another bagel half on her plate and slid it to her.

"Nick's right. We have the same scowl." She pressed her lips together, shaking her head as Adam leaned closer to her with his elbow on the counter.

"There's a lot of junk between us that isn't ours," he said. "I want to be in your life, but we both have to be willing to dredge up the pain."

Loren met his gaze. "I'll warn you now, I cry ugly."

***

The gate intercom buzzed shortly after breakfast, heralding the arrival of the detectives. The tight expressions Theresa O'Dowd and Gordon Carson wore when Loren opened the front door set off her internal alarms.

"Please, come in." She stepped aside, and Adam stood up from the sofa when they entered the great room. Graham stayed seated.

"I apologize for not rising to greet you. The altitude, you see," he told them, pointing to the ceiling. "When I get up, I get a wee bit dizzy." Carson snickered, and O'Dowd gave Loren a confused look.

"It's the painkillers. His jokes don't make a lot of sense right now," she said with a soft smile, then returned to his side. "Please, sit down. I have a feeling you don't have good news." Carson sat back on the sofa while Theresa perched on the edge, her dark eyes flicking to Adam.

"The Crown Court has reviewed our investigation," she said. "With your statement, Ms. O'Neill's and yours, Adam, their preliminary findings are that Mr. Jacobson was the aggressor and you were merely defending yourselves. He is being charged with several counts of aggravated assault against the four of you, and third-degree murder. The department will issue a statement later today but be assured, your names will be redacted."

"Is that the end of it?" Loren asked. The detectives glanced at each other, then both faced her, and her stomach bottomed out.

"No, I'm sorry to say," Theresa replied. "Mr. Jacobson has testified he knew Mr. Lalonde for some years, and that Lalonde hired him to follow you when you left the US. We've conducted a search of Lalonde's flat and discovered photographs of you dating back from when you were in Colorado, which corroborate his statement." Carson cleared his throat then, and Loren focused on him.

"There are also photographs and video of you in your home, both on Badgers Close and on Essex."

Loren blinked. *I see you. I hear you.* She stood up and moved to the other side of the couch to cross her arms tightly over her chest. "Video, where? In my room?" Carson glanced away, but O'Dowd met her gaze.

"Yes."

"Oh god," she groaned, covering her mouth to fight the urge to throw up.

"Loren." The anguish etched on Graham's face brought her to him. She clutched at his hand. She faced the detectives, her fist in her stomach. "What about my roommates? Were there pictures and videos of them, too?"

"No," O'Dowd answered, her eyes flicking between the couple. "Most were of you alone. Some were of you with a dark-haired man, who I believe is Philippe Durand, and of you and Graham."

Loren choked. "Was I... were we..."

The DS nodded solemnly. "Yes, there is video of you being intimate with both." Loren sank to her hands and knees, unable to breathe. Graham was there, holding her, rocking her as she trembled.

"He was watching us." He pushed her hair out of her face.

"We'll get through this together. Come on." He helped her to stand, and they both stumbled around the sofa. Graham then glared at the officers as he gathered Loren to him.

"Who else has seen those? You cannot release any–." O'Dowd leaned toward them.

"I will make certain neither of you are compromised any further," she said.

"This can't be happening," Loren muttered, her hands covering her ears.

Carson coughed softly. "Graham, I'm sorry, but we have a few questions about your security agents, Derek Graves and Penelope O'Neill."

"What about them?" he snarled.

"Did they have prior contact with Mr. Jacobson?"

"Yes, in London and New York," he replied as Carson took out a small tablet from his jacket. Graham tightened his arms around Loren. "I came back from California to rumors that Loren and I had broken up. An evening out was arranged to quash it, and the paparazzi were tipped off. We were having dinner at the Plaza when Jacobson confronted me in the lav. I had him followed." He licked his lips.

"It was the same in New York. The press were given notice that we would be at a gallery event. Jacobson showed up, and O'Neill followed him at my direction."

"And assaulted him?" O'Dowd inquired.

"Penny was defending herself," Adam snapped at her. "He grabbed her from behind. I was there."

Her gaze narrowed. "You didn't share that in your statement, Mr. O'Connell."

"It didn't happen here," he shot back.

"O'Dowd," Carson muttered and they both stood. "I've ordered a uniformed officer to be posted at the gate to your house, to keep the riff-raff at bay, you know."

"Thank you. We appreciate that," Graham replied, and the detectives started toward the foyer with Adam escorting them.

"Let go of me," Loren growled and shoved Graham off. She stood and moved away, clutching at her shirt. *I can't do this.*

The ringing in her ears intensified. She tore open the slider, storming out to the deck to stalk its length, her nails digging into her palms. The monster was clawing at her insides, screaming for release.

"He was watching me," she groaned. "All this time, he was watching me. Everything I did! Everything I said!"

A red haze settled over her vision. She seized an Adirondack chair, lifted it over her head and slammed it repeatedly on the decking. Splintered wood flew in all directions, and Loren flung the broken pieces away. She grabbed another chair, screaming as she heaved it out into the yard, then picked up a third, spinning around to throw it even farther than the first.

She turned back, scanning the deck for something else to destroy. The glass-top coffee table came into focus and she started for it when Graham stepped in front of her.

"No, Loren. The table's expensive," he said, calmly. "Take another chair, or you can hit me." She clenched her fists, snarling deep in her throat and drew back to strike at him.

He flinched, and it was a kick in the stomach. The destruction she caused lay all around her. Her rage drained away to leave her gasping.

"What have I done?" A cold drip slid down the side of her left hand and she raised it to stare at the thick line of crimson against her skin. Graham stepped forward and gently covered the gash with his long fingers.

"I don't have a handkerchief this time." She her knees gave out, dropping both of them to the deck.

"I'm sorry," she sobbed. "I'm so sorry. I never meant for any of this to happen." His arms surrounded her, enveloping her in his warmth.

"We'll get through this, love," he murmured. "You and me, together."

***

Loren heaved a sigh and turned over to squint at the angry red 3:24 AM from the clock next to the bed.

"It's not just the mattress keeping you awake this time, is it?" Graham murmured.

"No, it's not," she replied, rolling to her back. He slowly came up on his elbow and brushed her hair from her face.

"You're frightening me, love. You haven't slept for more than an hour at a time, and you've barely spoken a word to anyone. Then disappearing on your bike yesterday without your mobile. Please, talk to me."

Loren gently brushed her fingers over his lips. The swelling was down, but pain etched lines around his mouth and across his forehead.

"I can't look at you and not feel guilty," she said, unshed tears choking her voice. "I close my eyes, and I see Jacobson hit you. I see blood on my hands. Then I see my mother and my sister. I hear my father's voice." She let out a sob and covered her face. "I don't want this anymore. I just want to forget again." Graham pulled her into his arms.

"It's not your fault, love, and no matter how many times I tell you, you won't believe me." He let her go to reach to the nightstand and came back with a business card in his hand. She scowled at the name on it and pushed him away.

"Dammit, Graham, I threw that in the trash."

"I fished it out. Loren, I love you so very much, and I wish I were enough to help you, but I'm not. Dr. Pallas can help."

Her mouth popped open. His words sounded like what she once told Anthony. She let out a breath and lay back into his embrace. *He's right. I'm gonna lose it if I don't do something.* "Okay. I'll call her."

***

Loren stared at the clock on the range in the kitchen willing time to move faster. When time finally dragged itself to 9:00 AM, she took a deep breath and picked up her mobile, but her finger hovered over the screen.

"Do it. Dial, dammit. Do it," she muttered and slowly pressed the numbers. But, when the call connected, she couldn't speak.

"Good morning, Counseling Service. May I help you? Hello?"

"I'm sorry," Loren coughed and covered her eyes with her hand. "I'd like to make an appointment to see Dr. Pallas."

"Of course. Are you a new patient?"

"Um, yes and no. I've been there before, for a meeting," she replied. "My name is Loren Mackenzie."

There was a brief pause. "Would you mind holding for a moment?"

Her brows went up. "Uh, sure." Music began to play through the speaker, but not long enough for her to identify the song.

"Miss Mackenzie, Dr. Pallas has an opening at eleven this morning. Would that work for you?"

She blinked. "Yes. I-I'll be there. Thank you." She disconnected, awash in different emotions, the strongest being relief. *This is good. I need this. I'm falling apart.* She sat down, only then realizing she had been pacing along the counter when footsteps came from behind her.

"I came out of the loo and you were gone," Graham said, sitting down next to her.

"Yah, I couldn't lie there anymore, and you needed to sleep." She flicked the card in her hand with her finger. "I have an appointment at eleven."

His brows went up. "Do you want me to come with you? Or Adam? I could ring Anthony." Loren leaned in and kissed his unbruised cheek.

"No, I can go by myself, but thank you," she said and stood. "If you're ready for some solid food, I can make you something."

"Thank you. I'm tired of drinking my meals," he groaned as his shoulders drooped. "Perhaps just a bleu cheese omelette."

She gave a crooked grin. "Scrambled eggs it is."

***

Loren rode into Stanmore on the A409, and her eyes went to a nondescript office building on her right.

I can't do it. She rolled the accelerator hard, weaving between two stopped vehicles stopped at a red light to escape. Shame rode behind her, tightening its grip on her midsection when her calendar reminder pinged in her ear. She had ten minutes before she was late and her detest at being tardy won out over her anxiety.

"Goddammit," she grumbled and took a hard left down a side street to turn around. The BMW rolled to a stop in the car park, and Loren removed her helmet to glare up at the plain brown office building. The large, half-moon window over the entrance reflected the gray clouds overhead. She sighed, ran a gloved hand over her face then shut off the engine.

Just get off the bike and go inside. Do it. Get it over with. Muttering under her breath, she dismounted. Each halting step toward the building and into the elevator cost her more than just physical energy.

Go. Inside. Press the call button. Do it! She was a trembling, sweaty mess when the elevator doors opened to the second floor, and she had to grab the frame to pull herself out of the car. A young woman at the reception desk smiled when Loren slinked through the office door.

"Hello. May I help you?"

"I have an appointment to see–." A door opened down the hall, and Loren stepped back from the desk. Dr. Pallas walked toward the lobby with a young man, speaking in lowered voices. They shook hands, and the man quickly headed out the door. Loren kept her chin down, wringing her leather gloves in her hands when Dr. Pallas approached.

"Miss Mackenzie? If you're ready."

The psychologist led her to a cozy but cluttered office where they settled across from each other in modern, high-backed chairs. Loren removed her moto jacket, her eyes skipping around to odd knickknacks on shelves piled with books. A skylight in the vaulted ceiling draped the room in soft light, but there was no desk or chaise lounge like she expected. A square coffee table separated the two women, and a pale pink area rug covered the beige Berber carpet beneath it. She brushed her fingers over the purple velour of the chair arm.

"I like the chairs."

"They're soft, like a kitten," the doctor replied. "I'm glad you came back, Loren." She raised her gaze to meet the green eyes of Dr. Pallas, then looked away.

"I'm not," she said, taking a breath, which turned into several. "I don't want to be here. I don't want to need help, but I'm being torn apart, and I don't know what to do."

"Asking for help isn't a weakness, it's a strength," the doctor told her. Loren nodded, absently picking at the bandage on her left wrist, then became aware of the thick silence in the room. She raised her gaze and her brows went up at the doctor's deep frown.

"What?"

"Did you harm yourself?" Dr. Pallas asked.

"Uh, well, yes, but not the way you're thinking," she retorted. "I broke one of the chairs on the back deck and I cut myself." The doctor's expression didn't change. "Do you want to see it?" Loren extended her arm, but Dr. Pallas waved her off.

"No, I believe you. What set this off?"

"The man who attacked me, Felix?" Loren bit her lip and couldn't speak for a moment. "He was killed," she choked, and a flash of surprise went across the psychologist's face.

"When did this happen?"

"A few days ago. It was on the news," Loren replied. "He said he was sorry and that he loved me." She clenched her shaking hands in her lap. "He asked me to forgive him, and in my heart, I did, but then I find out he had me followed. He put cameras in my house, in my bedroom. He saw everything I did. He heard everything I said." She dragged a shaking hand over her mouth.

"When he raped me, he had my body, but he didn't touch *me*," she pounded her fist on her chest, "but this… I feel stained, and it's spreading. I'm the whore he called me." She squeezed her eyes shut, breathing deeply to stuff every emotion she felt into the pink jewelry box in her mind. Her stomach calmed as the tension left her, and Loren opened her eyes to the raised brows of Dr. Pallas, holding a box of tissues.

"I was ready to hand these to you." She placed the box back on the coffee table. "You are astonishingly good at denying your emotions."

"I'm the Ice Queen," Loren replied flatly. "I've had to learn how to compartmentalize to survive."

The psychologist nodded. "Surviving. I agree. That's what you've been doing. But, is merely surviving how you want to spend the rest of your life, or do you want to live?" Loren thought of Graham, and two tears rolled down her cheeks.

"I want to live. I want to be free of it." Dr. Pallas leaned forward and offered her hand. Loren hesitated for a breath, then clasped it.

"Your hand isn't cold," she said, squeezing, then let go. "I see a woman seated before me, not a sculpture made of ice. A woman, that despite what horrors she's faced, she can still see light in the darkness. You have compassion and hope. You feel love and you can forgive." Dr. Pallas eased back into her chair. "I won't lie to you, Loren. You have a hard road ahead of you, but you can heal, and we'll start today."

***

After Loren left for her appointment, Graham remained in the kitchen icing his jaw while staring out at the Ridgeway.

A year ago, I was alone. How my life has changed. He sighed. "We are time's subjects, and time bids us begone."

"What does that mean?"

"Holy fuck!" He jumped at Adam's voice from behind him, then groaned at the pain in his jaw.

"Sorry," Adam chuckled softly. "I thought I was making more noise."

"Perhaps you were. I was a bit lost," Graham muttered, reapplying the ice pack and focused on the view outside again. "It means time moves us, whether we want to move or not."

"Ah. Did Loren go out? I heard the motorcycle."

"She went to see a psychologist."

"How did you get her to do that?" Graham turned at the note of disbelief in Adam's question.

"Constant badgering," he said flatly, and Adam snorted a laugh. "I told her the truth; that I'm afraid for her." Graham returned to the windows. "I could care less about the chairs she smashed or the cracked decking, but to see the storm raging inside her, and then to shut down as she has." He shook his head. "I want to help her, but I can't, and I also knew I couldn't drag her there myself like Anthony did."

"He did what?"

Graham lifted his head. "He and I met Dr. Pallas in the hospital, back in August. She works with the Special Victims Unit and runs a support group. Anthony stuffed Loren in his car and drove her there, then harassed her until she went inside."

Adam squinted an eye. "She let him do that?"

"Yes, well, they have a complicated relationship. She saved his life," Graham answered, meeting his gaze. "He's a vet, like you, and suffers from PTSD. He told me he tried to overdose, but she found him."

"Survivor's guilt." Graham nodded, then smirked a little.

"She stuck her fingers down his throat to make him vomit. He wasn't sure which was worse, the embarrassment of her doing that or that she had to clean him up." The two men were silent, and Graham refocused on the view out the windows.

"I talked to Anthony the other night," Adam said. "We were both in Helmand, but in different areas of the province. We got shot in the same month, but he went home before I did." He curled his lip. "You know, I could very easily hate him."

"I can't imagine why," Graham retorted, grimacing. "Broad shoulders, ruggedly handsome, a wounded soldier. The epitome of a knight in shining armor and every woman's fantasy." Adam gave him a soft punch on the shoulder.

"But she picked the stork. Or is it giraffe?"

"I'm sure Charlotte will come up with more," Graham chuckled, but it ended abruptly at Adam's narrowed eyes. "What?"

"I'm going to show you something, but if you tell Loren–." Graham pointed a finger at him.

"I'll have you know, someone much more formidable than you threatened to murder me and bury me in the back garden, so get in line." Adam pressed his lips together, and Graham shook his head. "That look," he chuckled. "You truly are her brother."

"Yeah, well," he muttered, then coughed. "She told me about a man she's dreamed of her whole life." He took a folded piece of construction paper from his pocket and slid it across the counter. "A knight she believed was going to come and save her." Graham unfolded the picture, and his mouth dropped open. He winced, holding his hand to his cheek.

"What is this?"

238

"That looks like you as Apollo, doesn't it?" Adam slid a photograph to him. "It's not though. It's this guy." Graham's mouth opened again and groaned.

"Ah, stop shocking me, dammit." He held the picture close to examine it. "Who is this?"

"It's Martin Garrett."

His eyes went wide. "The man who…"

"Yep," Adam popped his lips. Graham exhaled hard, his brain folding over on itself.

"What are you saying? She's only with me because of a fixation?"

Adam scoffed. "If that were the case, every boyfriend she's had would look like you, and I'm pretty sure they didn't. Except maybe the skinny beanpole part." He leaned in a little. "From what Anthony told me, and what I've seen myself, you know her better than anyone, except maybe Charlotte," he said, then curled his lip. "Dammit, I'm really going to hate him." He shook his head. "I don't know. Maybe she does have a type," Adam air quoted, "but when push comes to shove, *you* hold her up, not your face." Graham pursed his lips as much as he could.

"If my jaw didn't hurt so much, I would be laughing."

***

Loren entered the house from the garage, her brain still spinning from her visit with Dr. Pallas when the scent of Thai food smacked her in the nose. She walked into the kitchen and Graham rose from the sofa to meet her half-way.

"Is that Chu Chee I smell?" she asked.

"We didn't want to eat without you," he told her. "All's well?" She kissed him, then wrapped her arms around his waist.

"I don't want to go back, but I have to, on Thursday." He huffed a chuckle, and she let him go with a tight smile. "I need to get out of this leather," she said. "I'm already starting to overheat."

"If I weren't drugged, I'd be overheating as well," he said, flatly, and Loren shook her head, smiling.

"Go sit down." She headed for the bedroom and sat down heavily on the edge of the bed, her shoulders rounding to stare down at her boots. She closed her eyes and breathed slowly, focusing on releasing the tension in her muscles.

I can do this. I have to tell them. When she returned to the kitchen in joggers and a sweatshirt, Adam was seated at the counter with Graham.

"He told me where you went," her brother said. "You okay?"

"Yah. I'll be okay," she replied and sat down. Graham and Adam tucked into their lunch, but Loren pushed her chicken and cashews around on her plate, contemplating what she had to tell them. She put her chopsticks down and waited until Graham had stopped chewing before she put her hand on his forearm. He looked at her, and she took a breath to speak, but couldn't get the words around the lump in her throat. He put his hand over hers.

"Tell me." She gave a tearful smile and compelled her voice to work.

"I've spent my life avoiding, stuffing and forcing myself to forget what happened to me." She sniffled and raised her arm to brush her sleeve under her nose when he handed her a tissue.

"Thanks," she whispered. Dabbing her nose, she then turned to her brother. "I can't even tell you how much it means to me that you're here." Adam reached over and patted her hand.

"You're getting help, that's what's important," he said. "And I don't feel slighted you left me to babysit your boyfriend. It gave me some time to interrogate him, I mean, get to know him better," he added quickly. Loren huffed and looked at Graham, who patted his chest.

"Do I still have grill marks on me?" They chuckled and went back to their meals, but she could feel her brother's gaze on her. After a few minutes, Adam cleared his throat, and she huffed a laugh at the familiar look of uncertainty on his face.

"Go on, I'm listening."

"When you left New York, I didn't think much it would hurt," he said. "With you being here and me being there, it won't be easy to reconnect, so I talked it over with Graham." His eyes flicked across the counter. "The meeting I had was to discuss transferring to London." Her brows went up, looking from Adam to Graham and back.

"You would do that?"

"I told you, I'm not going to leave you behind again," Adam replied, then smirked. "And it was Graham's idea." She laughed and launched off her stool to hug her brother.

"Thank you," she whispered then let him go. Adam stood and cleared his throat, but she could see tears in his eyes.

"I'm going to head out for a run," he said, thumbing at the window wall. "All this sitting around eating bagels and donuts is bad for my waistline."

She chuckled. "Sure. There's a great trail behind the house." Adam headed to his room, and Loren went around the counter to Graham. She grasped the underside of the seat and slowly turned him toward her, then stood between his knees and gazed into his bright blue eyes. One was still a little bloodshot. She gently brushed her thumb across his bruised cheekbone.

"I love you with so much of my heart that none is left to protest," she murmured, and he gave her a look of utter dejection.

"I want to kiss you so very badly, but it's going to hurt too much."

"I promise, I'll be gentle." Loren kissed him on the forehead, his closed eyes then placed soft kisses on every bruise and bandage. "Thank you for being such a wonderful boyfriend." Graham smiled as much as his swollen cheek would let him.

"A much better boyfriend than Jude Law?"

Her smile brightened the room. "Much better than Jude Law."

***

14 December

Kamnik, Slovenia

Oskar Ryzak sat at a large mahogany desk, gazing at glossy photographs. He shuffled the images of a woman in a blue silk dress, reclining on a chaise lounge then chose one, but tossed it in a pile on the far side of the desk. He lifted another and studied it for a bit longer, placing it with several others before him. His head came up at footsteps echoing across the room, and a tall, well-built man dressed in a sleek blue suit entered.

"Maksim! You are finally home! Come and see," he called, waving him over. The younger man bent and pressed his cheek to Oskar's.

"Hello *Táti*. What is all this?" Maksim picked up a photo and his hazel eyes narrowed. "Who is this lovely creature?"

"That, my son, is the new face of our recovery line."

"So, this is Loren Mackenzie." His full lips curved downward. "Who was the photographer? Not that pig, Meyer."

"Yes, it was," Oskar replied, a dark frown pulled at his mouth, his gaze lingering over the images on his desk. "I regret not listening to you."

"Did something happen, *Táti*?" Oskar sat back in his chair, pressing his fingers together.

"Yes, but, before you go and do something rash, my son, Roman Meyer has been punished for his actions."

"Punished." A half-smile appeared. "Good. When do I get to meet her?"

"The team's training camp begins in January, in Majorca," his father replied.

"What a coincidence," Maksim drawled. "We'll already be there."

"That we will, however, there is another matter we need to discuss," Oskar said, tapping a newspaper photograph of a ponytailed man being led into a courthouse in handcuffs. "This needs to be dealt with. I cannot have anything threatening what belongs to me." Maksim picked up the article, then raised his gaze to his father.

"As you wish, *Táti*."

***

Acknowledgements

To Bob R., my editor, Jessica Bucher, all of my amazing Beta readers at The Women of Sufferlandria, and especially, my husband, Eric.

A special thank you to:

Phil Leggett, Paul Sherwin, Bob Roll and Jens Voigt, Sarah Connelly, Matt Smith, and Rochelle Gilmore, for your colorful race commentary.

USA Cycling, Union Cycliste Internationale (UCI), British Cycling, Ella Cycling, Vox Women and all of the news outlets highlighting women's cycling.

In honor of their inspiration, heart, and grace:

Kathryn Bertine, Annemiek Van Vleuten, Kelly Catlin, and Loren Rowney.

About the Author

Sara Butler Zalesky has never lacked for imagination, but it wasn't until the Fates gave the string of her life a tug to bring her romantic leanings together with her passion for the sport of cycling. The combination gave a unique voice to her first novel, *Wheeler*.

The author resides in the suburbs of Philadelphia, PA, with her husband and their son. She is a paralegal for a boutique law firm in Chester County, PA, an avid road cyclist and indoor cycling instructor at a national chain.

Follow the author at on Twitter @sarazalesky or her blog at sarabutlerzalesky.com for funny memes, GIFs, and other assorted writings about all kinds of other stuff.

She really does do a little dance every time someone follows her.

If you loved *In Darkness*, please be kind and leave a review!

Loren's story continues with *Wheeler: One Fire Burns Out Another's Burning*, set to be released in May 2019.

42813949R00139

Made in the USA
Middletown, DE
21 April 2019